DRUMFIRE

Geronimo smiled a bitter smile. "I could make my own way to Oklahoma. I am not so old that I couldn't do that."

Sundance smiled too. "And you're not so old that you couldn't make it back to Arizona and gather your people for another war."

"If I gave my word that I would live in peace?"

"The War Department doesn't want your word."

"True," the crafty old warrior said. "The War Department has no respect for honor."

BUFFALO WAR

"If the plan goes wrong you can shoot me," Sundance said. "Just tell your men to keep their heads down and be ready for anything. Tell them no more shooting." The Mexican-hatted man hissed the order. The big rifle from the house hadn't fired for several minutes.

"My men will do more than kill you if you are wrong," the man beside Sundance said. A man moved and the big rifle blew the hat off his head. After that it was silent again.

"Enough of this warning and threatening," Sundance said. "I knew what I was getting into. Now I'm in it."

SUNDANCE

DRUMFIRE

BUFFALO WAR

PETER McCURTIN

LEISURE BOOKS NEW YORK CITY

A LEISURE BOOK®

March 2000

Published by

Dorchester Publishing Co., Inc.
276 Fifth Avenue
New York, NY 10001

ISBN 0-8439-4701-2

Printed in the United States of America.

SUNDANCE

DRUMFIRE

BUFFALO WAR

DRUMFIRE

CHAPTER ONE

The old man sat at the table with his scarred hands folded in front of him. He looked up when Sundance came in, and for an instant there was a flicker of recognition in the fierce black eyes, and then it was gone. His uncreased black hat sat squarely on his head, and it was impossible to tell what he was thinking. Old age and old hatreds had made a mask of his flat, wide face; the years hadn't changed him much, and maybe they hadn't changed him at all. Though his coarse crow-black hair had gone completely gray, there was a wiriness, a ruthless strength that belied his age. Mostly it was in the eyes, Sundance thought: black and unfaded, they might have been the eyes of a young warrior.

"You are Geronimo," Sundance said. There was no need to say it, but the old man's presence seemed to call for a sort of formality. In a way, this was the moment Sundance had been waiting for throughout many years of his life. As much as any man he had been responsible for the defeat of Geronimo, fiercest of all the Apaches, the greatest strategist produced by any Indian nation. For well over a decade he had outfoxed and outfought the best officers the United States Army had sent against him. From his stronghold in the mountains of Sonora he had raided on both sides of the border, defying Mexicans and Americans alike. Finally, it had taken General George C. Crook to put an end to his reign of terror. With Sundance as his chief scout, Crook had pursued Geronimo with a calm ferocity that matched the Apache's own. Crook had hunted Geronimo and his band through the parched, waterless mountains, destroying his food supplies, shelling his positions with mountain guns, rounding up his women and children until, ragged and starving, his ammunition gone, his horses dead, he had been forced to surrender.

"I am Geronimo," the old Apache said in plain, functional English. There was little to indicate that he had spoken Spanish for most of his life. The long years of exile in Florida had taught him the hated language of his captors. The little room he sat in now was bare as only a room in an army post can be; the floor was scrubbed white and smelled of strong yellow soap; there were bars on the windows.

"My name is Jim Sundance. Do you know who I am?" Sundance thought it strange that he had never seen Geronimo before; at least not up close. During the long campaign in the mountains he had come close to killing the great Apache several times; always without success.

Geronimo regarded Sundance with calm black eyes that gave nothing away. "I know who you are," he said. "You fought me long and hard. If I had killed you it might have been different. Your friend Three Stars, how have the years treated him? You and Three Stars, you are the men who beat me. None of the others, you and Three Stars did what no one else could do."

Three Stars was what the Indians, hostile and friendly, called George Crook, and whether they hated or liked Crook, all had respect for the no-nonsense soldier who was ruthless in battle and generous once his battles had been won. After Geronimo's surrender there was a clamor for his execution; only Crook's forceful intervention had saved him from the gallows, the death an Indian feared most. Sundance wondered if this meant anything to Geronimo, but there was no way to tell.

"Three Stars is all right," Sundance said. "He is in command of the Department of the Missouri, but there isn't much fighting to be done these days."

Geronimo's brooding eyes showed a trace of amusement. "It is hard for a soldier not to have somebody to fight."

"Three Stars doesn't see it like that. He likes peace."

"A strange soldier. But you did not come here to talk of old battles."

Sundance shook his head. "I came to tell you that you can't go back to Arizona. There is still unrest among the Apaches and your memory is too strong. The War Department is afraid there will be a new war if you go back there. The War Department refuses permission and the President agrees with them."

Geronimo smiled for the first time. "The President remembers Geronimo? Who would think one old Indian is a threat to your United States? You spoke of peace. What you mean is the peace of the dead. You are a halfbreed. Does it not bother you to have killed so many of your mother's people? The sons of so many Indian mothers?"

Sundance said, "Sometimes when I think about

11

it, it bothers me. But if we didn't kill many others would have killed all. There still are men who would like to do that. Would that have been better?"

"They are killing us anyway. I have been a prisoner here in Florida for many years and have seen the things they do. They herded us here in cattle cars, lying in our own dung, eating the slop they threw us when they felt like it. Hundreds of my Apaches died of swamp fever and starvation. Hundreds of my bravest warriors died that way."

Everything Geronimo said was true, yet there was nothing that could be done about it. The long bitter history of the Indians was one of hypocrisy and lies, double-dealing and broken treaties. Coveting their tribal lands, the whites goaded the Indians into war and then sent the soldiers to slaughter them. But, Sundance thought, what was the use of talking about it?

"You can't go back to Arizona," he repeated. "The only way you can leave here is to go far from your own country. Three Stars has been able to get that much for you, and he had to work hard to do it. Do you know where Fort Cobb, Oklahoma is?"

"I know where Oklahoma is. This Fort Cobb. They would lock me up in another fort?"

"Not lock you up. You will be given land to farm. I don't know what the land is like, but it will become yours if you go there. You can live out your life in some kind of peace."

Geronimo smiled again. "Some kind! I will be watched by the soldiers from this fort?"

"You will be watched for a while. Maybe as long as you live. Oklahoma must be better than this."

"A farmer!" Geronimo spoke almost in wonder. "After all my years to root in the earth like a woman, or an old man who is good for nothing else. I did not think I would end my life in that way."

"You are an old man. Old enough anyway. Old or not, you still can live with honor. Other good men have done it. You will not be on a reservation, the land will be your own. But you must make the decision. No one will force you to go. Many men would be glad to keep you here until you die."

"Are they that afraid of me?" Geronimo seemed to derive satisfaction from the thought.

He's a vain old man, Sundance thought. A tricky and dangerous old man still dreaming of past glory.

Sundance said, "They don't want you in Arizona. Now I have come a very long way to tell you all this. I would like an answer before they change their minds."

Geronimo stared at Sundance. "You come from Three Stars?"

Sundance nodded. "He fixed it so you can go to Oklahoma, but he wants it done quietly. An army escort would get too much attention. Once the newspapers got hold of it there would be an uproar. Here the army has given you protection, but away from this place you have many enemies who would like to kill you. It hasn't been so long that the things you did are forgotten."

Geronimo smiled another bitter smile. "I could make my own way to Oklahoma. I'm not so old that I couldn't do that."

Sundance smiled too. "And you're not so old that you couldn't make it back to Arizona."

"If I gave my word that I would live in peace?"

"The War Department doesn't want your word."

"True, the War Department has no respect

for honor."

They had been talking politely for too long, Sundance decided. He knew the old Apache would take no offense. First you said it politely—the Indian custom—and then you spelled it out in hard words. Looking at Geronimo, he knew this latest job Three Stars had given him wasn't going to be easy. On the long journey south to Florida he had hoped to find Geronimo mellowed by age, wanting only to live the rest of his life with some measure of peace.

Now he spoke plainly: "If you want to go to Oklahoma I'll see that you get there. I have given *my* word to Three Stars and intend to keep it. We will try to go as secretly as we can, but that won't be possible. Not for long. I can't let you get killed because the Apaches will break loose when they hear of it. You know what I think? I think maybe it's a mistake to let you out of here."

"Hard words, Sundance."

"No more than the truth. I'll do my best for you because of Crook, but if you try to run out on me I'll bring you back here in irons. If that happens you'll never again see the light of day. It's time to change into a wise old man, Geronimo. Take what's being offered to you and make the best of it."

Geronimo unfolded his hands to adjust his hat though it was sitting perfectly straight on his head. "We will go to Oklahoma," he said. "Who can tell what will happen on the way. Every man's life changes from day to day."

Sundance said, "Don't try to change it too much. Now I have to get the colonel to sign these release papers." Sundance touched his shirt pocket. "These will get us through if we're stopped by the army. But it's not the army I'm thinking about. You

14

got any stuff you want to take along?"

The old Apache's eyes glittered with sudden arrogance. "After fifteen years here I have nothing. When I was a young man all I ever needed was a pony and a rifle."

Going out, Sundance said, "You sure as hell won't get any rifle from me."

Colonel Carson was a big man not far from retirement age. All the windows of his office were open, but he was sweating hard in the steamy heat of southern Florida, and he treated Geronimo with a hearty condescension that Sundance knew was entirely misplaced.

Geronimo stood waiting while the colonel scratched his signature on the release papers. "There you go," he said, waving the ink dry and handing the papers back to Sundance. "Wish to hell I was going to Oklahoma with you. You know where I'm going when I retire? Back to northern New Hampshire, is where I'm going. There's not a day in this stinking heat I don't think of all that ice and snow. Gets down to twenty below on the good days."

Sundance folded the release papers and put them in his pocket. "You sure word of this hasn't got out yet? I'd like to keep it quiet as I can."

"It hasn't got out from me," Colonel Carson said testily. "I don't want Crook after my hide." He looked at Geronimo. "It's been fifteen years this old rascal has been a guest of Uncle Sam. Maybe nobody will recognize him."

Old rascal! Sundance didn't smile at the colonel's stupidity because he was just a blustering old man

15

trying to get along as best he could. Either the colonel's memory had gone soft, or he didn't want to remember all the things Geronimo had done. Fifteen years before, thanks to frontier photographers, Geronimo's savage face had been as famous as the President's. Sundance remembered the most famous picture of all, made during a temporary truce; it showed Geronimo aiming a Winchester directly at the camera. There wasn't a hope in hell that Geronimo wouldn't be recognized somewhere along the way.

"Where's the nearest telegraph wire?" Sundance asked. He knew they were building one to the military camp, but it hadn't been finished yet.

"Closest one is Lakeport," the colonel said. "Why do you ask?"

Sundance said, "I'm thinking one of your men will get over there and make some money from the newspapers."

"Then I'll try to keep them busy. That's not to say they won't get some civilian to go in their place. I've got no control of civilians. But I'll do the best I can."

Colonel Carson came over to Geronimo and held out his hand. "Behave yourself, you old ruffian," he said.

Geronimo shook the colonel's hand and turned away quickly. The colonel said to Sundance, "You won't have any trouble with him. When they first brought him here he ran off in the swamps a few times. After the fourth or fifth time he gave it up. I guess he got flogged pretty good, but that was before my time. The two of us have always gotten along pretty good."

Sure, Sundance thought, I'll bet you have.

Outside Eagle was saddled and waiting and when the colonel gave the order a trooper saddled an army mount for Geronimo. The trooper stared at Sundance with curious eyes, wondering who he was and what he was doing with Geronimo. Sundance didn't mind the curious stare. With his copper skin and shoulder length yellow hair and buckskins he had long grown accustomed to being stared at. He wore a beaded weapons belt from which were slung a long-barreled .44 Colt, a razor-edged Bowie knife, and a straight-handled throwing hatchet.

When the trooper finished the colonel waved him away. It was blistering hot in the compound, with hardly a breath of air. Out past the army post the swamps stretched away for limitless miles. Sundance hated this steaming swamp country, with its water moccasins and alligators. It was so different from the clean, hard Southwest where he had spent so much of his life. He sensed Geronimo's hatred too.

The colonel waved goodbye and went back inside. Geronimo stood for a moment and looked around the merciless place where fifteen years of his existence had dragged by, one despairing day after another. He turned to look at Sundance, who was mounted up and waiting.

"I want to remember this place forever," Geronimo said. "I want to burn it into my brain like a hot iron."

"You'd do better to put it behind you."

The old Apache's eyes flashed with anger. "Not while there is breath in my body."

Sundance touched his heels to Eagle's flanks and started for the gate of the post. "Do what you like," he said.

Going out through the gate, Geronimo turned again and spat and for a moment his impassive face was contorted with incredible hate.

"You ride ahead of me," Sundance said.

CHAPTER TWO

Heading west toward the Gulf Coast, Sundance figured the best way to do it would be to take a boat from Tampa to New Orleans. The coast boats from Tampa sailed directly from Tampa to New Orleans, so at least they'd be cut off from the world for a few days. The railroad would be faster, but the trains stopped at too many places. Besides there was no way to outrun the telegraph. New Orleans was a big city and the passions of the frontier had no part in its life. Once they got there he would figure out the next part of his plan. But when he thought about it, he knew he had no plan at all. It all depended on what happened, how much the world knew about the release of Geronimo.

Sundance knew there was no way to keep it a secret. First the news would get to Lakeport from the fort; after that the telegraph lines would start humming, and he could just about hear the excited messages as they clicked their way from the telegrapher's key. In the end it would boil down to one statement: Geronimo was on the loose again. Naturally, in the cities, that wouldn't mean a thing—just another item for the newspapers. But even in the cities they would blow up the story, make it out to be more than it was. From the cities the news would be tapped to the small towns and settlements of Arizona; that's where the real panic would be and, when he thought about it, there was good reason to be, for fifteen years wasn't a long enough time to obliterate the dreaded name of Geronimo.

In recent months there had been sporadic Apache raids along the border, but from all reports the raiders were poorly led and badly organized. The threat of Geronimo's return would sweep through Arizona like a brush fire. The politicians and the panic-mongers would feed that fire to their own advantage. But, Sundance thought, they weren't entirely wrong. If Geronimo broke loose and got back into the mountains, it would mean a long and bloody war. There was no doubt that the Apaches would lose, but while the war lasted—and it could last for years—it would take an enormous toll in misery and bloodshed.

Late at night they rode through a town and a man with a badge pinned to his shirt came out onto a porch and looked after them. The village constable, or whatever he was, didn't challenge them, and they kept going. On both sides of the narrow road the swamp quaked in the darkness; they listened for sounds of pursuit, but heard nothing but the croaking of frogs and the strange barking of night-hunting alligators. They traveled all night and well into the next day. In the afternoon they slept for a few hours on a sandy island in the swamp.

Before they lay down Sundance said, "I don't want to tie you. Give me your word you won't try to run off and I'll believe you." Sundance realized that the Apache was very much afraid of the swamp. To Geronimo his only country—his nation—was southern Arizona. Everything else was strange and menacing.

Geronimo looked around at the dark, oily-looking water that surrounded the little patch of dry ground. "In this place you can have my word. I would not know which way to go from here. How do you know the *abortos* will not devour us in our sleep?"

Aborto was the Spanish word for monster. "You mean alligators?" Sundance asked. "They won't eat you in your sleep. Alligators seldom attack humans unless they're crazy or starving. Get some sleep now and I will watch the monsters."

An hour later Sundance woke up when Geronimo cried out in terror. Sundance drew his Colt. "One of them is coming, I hear it," the Apache cried.

Sundance looked where Geronimo was pointing and saw a big gator crawling out of the water and up onto the sand. Picking up a chunk of deadwood, Sundance threw it at the gator's head. The gator opened its mouth in a snarl and splashed back into the swamp.

Geronimo looked at Sundance with wonder. "You did that. If I had not seen it I would not believe it. You had a gun but you did not shoot."

Sundance smiled at the Apache. "We better move on before any more monsters try to get in bed with us. I'd worry more about snakes if I were you."

The fierce old warrior shuddered. "I will be glad to leave this terrible land. The god who made this place was an evil god."

"Let's get going," Sundance said.

Once again they rode all night and by morning the swamp and jungle gave way to a coastal plain that ran down to the bright blue waters of the Gulf. After the stink of the swamp the clear salt air felt good in their lungs. Geronimo's eyes widened as he looked at the immensity of the Gulf of Mexico; after a lifetime spent in deserts and swamps he had never seen the ocean before. He pointed toward the horizon.

"What is beyond that?" he asked.

Sundance said, "Depending where you want to go. Texas, Mexico. We're going to Louisiana. And you're not going anywhere but Oklahoma."

Geronimo's eyes took on a crafty look. "Louisiana is not so far from Texas."

"And beyond Texas there's Arizona. Forget it. Remember you gave your word back on that island."

"On the island, yes. Here there are no monsters and no snakes." Geronimo looked at the sea again.

Sundance slapped his holster. "This will kill you quicker than any snake if you try to double-shuffle me. Go on now, ride in front of me and we'll be in Tampa in no time."

Tampa was no more than ten miles along the long empty beach, and in another hour they were able to see the church spires in the town, and when they got closer a steamer was putting out to sea, leaving a long trail of black smoke behind it.

Geronimo watched the outgoing steamer for a long time. "I have much Mexican gold hidden in the mountains," he said.

"What gold?"

"There was no time to take it when Three Stars attacked us so suddenly. The others who knew about it were killed by the soldiers, so the gold is still there."

22

"If it's still there why didn't you try to bribe your way out of jail with it?"

"The white soldiers would take the gold and kill me so I could not talk about it. But I swear to you it's still in the mountains, in a place to which a goat could not climb. Take me there and you can have all of it. I just want to go back to my country. Oklahoma is like the end of the world to me. The money is there, Sundance. Let me go free and you will be a rich man."

It was likely enough that Geronimo had Mexican gold hidden away in some remote mountain cave. Lord knows he had stolen enough of it in his time, which was the main reason that he had been able to buy the latest repeating rifles. And he could buy more if he hung onto the gold. On both sides of the border there were gunrunners who would sell him all he needed.

"I don't want your gold," Sundance said. "I'll never be rich and you'll never start another bloody war. I'll kill you before I let you get away from me."

"We will see," Geronimo said.

In less than an hour they reached the outskirts of Tampa, a bustling port with long wharves running out into the sea. Close to a breakwater a ship with steam up rode at anchor. They rode into town from the south end and had to skirt some tobacco warehouses owned by a Cuban cigar-maker before they got out onto the breakwater. At the end of it was a ticket seller's hut and a stack of crates.

"You left it mighty late," the ticket seller complained when Sundance asked for two tickets to New Orleans. "And you say you want to ship two horses as well. That's going to cost you extra for

23

holding up the ship.''

Sundance put the ticket money on the counter, then added another twenty dollars. It was all War Department money and he wasn't about to argue about the cost.

''Just get the horses on the boat,'' he said.

After a short argument, and the passing of some money to the first mate, the horses were aboard and orders were given to cast off. Standing at the rail, Sundance looked up quickly when two men in dark suits drove a spring wagon down to the dock at breakneck speed. Instead of buying tickets, they left the wagon unhitched and dashed up the gangplank just as it was being drawn in. The ticket seller yelled after them, but they took no heed. The first mate bore down on them with a truculent air. One of the men, young and burly, shoved money at the mate, saying something about urgent business in New Orleans. The mate took the money, shrugged, and walked away.

The two men went below without looking at Sundance. They might be what they said they were, two sweating moneygrubbers running to catch a boat. Geronimo, made nervous by the sway of the steamer, hadn't noticed them.

''It's not going to sink,'' Sundance told him. ''And if you get sick you won't die. You'll think you're going to die, but you won't.''

The steam whistle let loose with a few blasts and the boat eased away from the dock. In a few minutes Tampa began to drop away behind them. The wind picked up as they steamed out into the Gulf and Geronimo gripped the rail so hard that Sundance had to pull hard to make him let go.

''Loosen up and you'll feel better. We'll go below

so you can lie down.''

As the sea grew choppier, Geronimo's face turned a gray color and there was an imploring look in his eyes. He said, ''Sundance, I do not like this boat or this sea.''

Taking the old Apache by the arm, Sundance steered him down the companionway to their cabin, and Sundance had to call a steward to get him to unlock the door. There was no sign of the two men who had come aboard in such a hurry. The portholes were closed and the tiny cabin was hot and airless. Sundance got the portholes open and got Geronimo to lie down on one of the bunks. Lying there gray-faced, the Apache looked nothing like the fearsome warrior everybody said he was.

Thirty minutes out from Tampa, the Apache vomited into a china chamber pot that Sundance pulled out from under the lower berth. After that he still felt sick, but not as sick as he had been. Not much later the old man fell asleep, moaning as he turned uneasily from side to side. Sundance sat and watched the door.

The steamer was running against a heavy sea in a strong wind, and the vibration shook the boat from stem to stern. Spray splashed in through the portholes, but Sundance left them open. He continued to watch the door of the cabin, but nothing happened. But if something happened he'd be ready for it. There was something about the two so-called businessmen that wasn't right. They had been too loud in stating their business to the mate, and abandoning a new-looking spring wagon and a young horse wasn't right either. So either there was an awful lot of money at stake in New Orleans, or they wanted to get on the steamer for an even more pressing reason. Sundance knew he was being overly suspicious, but that came with the dangerous trade he followed. At times he had been wrong about people—no one was right all the time—but he knew without conceit that his betting average was pretty high.

The day wore on and they were far beyond the sight of land, and as the aging steamer battered its way on a northwesterly course the wind increased in force; at times the sea got so rough that the driving screw of the ship was left clear of the water. When that happened the entire ship shook and lost some of the power that propelled it. But always it regained its drive as the screw took hold again.

It was close to dark when Geronimo woke up and lay there with his eyes closed. Sundance knew the old man was over the worst of it. A knock came on the door and Sundance brought his gun out and called out, "What do you want?"

A voice came back. "It's the steward. You want me to light the gas lamps?"

Sundance said he would do it himself and he heard footsteps going away. He waited a little longer before he struck a match and held it close to the fragile burner of the gas lamp. He turned the screw and the gas light popped into life. Geronimo opened his eyes and stared at the light.

"How do you feel?" Sundance asked him.

Geronimo wiped sweat from his face and lay back on the pillow. "I am sick, I need whisky."

Sundance went to the door of the cabin and listened but didn't open it. If they were waiting out there to kill him they could do it as soon as he turned the knob. There wasn't a sound in the walkway, but that didn't mean they weren't out there. It was a good thick door. That didn't mean that a barrage of bullets from two big-caliber pistols wouldn't blow it down in no time flat.

Sundance got away from the door. "No whisky," he said. "I don't want you going wild on me. You have a bad reputation when it comes to whisky. I mean no disrespect by that, Geronimo. My own reputation is no better than yours. When you get to Oklahoma you can stay drunk for the rest of your life."

Geronimo said, "If I have to go to Oklahoma that's what I will do. Why are you sneaking around like a thief? Drawing your pistol and listening for strange sounds?"

Sundance sat down facing the old man. "There are two men on this boat I think may have been sent to kill you. They were sent to kill you or kill me. You didn't see them because you were too busy being sick like a woman with a three months' baby in her belly."

Sundance's sarcasm roused the old Apache from his apathy, as he knew it would.

"And that is why you sneak like a thief because you are afraid to go out and face them? Give me a gun, even a knife, and I will kill them for you."

"I thought I would let them come to us. That's one way to do it."

Geronimo said, "The way to do it is to attack them before they attack us. That is how I would do it. That is how I have always done it."

Suddenly Geronimo smiled, knowing what Sundance was up to. This time there was no craftiness in his smile. "You have made me angry, Sundance, and that is what you meant to do. How soon do you want to kill them?"

"We could be wrong about them." Sundance smiled. "We could be going out to kill innocent men."

"In my eyes no white man is innocent. But if they are innocent you can feel sorry for them. I will be happy I killed them. I would like to use the throwing hatchet. It has been years since my hand grasped the haft of such a weapon. Though I am an old man, I will show you how it is used."

"Just don't throw it at me, Apache."

Geronimo's smile was grim and final as death itself. "There may come a time for that. If I do, I won't miss. How do you want to do it?"

Sundance said, "I will go up on deck and they will follow me. They will follow because they will want to kill me first, thinking my vengeance will be terrible if they kill my good friend Geronimo before they kill me."

"You're full of shit, Sundance."

"Where in hell did you learn to talk like that? True, you have learned to talk English very well, but there is no dignity in talk like that." Sundance smiled.

So did the treacherous old Apache. "For fifteen years I heard nothing else from the soldiers at the post. If one suspected another of not telling the truth, he said, 'You're full of shit.' "

Sundance stood up and handed the throwing hatchet to Geronimo, who handled it lovingly while looking at Sundance's skull. He hefted the keen-bladed weapon, testing its balance.

Watching the old murderer, Sundance said, "Don't get any ideas. You can't kill me in the middle of the Gulf of Mexico—and you can't swim."

Geronimo said, "You have no trust, Sundance.

28

There are times when men must fight common enemies so they can have their own fight later."

This time Sundance didn't smile. The time for cautious banter had passed. He said, "I'll go up top and draw their attention to me. Even two-to-one I think I can kill them, but there's no use taking chances. They must be good at killing or they wouldn't have been sent—by whoever sent them—to do a job like this. I can't take a chance on being killed before you become an honest farmer in Oklahoma."

Geronimo fingered the throwing hatchet with its long narrow blade. "Do not dwell too much on that, Sundance."

Ignoring the threat, Sundance said, "I will draw them up on deck. They will come after me and you will come after them. I will take them from the front, you will take them from the rear."

"All is fair in love and war," Geronimo stated.

Sundance said, "You learned too much English in fifteen years. Full of shit and now all's fair in love and war. That last part doesn't sound like troopers at the camp."

"That didn't come from white soldiers but from a white woman, Colonel Carson's woman," Geronimo said. "Mrs. Carson felt sorry for me and decided to teach me English eleven years ago. At first I resisted her attempts before I saw the advantages of learning to talk the language of my enemies. I was sorry—almost sorry—when Mrs. Carson died of blackwater fever. I was not young, not very young, eleven years ago, but I think the Colonel's lady liked me better than her colonel."

Sundance checked the loads in his Colt before he went out. At the door he said, "You're full of shit, Geronimo."

29

CHAPTER THREE

Sundance didn't have to pass through the bar to get to the deck. But he went that way to see if the two men were there, and they were, sitting at a bolted-down table with two tall whisky and mint-sprig drinks in front of them. To Sundance their indifference to him was a dead giveaway, and he climbed the companionway, up into the night wind and the loud crash of the sea spray along the sides of the boat.

Out in the open air it was chilly even for the Gulf of Mexico in the first days of June. The steamer beat on in the darkness, its running lights the only bright things in all that immensity of dark and froth-topped sea. Kerosene lanterns burned dimly on deck, but the deck itself was deserted because of the spray and the wind. It was getting late and most of the passengers had retired to their cabins to be sick or to sleep or to be sick from drinking their own liquor, which was the cheap way to get drunk, since the coast boats charged all the traffic would bear.

Even if he had been wearing nail-shod boots the sounds of sea and wind would have been drowned out as he walked past the shadow of the yellow-lighted bridge and back toward the stern of the boat. Far back as he was, cold salt spray was carried on the wind. It wet his back. It revived him, made him more alert than he had been. He was glad of the feeling. And then he heard them. No, he sensed them—he sensed them coming. He whirled with his gun drawn, but they had their guns drawn and were aiming them. One fired before the other and he felt the wind of the bullet in his face. he fired and the first shooter dropped like a stone. The boat lurched and when he fired at the second shooter he missed and after he did that he straightened up to fire again, but before he got off a shot the second killer jerked upright and then fell forward on his face; and only then did he see the haft of the throwing hatchet projecting from the back of the dead man's head. The hard-thrown hatchet had killed him faster than any bullet.

Geronimo came out of the shadows and stood over the man with the split skull. "Like a melon," he said with quiet satisfaction, like a man who had rung the pin in a horseshoe pitching contest.

Tensed up but calm, Sundance waited for sounds from the bridge. Nothing came—nothing but the heavy throb of the engines, the crash of heavy seas, and the constant whip of the wind.

Geronimo's old man's yellow teeth were yellower in the flushed light of the deck lamps. He was grinning. He said, "The colonel's lady, my English teacher, always said, 'If it's worth doing at all it's worth doing well.'"

Sundance had to pull hard to get his hatchet out of the dead man's cloven skull. He wiped the blade on the dead man's coat. "Forget Mrs. Carson's wise remarks and let's get these bastards over the side."

31

They dragged the dead men to the aft rail and dumped them into the churning sea, and after they hit the water they disappeared from sight, driven deep by the force of the ship's screw. The great white sharks that ranged the Gulf would do the rest. Nothing would remain of the two killers—whoever they were—and the increasingly heavy spray had already washed the blood off the deck.

"I guess they committed suicide," Sundance said. Geronimo is having a good time, he thought.

"To get between you and me was the same as suicide," Geronimo said. "If only you had joined me instead of fighting me in the old days."

This was the first small gesture of friendship the old Apache had shown to the man who was his guardian—and his captor.

Wiping off the throwing hatchet after he held it in the sea spray, Sundance said, "We'd have conquered the world."

Geronimo didn't smile. "No. But we would have kept Arizona for the Apache. I didn't want to take Arizona for myself. I just wanted it to be free."

Sundance decided there was such a thing as hearing too much truth. What was the point of hearing it if nothing could be done?

"Too late for that," he said.

Geronimo turned away with a strange look on his face. He still thinks he can turn back the clock, Sundance thought. After all the years and all the changes, he still thinks he can alter the course of history.

They went back to the cabin and there was no one waiting there to kill them. The two killings had put life back in the old Apache; his seasickness had passed and he stood at the porthole staring out at

32

the dark sea. Five minutes passed in silence and then he turned to Sundance.

"They wanted to kill one of us," he said.

"Or both. But they weren't just men with an old grudge. Later you—we—will have to face that, but this was different. They heard about you too fast. That means they got word by telegraph. So they weren't just two men whose family you murdered long ago."

Being called a murderer didn't get any reaction from Geronimo. "Then who were they?"

"They could have been sent by the Indian Ring. I can't be sure. But it looks like the Ring. They like their Indians tame and you're far from that. I know for sure that they tried to block your release, arguing that you'd stir up the Apaches worse than before. And not just the Apaches, all the tribes in the Southwest, even your enemies. You could do the same in Oklahoma."

Frowning, Geronimo found that hard to understand. "But I would be a stranger—a foreigner—in that country."

Sundance said not so much anymore. "Even the Indians are changing, Geronimo. For years the whites encouraged their wars, set one tribe against the other. In Sonora the Mexicans use Apache scouts to hunt down and kill the Yaquis. Comanche against Kiowa. Maricopa against Pima. But like I say all that is beginning to change."

Geronimo said, "This Indian Ring, I have heard of it, as who has not. Even in the swamps there was talk of your fight against these men. When I got old and harmless"—Geronimo smiled—"they let me wander around the fort. Sometimes Mrs. Carson would bring me to the porch to teach me English while her husband and the other officers drank whisky and talked. Sometimes they talked of the Ring and of you. One young officer always said you should be shot."

Sundance said no. The men they had killed tonight had nothing to do with the army. "Soldiers get bored and they talk. I still think it's the Ring. They have the men and the money."

"They'll be waiting in New Orleans?"

Sundance said they would. "They'll want to know how their hired killers made out. They'll be right there on the dock when this boat pulls in. They'll have enough men there to blow us to bits."

"What can we do?"

"Get the hell off this boat."

"How will we do that?"

"Lifeboat," Sundance answered. There was no other way to do it. Like all desert Indians Geronimo didn't know how to swim. To the Apaches who regarded water as life itself—life measured in pints— the idea of swimming in it was as unthinkable as jumping off a cliff and trying to fly.

Just then alarm bells rang all over the ship and Sundance knew what it meant. The two men had been missed, and now the questions would start. Soon there was the babble of voices in the walkway, and Sundance heard the steward's voice as he went from one cabin to another, knocking on doors.

In moments the steward got to the door and Sundance opened it on the third knock. With the steward was the first mate, blue-uniformed and suspicious. The steward started to talk, but the mate cut him off; his eyes were hard and suspicious.

"You see two men, men looked like businessmen, got aboard in Tampa?" The mate tried to look

34

past Sundance.

Sundance said, "Two men ran down the dock just before we sailed," Sundance said, "What's all the racket about?" Sundance yawned.

The mate backed down a little in the face of Sundance's indifference.

"They're missing," he said.

Opening the door wide, Sundance said, "Well they're not in here. Maybe they're with one of the ladies."

The mate bristled because he thought he was tough. "We don't allow whores to work this ship, mister."

Sundance knew that was a lie. All the Gulf steamers had hooker girls sailing back and forth, plying their trade. The officers got a cut, and more than that when they felt like it.

Sundance feigned anger. "How the hell do I know where they are? It's your ship, you find them. Listen, commodore, if you're all through asking questions, my father here would like to get back to sleep."

The mate stuck his head in and looked at Geronimo, comparing him to Sundance. More or less satisfied, he went out, and in a moment Sundance heard him knocking on the next door.

"Your father!" Geronimo rocked with silent laughter as Sundance closed the door. "You think he believed you?"

Listening to the voices in the walkway, Sundance said, "I don't know what he believed. I think he looked harder than he had to. I get the feeling he'll be back with a whole bunch of monkeys from the engine room. But that won't happen till he searches the whole ship. That means the holds and the crew quarters.''

Geronimo stared out into the darkness. ''I would rather face the men in New Orleans than go out there. What about your stallion? I think you love that horse.''

Sundance had been thinking about Eagle and the years they had shared so many adventures. How many times had the great stallion saved his life with his courage and speed? Times beyond counting.

''A good horse,'' Sundance said. ''But there's no help for it. I have to leave him. Maybe later . . .''

The search for the missing men had moved from the passenger cabins to the depths of the ship. They went out after Sundance checked the walkway; the alarm bell had stopped clanging. When they got to the top of the companionway there was no one on deck. The wind was close to gale force, and there was no saying they'd get anywhere but the bottom of the Gulf. On both sides of the ship three lifeboats—small-sized because the ship was small and didn't carry many passengers—hung from davits. They swung with the ship as it dipped into the troughs and climbed the crests of the waves.

Sundance showed Geronimo how the lifeboats were lowered. The wind blew so hard that he had to pull the old man close to him so he could hear. ''There's a double pulley so they won't go down too fast. But we have to keep the pull steady. If we don't one end will hit first, the boat will sink. Now slip the knot at your end and we'll know in a minute.''

Geronimo was strong for an old man but the pull of the rope jerked him forward as the lifeboat started to drop. In the dim light of the deck lamps the muscles in the old man's neck stood out like cords. Then he gave a sort of silent yell and braced

36

his feet against the rail and the lifeboat went down inch by inch. It hit the heaving water and Sundance yelled, "Let go and jump!"

Sundance yelled again. "Jump, you old bastard!"

Below them the lifeboat was starting to drift away from the thrust of the ship. Geronimo stood as if he had lost the use of his legs. "I can't . . ." he started to say.

He struggled for a moment when Sundance grabbed him, lifted him, and threw him over the rail. He hit the water and went under. Sundance jumped and came up a few yards away from where the old man had gone under. He dived into utter darkness, his hands searching for the old man. At first there was nothing, then his hands touched Geronimo, got him by the shirt and, kicking hard, brought him to the surface. The old man had swallowed water and looked half-dead. Turning on his back, Sundance pulled the old man with him, letting the thrust of the ship push them back into darkness. Sundance turned his head and saw the lifeboat about fifteen yards behind, and moving fast. In seconds the ship had moved well away from him. Kicking his feet, Sundance kept Geronimo afloat until the lights of the ship began to fade into the darkness.

And then it was gone and they were alone in the wind-whipped sea. Behind them the lifeboat dipped and whirled in the sea. Swimming on his back, Sundance pulled the old man after him. His strength was going fast, and if they didn't make it soon, they wouldn't make it at all. Then the back of his head bumped against the lifeboat and, still holding Geronimo, he reached up and grasped the side of it and hung on. The boat spun in the wind but he hung on, his heart thudding against his ribs. If he lost his hold on the boat there was little chance that he would find it again. Taking a tight grip on Geronimo's hair, he launched himself from the water until his belly hung over the side of the boat. Still keeping the old man's head above water, he worked his way into the boat, and when he was in he dragged the old man aboard and turned him face-down on the bottom of the boat.

Geronimo began to splutter and his voice rose in the death wail of the Apaches. Sundance let him wail; there was no one to hear him. Up ahead in the darkness even the throb of the ship's engines had died away.

Geronimo kicked his way around until he was facing Sundance. "Am I dead?" he asked.

"Be quiet," Sundance said. "I have to get the sail up."

Sundance's muscles were quivering with exhaustion and he had to force himself to sit up. All around them was wind and sea and darkness. He felt for the collapsible mast and jerked it upright, then he let the short sail loose and secured it against the rip of the wind. After that he worked his way back to the tiller which was swinging wildly as the boat was buffeted by wind and waves. He steadied it and told Geronimo to keep the hell down out of the way. He had to wedge his body against the tiller to keep it steady. There was nothing to steer by: no moon, no stars. For now the best he could hope for was to keep them from capsizing. How he did it, he would never know, then or later. The boat was inches deep in water, but there could be no thought of bailing it out. Bail it with what? With no light to

38

steer by they could be going anywhere: far out into the Gulf where they would die of thirst. Toward New Orleans? Back toward the Florida coast. Sundance would have settled for the Florida coast, no matter what dangers it held. But he hung on, for to give up was to die.

Time passed and the force of the wind began to lessen. The wind dropped and then it dropped some more. Nothing could be seen in the great black emptiness of the Gulf. Old as he was, Geronimo had been sitting in silence with his head sunk on his chest. Now he raised it and looked at Sundance though he could hardly see him.

"It's not so bad now," he said wearily. "I have been in Florida fifteen years. I know how this wind blows. It can blow up into a hurricane or it can weaken and blow itself out. I pray that it will weaken."

Sundance was very tired. "Don't tell me you've turned Christian?"

"Mrs. Carson tried to teach me Christianity as well as English," Geronimo said. "When I prayed with sincerity she would feed me pork chops. I like goat chops better, but they kept no goats on the post. There was one goat on the post but it was a pet goat and belonged to the daughter of some captain."

It was all a crazy joke, Sundance thought. He was tired, so very tired. At this time of the year, usually he went to hunt bighorn sheep in the Little Rockies, in Colorado, with Three Stars. There in the Little Rockies, Three Stars had built a fine hunting lodge—fine for Three Stars, who liked things solid and simple, and fine for him, who wasn't fussy—and in the evenings, tired and hungry after the fishing and hunting, they would sit in front of the fire and fry fish or roast meat over it.

It began to get light and Geronimo's leathery face was red in the first rays of the sun. Cinched under his chin his hat was a shapeless mass of felt.

"Where are we?" he asked.

"In the Gulf of Mexico," Sundance said.

CHAPTER FOUR

Now it was hot and a fair wind was taking them north. No sailor, Sundance had been at sea before, in the Gulf of California and other places. There was no water in the boat and before long their lips were cracked and dry. Stiff with salt, their clothes had dried hours before.

The best he could do was steer by the sun and hope he was on the right course. Geronimo knew nothing of the sea; indeed this was the first time he had seen it. In the Arizona desert he could have traveled with his eyes closed; now he was faced with a mystery beyond his understanding.

The sun passed the noon mark. "Over there!" Geronimo said. Sundance looked and there was trash floating in the water: torn newspapers and other rubbish thrown from some ship. Sundance scooped up one of the torn newspapers; it was *The Tampa Times* from a few days before.

"Maybe we'll be all right," he said to Geronimo. "This must have come from the ship. We were most of the way to New Orleans when we had to jump off."

It was getting dark when they saw lights winking many miles ahead. Just a few lights and they seemed to wink on and off. Sundance knew it couldn't be New Orleans because the city wasn't on the sea but at the mouth of the Mississippi. It could be anywhere; it could be the lights of a ship.

But soon there were more lights and they remained steady, so it couldn't be a ship. Geronimo said nothing, for the Apaches had no belief in luck of any kind. In another hour Sundance saw the outlines of a coast, some coast. The wind drove them on and he knew they were heading for some small town. He guessed a small fishing port. The lights were strong now.

He ran the lifeboat up onto a rocky beach and they jumped into shallow water and waded ashore. A rickety wooden pier lay to the right of them and beyond the pier was a small cove protected from the sea by a crooked finger of land. In the cove fishing boats bobbed in the mild wind. Houses were grouped along the edge of the cove and on the high ground above it.

They made their way to the pier and climbed a ladder that went up to it. There was no one on the pier, but when they were passing a boathouse a drunken old man staggered out in front of them, belched, begged their pardon, and asked if they had a drink on them. He spoke English but with a Cajun accent.

"We're dry as a bone," Sundance said.

"So am I," the drunk said.

Sundance fished in his pocket for a wrinkled dollar and gave it to the rumpot. "What place is this?"

The drunk hiccuped. "You must be drunker than I am." He steadied himself and waved toward the collection of fishing shacks by the edge of the water. "Yonder is the town of Blind Bay."

"What state?"

"You are drunk! Louisiana, my friend.'

It took some more prodding to obtain the knowledge that they were on the southernmost tip of Louisiana; that New Orleans wasn't much more than fifty miles away.

The drunk said, "I been there so I know. I been there in jail. Horses! You won't find any for sale in Blind Bay, but Laveau the storekeep takes his wagon in there once a month for supplies. If this is Sunday he'll be going there early in the morning. Now I'll be off to slake my thirst, so I'll bid you goodnight."

Laveau, a clever-faced little man, ran the only store in Blind Bay, and he was still open. Unlike the drunk, he took great interest in their appearance, but didn't say anything. Sundance's weapons made him nervous; he didn't cheer up until Sundance put money on the counter, asked for food, a place they could sleep. Sundance guessed the storekeeper thought they were jailbreakers from some prison camp in Florida or Mississippi.

"You can sleep in the hayloft out back. I'll have to charge you for that. My friends, I'll have to charge you for everything. Money in advance." He named a price.

Pocketing the money, Laveau said, "I'll wake you at four o'clock in the morning. Got to get an early start. Time is money, as they say. No smoking in the hayloft, gents. I don't want to get burned out."

Later, eating thick meat sandwiches and drinking water in the sweetsmelling hayloft, Geronimo said, "You trust that little rat of a storekeeper?"

"Not trust him," Sundance said. "But he's mak-

43

ing money off us, so he'll want to make some more. To him we're just a couple of Indian prison breakers, and there's no money in turning us in."

The old Apache grunted. "We'll kill him on the road to New Orleans and take his wagon. You'll get your money back."

"The hell with the money! And we don't kill anybody we don't have to. On that road the storekeeper and his wagon are known to everybody. They won't give him a second look."

"Why go to New Orleans at all?"

"My horse will be there. I hope he's there." Sundance took another long drink of water. "Now get some sleep. Four o'clock comes early."

Nothing happened during the night. Sundance slept the light sleep of a man ever alert for danger. Geronimo muttered in Spanish in his sleep. Once Sundance woke up and went outside to look around. By three o'clock he was awake and checking his weapons. He always kept the Colt .44 well oiled, so no damage had been done to it by the sea.

Geronimo woke up with a start and reached for a rifle that wasn't there. Sundance said nothing. In a while Geronimo said, "I was dreaming of that last big battle in Sonora. The Caves. We could have held you off forever if the mountain guns hadn't brought half the mountain down on us. Was that your idea?"

"Yes," Sundance said. "You wouldn't surrender so we elevated the guns and brought the mountain down on you."

Geronimo drank water and ate the last of the meat. "I should have thought of that," he said without rancor. "You buried half my warriors alive." Suddenly the old man's admiration gave way to anger. "My two sons were sealed up forever. I have much to thank you for, Sundance."

"Don't mention it," Sundance said bitterly. Memories of the Battle of the Caves had remained with him for fifteen years. Even Three Stars had balked at the use of the guns to start landslides. But it had to be done and they did it. It was the one thing they never talked about, for what good was regret? But he too had his bad dreams.

"The storekeeper is coming, somebody is coming," Sundance said.

"Hello in there," the storekeeper called. "You all set to go to the big city?"

They climbed down and Laveau had his big wagon waiting in front of the store. The sky was streaked with gray and the morning wind had salt in it. Nothing else stirred in the town of Blind Bay. Sundance guessed the town didn't have a telegraph line, didn't have a newspaper, didn't have anything.

The freight wagon was a big one, with high sides and a canvas top. In it dried fish stank in crates. Laveau told them to make themselves to home. "Be obliged if you'd keep out of sight," the storekeeper said. "Where you come from and where you're going is absolutely none of this man's business. But I have to live here when this is all over. Now listen, gents, you'll want to eat on the way, so I'll have to charge a small fee for it."

"Sure," Sundance said, concealing his contempt. "A man isn't in business for the fun of it."

Laveau said heartily, "You bet your britches. I like a man that understands the business of business. You sure you got the money for the vittles?"

45

Geronimo was in a bad mood and he muttered in Spanish. Sundance told him to get a grip on his *lengua largo*: his long tongue. The storekeeper looked nervous.

Sundance said, "My father ate too much last night and has a sour stomach."

"Bastardo!" Geronimo muttered.

Laveau said, "What did he say?"

"He said it's a real bastard having a sour stomach. He'll get over it after a while. He always does."

They lay in the bed of the big wagon with stinking fish crates all around them, and the price Laveau charged for half a smoked ham would have paid for a whole pig. There was no charge for the water that came · ith the ham. The wagon, pulled by two big blacks, rattled out of the still-sleeping town, made its way past a small cemetery with lambs and simpering angels on the gravestones. The faces of the angels and lambs had been eaten away by the salt air from the Gulf. The wagon and the whole town stank of fish. In a few minutes the forgotten village fell away behind them.

Sundance wondered if he would find his horse again. By now the big stallion, a one-man horse, would be fretting in a pen somewhere on the New Orleans docks. Thinking about Eagle, Sundance rejected the idea that he was a sentimental man. The big stallion was as much a part of him as the weapons he used. Goddamn! he thought. I like that horse.

It was late in the day when they reached the outskirts of New Orleans. Worn out by his ordeal, Geronimo slept part of the way. Now Sundance shook him awake and told him it was time to part company with Laveau. The storekeeper didn't understand Spanish, but he turned when he heard them talking.

"You want off?" he asked.

When Sundance said yes Laveau reined in the horses.

Sundance pulled his Colt and cocked it and aimed it at the storekeeper's forehead. "This is just a reminder," he said. "You never saw us, we don't exist. Understand? Tell the world and I'll be back."

Laveau stared into the muzzle of the pistol. "Mister," he said. "Far as you're concerned I'm deaf, dumb and blind. You think you want your money back?"

Sundance let the hammer down and holstered his gun. "Keep the money and keep your mouth shut."

"Yes sir," the storekeeper said, sweat beading his clever little face.

The wagon rattled away and they were left at dusk on the dusty road with Negro shanties on both sides of it. Smells of cooking came from the shanties. It was a lot better than the stink of dried fish. Old men rocking on porches got up suddenly and doors closed as Sundance and Geronimo dropped off the back of the wagon. The wagon climbed a hump in the road and went out of sight. Sundance guessed they were safe enough for a while. The blacks wouldn't mix into any business but their own.

The road was unpaved and dusty and the trees that lined it were dusty too. Ahead lay the early evening glare of the city. "I think this is Gretna," Sundance said. It began to rain soft, warm rain; the falling rain made no sound in the thick dust of the narrow road.

Geronimo spat in the dust. "You don't know

where you are, Sundance. You—the great friend of generals doesn't know where he is.''

Sundance ignored the old man's sarcasm. "You want to knock on somebody's door and ask how to go?''

They hadn't gone far—it was dark now—when six Negroes of varying ages, but mostly young, stepped down from the porch of a whisky store and blocked their path. Sundance spoke in Spanish to Geronimo; told him to go easy.

A young black with a razor-scarred face said, "Talk American, you halfbreed son of a bitch.''

The young Negro had a loud check suit, candy-striped shirt, a light gray derby hat, gray Jefferson shoes with elastic sides.

An older Negro shoved him aside and told him to shut his fucking mouth. This man was about forty, thickened by food and by age and maybe whisky. Although not quite yet in middle age, his bushy hair was grizzled and gray. He looked tough. Sundance decided he was tough. Sundance guessed there was a gun in his waistband, under his stained black broadcloth coat.

"You want no trouble with us," Sundance said, thinking that if it came to trouble he would have to take on six of them. "Kindly make way and we'll go about our business.''

The tough Negro had been staring at Geronimo. Suddenly he said, "By Christ! It is you— Geronimo! Don't you remember me!''

Sundance tensed but kept quiet. Something was going on here that he didn't understand.

Geronimo stared at the big Negro. He said, "Are you the one?''

The Negro's face split into a wide grin. "Sure I

48

am! Sergeant Lafe Johnson, Ninth Cavalry."

Geronimo said, "The Buffalo Soldiers! After all these years! You could have killed me, but you didn't. Why didn't you? You fought us hard and well."

The Negro called Lafe Johnson had been drinking, but he wasn't drunk. Now he made a mock bow. "I betrayed home and country when I didn't kill you. Course you-all got to realize this ain't my home and this ain't my country. Lord but you led us a merry chase. Who's your friend that's been making hard eyes at us poor nigger folk?"

"Ugly, isn't he?" Geronimo smiled at Johnson. To Sundance he said, "Sixteen or seventeen years ago this brave man ran me down on a ridge. He killed my horse and I hit my head on a rock. When I woke up his carbine was in my face. And yet he didn't kill me, didn't take me prisoner. Why Johnson?"·

Johnson gave a booming laugh. "It was the Fourth of July and I was feeling patriotic."

"You would have been promoted," Geronimo said.

Johnson laughed again. "To what? Not to officer. Ever-body know the nigger soldier need the white officer to lead him, cause he too nigger-dumb to lead hisself." Johnson dropped the field hand talk. "Geronimo, you were doing what the niggers in this country should have done. You got out there and whipped the white man's white ass. Maybe the niggers will do it yet when they stop strumming their banjos and eating water melon and singing *Massa and Missy* and talking ass-backward for the white folks' entertainment."

Sundance said, "Geronimo's in the newspapers?''

"All the papers, on the front page," Johnson said. "The *Picayune* is getting a rupture trying to find headlines big enough. I guess it's the same all over the country. Even the Uncle Tom papers here in New Orleans are saying what a disgrace it is to let this wild man loose."

Geronimo smiled at Sergeant Lafe Johnson, late of the Ninth Cavalry, United States Army, the best all-black regiment the country had ever seen. Some years before, because of political pressure from the Southerners, the Ninth had been moved to the Northwest.

"This is Jim Sundance," Geronimo said.

Johnson said, "I was just funning before. I know who he is. He's in the papers too. Geronimo, there's a strong movement afoot, as the newspaper scribblers say, to send you back where you came from. There's even talk that you murdered two men aboard the *Gulfport Queen* and tossed their bodies overboard."

Sundance smiled. "It's all a lie."

Johnson's laugh rumbled up from his barrel chest. "Well sure it is. I know that. Murder aside, they got you down for stealing a lifeboat."

"We just borrowed it, Sergeant," Sundance said. "Now you think you can fix us up with some clothes so we can get into the city and get my horse?"

The big tough Negro disregarded Sundance's question. Instead he turned to Geronimo. "The papers say you're headed for some farm in Oklahoma. That doesn't sound like you." Johnson gave Sundance a quick look. "You don't have to go if you don't want. We could detain Mr. Sundance whilst you go on west. I would say that could

50

be arranged."

The other blacks grinned.

Sundance knew he couldn't take all of them, yet he meant to give it a try, if it came to that. Three Stars' good name and reputation were riding on getting Geronimo to a peaceful old age in Oklahoma. If Geronimo tore loose and started another war, it would be the end of General George Crook. Sundance didn't trust Geronimo, didn't trust him at all. The old Apache was a great fighter; also he was a great villain, justifying his misdeeds by all that had been done to his people. Even so, Sundance—at that moment—wasn't prepared to consider the rights and wrongs of history.

He decided to kill Geronimo, if that was what he had to do, and he knew he would die in a hail of lead from the guns of these black men while he was doing it, but in the end what else could he do? No personal honor was involved here, for he cared little for what other men thought of him. If he had to die, then it would be for Crook, perhaps the only real friend he had known in the thirty-eight years of his life. You had to die anyway, so it might as well be for something that mattered.

Johnson said it again: "You don't have to go to Oklahoma, Geronimo. Wouldn't be no trouble at all to get you back to Arizona. I'll bet the folks out there are just waiting for you to show up."

Geronimo turned to look at Sundance. He looked at him as if he never had seen him before. Sundance almost could hear the devious workings of the old Apache's mind. Geronimo's thoughts seemed to be a puzzle to himself.

Then he said, "Oklahoma will do for a start, Sergeant Johnson."

CHAPTER FIVE

Johnson and his men led the way through the maze of foul-smelling alleys that sloped down to the docks. The big Negro showed his teeth in a savage grin. "Me and the boys come down here now and then to borrow a few things. The po-lice sort of like to stay away from this part of N.O. When they do come they bring a whole platoon armed with shotguns. Course us boys got guns too."

Johnson took one of the new double-action, swing-out .38 Colts from under his coat. He pushed out the cylinder and checked the loads. "You can reload this litle beauty faster'n anything around. And when you hit a man with a hollow-nose— bam!—he don't do anything but die."

They moved on the darkness of freight yards and warehouses. They could smell the river now, oil-streaked and filthy, and soon they heard the slap of water against the pilings. After they got to the end of another alley, Johnson waved them behind a stack of empty barrels. Then he looked up cautiously.

"There's your boat," he whispered. "She'll be off again come morning."

Hawsered to the dock *The Gulfport Queen* was

dark except for the deck lights, and while they watched a thick-set man came out from the shadow of the bridge and went down the first companion-way.

"Watchman," Johnson whispered. "Now down there where it's so dark you can't see, that's where they pen the animals that come in on the boat. If they still have your horse, that's where he'll be. That's guarded too, but I never knew them to put more than one man on it."

Sundance stared into the darkness. "This time they could have added a few. More than a few."

"I was thinking that," Johnson whispered. "Honey to the flies. Shit! I wish we didn't have to cross so much open space. They could have ether lights all set up to flare. They catch us in the open we'll be meat."

Johnson's head jerked around as the watchman's heavy boots rang on the steel of the companionway. "Son of a bitch! What's he want back on the deck?"

From the cover of the barrels they watched while the watchman came to the aft rail and stood there filling his pipe. He stood his shotgun against the rail while he did it, and like all men with time on their hands, he did everything very slowly. First he tapped the bowl of his pipe on the rail. Johnson ground his big teeth together and Geronimo hissed curses in Spanish. Sundance did nothing but watch.

Now the watchman was scraping the bowl of his pipe with a penknife. A barge hooted out on the river. The barge splashed by the end of the long deck, pushed by a panting steam tug. "If I could get close enough with the hatchet," Geronimo whispered in English.

"Wait," Sundance said quietly. They were there to find a horse, not to murder a harmless watchman.

Johnson didn't agree. "Geronimo's right. The crew is up in the city getting drunk. The saloons'll be closing soon and they'll be all over the dock. If he don't get out of there soon I'll kill him myself."

"One more minute," Sundance said.

A match flared as the watchman lit his pipe, sucking on it vigorously. Then he turned his back and leaned against the rail. He turned once to spit into the river.

Sundance said to Johnson, "Geronimo and I will go across now. Look, we'll be all right. No sense the lot of you risking death. You got us here and I thank you for it."

Johnson grinned. "Thanks for thinking of us, but we ain't all that busy tonight. Move out now." For an instant the black gang leader sounded like the cavalry sergeant he had been so many years before. "But if that motherjumper turns for another spit it'll be his last."

Sundance nodded. Running fast on moccasined feet, he crossed the two hundred yards of cobblestoned dock to the other side. Crouched in the shadows, he drew his pistol and waited for the others. Geronimo came next, fast enough for an old man, making not a sound. Then, one by one, the six blacks came across. Johnson came last. It was dark and quiet.

"Now listen," Sundance whispered. "If they have a trap set up they won't be using city police or hired guards. The Indian Ring always uses its own men, the worst they can find. I just want you to know they don't take prisoners."

Johnson was impatient. "Neither do we. You know how many niggers fall accidental on purpose from the top floor of the Parish Prison? What we do now, we go down along the side of this warehouse and then there's an alley that goes to the horse pen. Then we get down on our bellies and listen."

"Sounds right," Sundance whispered. "Some one of them got to make a noise."

They found the alley and went through it, feeling their way through bottles and rusty cans. Rats ran away from them. Now that the big warehouse wasn't in the way, they could see the horse pen in the reflected glare of the city. Sundance's heart pounded when he saw Eagle moving fretfully in the center of the pen. A thick, three-rail fence ran around the pen, and there were no animals in it except the big stallion. Now he knew for sure that they were waiting to kill him: with no other horses in the pen they would have a clear field of fire. It was smart and at the same time it was a dead giveaway.

They waited in absolute silence, hardly breathing. Eagle must have sensed Sundance's presence because he began to run in frantic circles, closer and closer to the fence. He kicked at the padlocked gate and whinnied frantically. But then he quieted down again and did nothing more than paw at the ground. Sundance smiled. They even had him saddled.

In a while the clunk of metal against wood came from the river side of the pen. A long stack of lumber about four feet high stood about five feet back from the pen. "That's where they are," Sundance whispered to Johnson.

Johnson said calmly, "That's my thinking. I guess we can keep them busy enough, but what about that gate. It's chained and locked. You ain't going to break that chain or lock with a pistol shot. You got to get in there and then get out. How're you going to do that? No horse can jump that fence. Mister, I know about horses.''

''Maybe this horse can.''

''Then why ain't he done it?''

''I've got to tell him,'' Sundance said. ''As soon as your men open up I'm going over that fence. Lay it down heavy, I have to get set for the jump. If I make it Geronimo will have to ride double till I find something for him to ride. Then you men get the hell out of here.''

Johnson drew the .38 Colt with the hollow-nose bullets. ''You're crazy,'' he whispered. ''But I know how you feel. The white man drives everybody crazy.'' Johnson looked around at his men. They all had their guns drawn. ''You ready to go?''

Sundance jumped to his feet as the night was shattered by gunfire. It came so abruptly that the hidden gunmen were taken completely by surprise. Johnson emptied one .38 Colt and then he drew another. He passed the first one to a squinty little Negro, who was the ''loader'' for the gang. Using two half-moon clips he could reload a swing-out .38 in four or five seconds.

Sundance ran for the fence as the startled ambushers returned the fierce gunfire. It sounded like all Johnson's men were using swingout Colts. The loader was busy throwing them back and forth. Sundance got to the fence and vaulted up and over it. An ambusher's bullet clipped the wood where his feet had been a moment before. A repeating shotgun opened up from behind the pile of lumber and big lead pellets sang over his head. Johnson was yelling to his men to lay down a heavier fire.

In the pen Eagle was whirling wildly, but now he ran straight when he saw Sundance. The big stallion turned as Sundance sprang into the saddle and galloped his horse to the other side of the corral. Bullets came at him but Johnson's men kept most of the ambushers pinned down. Eagle gave a high cry of panic as a bullet creased his flank. At the far side of the pen Sundance turned his horse and started to make his run for the fence. From behind the stacked lumber a hoarse voice was yelling, "Kill the bastard! Kill the bastard!" After that the fire got heavier and Sundance knew he wouldn't get more than one try at the jump. Even in the saddle the fence looked higher than a hill. It came at him like a brick wall.

Sundance touched his heels to Eagle's flanks and the big stallion soared over the fence like a bird. Then Eagle's forelegs touched ground and they were over. Driven from cover by the hoarse voice of their leader, the ambushers were trying to make a frontal assault on Johnson's men. Johnson was yelling, "Come and get it, you whey-faced bastards!" But still the ambushers came on firing steadily. Sundance yelled at Geronimo to get the hell out of there and the old Apache came at a steady run. He cursed in Spanish as Sundance jerked him aboard and threw him across the front of his saddle. They were galloping away when suddenly Johnson's men stopped firing. Sundance jerked around in the saddle to wave, but there was nothing to wave at. He grinned savagely. Johnson and his men were gone, swallowed up in the maze of alleys and byways. God help the ambushers if they got brave and followed them in there.

With Geronimo kicking and cursing in front of

him, Sundance galloped away from the docks and kept going until the yelling had died out behind him. He listened for sounds of pursuit but heard none. It looked like the ambushers had figured on a quick kill when he came to get the stallion. Either they hadn't thought it necessary to have horses standing by, or they were city trash who wouldn't know how to stay on a horse if they had one.

When they had gone a safe enough distance Sundance found time to let Geronimo sit up straight in front of him. The old Apache was still mad at the unceremonious way he had been forced to leave the dock.

"All this is madness," he said.

Sundance wasn't too concerned about Geronimo's dignity, so he ignored the old man's complaints.

"Did Johnson lose any men?" he asked roughly.

"Two men," Geronimo said. "Two dead, one wounded."

Sundance said, "Good men, whoever they were."

"Good men," Geronimo agreed. "And what happens now?"

"You can't ride double all the way to Oklahoma. What happens now is we find you a horse. There's the railroad but I think they'll be watching the depots. Maybe we'll take the railroad later. First we have to get out of the city."

Geronimo stiffened at the thought of traveling by rail. "I was on a train just once in my life. That was when they caged me and took me to Florida like an animal."

"This time will be different, if we go that way."

Geronimo said, "Johnson and his men would

have killed you if I had given the word. I saved your life tonight."

"Why was that—if you want to get back to Arizona so bad?"

"Because you saved my life in the sea."

"You think that makes us even?"

"That is possible, Sundance."

"But then there is the boat. If I hadn't been along those two men could have killed you. I could have killed you while you were puking. That is more than possible."

"You would do well to let me go. I have so few years left what does it matter?"

Sundance grinned. Geronimo was a rogue no matter what age he was. "You can't be more than eighty," he said, knowing that Geronimo was not much more than sixty-five.

"Maybe I'll live longer than you," Geronimo said. "I have no great longing to grow corn for the rest of my life."

"How about potatoes?" Sundance asked.

Geronimo gave his answer to that—he spat.

Sundance knew it would be dangerous to try to buy a horse in the city. Geronimo's battered face was on the front page of too many newspapers. By now they'd be digging up all the famous old photographs. The best thing to do was to get to Oklahoma as quietly as they could. A lot of that would depend on how Geronimo behaved, and there was no chance that he wouldn't try to make a break for it. Once again he decided to kill the old warrior, if that was the only way to stop him. Kill him and bury him in a lonely place where his body never would be found. It would be a hell of a thing to do, but he was ready to do it.

Keeping to the outskirts of the city, they made their way along the southern shore of Lake Pontchartrain. It rained heavily for a while; the rain gave them the advantage of being able to travel without being seen. The rain rippled the surface of the huge lake and it was late and dark. The road west and north was deserted, and only once did they have to ride off the road when a bunch of drunken Cajun revelers in a wagon came the other way, heading for the city. They had to wait a long time, with Eagle standing fetlock deep in stagnant water, because there were many singers in the heavy wagon and the two mules pulling it were tired and old.

An hour later they reached a small town called Laplace. Shrouded by rain and fog, the town showed hardly any lights. At the far end of town they came to a harness maker and livery stable with a storm lantern burning under a tin shade above the door; and it took some hard knocking before the door swung open and an old man in a dirty nightshirt blinked and yawned himself awake. He was Cajun like the rest of the town. He looked suspicious when he saw what they looked like, but he let them in. To reassure him Sundance took out a roll of bills and peeled off a few.

Yes, the harness maker said, he could sell them a fine horse. There were horses in some of the stalls; none of them was fine. Sundance asked the stableman to turn up the light so he could see what he wanted to buy. In the end Sundance settled for a ten-year-old gray that had been given hard use in his time.

"And a saddle," Sundance said.

"You are going far?" the stableman said, yanking a fair-looking saddle from a rack.

"We are going on our own business," Sundance said, throwing the saddle on the gray. Geronimo talked soothingly to the horse while Sundance saddled it.

The stableman raised his hands in a French gesture. "Of course—your own business." He went into his sleeping quarters and wrote out a bill of sale with his name and business at the top of it. He did it quickly and it was clear that he wanted them to be on their way.

It still was raining when they rode out of Laplace in total darkness. The town was well beyond the city, but they had to get a lot farther by morning. Only then would they look for a dry place to sleep, but for now they had to push on. Sundance knew that the agents of the Ring wouldn't give up. First they would comb the city, especially the Central American quarter where two Indians wouldn't attract too much attention. Other paid killers would be hanging around the railroad depot, poking through the coaches and baggage cars of the outgoing trains.

The rain beat down hard and cold, but Geronimo rode without complaint. In the dark Sundance couldn't see the old Apache's face. He guessed it was set in its usual grim lines. Sundance knew the old man was tired, but for now there was nothing to be done about that. Stopping once under a dripping live oak they ate the fried chicken Johnson had given them. The chicken was wet and greasy, but it was food. By the time they started out again, the rain had stopped and a big watery moon drifted through the rolling black clouds. The road still ran west and they were able to make better time now that there was light.

This was all strange country to Geronimo, but his instincts didn't fail him. "We are not going north," he said.

"West, for now," Sundance said. "Unless I'm wrong they'll figure us to go north through Mississippi, then cut over into Arkansas. That's the shortest way to go. They'll be watching the roads up that way."

"Then where? How do we go?"

"By way of Texas," Sundance said. "We're heading due west to Beaumont, Texas. The railroad goes north from Beaumont. If it looks good we'll take the train from there."

"How do you know they won't be waiting in Beaumont?"

"No way to be sure."

Geronimo said, "They don't like me in Texas."

"They don't like you anywhere," Sundance answered. "If they kill us in Beaumont we'll be just as dead as in Natchez."

"They wouldn't hang me—lynch me—in Natchez. That is not in Texas."

"Mississippi," Sundance said. "I'll try to keep you from getting killed anywhere. And I'll shoot you before I let some town mob lynch you."

"Thank you," Geronimo said, and lapsed into silence.

Sundance knew what Geronimo was thinking, and he wasn't entirely wrong. Beaumont was in East Texas, where there hadn't been any Indian trouble for a great many years; still, a mob with enough liquor in them, enough Indian Ring money in their pockets, could easily be worked up to lynch the old Apache. Both of us, Sundance thought. But heading west was the best idea he had at the moment. Plans were made and plans were reshaped, depending on the circumstances. He would have to decide about Beaumont when they got close to it. Fact was they might not get there at all. Their greatest enemy was the telegraph; in a few minutes a message could travel hundreds, even thousands of miles. The telegraph talked fast, but the money of the Indian Ring talked even faster. Honest men who would spurn a bribe of fifty dollars would turn killer for five hundred.

Death could come out to greet them at any stretch of this lonesome road.

CHAPTER SIX

Three days later, avoiding the small towns they came to, buying some of their food from farmers, they were only a few miles from Crowley, Louisiana. So far their journey had been uneventful, and the few farm people who saw them took little interest in their appearance, for southern Louisiana was country where many races were mixed. Whenever possible Sundance bought their supplies from Cajun or mixed-blood farmers. Outsiders in their own land, they had little to do with the "Americans," who ruled Louisiana. It rained several times a day, as it always does in Louisiana in summer, but when the sun came out the low-lying country steamed bright green in the sunlight. If it hadn't been for the threat of the Indian Ring, it would not have been an unpleasant journey.

Sundance sensed the restlessness as they got closer to the Texas line. Now and then some farmer offered to let them stay the night in his barn after taking Sundance's money. But always Sundance said no because he trusted few men he knew and didn't trust strangers at all. The Cajun country fell away behind them; the land was drier, the air less humid. Sundance could see that Geronimo was toughening up very fast. Unaccustomed to riding for so many years, he looked tired and stiff for the first few days, and there was no need to watch him closely at night because he fell asleep once they had made camp and eaten. But now he rode without fatigue and on the fourth day he said he didn't need the saddle anymore, a sure sign that his wiriness and strength had returned. They traveled long days, starting out before sunup and bedding down long after dark, and he matched Sundance mile for mile. Now there was arrogance in his bearing; and though another man might have found this remarkable, Sundance was not surprised. If he wondered at all, it was because the change in the old man had come so quickly.

At times the old man was reasonable enough, or at least he held his arrogance in check. He was given to sudden shifts in mood; when the arrogant mood was on him he taunted Sundance for his way of life, saying that his fight against the Indian Ring was hopeless. Many of the things he said were true, but Sundance took no offense. Maybe the fight against the Ring was hopeless; that didn't mean he was going to give it up because a bitter old man spoke a few half-truths.

Sundance took no offense, but now he watched Geronimo all the time. All the signs were there: Geronimo was going to make a break, the first chance he got. He hadn't started tying the old man up at night. That would come, he knew, though for the moment he was reluctant to do it, for this was the greatest of all Apache warriors. In his way he was the last Apache, and no wonder the Ring was so afraid of him. Sundance's emotions warred one against the other as he thought about Geronimo.

The wild, the Indian side of his nature wanted to let the old man go. Geronimo yearned for one last glorious campaign against the "Americans." And so, in his way, did he.

On the night they were camped in a sandy-floored cave outside the town of Crowley Geronimo tore at his meat with strong brown teeth. Drinking water from his canteen he stared at Sundance across the small, carefully shielded fire. Sundance was used to the old man's changes of mood and took no heed of him. For a long time there was silence, then Geronimo said, "I owe you a debt from the boat, so now I will tell you this. You no longer have my word about anything. That is my warning to you. You know what I am saying?"

Sundance threw a few chips of deadwood on the fire. The light from the fire threw their shadows on the walls of the cave. "I know what you're saying," Sundance said.

Geronimo's dark eyes glittered. "You don't know what I am saying."

"What are you saying?"

"I am giving you a chance to kill me now."

"I don't need a chance. I can kill you anytime I like."

"You would kill me if you weren't a half-white fool. I am saying you better kill me now. That is the only way I can pay my debt. I won't pay it by going to Oklahoma."

It's getting very close, Sundance thought. "You mean to kill me, is that it?"

Geronimo said quietly, "Yes, if that's the only way. So now you are warned."

"You didn't escape from Florida," Sundance said. Sometimes pride could be broken down by contempt. "If I had been there for fifteen years I would have found a way to escape. You were too busy eating pork chops and taking English lessons from the colonel's lady. Were you too fond of the pork chops or too scared of the monsters in the swamp?"

Geronimo jumped to his feet and Sundance's pistol came out fast. "Sit down, you eater of pork chops," Sundance said.

Geronimo got ready to spring across the fire. "Now you'll have to kill me."

Sundance aimed the pistol at Geronimo's knee. "Sit down or I'll shoot the legs from under you. Then I'll let you go to Arizona—on crutches! You can shake your crutches at the soldiers when you start your war. But who will you lead? What young warrior will follow a cripple? Go back on sticks and they will leave you to die, as they do the old and useless."

Geronimo remained standing, still stiff with his old man's pride. "You have no honor," he said. Then he sat down.

"My own kind of honor," Sundance said. "You know what's wrong with you? You're an old man but you can't face being old. Where is the honor in that? When you die you want the whole Apache nation to die with you. It's not going to happen."

Geronimo spat. "You will never hold me, you bastard halfbreed." Then, hissing Spanish curses, the old Apache rolled himself in his blanket and went to sleep.

Sundance moved away from the fire and sat with his back against the wall of the cave. He slept with his Colt in his hand, ready to wake up at the slightest sound. He knew he was taking a chance because this was no ordinary man he had. Old though he was, Geronimo had lived by treachery and stealth for most of his life; and this was one time when he could not depend entirely on his highly-developed instinct for survival. During the night a sound like the snapping of a twig jerked him awake. He drew the Colt and cocked it and saw Geronimo looking at him from the far side of the fire. The old man was holding a broken twig between his fingers.

"I would go outside to piss," Geronimo said.

"Piss out the door," Sundance ordered, suppressing a smile, for there were some things you could not joke about with an Apache.

The rest of the night passed quietly.

In the morning Geronimo had nothing to say. Squatting by the fire, he took the food Sundance gave him without a word. First light was glimmering when Sundance kicked sand on the fire and said they were moving out. Geronimo just grunted.

Anytime now, Sundance thought.

They were cutting down through the trees about a mile from the road to Crowley when Geronimo got his chance. They rode as they always did, with Geronimo about twenty feet in front. Then it happened! Geronimo had gone through a patch of brush when, without warning, a fat-bodied diamond-back rattled and struck at Eagle. The big stallion reared up whinnying in alarm, his forelegs kicking at the striking snake. The snake struck again and Sundance missed with the first shot. He fired again and blew the head off the rattler; and even before the echo died away he heard Geronimo galloping away. Still panicked by the snake, Eagle plunged and kicked before Sundance was able to gain control. By the time he got through the brush Geronimo was long out of sight; in moments the sound of his horse had died away. Kicking Eagle to a gallop, Sundance rode downhill as fast as the heavily wooded slope would allow. The old son of a bitch was heading straight down to the Crowley road instead of away from it. The town was only a few miles away and would be awake by now.

By the time he got to the road Sundance knew he had lost the old man. Tracks crossed the road and he followed them. Then they doubled back and crossed the road again. He followed them back to the road a second time and there they were lost in wagon ruts. He tried to pick them up again and failed. In open country he would have run down the old man in no time; here rolling hills scattered with trees and rocks ran down to the road on both sides.

There was no use searching all over the country—Crowley was the first place to look. Staying on the road, Sundance rode on until he was close to town. Before he got to town he climbed a steep bare hill that overlooked the main street. He stood up in the stirrups and—goddamn it, they had him!

A crowd of men were dragging Geronimo down from his horse, and even at a distance Sundance could see the old man kicking wildly. Then three men got a grip on him and knocked him to the ground. When he was down they began to kick him. Sundance galloped down the hill, keeping his pistol holstered but ready to use it. The men punching and kicking Geronimo turned when they heard him coming. A middle-aged man with a badge pinned to a storekeeper's apron stepped into the street. He hiked up his apron until he was gripping the butt of a gun.

Other men were crowding into the street when Sundance reined in. A few of them had guns, mostly shotguns. The storekeeper with the badge came forward still gripping his beltgun. Some of the shotguns were beginning to point at Sundance.

The storekeeper-constable didn't look too determined. More than likely his half-eaten breakfast was waiting for him on the kitchen table.

"What in blazes is going on here?" he wanted to know. He nodded his head at Sundance. "And who are you?"

"I see you got him," Sundance said.

"Who did we get?"

Sundance pointed to Geronimo still struggling in the grip of four men. "That old man there stole my horse. I've been following him for days."

One of the men holding Geronimo said angrily, "The hell with the horse. This goddamned Injun near kilt two ladies crossing the street. Rode right down on top of them. They screamed when they saw him coming. Old bastard didn't give a damn they were there or not. We got ways of dealing with women-killers in this town."

"Go easy now," the constable said. "Keep a grip on him till I get the straight of this." He turned back to Sundance. "What's all this about stealing your horse?"

"My horse," Sundance said, taking the bill of sale from his pocket with his left hand. He leaned down to give it to the constable. "Description of the horse is all there. The frost-cropped ears, the white markings on the chest. Like I said—my horse."

The constable had to push wire-rimmed glasses

on his nose to read the bill of sale. Now and then he looked up to compare the horse to the written description. Finally he folded the paper and handed it up to Sundance.

"Looks like it's your horse all right. That makes it horse-stealing. I guess I'd better lock him up."

"No need for that," Sundance said, knowing it could go two ways. If it went the wrong way he wasn't sure what he would do. It would be hell to get into a gunfight with a bunch of thick-headed farmers. Maybe he could get one or two before they blasted him with the shotguns. A man didn't have to be a marksman to kill with a shotgun.

"The old man is half crazy," Sundance went on, hoping it wouldn't come to killing. No one had mentioned the name Geronimo. Crowley was the kind of farmer town that read last week's newspapers, if they read them at all.

Sundance said, "The old man worked for the liveryman back in Laplace. I bought that old horse for my woman to ride. Look at that old horse! Who'd steal a horse like that except a crazy man."

One of the men asked, "What about the women he nearly kilt? They could be broke up inside." He pointed to two middle-aged women being comforted by other women.

"Jeb has a point there," the constable said.

Sundance took a roll of bills from his pocket. "What would you say to giving the ladies fifty dollars? I'll take the old man back and make him work it off. Consider it a fine, if you like. I'll guarantee he never comes this way again."

Sundance waited while the constable conferred in whispers with the other men. The two ladies were called over and the conference went on for a few

71

more minutes.

"Is that fifty dollars apiece?" the constable asked.

"Why not!" Sundance said. "I'll work this old bastard to the end of his days."

"All right." The constable nodded, glad the trouble had passed.

Sundance got down to make it look right. Then he gave the money to the women; the other women gathered around them protectively.

"Turn him loose," Sundance said.

One of the men was still holding Geronimo's horse. Geronimo stood glaring at Sundance.

"Climb aboard, old man," Sundance ordered.

Geronimo turned and Sundance kicked him in the backside and he went sprawling in the dusty street. His leathery face was so contorted with hate that some of the men backed away from him.

"He is crazy," one of them said.

"I can handle him," Sundance said. "He won't bother you again."

Geronimo got on his horse and they rode out the way they had come in. Jeering children followed them part of the way, throwing sticks and rocks. They got tired of it after a while.

At the end of town Sundance said, "We'll have to circle the town after we get out a bit. You got your chance and you took it. You won't get another. If I hadn't looked for you in that town you might be dangling from a hay-hoist by now."

By way of thanks Geronimo spat.

They rode out three miles before he circled the town. Geronimo's face was a mask of hate. In spite of all that had happened Sundance felt like smiling. The great chief of the Apaches had been belted around by a bunch of farmers and kicked in the ass. Maybe it wasn't so funny. In saving Geronimo's life he had made sure that Geronimo would try to kill him. But when he thought about it, he decided it was just as well. Up till now there had been a sort of wary regard between them. They were on the same side in their different ways. Now all that was over.

It still was early morning and there was a whole day ahead of them. Sometime after noon they stopped to rest and water the horses. This was well-watered country, but Sundance told Geronimo when to drink, when not to drink. It was a small point, but one worth making. Geronimo didn't miss it. He did what he was told.

They ate in silence, with Geronimo never taking his eyes away from Sundance. He's wondering how he's going to kill me, Sundance thought. The idea didn't bother him. In fact, it made everything that much simpler. Now that the old villain had made his break he could treat him like the captive he was. Sundance would deliver him to Oklahoma, trussed like a Christmas turkey if he had to. After that he was the army's business. He could go to Arizona! He could go to hell!

That night they camped by a river bottom in a cottonwood grove. Still burning with hate, Geronimo ate in absolute silence. In the gathering darkness the river had a peaceful sound. Before he tied up Geronimo for the night Sundance piled green wood on the fire to keep the mosquitoes away. He roped the old man's hands behind him and rolled him over on his side before he covered him with his blanket. Geronimo remained silent. Oddly, now that Geronimo was securely tied, Sundance began to feel danger, real danger, for the first time. He sat with his back to a tree watching the still form under the blanket. He knew Geronimo wasn't asleep. Finally he slept himself but for the first time in years his sleep was uneasy. During the night he woke and Geronimo hadn't moved but when he went over to make sure he found the old man's dark eyes staring up at him. Nothing was said.

Sundance sat down again to wait for dawn, something he never did. It was going to be a long night.

All the nights were going to be long from now on.

CHAPTER SEVEN

In the morning Sundance risked a small fire to boil up a pot of coffee. They were far enough off the road to risk a small fire and he craved good strong coffee as nothing else. In the days before he gave up whisky under the threat of being shot, personally, by Three Stars if ever he got drunk again, coffee had meant nothing to him. Now it was something he smelled even before he woke up; something he longed for even before he made it. Three Stars drank strong black coffee by the gallon and smoked long-nine Havanas by the boxful. Three Stars never had been able to interest him in cigars, but after the whisky, coffee had become the light of his life. The blacker the better.

Geronimo squatted by the fire rubbing his wrists and his anger at the previous day's humiliation seemed to have settled. He's going to try something else, Sundance thought. It came after a few minutes.

"I know you had to kick me yesterday," the old man said with hooded eyes. "They might have changed their minds and come after us if you hadn't. Yesterday I felt only hate for you."

Sundance pretended to go along with this new

reasonable attitude. He dished up fried bacon on a tin plate and gave it to the old man.

"That's all right," Sundance said. "I'd get mad if somebody kicked me."

"I think they would have lynched me."

"Maybe not right away. If they got worked up enough they might have. If it happened in Texas I wouldn't have been able to save you." I'll have to watch him even more carefully, Sundance thought.

Geronimo ate the bacon with his hands, wiping the grease on his arms, believing as the Apaches did that it would give him extra strength. He gulped the scalding coffee without letting it cool.

"You think you could have tracked me?" Geronimo said.

"In time," Sundance said. "I'd follow you to Arizona if I had to. You still want to kill me?"

"No. Fifteen years ago you would not have been able to track me. You are right—I am getting old."

Geronimo began to ask Sundance questions about Oklahoma. Was it desert land there? He asked the names of the tribes that lived there. Who were the great warriors?

Nowadays the Indians there were mostly farmers, Sundance said. Once again he explained that the Indians there were not on reservations but owned their own land. He said there were newspapers in the Indian language. The biggest problem the Indians had was the whisky sellers who preyed on them. U.S. marshals from Fort Smith hunted them down, killed them or jailed them.

Geronimo feigned interest, but his eyes gave him away. Oklahoma might be the Promised Land, for all he cared. Sundance knew he was dreaming of the bleak sun-blasted mountains along the border where every day was a struggle just to stay alive. It was a merciless land, but the old man loved it.

"It will be hard to be a farmer," Geronimo said, hooding his eyes again. "I do not know how to do it."

"It's not that hard to learn. There are men who will show you how. You will be given a house of your own. Three Stars has seen to that."

Hate flickered for an instant, then it was gone. "A house," Geronimo said. "I have lived under a wooden roof for fifteen years. And now there will be another house."

"Does that mean that you won't try to run off again?" You foxy old bastard, Sundance thought.

Geronimo smiled and it was like seeing a rock crack open. "I will answer you this way, Sundance. If you get drunk and fall asleep leaving your horse and weapons unguarded, then I will run away. If that does not happen I will not try to escape."

Sundance gave Geronimo a second cup of coffee and he heaped it with coarse brown sugar purchased from a farmer's wife. It was strange to see that such a fierce warrior had a sweet tooth. "Well that's better than nothing," Sundance said. "That doesn't mean I won't be watching you all the time."

Geronimo devoured the rest of the bacon. "I would expect that," he said, greasy faced. He scraped the bacon bits from the skillet with a hard biscuit.

"That's what you'll get," Sundance said.

They rode west toward the Texas line, keeping away from the towns. It was going good, Sundance thought, maybe too good. Now and then Geronimo talked of the gold hidden in the mountains, looking sideways at Sundance as he did so. He said he didn't

77

know how much gold there was—there was so much of it. Sundance let him talk, not at all surprised that the old man was so talkative. Among whites the Indians might be silent, wary of giving themselves away; they talked all the time when they were among their own kind.

Sundance smiled as the old man talked on about the gold. "I'll make a deal with you about the gold," Sundance said at last. "Tell me where it is, how to get it, and I'll bring your half to Oklahoma. If there is so much gold you'll be the richest Indian in that country. You can have your own herd of horses and you won't have to steal them."

Geronimo thought for a while. "I think I will let the gold stay where it is. It is best to leave it in the mountains."

He really thinks he's going to get back there, Sundance thought. Get the gold and start a war. Sundance wondered if Three Stars might not be making the worst mistake of his long career. The soldiers at Fort Cobb might keep their eye on Geronimo, but short of locking him up there was nothing they could do to keep him from slipping away. To get to Arizona he would have to travel clear through Texas, where the other tribes hated the Apaches. Still, if he made up his mind to do it, he would get home to the mountains. Of course Three Stars might be convinced that fifteen years had changed Geronimo. Or it could be that he was gambling that once Geronimo saw his new home he would give up any further thought of war. It was a hell of a gamble. Crook wasn't so short of retirement and he never had been one for saving money. Crook had more needy relatives than any man alive, and though he grumbled at the poor mouths they made, he never turned them away empty-handed. It would be a hell of a thing if he got booted out of the army at this time in life. The Indian Ring hated Crook with a vengeance and would do anything to see him disgraced. Sundance thought of trying to explain that to Geronimo, but changed his mind. The old Apache would see that as weakness; in the end the only way to treat Geronimo was with his own kind of ruthlessness.

They were a day's ride from Beaumont when Sundance decided they would have to risk going into town. They had been out of touch with the world for well over a week; it was time to see what was going on. The newspapers would tell some of that, though not all of it. And maybe Beaumont was the last place the agents of the Ring expected them to go. Anyway if they were going to board a train to the north, then they would have to load their horses at the depot. Up the line from Beaumont that might not be possible.

"We'll go in at night," Sundance said that evening when he was gathering chips of wood for a small fire. This was farm country here, rolling green hills, herds of fat cattle. It was a hot bright night without a breath of wind. Scorning woman's work, Geronimo did nothing to help with the gathering of wood or the scouring of the dishes. He sat—or squatted—like royalty while Sundance did all the work.

"Then we go by train?" Geronimo said.

Sundance opened a can of soldier beans and set it on the fire. He cut thick slices of bacon and put them in the skillet. When the beans began to simmer he added them to the bacon and stirred it up.

"Maybe we'll go by train," Sundance said. "It

depends on what's going on in town." He looked Geronimo over and except for his grim, leathery face he could have been any old Indian. The clothes were white man's clothes; at least that would be a help. But that goddamned face! It was the color of an old smoked ham, with black pebbles for eyes, a knife slash for a mouth. Nothing—absolutely nothing—could be done about that face.

"Try not to look so fierce all the time," Sundance said, dishing up the bacon and beans. He pulled the steaming coffee pot off the fire and watched while Geronimo dumped brown sugar into it.

"I will do my best," Geronimo said, shoveling bacon and beans into his mouth with his fingers.

As dusk came down the next night they could see the lights of Beaumont. "We'll give it another hour before we start in," Sundance said.

They rode into town in darkness. Beaumont was a fair-sized place. Sitting squarely on the Texas-Louisiana border, it looked more Southern than Western. Shade trees lined the streets and there was a big white courthouse with a Confederate flag flying alongside the Stars and Stripes. On the courthouse lawn stood a cannon and a stack of rusting cannon balls. The railroad depot was right in the center of town, and a long line of cars pulled out as they rode down the main street. It was a farmer's town with a settled look. Two ladies in a fancy buggy driven by an old Negro in a top hat turned to stare at them. The town had plenty of Negroes, very few Indians. The Indians looked tame and beaten down. Geronimo spat and Sundance warned him not to do it again. "Don't go looking for trouble.

We may find more than we bargained for."

"I am hungry for goat chops," Geronimo said. "Are there Mexicans in this town?"

"The Mexican quarter is where we're going," Sundance said. "We won't stand out so much there—and you can get your goat chops. Maybe if we're lucky there will be a train out tonight. If not we'll hole up and wait for morning."

The small Mexican section was on the other side of the tracks, a few narrow streets with pens for pigs and goats behind the houses or between them. The hot night air was filled with the smells of chili and spices. Half-starved dogs ran yelping behind them. In one house bare-breasted whores sat at the open windows making sucking noises with their mouths. Geronimo looked at the fat whores and smiled his grim smile.

"I have raped many Mexican women," he said.

"Not lately you haven't," Sundance said. "Here you have to pay. Later if you want a woman I'll stake you to one." He smiled. "You think you'd still be able?"

Geronimo just glared.

The widest street had the biggest cantina, a low-roofed dirty place that stank of beer and mescal. A few loungers stood outside and made way slowly after they hitched their horses. "The stallion will kick you to death if you bother him," Sundance said in Spanish.

Nobody answered and they went in. The place was nearly empty. A short fat Mexican stood behind the bar, and from the glassy look in his eyes he was his own best customer. He did his best to straighten up when they got to the bar. He bowed and smiled and reached for a dusty bottle of rye whisky. A fat woman looked out of a smoky kitchen, then went back to what she was cooking.

"No whisky," Sundance said. "We will have beer. The best beer you have." He knew Geronimo wanted whisky; that would be like trying to lead a mountain lion on a watch chain. "And a lot of food. Goat chops for my friend. I would like the biggest steak you have."

' The bartender uncorked two bottles of warm beer and set them on the bar. A few Mexicans sat at a table by the wall drinking mescal and playing cards with a greasy deck. They looked like farm workers or goatherders. They had been talking loudly; now they kept their voices low. No one at the table looked like a gunman of any kind.

They took their beer to a table and waited for the food. Geronimo emptied his beer mug in one long swallow and a smile spread across his face. Sundance told the bartender to bring two more bottles.

"You got any newspapers around here?" Sundance asked the Mexican.

"There is a Spanish paper from yesterday. I will get it."

Sundance gave the Mexican a dollar and told him to send someone for the "American" paper. "Tell him not to take all night."

The Mexican was curious, but didn't say anything. "He will bring it like the wind," he guaranteed. He whistled and one of the loungers came in. The bartender gave him a coin and he slouched out. "See! Like the wind!" the bartender repeated.

"Go easy on that beer," Sundance warned Geronimo, who was guzzling the second bottle.

Geronimo just smiled.

Sundance looked through the Spanish paper and

there wasn't a word about Geronimo. It was just as Sundance had figured. Beaumont was too far removed from the frontier to take much heed of Indian trouble. He folded the paper and thanked the bartender, who was knocking back a glass of mescal. The fat woman came in with the food. She stared at Geronimo before she went back to the kitchen.

"Another beer?" Geronimo said, smiling.

"Eat your food, then we'll see," Sundance said, digging into his steak. It was cooked a little too much for his liking, but for a Mexican cantina it was a good steak and he didn't have to saw at it. Anything was better than bacon and beans.

It took a while for the man to come back with the *Beaumont Star*. Sundance looked at the date; the paper had come out that morning. Geronimo was tearing into the plate of goat meat like a man who had been starved for a month. Paging through the paper, Sundance finally found an item about Geronimo on page 5. It said the whole country was wondering about the whereabouts of the notorious Apache. Geronimo may or may not have been drowned at sea, but there were reports of two Indians being seen in southern Louisiana. Nothing was said about the gunfight on the New Orleans docks. So far as it could be ascertained "the savage redskin" was in the company of the equally notorious Jim Sundance, an adventurer and perennial thorn in the side of the authorities. General George C. Crook was coming under heavy fire for his part in the release of "this bloody-handed murderer." The newspaper writer went on to say that several congressmen and senators had demanded that Crook be dismissed from the service. Senator

MacGhee went so far as to say that "George Crook is unfit to wear the uniform of our glorious country." Senator MacGhee demanded that Geronimo be recaptured immediately and returned to the military prison in Florida.

Geronimo looked up from his plate and gestured toward the newspaper with a well-gnawed bone. "You are reading about me?"

"They think you should be sent back to Florida. You've got them all stirred up in Washington."

Geronimo started eating again. "Important men?"

"Men with power," Sundance said. "A few may think they have good reasons. The others are crooks working for the Ring or they're part of it. They'll keep beating the drums as long as they think it will do any good. The only good thing—it isn't all that important here. So we have a good chance of getting on some train."

Sundance called the bartender over and ordered another beer for Geronimo. "You know about the trains?" he asked the Mexican. "The trains going to the north?"

"Yes, all the trains. I worked for the railroad before I opened this fine cantina. I know when the trains come, when they go."

"Does one go tonight?"

The Mexican was drunk and sympathetic. "The evening train has gone," he said. "Maybe an hour ago. My friend, you will have to wait till morning. There is a train at six o'clock. You have a place to stay for the night?"

Sundance said, "I was about to ask you, my friend. We would be honored if you could find us a place to sleep. It doesn't have to be fancy."

The Mexican rubbed his hands together. "I have just the place for you. My dead brother's room. He was of considerable skill with a knife. Alas, he met someone with even greater skill. But I must tell you the bed is narrow, only wide enough for one man."

Sundance inclined his head in thanks. He said in Spanish, "It is of no matter. I will sleep on the floor."

The Mexican nodded toward Geronimo. "It is good to show respect for age."

Geronimo muttered into his beer mug.

The bartender said, "As soon as you have eaten I will show you to my dead brother's room. Behind the house there is a stable for your horses. They will be safe. In the morning my woman will cook a good meal before you go."

After taking the money Sundance gave him, the bartender backed away. Then he went to the kitchen to talk to the fat woman. She came out with a broom and went up to the second floor. Sundance finished his steak and waited for Geronimo to get through. The old man gnawed at the bones until there wasn't a shred of meat left. It had been a huge meal, yet he looked regretfully at the empty plate. He poured a dribble of beer from his bottle and swallowed. He drained Sundance's bottle too.

"That's enough," Sundance said, pushing his chair back. "With all that beer and food you ought to sleep like a stone. Come on now, it's time for bed."

Upstairs the fat woman had moved the dust around with the balding broom. The room was small but it would do. There was a narrow cot, a rickety table, a chair. The window had a torn oiled paper shade on it. Sundance opened the window and pulled down the shade and some of the stale air drifted out of the room. The only light came from a candle guttering in a china holder.

Geronimo lay down and allowed himself to be tied. Sundance turned him on his side and he went to sleep, belching loudly. There was no lock on the door, so Sundance set the chair against it. He stretched out on the floor after blowing out the light. After a while, with the Colt in his hand, he slept.

In the middle of the night he heard Eagle whinny a warning.

CHAPTER EIGHT

Eagle whinnied again by the time Sundance got to the window with the Colt in his hand, and from where he was he could see the stables behind the cantina. It could be just a rat that was disturbing his horse, but he didn't think so. Most stables had rats and usually they didn't bother the horses. All he could see was the outline of the stables, because there was no moon.

It was a short drop from the window and he landed making almost no noise on moccasined feet. He drew the Colt again and ran forward at a crouch, and for a moment he stood with his back against the wall just beside the stable door. Now he heard movement, and it wasn't any rat. A dark lantern threw a thin beam of light, and then went out. He heard movement again. It could be a horse thief, it could be someone sent by the Ring.

Whoever it was had moved away from Eagle and was looking at Geronimo's horse. Eagle made no sound as Sundance edged into the darkness. The dark lantern shone again and the beam of light went from the horses to the saddles. He saw a tall figure with a hat.

"Move and you're dead," Sundance said, cock-ing the revolver to make his point. The *kik-kak* of the hammer going back seemed loud in the stable. "Put your hands up and shine that light at the wall."

The light hit the wall and he saw a tall woman standing unafraid in front of him. He couldn't see much else because of the way the light was directed.

"Hold that light high and come out of there," he ordered. "Try blinding me and I'll kill you."

The woman came forward still holding the light. "There's no need for all this Mr. Sundance," she said in a husky voice. "I'm not trying to steal your horse, if that's what you think."

"Outside," Sundance said.

The back door banged open and he heard the excited voice of the cantina proprietor, the twin hammers of a shotgun being eared back.

"Easy with that shotgun," Sundance said in Spanish. "We're coming out so don't shoot."

The Mexican had the shotgun raised to his shoulder when Sundance came out behind the woman.

"I caught her sneaking around the horses," Sundance said. He took the dark lantern from the woman and put the light in her face. It was good-looking though hard and angular. "You know who she is?"

The Mexican came closer and gave a grunt of surprise. "Miss Baxter!" he said. "What's going on here? In my stable in the middle of the night."

The woman called Baxter replied in Spanish that was very bad. She mixed Spanish with English. She said she could explain.

"Who is she?" Sundance said.

"You can ask me," the woman said with no embarrassment. "My name is Dora Baxter and I work for the newspaper here. *Beaumont Star,* the one you were reading tonight. I know who you are and what you're doing in town. Tell him who I am, Francisco.''

"She is Miss Baxter," the Mexican agreed.

"Get a light on in the bar," Sundance told the Mexican. "All I see here is a horse thief."

"Oh come on," Dora Baxter said.

"Follow him in," Sundance said, holstering the pistol. He pushed her hard.

In the cantina, with the oil lamps up, Sundance told her to sit at a table. He sat down opposite her while the Mexican stood nervously with the shotgun in his hands.

"Tequila," Dora Baxter said. "We're in a bar, we might as well have a drink. "They tell me you don't drink much, Mr. Sundance?"

"I'll ask the questions," Sundance said. "What the hell did you think you were doing out there? You're lucky my horse didn't kick you to death."

The Mexican brought a bottle and a glass and set them on the table. Then he went back behind the bar and tried to look less puzzled, and while he was doing it he had a drink.

Dora Baxter sprinkled salt on the back of her hand, knocked back a shot of tequila, and licked the salt. Her hat was pushed back and she had very black close-cropped hair, almost like a man's. If she hadn't been so hard-faced she would have been beautiful.

Dark eyes regarded Sundance with something like amusement. "I was checking up on you," she said calmly. "That's what reporters do, check up on people and things. I wanted to be sure you were who I thought you were. Not that there was much need to do that. You do stand out, Mr. Sundance. You see, I know all about you. What do you know about me?''

''A little, if you're the same Dora Baxter. What's a famous *New York Sun* reporter doing on the *Beaumont Star*?''

''Then you do know who I am?''

''I can read.''

''I got fired,'' Dora Baxter said. ''I wrote a long article about some politicians who were grafting more than usual. The *Sun* refused to print it so I gave it to John Fanning of the *Herald*. He was planning to print it but Tammany put too much pressure on him. After that I couldn't get a job anywhere. You know, the grapevine. I tried Philadelphia, Chicago, even San Francisco. No big city paper would hire me. So I ended up on the *Beaumont Star*.''

Sundance looked at her while she had another drink of tequila. ''So you want to write about Geronimo for the local paper?'' Somehow he didn't think so.

''Not for the *Star*. Every newspaper in the country—well, most of them—is wondering where Geronimo is. I'm the only reporter who knows. That gives me an advantage. You think it doesn't?''

''Maybe it does,'' Sundance said, trying to think of all he knew about this nervy scribbler. One thing was sure: her muckraking articles had sold a lot of newspapers for the *New York Sun*. He remembered one story about some Chicago meat packer who was selling rotten canned beef to the army. Then there was another series of articles drumming up support for the rebels in Cuba. He had heard her called a jumped-up bitch. A bitch she was. How jumped-up he didn't know.

"You think Geronimo will get you your job back on the *Sun*?" he said.

Again there was that amused look. "Just any old story won't do that, Mr. Sundance. I offended a lot of important people, so what I write about Geronimo has to be special. It has to be a story that no one else could possibly write."

"How so?"

"I want to go along with you when you take Geronimo to Oklahoma. I want to write a day-to-day account, all the excitement, all the danger. The perils you have to face, the obstacles you have to overcome. Your enemies in the Indian Ring."

Dora Baxter's voice quickened with excitement. "You're just as notorious as Geronimo, Mr. Sundance. There are people who regard you as the most dangerous man in this country."

"Thanks," Sundance said.

"I'm not joking. Don't tell me you didn't kill those men on the boat, those Indian Ring thugs in New Orleans. Oh I wish I could have been with you since the start of your journey. The way you risked your life to get back your beautiful stallion. On the way to Oklahoma I want you to tell me everything just as it happened."

Nervy was the word for her all right. "There's a catch," Sundance said. "You're not going to Oklahoma."

"Why is that?"

"Because I won't take you."

"I think you will after I explain a few things," Dora Baxter said, sounding like a lawyer in court. "You came by way of Beaumont—the long way —because you want to dodge the Indian Ring and anyone else who might want to kill Geronimo. Is

91

that right?''

Sundance said drily, "You talk and I'll listen . . . for a while."

She answered her own question. "Of course it's right. I'm the only one who knows you're here and how you plan to go after you leave here. As long as I don't write you up in my newspaper, you're safe for the moment. But once the story is in the paper— that's tomorrow's paper, by the way—the news will be on the telegraph wires to all points. Any advantage you have will be lost. Come to think of it, you may be worse off in Texas."

Now Sundance's eyes were just as hard as hers. "You'd do that for a piddling newspaper story?"

Dora Baxter laughed mockingly. "Piddling to you perhaps. Not to me. I want to go back to New York. Go back where I ought to be. Geronimo is a way to do it. For me it's that simple. And don't give me that steely gaze of yours. It won't work. I don't care what you think of me. I don't care what anybody thinks of me except that I deliver the goods."

It was hard to know what to do with her. "How about if we make a deal," Sundance said. "Keep quiet about Geronimo and I'll come back here and give you the whole story after I deliver him to Oklahoma. A day-to-day account, like you said. I'll write the whole thing down if you like. That way you can write it as if you were with us all the time. Is it a deal?"

"No deal, Mr. Sundance."

"You think I wouldn't keep my word. You say you know me, so you ought to know I do what I say."

"That's not the point. What you're proposing wouldn't be honest."

92

"That's a funny thing for a blackmailer to say."

"Call it what you like. When I write a story I don't do it from somebody's memory, somebody's notes. I'll tell you something about me. Once I wrote an article about what it was like to be a kitchen maid in a great house. That's about the worst job I can think of. But I didn't just go around asking questions. I got a job as a kitchen maid. I worked twelve hours a day seven days a week. I mopped, scrubbed pots, peeled potatoes, washed dishes, anything you can think of. I wrote another story exposing the rotten conditions in a Chicago packing plant. To do that I stood ankle-deep in blood and filth. You get my meaning?"

Behind the bar the Mexican was having another drink. Sundance opened his watch and looked at it. It was three o'clock. The train left at six. "I get your meaning, but this is different.'

"Different, how?"

"Look, Miss Baxter. Geronimo spent fifteen years in a Florida hellhole. The swamps. Fever. Absolute misery. Don't you think fifteen years is long enough to pay for his crimes? If they were crimes. For Christ's sake, give the old man a chance. That's what I'm trying to give him. Can't you do the same?"

Dora Baxter looked surprised. "I'm not trying to take away his chance. Why should I? All I want to do is write my story, get my job back. I'm a damn good reporter. Even the men who said women didn't belong in the newspaper business except as clerks and copyists have to admit that now. I'll tell you a secret, which is that I'm a better reporter than most men."

"Good for you. You're still not going to Oklahoma. By yourself maybe, not with us."

"Now you're angry and there's no need. But if that's the way you want it—fine. I'll just get back over to the paper before they lock up the type."

Sundance's gun snaked out as Dora Baxter started to get up. She stared at the cocked pistol. "You're not going anywhere," Sundance said. "You're not going to write anything about Geronimo."

Behind the bar the frightened Mexican said, "Please, senor."

"Are you planning to kill me, Mr. Sundance?" Dora Baxter asked. The pistol didn't seem to frighten her. "Come on now. Put that thing away and let's talk some sense. I know you have a fearsome reputation, but you won't kill me."

In spite of his anger Sundance was forced to smile at her. "No, I'm not going to kill you. I'm going to take you out of here, rope and gag you, and leave you in a ditch. We'll be long gone by the time somebody finds you."

"Will you now? I'm sure you can do all that, but what happens when I get free? I'll tell you what. I'll turn every newspaper in the country against your beloved General Crook. Oh, a lot of people don't like me, but you'll find that newspaper people stick together. They won't like one of their own, especially a woman, being abducted and abused and raped by the general's hired gunman. The newspapers will blast your friend right out of his job."

Sundance holstered the Colt. "If you're going to accuse me of rape, then maybe I should rape you."

Dora Baxter laughed in his face and helped herself to another drink. "Don't be a horse's ass, Mr. Sundance. You're not going to do anything but take me to Oklahoma. Those are the facts. Face them."

Sundance guessed that was what he was going to do, but he made one last try. "It's too dangerous," he said. "The Indian Ring agents will catch up with us sooner or later. If you're with us they'll try to kill you too. They don't like to leave witnesses—especially newspaper reporters—around after they do their work. Geronimo has other enemies. You could get shot."

"Rubbish," Dora Baxter scoffed. "I've been shot at before. I was right in the middle of the fighting in Cuba. I was with a crowd of miners in Leadville, Colorado, when the Pinkertons fired on us during the strike. When I was writing that story on Tammany Hall—the one that got me fired—I got a note saying I'd be found floating in the river."

Sundance held up his hand. There was no point going on with it. "All right, if that's what you want," he said. "You're going to Oklahoma—if we get there—but you're going to take orders from me. Get in my way, do anything at all, and I'll . . ."

She laughed again. "You'll do what? Enough of these threats. There's no need for them. I'll do what you say as long as it's reasonable. Can't you get it through your head that all I want to do is write the story of you and Geronimo?"

Sundance told the Mexican to make a pot of coffee. "Fry up some steaks while you're at it. You want steak?" he asked Dora Baxter.

"Sure," she said. "But I'll do the cooking."

"Maybe you better go home and get your things together."

"My things are together. You'll find my bag out in the stable."

"You find it. Nobody's going to fetch and carry

95

for you on this trip."

"Oh go to blazes," Dora Baxter said.

When the steaks were ready she brought them in, then went to get the coffee. Sundance had been in some peculiar situations, but this one beat all. Now that it was decided, there was nothing to do but make the best of it. Bitch or not, she knew how to cook, and that was something he would not have expected of one of these newfangled emancipated women.

Cutting his steak Sundance said. "How did you get onto us?"

"By being a reporter," Dora Baxter said. "At night I walk around town and talk to people. Anybody at all. The mayor. The town drunk. I ask them if anything odd or interesting is going on. Last night I asked the man that sells the *Star* in the town square. He told me one of Francisco's card players came running to get a copy of the *Star*. It didn't seem like much, except that Mexicans don't read the *Star*. I had to go back to the office to do some work. By the time I finished this place was closed for the night. I tracked down the man who bought the paper and he described you. Then I went home and packed my bag. Pretty smart, don't you think?"

"Smart of you, stupid of me. I wouldn't have you bothering me if I hadn't bought that goddamned paper."

"Oh come on now." That seemed to be one of her favorite expressions. "Come on. I'm not that bad, am I?"

At any other time she would have been easy to take. Well, easy enough. She wore a soft leather skirt, the kind some hardy women favored in range country, and a dark blue wool shirt. The skirt covered the tops of her knee-high boots. Now that she had her hat off, he saw that her hair was curly. But it was her eyes that interested him. In the lamplight they were almost as black and shiny as her hair, and they looked at the world with supreme self-confidence. In spite of the hardness of her face she was so close to beautiful that it didn't make any difference. He guessed she must have had to fight pretty hard to get ahead in her profession.

"You didn't answer my question," Dora Baxter said. "I'm not that bad, am I?"

"You're a ruthless bitch, Miss Baxter," Sundance said. "But you fry a good steak."

She said, "I don't mind the bitch part. Just don't expect me to cook for you on the way north."

"Who the hell asked you?"

Dora Baxter held up her hand in the Indian peace sign. "Look, we're going to be together for a long time, so why don't we smoke the peace pipe?"

Sundance said he didn't smoke.

"I do," Dora Baxter said. "I smoke and I drink. I do all the things men do."

"Not all of them."

"If that's supposed to shock me, you're wasting your time. My father ran a saloon and dance hall on the Bowery and there's nothing I haven't seen. McGurk's Suicide Hall was in the same block. I don't know why so many whores picked the balcony of McGurk's saloon to drink their cyanide, but they did. McGurk kept trying to chase them until he discovered it was good for business. People came there in the hopes of seeing a streetwalker doing the Dutch act."

"Don't be so tough," Sundance said. "You don't have to convince me."

Dora Baxter went on as if she hadn't heard him. "McGurk and his whores put a crimp in my father's business but there was enough money for me to go to college. My father couldn't see the use of it. Still, he didn't put up much of a fight. He thought when I got out I'd get married and settle down, as every good and sensible girl is expected to do."

This was one hell of a conversation, Sundance thought. He said, "You should have done that instead of working as a kitchen maid and meat packer. What the hell kind of life is that for a woman?"

"An exciting one," Dora Baxter said. "I wanted more for myself than that. My Uncle Ned worked in the composing room at the *Sun* and he got me taken on as a copyist, later a typewriter girl. When things were slow I wrote articles and when they found out about it, it nearly got me fired."

"You're always getting fired," Sundance said, smiling in spite of himself.

"Eat your steak," Dora Baxter said. "Anyway, I buttonholed an assistant editor on the day I was supposed to get the gate. I had to fight to get him to read my writings. But he did and so I wasn't fired after all. They put me on as a very junior reporter, but I didn't stay there."

"No," Sundance said. "You're here. Let me tell you something else . . ."

From upstairs came a crashing sound followed by loud cursing. Dora Baxter looked at the ceiling.

"What on earth is that?" she asked.

Sundance smiled. "I think Geronimo just fell off the bed."

CHAPTER NINE

Geronimo was still kicking and cursing when Sundance went upstairs and untied him and hauled him to his feet. The old man picked up his hat and put it squarely on his head, in the manner of all Indians. In the holder the candle had guttered down to a stub, and by its feeble light Geronimo looked very grim. He rubbed his wrists and Sundance thought it was a good thing the old bastard didn't have a weapon.

"I woke and you were gone," Geronimo said. "I tried to turn and see where you were and I fell. Where did you go?"

"Downstairs," Sundance said. "It's nearly five o'clock. The train leaves at six. You must eat before we go. Yes, I know—goat chops."

"And beer," Geronimo said.

They went downstairs and Dora Baxter's eyes lit up when she saw the old Apache warrior. Behind the bar the Mexican was snoring and Sundance wasn't able to rouse him. In the street there was early sun and the town would be awake before long. Geronimo stared at Dora Baxter without saying anything.

"She's going with us," Sundance said. "This is

Miss Baxter who is going to write about our journey for the newspapers. She is a famous newspaperwoman and has great interest in you. Her words are read by tens of thousands of people."

Sundance was about to say "millions of people" until he remembered that such a number was beyond the understanding of an Apache. One of the reasons the Apaches fought so hard was that they had no idea of the vastness of the country. For them, the world was the desert country of the border.

"I am honored to meet you, Mr. Geronimo," Dora Baxter said, standing up."

Geronimo just stared at her.

"Drop the *mister*," Sundance said.

Geronimo spoke to Sundance in Spanish: "Why is she going with us?"

"I told you," Sundance said. "To write your story."

"My disgrace. I do not want her with us, Sundance. Send her away from here. You will have much trouble with me if you do not."

Dora Baxter said, "I understood some of that."

Sundance warned her to be quiet. "Geronimo," he said. "It is not as you think. This woman will disgrace your enemy and friend Three Stars if we do not take her. Three Stars saved you from the hangman's rope, he got you out of prison. Would you have him disgraced because of your own pride?"

Geronimo looked at Dora Baxter. "This woman could do that?"

"This woman could. This woman and her newspaper could do that."

Geronimo looked at Dora Baxter again. "Then

why don't we kill her?"

"I can't do that," Sundance said.

Geronimo looked at Dora Baxter again. "The white half of you is weak, Sundance. Give me the knife and I will do it."

Dora Baxter knew enough Spanish to realize the old man's intent, and for the first time she looked nervous. Sundance was glad to see she wasn't tempered steel, as she thought she was. In the end they never were, though it was easy to see why any woman—any man—might be afraid of Geronimo.

"No knife and no killing," he said. "Three Stars would have to answer for anything you do. I said no more talk of murder. Do you want the meat or not?"

"And beer," Geronimo said.

Sundance nodded toward the kitchen. "A lot of goat chops for *Mister* Geronimo here. Maybe he'll like you better after that. I'll get the beer. When I say a lot I mean an awful lot. Make it ten or twelve. Fried goat's been on his mind for fifteen years."

Sundance went behind the bar and uncorked a bottle of Pearl beer and brought it to Geronimo. He didn't bother with a mug.

Geronimo swigged down the warm beer while the goat meat began to sizzle on the stove.

"I don't like what you are doing, Sundance," Geronimo said. "You said nothing of this woman."

"Have another beer," Sundance said, going to get it.

He brought it back. "What I am doing is necessary. I think this woman is all right. But right or wrong, she's going with us to Oklahoma."

"Is she your woman?"

"Hell no."

"You have no claim on her?"

"I told you no."

"Then she can come with us."

The old man smiled an evil smile and sucked the last drop of beer from the bottle. Dora Baxter came in from the kitchen with more meat than Sundance had seen on a single platter. The huge platter of meat steamed up against the hanging lamp now growing pale as the sunlight from the street grew stronger. All goat meat had a strong smell, even when the meat came from a fresh-killed kid. Sundance decided this goat must have been pretty old, because the smell of the steaming meat chased away the sour smells—old beer, old mescal, old vomit—of the cantina.

After Dora Baxter put the heaping platter in front of Geronimo he lost all interest in her. Behind the bar, on the floor, the Mexican was mumbling in his sleep. Sundance took out his watch and pressed open the silver face-cover. It was 5:15.

"Is he always this fierce?" Dora Baxter whispered to Sundance.

"This is one of his good days," Sundance said. "You should see him when he's in bad humor."

Geronimo made grunting noises of satisfaction as, holding the goat chops two-handed, he tore at the meat. Only five minutes had passed, and half the meat was gone.

"How do you like him, Miss Baxter?" Sundance asked. "Noble as hell, isn't he? Tall, copper-skinned, eagle-nosed, full of quiet dignity. Or is he short, squat, flat-faced, and dirty? Answer me, Miss Baxter, how do you like him ?"

Her answer surprised Sundance, who had expected her to be disappointed.

"He's still Geronimo," she said.

"So he is," Sundance agreed. "That grimy old man over there gave the United States of America a lot of trouble for a lot of years. They took his country but they didn't do it easily. If he had more than a few hundred men they wouldn't have done it at all. You newspaper people used to call him General Geronimo. A joke. But that's what he was —the best."

Dora Baxter didn't answer.

At the table Geronimo threw down the last sucked-on bone. "I am ready," he said.

Sundance opened his watch again: 5:25. He put money on the bar for the Mexican and they went out to get the horses and after the cantina the sunlight was strong and it was good to be in the clean morning air and the sun. Dora Baxter picked up her leather bag and waited for them to sling the saddles over their shoulders and lead the horses from the stable. Somewhere in the town a church bell was ringing, though it wasn't Sunday. On the way out of the Mexican quarter they passed a pen filled with half-wild pigs.

"You still want to go along?" Sundance asked Dora Baxter. "This is a nice quiet little town and maybe you'd be better off here. I told you they'll catch up with us somewhere along the way. You won't like it when they do. It won't be like Cuba. They'd only kill you in Cuba. These men will do worse to you if we fail."

"In for a penny," Dora Baxter said.

They went to the railroad depot through the streets of the drowsy morning town and there Sundance paid for tickets to Oklahoma City. Dora Baxter insisted on paying for her own ticket. Looking at Geronimo's old nag, Sundance wondered if he shouldn't just leave it behind. That was before he decided they might never get to Oklahoma City. There might come a time when the aging and badly used animal would come in handy.

Not too many people were waiting for the north-bound train: a few farm couples with kids, the usual traveling salesmen boisterous in their loud suits and wearing their hangovers like a badge of honor. Most of the others were cowboys of one age or another. One traveler was a first lieutenant of infantry who looked sleepy.

Sundance watched one and all, mindful that any one could be an Indian Ring agent, a spy for the Ring—or anything.

Early though it was, some of the traveling men were swapping bottles, swapping dirty jokes, and though all the jokes were old, as all jokes are, they laughed at them anyway. Sundance thought it was odd to be standing in the sun-warmed depot with Geronimo and a lady reporter from New York. Some of the travelers, those not too tired to show interest in anything, stared at Geronimo and at himself, and at Dora Baxter because she was with them. But after all the train was going north toward Oklahoma—Indian Territory—and the gawkers lost interest after a while.

The train came clanging in and they waited until the horses were on board. Sundance had to stay with Eagle or the stallion would have gone wild if a trainman had tried to throw a loop on him.

On the way north from Beaumont Geronimo sat in a seat by himself and pulled his felt hat down over his eyes and fell asleep; his way, Sundance thought,

104

of shutting out the bad memories of the cattle cars that had taken him to Florida fifteen years before.

The coach was shabby and smelled of a thousand trips and its red plush seats were dusty and there was spittle on the floor. Even with the windows open the air was rank with stale tobacco fumes and spilled whisky. The traveling salesmen were still at their dirty jokes, one trying to top the other. The cowboys and farmers rode in silence, not even looking out the window at the flat, featureless Texas farmland that stretched away as far as the eye could see. Hot air blew in the windows without doing anything to get rid of the smells. Everything rattled: the windows, the seats, the frame of the coach. Smoke and ash trailed behind the locomotive, dirtying hands and faces.

This was no express and the train stopped at every town and village it came to, and always when it did, Sundance watched the men who got on board. So far they were as nondescript as the train itself: more farmers, more cowhands without horses. Most of the cowboys carried their own saddles; a cowboy who didn't own his own saddle was a man without pride, an object of ridicule—a tramp.

"Well nothing's happened yet," Dora Baxter said.

"We haven't gone far," Sundance said. "You sure that Mexican in Beaumont is to be trusted? You said he was."

"Francisco? Of course he is. He's a friend of mine. I helped to get one of his children into the local hospital. They don't like to take Mexicans. Why is it that nobody trusts Mexicans?"

"Because you can't, most of them."

"I wouldn't have expected someone like you to

say that."

"I didn't mean it the way you think. Nearly all Mexicans are poor. That makes them practical. When they're offered money they take it. Your friend will talk if the agents of the Ring get to him."

And before she could argue about that, Sundance added, "Won't make any difference. If they track us to Beaumont they'll know what we're up to. Somewhere somebody has a map out and is drawing lines on it. It's not so hard to figure out."

The conductor, a gaunt man with a prominent Adam's apple, came through. The traveling salesmen all called him Uncle John and he scowled at them, tired of looking at them year after year.

Dora Baxter said, "Then you're sure they'll try again?"

Sundance nodded. "That's what they're paid for. I don't think you know what the Ring is like, or you wouldn't be here. You know they're powerful, but everybody knows that. You know they have their hired thugs, like your New York politicians. But the Indian Ring is more than a gang of rich thieves. It's an organization and not just in the West. It's wherever Indians are. The Bureau of Indian Affairs controls the Indians, tries to, and the Ring controls the Bureau. Every year they divide up millions, so they can bribe, kill, do anything they like. All it takes is money and they've got more than they need."

"Why aren't you dead?" Dora Baxter said.

"They've tried to kill me often enough. I guess they will someday, but I'm going to fight them as long as I can. Maybe the country will wake up by then. When they steal from the Indians they steal from everybody. The Ring is like a huge cancer that

106

keeps spreading. They have spies and agents everywhere. They pay well and they don't like mistakes."

"You're not just trying to scare me off this train?"

"I'd like to do that, but what I'm saying is true. In time they'll find us. They even work with the detective agencies like Holmes and the Pinkertons. Be smart, get off at the next station. Find some other way back to New York."

"This is the only way. I'm staying."

"All right. Can you shoot a gun?"

"Oh come on! Of course I can. When Tammany was after me a detective I know bought me a pistol and taught me how to use it. I learned to use a rifle in Cuba. The rebels taught me."

Sundance looked at her bag lying on the floor between her feet. "You have the pistol now? Keep your voice down."

"It's where you're looking. A five-shot English Webley. The Bulldog model, a .45. Break-top. It saved my life in Cuba. The Spanish infantry overran the rebel positions and an infantryman tried to bayonet me. Put three bullets in his belly and got away. I love that stubby gun."

Sundance glanced over at Geronimo. "Don't let the old man know you have it. It could get you killed. Me, too."

"But you've been keeping him alive. You risked your life for his."

She might be a tough, gun-toting lady reporter, but she sure as hell didn't know anything about Apaches. "Geronimo wants to get back to Arizona and I'm in his way. But I know in his heart he wants to be a farmer."

"I don't believe you."

107

"Suit yourself. Like they say in Washington, the official position is that Geronimo wants to grow corn and sit on his porch in the cool of the evening looking out over his fields and feeling the contentment that comes with honest toil."

Dora Baxter laughed. "You're a strange man. Sometimes you talk in grunts, then you say something like that. Don't be offended, but what were your parents like? Your mother was a Cheyenne, wasn't she? And your father an Englishman?"

The train rattled on through East Texas. Soon the farmland would give way to arid country.

"My father went to Oxford but he did something bad—I don't know what it was—so they shipped him off to America and warned him never to come back. A remittance man, except the family didn't send him any money. He worked at a lot of jobs before he drifted west. My mother was of the Northern Cheyenne. Somehow he met and married her and remained with the Cheyenne for the rest of his life."

Dora Baxter didn't look at him when she said, "You don't have to tell me the rest of it. I know what happened."

"I wasn't going to tell you," Sundance said.

And he didn't, but as the train rattled on he thought of his father and mother, the white and Indian renegades who had murdered them. His mother had been raped repeatedly; both had been tortured. Two people who had never harmed anyone in their lives. Hardly more than a boy but already skilled in the ways of a Cheyenne warrior, he pursued the killers until he found them, one by one. The gang had broken up, scattered in all directions, but he found them anyway. And then he killed them but not with a merciful bullet. He used fire and the knife; they died screaming.

It was the first and last time he had killed like that.

Dora Baxter put her hand on his arm. "There's no use thinking about it. I'm sorry. I shouldn't have brought it up."

"That's all right. I think about it anyway. Sometimes I do. Looks like we're coming into some town."

The train was entering the ragged edges of a place that looked bigger than the other station stops.

Uncle John, the conductor, stuck his head in the door and called out, "Brimmerton! Brimmerton! Them that wants to eat, they'll be a twenty minute stop! For them that wants to eat . . ."

Jerked from his sleep by the conductor's bellowing, Geronimo didn't seem to know where he was. He jumped to his feet and once again Sundance was reminded of how tough and wiry the old man was, and he found himself wishing that Geronimo was less agile.

"You want to eat?" he asked Dora Baxter. "I know the old man does."

"Why does he eat so much? The army couldn't have starved him that much."

"They didn't starve him at all." Sundance smiled. "Apaches eat like pigs every chance they get. They don't get that many chances."

Geronimo looked sour when Sundance told him there would be no goat chops in the Harvey House.

CHAPTER TEN

The Harvey House in Brimmerton wasn't on a main line, so they didn't have waitresses. But the sandwiches were fresh and the coffee was all right. All Harvey Houses looked the same, though their size depended on how many travelers they had to feed. You couldn't get a steak because on the railroad it was eat and run. But there was beef stew and sandwiches: roast beef and fresh ham and ham-and-cheese. And four kinds of pie.

The frame building was crowded but clean and there was a sign about spitting anywhere except in the cuspidors. All the traveling men got off the train to eat; the farmers and cowboys stayed on, eating fried chicken or cold corn from waxed paper.

Sundance fought his way to the counter and got two bowls of beef stew for Geronimo, sandwiches and coffee for himself and Dora Baxter. They had to sit with the traveling men, who took no notice of them. There were no surprises for drummers. Because Dora Baxter was at the table, they dropped the dirty jokes and talked about business conditions in Texas and all over.

Ladling meat and potatoes into his mouth, Geronimo stared at Dora Baxter until Sundance felt sorry for her. The old bastard hadn't spoken to her since they started the journey. He didn't speak to her now. Then he did something that startled even the salesmen. He dipped his grimy fingers into one of his stew bowls, found the biggest chunk of beef and held it out to Dora Baxter: an offering.

"Eat," Geronimo commanded.

The salesmen gaped.

Dora Baxter, smiling nervously, opened her mouth and Geronimo thrust the chunk of stew beef into it.

One of the salesman began to laugh but out of politeness he changed it to a cough.

Geronimo, grim-faced as ever, watched Dora Baxter while she chewed and swallowed. It was a big piece of meat and she gasped and tried to smile.

"Good. Very good," she said, a little red-faced.

Geronimo smiled at Sundance and went back to devouring his stew.

Uncle John, the conductor, opened the door of the restaurant. "Five more minutes, folks. The train goes with or without you. Five minutes!"

Geronimo finished his stew, wolfed down four wedges of pecan pie, drank three cups of heavily sugared coffee—and there was still plenty of time to get back on the train.

Back in his seat, Geronimo frowned at the floor until the train left Brimmerton behind. The salesmen were passing a bottle and were back to the dirty jokes. There was a constant parade, back and forth, of farmers going to get a drink from the water bottle at the end of the car.

Geronimo looked over at Sundance and spoke in Spanish mixed with Indian words from Apacheria, the country along the Arizona-Mexico border.

111

Geronimo said: "This woman you have no claim on, she thinks I am a great warrior and wants to write about me. You have said that and so it must be true, for all men know that the famous Sundance does not lie. But I would ask you again: does this woman truly admire Geronimo and all his great deeds in the past, and to come?"

"It's true," Sundance answered, not sure that he liked any of this. Geronimo was a savage but he was a sly savage, and nothing he did was without a reason.

"Good," Geronimo said. "And is it true—as you said in your great honesty—that she wants to know everything about Geronimo so that she can write it in her newspaper?"

The old weasel was up to something. Anything Geronimo was up to was always nasty. "True," Sundance agreed.

With a grim smile Geronimo played his ace. "Then I would like you to tell this woman that Geronimo wants to prove to her what a man he is. In the man and woman way. You will tell her that is what Geronimo wants."

Sundance didn't smile because there was nothing funny about it. Now and then he could find something funny about Geronimo. Something very small. This was something else entirely. The crazy old bastard's pride was involved, and that made it downright dangerous.

"They wouldn't print that in the newspaper," Sundance said, hoping to head him off. "The man and woman thing. No newspaper would print that, so why bother with it? Let this woman here write about Geronimo's great campaigns, how he defied the Mexicans and the Americans for so many years, though his force was small and theirs great. How they were so afraid of him that time and time again they tried to make peace. Let her write how Geronimo survived fifteen years in the Florida swamps while other, lesser men died of fever and hardship."

Geronimo scowled in spite of this recital of his magnificence.

Sundance went on. "Let this woman write how Geronimo was drowned in the Gulf of Mexico and came back to life. Let her say how Geronimo is so famous that an equally famous American general interceded on his behalf—because of respect—to get him out of prison. All these things can be said. Geronimo knows how to read and he can read them when this woman puts them in her newspaper."

Geronimo wasn't about to be put off so easily. "Tell her, Sundance. It is not for you to say what she would like to do. If she admires Geronimo the knowledge of what a man he is—man and woman—could be for herself. Tell her, Sundance."

Why not? Sundance thought. It might take her down a peg, something she badly needed. He nudged Dora Baxter, who was dozing with her head against the window frame.

"What is it?" She yawned and rubbed her eyes. There were smudges on her face from the trailing smoke.

Sundance looked across the aisle at Geronimo and he was facing straight ahead. Sundance knew he was listening, the old son of a bitch.

"Geronimo wants you to know what a great man he is," Sundance said.

"I know he is. I know he's a great warrior."

"He didn't give you that chunk of meat for nothing. The old boy's taken a shine to you, if you know what I mean."

Geronimo bristled at being called an old boy.

"Tell him I'm flattered," Dora Baxter said.

"You still don't get it," Sundance said. "He wants to show his stuff with you."

"Oh come on!"

"You know the Spanish word *cojones?*"

"Of course I do."

"That's it," Sundance said. "Geronimo wants to show you that he's got *cojones.*"

Dora Baxter looked over at Geronimo who seemed to be looking at one of the drummers puking out the window. The other salesmen were cheering him on.

"If you're joking, it's a rotten joke," Dora Baxter said, coloring slightly. "If he did say that I'm sure you put him up to it."

"That sounds like the joke—the drummer joke—about the midget whose friends helped him make love to a tall woman. Listen. Say yes or no, but don't say it's a joke. You're the one who wants to know everything at firsthand. Kitchen maid. Meat packer. What else did you say you did? Dance hall girl on the Bowery?"

Dora Baxter saw Geronimo staring at her. "Oh God," she said desperately. "Perhaps I do talk too much. Sundance, I hate to ask your help, but you have to help me. I do admire Geronimo and don't want to hurt his feelings—but *that*! Can't you explain to him that reporters just write about their subjects; they don't get involved with them. Say that's the first thing they teach you when you go to work for a newspaper."

"Geronimo wouldn't understand any of that.

114

Geronimo never worked for the *New York Sun*."

Still staring at Dora Baxter with his dirty face, Geronimo smiled again. Sundance thought, not even a scrubbing brush and a bar of lye soap would get six decades of dirt off that face.

Dora Baxter grew even more desperate. "Please, Sundance, you have to help me. I feel so bad about this whole thing."

It was time to put an end to it, if he could. "All right," Sundance said. "I'll do my best."

Then, speaking in Spanish, he said to Geronimo, "There are certain difficulties here . . ."

He explained that Miss Baxter was a devout *catolico*—like the pure young virgins of Old Mexico—and was affianced to a fiercely jealous young man who would have her examined by a doctor—as was the custom among devout *catolicos*—before the marriage could take place.

Sundance said he knew such a great man as Geronimo would not wish to spoil the happiness of this fine young woman who was so interested in his life story. There could be no doubt that she was pleased—and honored—by Geronimo's offer, but what he offered was not possible.

Geronimo just turned his head away.

"I'm so sorry," Dora Baxter said. "He's such a fine old man."

Sundance told her to shut up.

She didn't. "You were talking so long. What did you say to him?"

"Spanish takes twice as long as English," Sundance said. "You want to know, I'll tell you." Sundance told her.

Her face flushed. "You bastard. You rotten dirty bastard!"

"Shush now. Don't let him hear you or he won't believe you're not a devout *catolico.*" Sundance smiled. "Like the pure young virgins of Old Mexico."

"I'm going to sleep," Dora Baxter said. "I've had enough of your jackass humor."

But when she woke up she grinned at him. Geronimo was asleep. "Why did you make up such a ridiculous story?" she asked.

"I had to tell him something. I'm not sure it did any good. Probably wouldn't have made any difference what I told him. You turned him down and he doesn't like it. Your fault, not mine. Some advice. Next time you meet a wild Apache don't tell him what a great man he is. A good thing you have me along."

"Why is that?"

"He'd rape the bloomers off you."

"Oh!" Dora Baxter said.

There was some humor in the situation, Sundance thought. About an ounce and a half, though he was sure Dora Baxter would treat it as very funny when she regaled her newspaper friends with the story in years to come.

Dora Baxter knew that all men were vain; what she didn't understand was that Apache men were vainest of all. To Geronimo, her interest in him could mean only one thing, for as all men knew women were interested in nothing more than what was between a man's legs. All else was foolishness, in the Apache mind. Vanity was the key to the Apache's thinking. Apache men—with all their beads and ornaments, their face paint, their dancing and ceremonial strutting—were vainer than women. Now Dora Baxter, through no fault of her

116

own—that wasn't true either—had insulted Geronimo, and he would have to deal with that, too.

Still sleeping, Dora Baxter had a faint smile. Geronimo was awake and wasn't smiling at all. Sundance moved over and sat beside him. He could see that the old man wasn't inclined to talk. He hoped he could change his mind.

"I was thinking," Sundance said.

"What were you thinking?" Geronimo's bitter old face was turned away.

"Remember back in Beaumont you were talking about whores?"

"I said I raped many Mexican women."

"You don't have to do any more raping. You want to go to a whorehouse, Geronimo?"

"Whores are women," Geronimo said. "That was your promise. That we would go to a whorehouse. You made a promise, Sundance. You will keep your promise? After fifteen years in that swamp I want a woman. This woman you say you have no claim on does not want Geronimo. . . ."

"No claim," Sundance said. "That's the truth."

"Then maybe she claims you and you don't know it."

"The whorehouse," Sundance said. "You want to go or not?"

"A woman is a woman. I am telling you it has been fifteen years."

"I know it has."

"You think I am all dead down there?"

"No," Sundance said. "I think you are still a great warrior down there. Geronimo, you must listen to me. This newspaper woman is not worthy of you. She is skinny and too tall and has a hard and

117

not a pleasing face. She is too old. She must be thirty, or even past thirty.''

Geronimo's smile was less grim than usual. "Not a pure young virgin of Old Mexico.''

"I lied to you.''

"I know you did. You want her for yourself?''

"No.''

"I would not have minded her," Geronimo said. "I think she is a mean woman, but I would not have minded her.''

"I don't want her," Sundance said.

"Then you're a fool," Geronimo. "Any man not a fool would want that one. To not want a woman like that, is that what it means to be a stupid halfbreed?''

"I think so," Sundance said, pleased that the old man was insulting him. It was all right to take an old man's insults, and the acceptance of the insults would make Geronimo feel better, and thus his sense of insult would grow less.

"You think," Geronimo said. "I do not have to think. I would like to have that woman over there. That one is a bad woman. I can tell. I like bad women. I tell you this, Sundance. I like bad women better than bad men, for what can a man do with bad men except kill them?''

"True.''

"What do you know about truth, Sundance? What will you leave behind when you die? All your life you have been caught between two worlds, not knowing which way to turn. You are of the Indians and you are not. You talk the white man's language and you know his ways, but he doesn't want you.''

"True," Sundance said.

Geronimo showed impatience, unusual in an

Apache, especially an old one. "You, the great killer, can't say anything but 'true.' You helped to kill my children but I do not hate you for that. It was a war and your Crook gave me a chance to surrender before he brought in the mountain guns. . . ."

It was going good, Sundance thought. The old bastard was getting rid of his hate in insults. But he knew the hate wasn't for him. It was for Dora Baxter with her curly coal-black hair, her eyes just as black; and the lanky stretch of her body, her long, lean legs. If Geronimo talked long enough he would convince himself that what he wanted was some prostitute in some house along the way. Yet he remembered Geronimo's words. *You have to be a halfbreed fool not to want that one.*

I guess I do, he thought. And he remembered Geronimo's other comment: *I like bad women.* When he thought about it, Sundance had to admit that he liked bad women, too. Whatever "bad" women meant. But forget about the meaning. He liked them, too. There was something about a bad woman, a mean woman, a cruel and selfish woman that stirred the blood. They kept you hopping and off-balance all the time; the frantic pace and the loss of equilibrium was worth it.

Certainly Dora Baxter was a selfish woman; it would be hard to find a woman who was more so. He guessed a lot of newspaper people were like that, always thinking of themselves rather than the public whose interests they were supposed to be looking out for. There was something about Dora Baxter that spelled trouble, a craving for danger that went far beyond her work as a reporter. She said she loved her "stubby little gun," the five-shot Webley Bulldog. That was the key to what she was really

119

like, because no sensible person loved weapons for their own sake. At least you didn't love them in the way she meant. You appreciated their efficiency, and you cared for them as you would anything else you valued; anything more than that wasn't quite right.

But there was no getting rid of her, he knew; not for the moment anyway. That wouldn't come until the Ring picked up their trail. Then her blackmail would lose its force. Then he could safely leave her behind. As a man rather than Geronimo's jailer he wasn't sure he wanted to.

Geronimo had retreated into silence and Dora Baxter was writing furiously in her notebook, the pencil racing across the page with no hesitation. It was well into the afternoon and everyone in the coach was starting to get that look of boredom and fatigue that marks all travelers on a long train journey.

It was going to be a long night.

CHAPTER ELEVEN

It was getting dark when two men with deputy marshal badges got on with a prisoner, a chunky man of about forty with a jutting chin and a scar under his right eye. He was wearing handcuffs and the two men guarding him carried sawed-off shotguns and pistols. The two deputies were about thirty; lanky, slow in their movements. The conductor came in with them and moved some people from the last seat, so there would be no one behind them. Everybody gaped at them and one of the drummers, more than half drunk, yelled down the aisle, "Looks like you got a bad 'un there, boys. What did he do, kill somebody, rob a bank?"

The deputies took no notice of the drunk, but the prisoner spat at him. The two men slammed him into the seat and warned him to behave. One of them crooked a finger at the conductor and he stooped over to listen. A few minutes later he came down the aisle to take the tickets of the last passengers to get on. The drunken salesman stopped him on the way.

"Who's the badman, Uncle John? Has to be real bad, it takes two shotgun guards to take him for a ride."

"Bad is the right word for him. That's Cass Bains you're looking at. Murdered a whole family up in Oklahoma. They're taking him back to be hung. Damn! I wish I didn't have him on my train. Stay well away from him is my advice."

"Oh I don't know about that," the salesman said airily. "He don't look so tough to me. I never even heard of him."

"You're a drunk fool, Magruder," the conductor said and went on to take the tickets. After that he lit the gas lights up and down the aisle. Sparks flew past the windows as night fell and the train roared on, and in the aisle the waxed paper the farmers had discarded crunched underfoot every time somebody went to get a drink of water. But even that stopped, too, and even the loudmouth salesmen were quiet. People slept slumped over in their seats, their hats pulled down over their eyes. Soon the car smelled like a dirty bedroom in a cheap hotel, and when Sundance looked over at Dora Baxter she was still writing in her notebook, squinting in the bad light of the gas lamps.

Up ahead the two deputies sat with the prisoner between them. The prisoner had his eyes closed. An hour passed and then another. Geronimo grunted in his uneasy sleep, muttering in Spanish between grunts in no language. Sundance looked at the deputies at the end of the car. One had his eyes closed, the other was smoking a cigarette.

There was something about the prisoner that bothered Sundance, nagged at his memory. The name Cass Bains didn't mean anything to him. The West was full of killers of every stripe. It could be that Bains had a small reputation for villainy he didn't know about, yet he didn't think so. The

122

deputies sure as hell looked like deputies, and not just jobless cowboys with a badge but professional mancatchers, hard-eyed, slow moving, without mercy of any kind. Without appearing to, he studied the prisoner's face. It was that heavy jaw that awakened something deep in his memory. If he had seen the man before, a lot of years had passed since then. He searched back through his mind, trying to tie the prisoner's face to the towns and camps he'd been in. It wasn't until thirty minutes later that he saw the prisoner's face in another time, another place. Sure! That was it. Sixteen years before in Dodge City. There was a shooting at a poker table and two men got killed. The man who did the killing had a heavy jaw and he backed out of the saloon with a cocked pistol and got away before they could catch him. Now he even remembered the killer's name because somebody shouted it. Billy Dawes.

Geronimo woke up with a snort when Sundance pinched him in the leg. The old man glared at him. "Why do you disturb me? Sleep is the only hiding place I have."

"Keep looking at me," Sundance said. "Those men—the deputies and the prisoner—are killers. They are waiting for me to fall asleep. You understand what I'm saying?"

"I understand. You must give me a gun."

"My pistol," Sundance said, who was carrying it not in the holster but stuck in his belt on the other side, away from the old man. He reached over with his right hand and passed the Colt to Geronimo. "We have to kill them before they can use the shotguns. The prisoner will have only a pistol, so he dies last. You take the one beside the window, I'll kill the other one."

"How soon?" Geronimo asked.

"In a minute," Sundance said. "As soon as I warn the woman."

Dora Baxter looked up from her notebook and before he said anything else, Sundance warned her not to look away from him. Her head started to turn but she checked herself.

"What's going on?" she said calmly. "Is there somebody on the train?"

"We're going to kill the deputies and the prisoner. Don't look at them. They're gunmen and we have to get them with the first shots. A lot of people are going to get killed if they use the shotguns. Now open your bag like you're putting the notebook away. Take out the Webley and cover it. Don't cock it. Geronimo has my pistol. We'll kill the deputies, you take the prisoner. You shoot at him and keep shooting. Try not to kill any passengers."

"Sure," Dora Baxter said. "When?"

"Soon as you have the gun in your hand."

Sundance reached for the Winchester and held it across his knees. Geronimo was holding the pistol by his side. Across the aisle he felt the movement of Dora Baxter opening her bag. At the end of the car the two deputies were talking. The prisoner had his eyes closed.

Now! Sundance jumped to his feet, jacked a shell and killed the man on the left. The bullet tore through his face killing him instantly. Geronimo emptied the Colt at the other man, hitting him with three out of six bullets. Dora Baxter fired at the prisoner and hit him but he dived to the floor and came up with a single-barreled shotgun cut down to the size of a large handgun. He fired it and blew a farmer's head off. Another man jumped up yelling

124

hysterically. Sundance had to hold his fire. The yelling man tumbled into the aisle. The prisoner had a pistol out now and he fired it fast from behind the last seat. Sundance felt bullets all round him. The man fired again and this time Sundance got him in the head. He heard a gun being cocked behind him and he whirled with the rifle, trying to bring the rifle up in the narrow space between the seats. Before he could fire Dora Baxter spun around with the Webley and shot a man in the face. At close range the heavy .45 bullet drove him back with tremendous force. All over the car people were screaming and cursing and praying.

Facing different ways, they covered the car with their guns. There was a wild look on Dora Baxter's face. "You were a little slow just now," she said to Sundance.

"That I was," Sundance said. "Obliged to you, Miss Baxter."

"Dora," she said. "After this why don't you make it Dora?"

Now that the shooting was over the conductor came in shaking all over. "On my train! On my train!" he kept saying. He looked at the dead men. "Oh dear God! On my train!"

Sundance pointed the rifle at him. "Stop this thing. We're getting off."

"Oh yes indeed. You do that," the old trainman quavered. "But no more shooting and killing, please."

The train ground to a halt and they moved down to the box car where the horses were. Dora Baxter held the Webley on the conductor while they got the horses saddled and off the train.

"No hard feelings, Uncle John," Sundance said

125

while they mounted up. "You tell the law that the so-called prisoner was a man named Billy Dawes, a killer. There may be wanted posters out on him, the others too. If there's a reward, you claim it. They were on your train."

"Oh yes indeed," the conductor said. "I could use the money."

Sundance put Dora Baxter up in front of him and they headed out into the night. Geronimo gave the empty Colt back to Sundance, and was reluctant to do it. They had come a long way from Beaumont; there was a long way to go before they crossed the Oklahoma line. This far north the country was sparsely settled, but Sundance figured they'd be able to get a horse for Dora Baxter sometime the next morning. It was a warm night and the sky blazed with stars and after they left the railroad they entered a region of rolling treeless hills except where cottonwoods grew along a creek bottom. They had to put as much distance as they could between themselves and the railroad. The agents of the Ring would start where they left the train and try to track them from there. Still, he guessed they had a fair enough start.

"You can't leave me behind after this," Dora Baxter said. "I was in on the killing. Now they'll be after me too."

"You invited yourself," Sundance said. "But you're right. They'll be after you too. As long as you stay with us they'll be out to kill you. They won't try too hard to find you if you're by yourself."

"Don't start that again. I'm in this to the end. Who do you suppose told them we were on the train?"

126

"No way to tell. There was an army officer on board who got off when we went to the eating place. It could have been one of the drummers who telegraphed ahead. Geronimo's picture has been in a lot of barbershop magazines."

"What now?"

"We keep going, get a few hours sleep, and start in again."

"Doesn't sound like much of a plan."

"It isn't. First you run, then you think of a plan. That's how it works."

Dora Baxter said in sudden excitement. "You know that's the first shooting I was in. I've been under fire, but that's different. It was a good feeling standing there and firing back, knowing I wasn't going to throw myself on the floor with the rest of them. It was the feeling of not being afraid. Now I know I'll never be afraid of anything."

"That's a dumb thing to say. You don't put yourself in the way of danger."

"But you do it all the time."

"That's different. I get paid for it. Paid well."

"You're not getting paid for this."

Thinking of Crook's past friendship, his immense kindness, Sundance smiled. "I got paid in advance."

They traveled on into the night. This was easy, rolling country and they traversed the range of low hills without any difficulty. Dora Baxter talked herself to sleep and Sundance held her in the saddle. Geronimo rode tirelessly, and in silence, still angry at having the Colt taken away from him. There was nothing Sundance could do about that. The closer they got to Oklahoma, the less he could trust him.

Down from the hills they picked up a little-used

127

road going west. There was no sign that anyone had been along recently. Far off from the road they saw the lights of a house; some farmer getting up early. It was five o'clock and the stars were glimmering out when they came to a place where the road went through a creek, and Sundance said they would take the horses into the water and ride upstream and look for a place to make cold camp.

In places the water was deep but not so deep that they couldn't take the horses through. Dora Baxter woke up when the water in a deep pool wet her feet.

"My God! It's morning," she said.

Sundance pointed to a grove of cottonwoods still in deep shadow. "We'll sleep in there for four hours. It's as good a camp as any."

"Strong hot coffee, that's what I want," Dora Baxter said.

"No coffee, no fire," Sundance said. "You have a choice of breakfast. Jerked deer meat or cold bacon."

"Just a small fire?" Dora Baxter urged, still thinking of the coffee she wasn't going to get. So was Sundance. After a long night in the saddle he craved a cup of scalding black coffee more than anything else.

"Can't make any kind of fire," he said. "Smoke could be spotted."

"But they can't be that close behind us, can they?"

"Probably not. But if some farmer sees smoke he can tell them where he saw it. And when they know where we've been, they can figure out where we've gone. They may track us anyway, but we don't have to give them help. For now we travel by night and keep out of people's way."

The sun was flooding up full by the time they unsaddled the horses and rubbed them down with handfuls of grass. Geronimo put his horse on a long tether, hitching the end of the rope to a tree root. Eagle grazed at will but stayed in the shelter of the trees on Sundance's command.

Under the trees the ground was spongy, a good place to sleep. Birds flew away when they approached but came back and twittered in the branches. Down from where they were cattails waved along the banks of the creek and the morning wind was getting warm.

"Food," Geronimo demanded.

Sundance unwrapped the slab of bacon from its oilskin covering and cut off a chunk for the old man. He gave him hard biscuits to go with the bacon. Geronimo tore at the salted, fatty meat with his strong brown teeth, crumbled the biscuits and filled his mouth until his cheeks bulged. Everytime he swallowed his eyes closed in contentment.

Turning with the bacon and Bowie knife Sundance asked Dora Baxter if she wanted breakfast.

"Slice the bacon very thin, will you?" she said. "I'll wrap it around the biscuits and pretend it's crisp-fried. Raw bacon and creek water for breakfast. If the boys in the city room at the *Sun* could see me now."

Geronimo demanded more bacon and Sundance gave it to him.

"You'll get used to it," Sundance said. "Or maybe you won't."

"I'll get used to it," she said.

Geronimo finished eating and stood up to be tied.

"What are you doing?" Dora Baxter said, startled when Sundance shook out the rope. "You can't do that. Ask him to give you his word."

"His word's no good," Sundance said. "I know because he told me. I had no sleep last night, very little the night before. I'd like to sleep now without having to wake up every fifteen minutes to make sure he's here."

With his back turned Geronimo growled, "Stop talking and tie me, Sundance. I am tired and want to sleep. You and this woman can talk when I am asleep. You can be cow and bull when I am asleep."

Dora Baxter said, "I'll watch him. I've had some sleep. I'm all right. I have the Webley."

"He'd just take it away from you and kill us. Mind your own business and go to sleep."

Sundance finished roping Geronimo, wrists and ankles and throat. Then he laid him down and covered him with a blanket. The old man was snoring before he stood up.

Dora Baxter looked unhappy. "All that roping is inhuman. Wouldn't handcuffs do just as well, if you have to use anything at all. Putting the rope around his neck. That's awful."

"He doesn't mind the rope so much," Sundance said, putting the blanket and the saddle where he was going to sleep. "Sure I could use handcuffs but that would drive him crazy. Apaches—all Indians—hate irons because there's no way to get out of them. They know ropes, know what they feel like. With a rope they always think there's a chance to work themselves loose."

"Then why use it?"

"Because Geronimo knows that when I tie him he stays tied."

Dora Baxter took the notebook from her bag and began to write in it, but she slumped over before she

130

got to the end of the page. Sundance smiled and covered her with a blanket after he stretched her out on the soft dry ground. Her sleeping face lost some of its hardness, though she hugged the leather-bound notebook to her breasts, like a mother with a child.

Behind the stand of cottonwoods a hill rose up to not more than seventy-five feet and Sundance climbed it with the sun warming his face. Lying on the hill, he uncased his small brass-framed binoculars and scouted the creek all the way down to the road. Here and there along the creek there were jackrabbits hopping and running in the grass. No one was on the road.

His belly rumbled with hunger when he thought of a plump young rabbit dripping fat on a spit over the fire they didn't have. He stuffed a handful of dried meat into his mouth and came down from the hill. Their pursuers might be closer than he thought, or they could still be following blind trails in the hills. But he had no doubt that they would come, inexorable as fate itself. All they could do was run and fight when they had to. Dora Baxter seemed to believe that courage always won out in the end, if you had enough of it. But he knew better, as she ought to know, and didn't; but then to her the whole thing was a strange game of some kind. Something not quite real.

He lay down and went to sleep.

CHAPTER TWELVE

It was past ten when they started out again after a second, quicker breakfast of cold bacon, biscuits and creek water. They stayed off the road. Having to ride over broken country slowed them but Sundance couldn't see any help for that. By noon they hadn't covered many miles but then when they topped another ridge, far below they saw horses in a square pasture not far from a big house of wood and stone. On the far side of the house a valley dipped down and in the center of it cattle were spread out like a dark stain around a prairie pond that glinted like old silver in the sun. There was no one guarding the horses in the pasture.

"You think you can get one for the woman?" Sundance asked Geronimo. "If you think there is too much danger I will do it."

The old man glared at him. "I was stealing horses before you were born, Sundance. For you to steal a horse with success it would have to be in a thunderstorm in the dead of night with everyone drunk."

He took the binoculars from Sundance and glassed the horses in the pasture. "This woman you do not claim as yours, I think the chestnut down there is a good horse for her."

Sundance nodded. "That's the one to get."

From the ridge they watched while the old man worked his way down to the flat. Past the house, by the pond, men on horses were herding cows away from the pond, giving others room to drink.

Geronimo was like a shadow as he ran toward the pasture, and the horses hardly moved at all when he came close.

Dora Baxter gave the binoculars back to Sundance. "Why is he taking so long?" she said anxiously. "He should be out of there by now."

"He's letting the horses get used to him. Don't worry about it. Geronimo knows horses better than anything except killing."

And while they watched the old man came out of the small horse herd with the chestnut. There was a rope on the chestnut, but the old man was hardly using it. Sundance smiled. The old thief. But even so he pulled the Winchester from its beaded scabbard and made ready to give the old man cover if he needed it. The men by the pond, far off, were still moving the cows around.

Geronimo took the chestnut along the bottom of the ridge, then down over a hump in the ground where he could no longer be seen from the house.

"Time to go," Sundance said.

They went back down the blind side of the ridge and crossed it closer to where Geronimo was waiting.

Geronimo glared at Sundance. "That is how it is done, halfbreed."

Sundance took the saddle from Eagle and put it on the chestnut. Geronimo held the chestnut's head while he did it.

"They won't miss it for a while," Sundance said.

133

"When we're far enough along we'll turn it loose and get you something else to ride. Don't argue about it unless you want to know how it feels to be hung, like everything else you want to know about."

"Oh come on!" Dora Baxter said. "You wouldn't hang a woman just for stealing a horse."

"In Texas they would."

After that they made somewhat better time. The chestnut was a three year old, and gentle, and Dora Baxter had no trouble staying in the saddle, although she was far from an expert rider. But she was pretty good for a city-bred woman, Sundance thought. This woman was pretty good at everything she did.

In the early afternoon they ate more cold bacon but they stayed in their saddles, moving on all the time. The sun was hot and the bacon was soft from the heat and tasted worse than it had in the early morning. Dora Baxter had sweat stains in the armpits of her shirt.

The horseflies were thick and when they stopped to rest again Sundance asked Dora Baxter for one of her small unladylike cigars.

"So you smoke after all," she said.

"For the horses," Sundance said, and as she watched in astonishment he broke the cigarillo between his fingers and chewed it until it was brown-running slop. Then he took a swallow of water and spat some of the mixture into his hand. He rubbed down the horses, and when he ran out of tobacco juice he asked Dora Baxter for another cigar. The horseflies buzzed but didn't bite.

An hour later they had to get back on the road because the country became too fissured and rocky.

It was close to nightfall when they came to a cross-roads with a weathered signpost. One of the arms of the post pointed to McDade, 15 Miles.

"That's where we'll go," Sundance said.

"You ever hear of it?" Dora Baxter asked.

Sundance said no. "But it's north and we have to head that way sooner or later. You still thinking of coffee and hot food?"

"That's all I've been thinking about."

"Let's make tracks then before it gets too late. These small towns aren't too neighborly after they go to bed."

It was just past eight o'clock when they saw the lights of McDade up ahead. It stood in the middle of nowhere, but it was bigger than Sundance had expected. There would be no telegraph line in a town so far from the railroad so maybe they could find a place to spend the night. The main street was shaded by trees and at least some of the town was awake as they rode in. Halfway down the street between a harness store and a barbershop was the McDade Saloon & Hotel, Prop. Mamie McDade. In front of it was a wagon with an old woman asleep on the seat. There were no horses anywhere around.

The hotel was a three-story building painted yellow, and there was a sign proclaiming that it had been in business for a tenth of a century. They hitched their horses and went in and saw a fat woman behind the bar, and in front of it was an old man so drunk he was hardly able to stand. If the woman thought they were an odd-looking group it didn't show in her face.

"Sit yourself down, I'll be with you directly," the fat woman called out, and went back to telling the old man he ought to go home.

"Nope," he said with great solemnity, pouring himself another drink from the bottle on the bar. "I ain't drunk enough yet to go home."

"You're a disgrace," the fat woman said amiably, and came over to the table to see what they wanted.

"That's me on the sign out there," she told them. "Mamie McDade. Now what can I do for you?"

"Got anything to eat?" Sundance asked.

"Bless your heart, stranger, I got plenty to eat. Horse auction starts the day after tomorrow. We have one every month and make it last most of a week. Town may look dead right now. You should see it on auction week. Make enough money in one week to last me the month." She looked at Geronimo. "Listen, stranger. No offense but I can't sell this feller any whisky. Beer's all right though. No law against selling him beer."

"Bring him a beer then. Whisky for the lady. Coffee for me. After that keep the steak coming. We'll tell you when to stop. Anything that goes with steak, bring it along."

"That's the kind of talk I like to hear," the fat woman said, yelling to the cook. A mournful-looking man in a white apron came out of the kitchen in the back of the bar and kept nodding while the fat woman ticked off a long list of side dishes: fried potatoes, corn, mashed turnips, creamed onions. When she got through she went to get the drinks.

"Go on home, Lemmy," she told the old man, who took no notice of her.

Geronimo guzzled his mug of beer as soon as it was set down.

"Bring him another," Sundance said. "Maybe you can tell us how far the Oklahoma line is from here.''

"Going up to the Territory, are you? Well now, let me see. I'd say it's a good three-day ride, depending you put in a full day in the saddle. Four, if you dally. Was there once twenty-three years ago. Time does fly, don't it?''

The fat woman was on the shady side of fifty and good-looking in a puffy sort of way. She had the easy, offhand manner of someone accustomed to dealing with men. Geronimo kept looking at her. While she was getting the beer, two girls came out on the balcony that ran around the rear of the saloon. Dora Baxter looked up at them and smiled at Sundance.

"Mamie is a madam,'' she said, lowering her voice.

"Just as long as the steak is good,'' Sundance said.

The two girls giggled and the fat woman clapped her hands at them and they disappeared, still looking back. When the coffee was ready the cook brought it in.

"Grub's just about ready,'' he said, staring at Geronimo.

The fat woman helped bring in the dishes and she yelled at the cook for being so slow. "Eat hearty,'' she said, and went back to her post behind the bar. "Go on home, Lemmy,'' she said again.

As usual Geronimo ate like a wolf, heaping his plate with enough food for three men. Now and then he looked at Mamie McDade. But he never stopped eating.

Dora Baxter inclined her head toward the bar. "You think she'll let us stay the night? I didn't see anything else that looks like a hotel.''

"Hard to tell," Sundance said. "There may be a girl in every room. We'll ask her when we get through."

Dora Baxter giggled. "I've been in a lot of places, never in a whorehouse. No wonder she does such good business when the horse auction is in town. You think she's rich?"

"I would say so." The steak was good and so was the coffee. There was nothing like farm country for getting a good steak. Geronimo was gnawing on an ear of corn.

"You been in many whorehouses?" Dora Baxter asked, smiling at Sundance. "I'm asking as a reporter."

"I've been in a few. There's nothing very special about them. They're like stores. They sell and you buy. Better stop talking and eat. There won't be anything left if you don't."

Geronimo was starting on his third steak.

In a while the fat woman came over and regarded the empty dishes with approval. "I do admire folks that know how to eat," she said. "Anything else I can do for you?"

Sundance said, "Maybe you can rent us some rooms for the night. Two rooms?"

"Well, I don't know . . ." the fat woman started off, trying to be as delicate as she could.

"Anything at all," Sundance said. "We've been on the road a long time and the lady here is tired. No need to explain the setup here. Doesn't bother us a bit. Fact is, you've got a nice-looking place here, Miz McDade. When the food's good you know everything else has to be fine."

"Well thank you, sir," the fat woman said with the pride of ownership. "I like to give value for money. Nobody ever said Mamie McDade didn't give them a fair shake. Things are slow tonight. Not a soul here but me and the girls and that drunk fool over yonder at the bar. And the cook. Why sure, why not?'' She looked at Dora Baxter. ''You'll have to sleep in one of the girls' rooms. She can double up. Same goes for you fellers.''

''That'll be fine,'' Dora Baxter said.

The fat woman was turning away when Geronimo spoke in Spanish to Sundance. ''I want a woman. There are women here.''

''I'll see what I can do,'' Sundance said. He got up and steered the fat woman away from the table. She looked surprised at the expression on his face.

''Something not right?'' she asked.

''You may think so when I tell you. Look, this is kind of awkward. The old man with me wants a girl. You got anybody here willing to take him on. I'll pay whatever you say.'' Sundance peeled off some bills. ''Is fifty dollars enough?''

''Good lord yes. More than enough. Wouldn't think of asking that much, but the girl I have in mind is going to holler blue blazes. Jenny'll take on just about anybody, but . . .'' The fat woman shook her head. ''I guess she'll do it though.'' She glanced over at Geronimo, who was eating the last of the food. ''You think the old boy is able?''

Sundance smiled. ''He thinks he is.''

''Wonders never cease, do they? I'll tell you this. He'll have to take a bath before Jenny lets him in her bed. No bath, no girl.''

''He'll take a bath,'' Sundance said, handing over the fifty dollars.

Sundance came back to the table while the fat woman went upstairs to make the arrangements.

139

Dora Baxter was drinking coffee and smoking a cigarillo and she looked up inquiringly. "What's going on?"

"I'll tell you in a minute." Switching to Spanish, he told Geronimo about the bath, knowing full well that the only bath Geronimo ever had was in the Gulf of Mexico. "No use scowling at me, Geronimo. No bath, no girl, that's what she said. You do what you like. Makes no difference to me."

"All right," Geronimo said after he thought about it for a long time. "I will do it."

The fat woman and a big Swedish-looking girl came out onto the balcony. After she looked over Geronimo, the girl shrugged and went away.

"He can come up now," the fat woman called. "Bath's in the room the end of the hall. I'll show him where it is."

Geronimo stood up like a man going to be hanged.

"Leave your boots," Sundance said. "That's right, take the boots off and leave them here. I don't want you ducking out some window."

In the old days it wouldn't have bothered Geronimo to go barefoot over rough country, but after fifteen years in Florida he was used to having his feet protected. Dora Baxter did her best not to smile while Geronimo pulled off his army boots and put them under the table. At the top of the stairs the fat woman was waiting. Geromino went up.

"Too bad I can't put all this in my story," Dora Baxter said. "Perhaps it isn't. Who would believe it? Geronimo in a whorehouse. And taking a bath. Why don't you want a girl?"

"Who said I didn't?"

"The ones I saw aren't very good-looking."

140

"You don't come to a whorehouse to get married."

"I wonder what it's like to be a whore."

"Why don't you stay on with Miz McDade and find out."

Dora Baxter laughed. "They'd never print it if I wrote it. Must be strange, though, being a whore. All those men. You finish with one and you have to service another, never knowing what he's like. never knowing what he's going to ask you to do. Still, it must be interesting in a way. There used to be a saying that whores make the best wives. You think that's true?"

"I never married a whore," Sundance said. "I'll let you know when I do."

The fat woman came back to the balcony and said they could turn in any time they were ready.

They went up, Dora Baxter carrying her bag, and the fat woman opened the door to a room with the number 5 on it. A kerosene lamp with a frosted chimney decorated with birds and flowers stood on a table beside a bed that looked as if it had just been made up. There was a chair and a wardrobe for clothes. On the walls were pastoral scenes of some country far from Texas.

"A very nice girl works here," the fat woman said before she caught herself. "What I mean is . . ."

"It's fine," Dora Baxter said. "It's very nice."

"Thank you," Mamie McDade said. "Little Mary will be pleased to hear you said that. Your room is right next door, Mr.—"

"Starbuck," Sundance said. "This is Miss Philips. The old boy taking the bath, we call him Uncle Jerry up in the Territory."

141

"Please to meet you," the fat woman said. "Let me say it's a pleasure doing business with you, Mr. Starbuck." _____

"Likewise," Sundance said.

Sundance's room was exactly like Little Mary's except that there were no prints on the walls. He put Geronimo's boots in the wardrobe and went down the hall to see how he was coming with his bath.

He opened the door and Geronimo was still in the galvanized iron tub. The window was steamed up from the hot water; there was a copper boiler with a small charcoal fire burning under it. Geronimo was scrubbing his feet with a long-handled brush.

"How are you coming along?" Sundance asked, restraining the urge to smile.

"You see I am taking a bath. Does that have to be explained to you, Sundance? You see I have not ducked out a window. Do not be a pest, halfbreed."

"Have a good time," Sundance said. He could see that the old man was enjoying his first bath. The fat woman was right: wonders never ceased.

Down the street from the hotel there was a livery stable and he caught the stableman just before he went to bed.

After he saw to the horses Sundance went back. In front of the McDade Saloon & Hotel the old drunk called Lemmy was reeling all over the street while the old man in the wagon cussed him out.

When Sundance went back upstairs the door to Dora Baxter's room was closed.

CHAPTER THIRTEEN

Sundance put the Winchester in the wardrobe and hid the key before he stretched out on the bed. There was no point in putting temptation in the old man's way. After he finished with the big Swede girl, one way or another, he might decide to go foraging for weapons. No sound came from Dora Baxter's room and he guessed that she had gone to sleep. He smiled, thinking maybe she had a point. Maybe he should use one of the girls. There was a whole whorehouse to choose from, and yet he found himself thinking about her. She was something to think about, he admitted. Geronimo was right. It was dumb not to want her, and for all her contrary and difficult nature she was much woman, as the Mexicans said. But things were just as well as they were. God! He was tired. So keep it simple.

He woke up and drew the Colt when the door opened. Dora Baxter stood there with a wild look in her eyes. She was naked.

"I want to know what it feels like to be a whore," she said. "In that bed—thinking of all that's happened there—I couldn't sleep."

She closed the door and came forward when he swung his legs off the bed. "No, don't unbuckle your belt, I'll do it," she said. "I want to do every-thing for you. You'll like me, Mr. Starbuck."

Sundance smiled at this crazy woman and her wild ways. "Sure I will, Miss Philips. Just don't spell my name wrong when you put it in the paper."

She took his clothes and boots off in a way that was better than any whore's. Now and then she gig-gled. But the giggling stopped when they got into bed and he drove into her. There was no more play-acting then.

"Oh my God!" she cried out again and again, and she clung to him with a sort of desperation that wasn't entirely because of what he was doing to her. "Oh it's good, Sundance! It's so good!"

And when they were done, after he had satisfied her many times over, she lay beside him running her forefinger along the many old scars that covered his body.

"I've always wanted to go to bed with you," she said. "Every time I read about you I wanted to go to bed with you. You know something. You're the way I thought you'd be. And yet you aren't. You aren't rough with women. You're gentle."

"Don't tell Geronimo."

"I'm not just saying that."

"You wanted me to be rough?'

"I thought I did. Now I don't. Here we are and two days ago you didn't want me to come along. Have you changed your mind?"

"No."

"How can you say that—now?"

"I don't want to get you killed. You like danger too much. How long have you been in this business of yours?"

"You're just trying to find out my age."

144

"I'd figure you're around twenty-eight."

"That's not very gallant, sir. All right, I'm twenty-eight, but I've never been kissed until now. You believe that?"

"No."

"You're not under oath, Sundance. Ladies like to be lied to about some things. I've been a reporter for eight years. That doesn't make me an old lady. I'm going to be the most famous reporter that ever lived. Perhaps I'll even write a book about all this."

"We better get some sleep now," Sundance told her. "The night is wearing on and we have to make an early start."

Beside him he felt her shaking with silent laughter. "I wonder how Geronimo is doing with the Swede?"

Sundance said, "She hasn't thrown him out, so I guess he's doing all right. I'm hoping that a night with a woman will settle him down. I just want to get him to Fort Cobb with no holes in his hide."

"Suppose you get him there, what's to stop him from breaking out again?"

"Three Stars—Crook—seems to be gambling that he'll change his ways once he sees his own land. Knows it belongs to him. The soldiers at Fort Cobb will keep an eye on him, not that he won't break out if he has a mind to. I'm not sure I won't be fighting him in the Sonora mountains before the year is over. If it comes to that, I'll catch him all over again."

"You mean you'd take him back to that Florida prison?"

"No, I'd just kill him. If he breaks out this time, he'll get the rope for sure. The army will hang him where they catch him. If it's me, I'll finish him with

145

a bullet."

Dora Baxter's voice was tense with excitement. "What a story that would be. The last great Apache fighting for his freedom. Hunted by the men who befriended him."

"Don't include Three Stars in that," Sundance said. "I'll hunt him, but I doubt that Three Stars will be in the army, if Geronimo breaks out again. They'll nail Three Stars to the cross and be glad they have the chance to do it. I'll make Geronimo pay if that happens. I'll understand what's in back of it, and I'll still make him pay."

"But what a story!"

"Go to sleep," Sundance said.

Mamie McDade was up and around before they came downstairs before first light. Her face was puffy with sleep and her gray-blond hair was carelessly pinned up. The saloon smelled the way all closed-up saloons smell early in the morning. Stale beer mixed with the sharper smell of whisky. Sawdust and tobacco smoke. In the kitchen the cook was banging around talking to himself.

"I figured you'd be making an early start," the fat woman said, patting her untidy hair. "What I mean, the Territory being so far and all. Funny how a town wakes up, ain't it. In some towns you know it's awake for the day when somebody does this or that. Like the blacksmith starts hammering away. In this town it's when the sheriff comes in from his place outside of town. Once you see Mr. Haydock riding in, you know the town is open for business."

There was no way to miss what Mamie McDade was telling them. Be on your way before Mr.

146

Haydock comes around asking questions. She thought they were on the dodge from the law.

"Mr. Heydock is like a clock," she went on. "Right on the dot of six-thirty he'll be coming down that street. A man of habit, like they say. First he puts his horse up at the livery, chats a minute with the stableman, then heads for his office."

Sundance looked at the saloon clock. It was 5:15. Cooking smells came from the kitchen.

"Fixed you some steak and fried eggs," the fat woman said. "Something that'll stick to your ribs for the long ride ahead."

"Kind of you," Sundance said, wondering if the fat woman would be just as kind to the Ring killers when they came along. He knew they would. When they came to that crossroads they might split their force and send a few men on the road going west. They might not.

Geronimo came downstairs and Sundance gave him his boots. Dora Baxter hid her smile behind her hand. The cook brought in the food. There was plenty of it.

Geronimo looked at Sundance with grim satisfaction and said in Spanish, "I am not all dead down there, halfbreed."

Dora Baxter had a sudden fit of coughing. Then, wiping her eyes, she said. "Damn tobacco."

Later, at the livery stable, Sundance asked the man if he had a good horse for sale.

"You mean to make a trade and cash on the old gent's horse?" the stableman asked, looking at Geronimo's nag. "Can't allow you much cash-trade on that animal. You see the way it's all stove in."

"I mean the chestnut," Sundance said.

147

The stableman's eyes narrowed with quick suspicion. "What's the matter with the chestnut? Looks all right to me."

"Nothing's wrong with it. Doesn't belong to us, is all. Found it wandering on the road. The lady's own horse broke a leg and we had to shoot it. So when we found the chestnut we thought what's the harm of using it till we get to a town?"

"You don't say. Is that a fact now? Course you don't own the animal, I can't make any trade. You just leave it with me, mister, and I'll make inquiries as to its rightful owner."

"You got it right," Sundance said. "Now what have you got for sale?"

Sundance picked up a four-year-old gelding for Dora Baxter, and a saddle to go with it.

Geronimo looked from the gelding to his own nag. "I want a better horse, Sundance."

Sundance said not a chance. "You'll keep the one you have. It can't run too fast. When we get to the Territory you can have any horse you like. Don't argue, I won't listen."

As they rode out of McDade, heading north, Dora Baxter said, "I was beginning to like that chestnut. I hated to give it up."

"Better than having a posse after us. What we have to face is bad enough."

It was a bright clear morning without a cloud in the sky. High above kites soared and banked and the wind, still cool, was fresh in their faces. Geronimo wore his usual grim expression; he wore his face like a mask hiding another face, a real face, underneath.

In the days to come, Sundance knew, the old Apache would try to make his final break. If he did

148

break out he might just make it all the way back to the mountains, yet even for a man as tough and wily as Geronimo that would be a tremendous undertaking. All the way back, traveling across the immensity of Texas, he would be utterly alone, without friends, without money. At the moment their company afforded him a sort of protection. Alone, his very appearance would attract attention and suspicion. He would have to steal in order to live. The horse he had would never make it, so he would have to steal another unless he wanted to travel on foot. Sundance guessed he could do that too. Fifty years before, a mountain man by the name of Glass had crawled a thousand miles after he was crippled in a fall. A man could do anything if he had the will and the courage. And who could doubt that Geronimo had both? Sundance knew he would have to watch him closely in the days to come. Watch him all the time. Other Indians, the fiercest of warriors, had been broken by their years in military prison camps, and were living in peace in the Territory or on reservations far from their homelands. A few, even some of the most famous, had been allowed to join Wild West shows where they were dressed without regard to their tribe and put on display, whooping and doing fake war dances for the paying customers. But, Sundance knew, Geronimo was different from all the others. Of course that's why they were so afraid of him. There was, in the end, only one Geronimo.

Dora Baxter broke in on his thoughts. "I was thinking. Why don't they just wait until we get to Fort Cobb? These killers, why don't they do that, instead of chasing us all across Texas?"

A farm wagon with children in the back of it passed them going the other way. The children made faces at Geronimo, who took no heed of them.

"They may do that yet," Sundance said. "Though usually they try not to tangle with the army. At Fort Cobb Geronimo will be under the army's protection."

"But he'll be alone on his farm. What's to prevent someone with a rifle from killing him?"

"Not much," Sundance said. "Except that if he remains on the farm the Ring will lose interest in him. They like their Indians tame. Right now they want to kill him because they think he'll get back to the border country and start a war. If there is a war some of the reservation Indians will break out. That will be bad for business. Ring business. If there is no war the Ring can go on stealing and grafting. The Ring would like it very much if Geronimo settled down and raised corn. So would I. This is the first time the Ring and I have been on the same side."

"You think there's much chance?"

"Three Stars seems to think so, and he's a pretty good judge of men. He'll be farming himself if he's wrong. The hell of it is Three Stars' whole life is the military. But he's no tin soldier like Custer, no Indian hater like Phil Sheridan. If Sheridan had his way he'd wipe out every Indian in the country. And he doesn't just mean the hostiles. Sheridan means every Indian, man, woman and child. The army needs men like Three Stars to balance madmen like Sheridan. If Three Stars goes it'll be a sorry day for Indians everywhere."

Dora Baxter frowned. "Then why is General Crook taking such a chance. Geronimo is just one man."

Sundance looked at Geronimo riding ahead of

them, an old man on a beat-up horse.

"I think Three Stars feels bad about Geronimo and always has. Three Stars is like that. There are times when I feel bad about him, but I don't let myself think about it. Through all the years Three Stars has never talked about what we did together, what we did in the Sonora Mountains. At the time it seemed necessary. I still think it was. I like to think it was."

"You beat him. It was a war and you beat him, forced him to surrender."

Now, fifteen years later, Sundance could still hear the mountain coming down on the Apache position, sealing off the deep caves where the women and children were. Come to think of it, Phil Sheridan, the Indian hater, had never done anything like that. For days they had pounded the Apache fortifications wth the mountain guns hauled by army mules over the worst country in the world; country so bone-dry and jagged and broken that only an Apache could love it. Day after day the guns boomed and when the endless cannonade was over the Apaches were still there high in the rocks, defying every attempt to dislodge them, pushing back every attack with the new repeaters Geronimo had bought with stolen Mexican gold. The Mexican officers who accompanied Crook's force were supposed to be on the side of the Americans. They were there to observe, to make sure that Crook's force didn't penetrate deeper into Mexico, below the border country, if the Apaches retreated to the south. They were there to preserve Mexican sovereignty, it was stated at the time. But Crook knew the Mexicans didn't want the Americans to win, much as they hated the Apaches. Sundance knew it too. An

American defeat would be a sort of lefthanded victory for the Mexicans, still smarting from the Mexican war of just over twenty years before.

"We didn't kill all the women and children," Sundance said at last, the picture of the mountainslide still vivid in his mind. "Many got out, but many died. We killed many so we didn't have to kill all. Or have them killed later by a much larger force. It was my idea to elevate the guns and bring the mountain down on them. But Three Stars was in command and it was up to him to give the order. I was chief scout. I didn't give orders except to the other scouts. The guns had just finished firing and the Apaches had thrown back another attack. Our men were lying dead or wounded in the sun. When the guns stopped firing, when the attack was stopped, we could hear the women and children howling in the caves. The echoes of the caves doubled the sound. More than doubled it. You could hear it from down where we were. The sound came out of the caves and rang in the mountains. I remember how the Mexican officers were smiling. Three Stars was walking up and down with that shotgun he always carries on campaigns. He looked at me, then he looked away from me. 'Elevate the guns,' he said."

"But it ended the war," Dora Baxter said. "The Apaches who were set to join Geronimo didn't join him. Their lives were spared. There were so many who would have died if they had joined him."

"Probably," Sundance said, not feeling any better. "I want to believe that. But there are times when I think—I wonder if—we could have beaten Geronimo some other way. A retreat to the south into Mexico, that's what Three Stars wanted to prevent. There would have been trouble with Mexico if we had allowed Geronimo to escape to the south. But there just weren't enough men. The War Department never gave Three Stars enough men. Maybe we could have starved them out. I don't know what we could have done. Done other than we did. It's too late now to think about it."

"But you'll still hunt Geronimo down if he escapes?" Dora Baxter said.

"Yes."

"Even after what happened in Sonora?"

"That's right."

"Perhaps your friend Crook wants him to escape. Have you ever thought of that? Sometimes when a thing preys on a man's mind he wants to set it straight. Make up for it in the only way he can. You can't say for sure that Geronimo will start another war if he gets back to the border. Perhaps your friend Crook is wiser than you are. Perhaps all he wants is for the old man to be free."

"No 'perhaps' about it. If Geronimo gets loose he'll start another war. It's the nature of the man. But he won't get loose and he won't start a war. He won't ruin Crook."

"You sound so sure about everything."

"I'm sure about one thing. I'll kill him if that's the way it has to be."

"So you say," Dora Baxter said.

Nothing happened all day and no matter how many times he checked their back trail there was nothing to see. Now and then he climbed to high ground and glassed the country behind. Nothing. In the late afternoon they came to Richmond City: four houses and a general store. The storekeeper had a keg of beer with a tap and Geronimo drank

153

three cups of it before Sundance said that it was all he was going to get. Dora Baxter drank sarsaparilla instead of beer. She didn't like beer.

That night they made camp off the road. Sundance gathered some deadwood to make a small fire. But the night passed as quietly as the day. During the night a wagon went by on the road, but that was all.

"Looks like we're in the clear," Dora Baxter said the next morning while the coffee was boiling. "Your Indian Ring badmen aren't as invincible as you say they are."

"I just said they never gave up. How are you coming along with that story of yours? You getting it all down?"

"Everything that happens. I wish I could draw."

"Tell them to use one of Geronimo's old photographs. There are some good ones by Tim O'Sullivan."

"I know the ones, but I'd rather be able to draw Geronimo as he is now." Dora Baxter laughed. Geronimo was pissing behind a rock only a few yards from camp. "Well, not *right* now. You know what I mean." ·

Sundance kicked dirt on the fire and they started out again on the long road to the Oklahoma line. Now the road passed through hilly country. Sundance waited on a high place while the others went on. But all his glasses picked up on the road behind was a very old man riding a swaybacked mule.

"I don't think they're coming," Dora Baxter said when Sundance caught up again. "I don't know why, but I get the feeling there's no one following us. You think that?"

Maybe she was right, Sundance thought. There

154

was no feeling of pursuit, no sense of danger. Over the years he had learned to trust his instincts. Usually he was right. Not always though. "I don't know what I think," he said.

"We may get to Fort Cobb without firing another shot. The shooting on the train seems like a long time ago."

"Not long enough for me."

"Would you miss it if you didn't have to do any more killing?"

"You mean now?"

"No. I mean ever."

"Not a bit," Sundance said, then wondered how true that was. Killing had been a part of his life for so long. But it was hardly worth thinking about: men had to be killed and he would kill them.

Frowning, Dora Baxter said, "I think I'd miss it. The life you lead, I mean. I think I'd like to be you, Sundance."

She said it so seriously that he had to smile. "I like you the way you are."

"I like the way you say that. I'd like to have you in me right now."

"You'll have to wait till it gets dark," Sundance said.

CHAPTER FOURTEEN

That night, while Geronimo snored, they lay together under a blanket in a dry, sandy place surrounded by brush. They could see the moon through the branches and it was good to be under the blanket with a cold wind blowing from the north. A ground nesting bird made tiny sounds not far away.

"You could take me with you when you leave Geronimo," Dora Baxter said. "Where will you go after this?"

"Texas Panhandle. Buffalo hunters are invading Comanche and Kiowa country and slaughtering the last of the buffalo herds. The army used to keep them out. Now it looks like the army isn't trying too hard. Three Stars says there will be an Indian war—maybe the last—if they aren't stopped. If the tribes band together it'll be the worst war in years. Three Stars wants me to go there and take a look."

"I want to go with you, Sundance."

"Can't be done. Anyway, I thought you wanted to go back to New York?"

"I meant I want to work for the *Sun* again. But I don't have to be there for that. I can telegraph that I'm sending the story and wait for their answer. I

156

know they'll take me back. People back East are always wanting to read about the Wild West."

"How do you like it?"

"Oh I love it. Take me with you, Sundance. I said I wouldn't cook for you, but I will. And when there's danger I'll back you up like I did on the train."

"I can't take you. If the tribes are at war by the time I get there, it'll be as bad as it can get. The men I'm going after are scum. But the Comanches and Kiowas are worse, in their way. If you go with me you may be captured. The bucks will rape you until you're half dead. Then they'll give you to the women and they'll beat you and stone you and burn your hair off. You'll eat what the dogs eat, entrails and greasy bones. You'll be of less value than a dog. The men will rape you and you'll be pregnant. And then when you're scarred and battered and you smell, the bucks won't want you anymore. They'll let the old men have you. The old men are worst of all. They'll do things to you and you won't even care. You'll try to kill yourself but they won't let you."

Dora Baxter shivered. "I still want to go with you. I can write about your work. It will be good for the Indians."

"Some things I do can't be put in the newspaper," Sundance said. "Some of the things I do could get me hung. Look, we're having a fine time here, wherever we are. Don't spoil it with arguments. The kind of work I do is dirty, dangerous and no good for a woman. Go back to your own kind."

"But you are my kind, Sundance. I didn't know it at first. Now I do. Getting back to New York was all

I thought about. That was before."

They were camped again for the noon meal and Sundance was cooking bacon and heating beans and Geronimo was hunkered down by a tree. Writing in her notebook, Dora Baxter glanced at him now and then. She frowned as she turned page after page.

The meal was ready and Sundance was turned back to the fire when he heard the deadly rattle. He whirled and fired at the fat-bodied rattler, but it had already struck the old man high in the chest. The rattler died with its head blown away, still writhing. Before Sundance could get to him Geronimo's face had turned a strange color and his eyes began to stare as if he couldn't see.

Dora Baxter ran over too. "Is he going to die?"

Sundance held Geronimo against the tree and slit his shirt. The puncture made by the bite was deep; the snake was big.

"Answer me," she said. "Is he going to die?"

"Maybe. He's not young. Now be quiet for a minute."

Working fast, Sundance made a deep cross-cut in the shoulder and sucked the blood out when it came. He sucked and spat until the flow of blood began to cease. Then he felt the old man's heart. It was rapid and weak; the eyes glazed, the breathing shallow.

"Get the coffee over here," Sundance said. "You carry any liquor in that bag?"

"A flask of brandy."

"Fill half a cup with brandy, the rest with coffee. Hurry up."

"What are you doing?" she cried when Sundance drew back and punched the old man in the chest. He did it again.

"You're crazy, you'll kill him."

"His heart is faltering. Bring the coffee and brandy and stop wasting time. Get that snake away from here. Use a stick."

Sundance forced the old man's mouth open and let the brandy-laced coffee trickle in. His throat worked and he coughed. But his eyes stayed closed.

Sundance put his ear to Geronimo's chest and listened to the sound of his heart. It was weak. Still holding the leather-covered silver flask, Dora Baxter hooked the dead snake with a branch and tossed it into the brush. Her face was tight and pale.

"God! This is awful," she said, staring at Geronimo. "We've come so far to have this happen."

"Drink what's left in the flask," Sundance ordered. "I'm not going to give him any more. Wouldn't do any good."

There was the quick gurgle of the flask and she asked the same question: "Is he going to die?"

Sundance said, "Don't keep up with that. I just don't know. Get all the blankets and lay them out by the fire. He's starting to get cold. That's how snake bite works."

Sundance put the old man on the blankets and wrapped him from head to foot, putting a saddle under his head. Then he built up the fire with deadwood until it blazed high.

"Now all we can do is wait," Sundance told her. "Eat your food. It's going to waste."

Her face was sullen and unhappy. "I don't feel like eating. You eat, if you can."

"Do what I tell you. Yes, I can eat. Not eating won't do a thing for him."

"What's going to happen if he dies?"

"It's going to be bad. The Apaches will think I murdered him. They sure won't believe any rattlesnake story. All I can think of is to bury him deep where nobody goes."

Her face grew more sullen. "You'd hide his death? I won't let you do that."

Sundance filled a plate of bacon and beans and pushed it at her. "Then maybe I should bury you too. That would be better than an Indian war."

She picked up a strip of bacon and began to chew. "Oh come on! You wouldn't kill me. You're not a woman killer. Anyway, I saved your life on the train."

Sundance gave her coffee. "No, I guess I wouldn't kill you at that. How about if I get Three Stars to put you in a military prison till this cools off? You could write a story about your experiences behind the walls."

She made a sour face. "Nobody's going to put me in any prison. I'd smuggle word out to the *Sun* and your general would be ruined. Why in blazes doesn't the army get out of Arizona? The settlers too? There's nothing there but rock and sand and cactus."

"And gold and silver and copper. A lot of things the white businessmen want. Nobody's going to get out but the Apaches, if they start another war. This time they'll be facing a real army. If someone like Sheridan or MacKenzie commands it he'll wipe every man, woman, child. Even the old ones. These businessmen have invested too much money in their mines to let the Apaches bother their operations. A

160

lot of whites will die, but they'll win. They always do. Another thing. Don't tell me about the plight of the poor Indians. I've been working on it longer than you."

Dora Baxter had found her appetite in spite of her anger. "That's a rotten thing to say. I've been writing the best story of my life about Geronimo and his exile."

"Not this part, not if he dies."

"But I'll be a witness to what happens here. Wouldn't that be enough?"

"The Apaches are not acquainted with your reputation for honesty. All they'll know is their most famous leader was murdered somewhere in Texas. By a halfbreed they hate and a white woman they don't know. Then you'll see the worst uprising in years. There'll even be trouble with the Mexicans. They objected to ever letting Geronimo out of prison."

"He's stirring a little," Dora Baxter said.

The old Apache's eyes were fluttering and when Sundance felt the pulse in his neck he found it slightly stronger but still rapid. And his face was cold.

"You shouldn't have let me drink the brandy," Dora Baxter complained.

"He's had enough. Too much and his breathing might stop. What he needs is more coffee. A lot of it. Anything to keep his body heated up. The venom has to work its way out."

Sundance boiled up the coffee again and fed a cup to the old man, whose body jerked from the fierce heat. Then, suddenly, his eyes opened.

"The snake," he muttered.

"A big one," Sundance said. "How are

you? Cold?''

"Very cold. I taste brandy. You have more brandy? It would cure the sickness.''

"Brandy's all gone. I will give you strong coffee to keep you warm.''

Geronimo scowled. "Then coffee.''

"Hot and black. Then if you can eat I will feed you.''

The old man's glare became stronger and something like the old glitter returned to his black eyes. "I will not be fed like an old blind woman.''

"You have to stay wrapped up,'' Sundance told him. "You want to die, Apache?''

"No, halfbreed,'' Geronimo growled, turning his head away.

Sundance turned his head back and let him drink more coffee. Then he forked bacon and beans into his mouth. Geronimo ate stolidly, keeping his eyes closed.

After that he fell back into fitful sleep, with sweat dripping from his face and hair. But he shivered at the same time.

He still might die, Sundance thought, though he didn't say anything about it. Venom from the five-foot diamondback, one of the few reptiles that attacked without provocation, was hellish. The deadliness of the venom matched the viciousness of the snake itself. The bad thing was Geronimo's age. Children and old people usually died when the diamondback struck. But he'd seen strong young men die too. It depended on how the body reacted to the poison. And, too, he'd seen men who looked like they were recovering go white-faced in an instant, shudder a few times, and die.

If the Ring agents came now they'd be in one hell

of a fix. But they had to stay and they needed a big fire. It was getting dark and he told Dora Baxter to check her revolver. Then he watered the horses and took them to a grassy place far back from the camp.

When he had fixed the same monotonous bacon and beans he opened a can of peaches. The shrill, vibrating sound of cicadas came through the gathering darkness and May flies buzzed in the bright light of the fire.

Dora Baxter, eating peaches, was in an irritable mood. "This shouldn't have happened. Why didn't the army just send him to Oklahoma guarded by a squad of men? Go by rail with, say, ten trained soldiers?"

Sundance wiped Geronimo's face with a piece of cloth. Most of the sweating had stopped and the skin was coming back to its natural temperature.

"Because a squad of riflemen and an old Indian riding in a coach would cause too much attention."

"Then why not a closed military train? With men well-armed."

The United States Army doesn't spend money on special trains for one old Indian. Besides, he'd try to break out and they might have to shoot him."

"The hell with the United States Army!" Dora Baxter opened her notebook and leaned into the firelight to write. Just then the old man snorted himself awake.

"Food," he said.

Nine hours had passed since the attack by the snake, and Sundance decided to let Geronimo sit up so he could dry his clothes, which were sweated clear through. If he didn't he might catch a chill that would kill him in weakened condition.

"I can fix you a broth of dried meat and wild

163

onions," Sundance said.

Geronimo growled, "I will eat the snake that tried to kill me."

While Dora Baxter stared in disgust, Sundance got the dead rattler from the brush and carried it back to the fire. There he cut off the head and tail and threw them in the flames. Next he gutted the carcass on a flat rock and separated the tender white meat from the backbone. The bacon grease remained in the fry pan and he cut the meat in small sections and put it on to cook. In the cool night air the sizzling meat smelled very good.

Turning the meat, Sundance looked across the fire at Dora Baxter. "Want a piece. There's a lot even for Geronimo?"

"No, I don't want any fried rattlesnake, thank you. You eat it."

"You bet I will. Tastes a lot like chicken. But I'll wait and see how our friend here makes out."

"I am not your friend," Geronimo said.

Huddled by the fire with the sweat steaming from his clothes Geronimo ate all the meat and drank a whole pot of coffee. Sundance hung the blankets on sticks to allow them to dry.

Geronimo gave out with a windy belch. "Do we move on tonight, halfbreed?"

"In the morning, very early. We will if you're all right."

Geronimo made a sound of contempt. "No snake can kill Geronimo. I am all right."

"You are not all right yet. So tonight I will not tie you like other nights, sick as you are. The poison, some of it, is still in you. If you run you could die. You know that?"

"I know. Do not tell me things I know."

"Sure you know it, but you may try something anyway. So I will take your boots. I have hidden the horses and will check on you during the night."

"I am not deaf, halfbreed."

"I can run faster than you can."

The old man grunted. "All men know what a mighty warrior Sundance is. And now that I have eaten my enemy I will sleep again."

Dora Baxter smiled and wrote in her book.

Geronimo spread his blankets by the fire and rolled himself up with great deliberation. Sundance asked him if the arm closest to the bite felt numb. He said no.

"Good sign," Sundance said.

Now there was nothing to do but sleep and wait for morning. The firelight cast shadows in the clearing where they were, and it was quiet except for the crackle of the flames and the old man's gluttonous snoring. Sundance heated water for the dishes and put them away. That done, he put more wood on the fire.

Across the fire, Dora Baxter closed her notebook with a snap and from the look on her face it was plain that she didn't want him to share her bed this night. Fact was, he didn't especially want to. Something was eating on her that he couldn't make out. What the hell! There was no way to figure women, and tonight—after snatching Geronimo back from death's door—he didn't give a damn what was bothering her. Maybe she'd be in a better mood in the morning.

But she wasn't. In the morning he knew she was awake while he was livening up the fire for first coffee. He let Geronimo snore on until the coffee was ready. The old man had to be weak or he wouldn't be sleeping so late and so soundly.

Dora Baxter rolled out of her blankets in the same bad mood in which she'd gone to sleep. And she just nodded when Sundance said the coffee was hot.

"No breakfast, just coffee," Sundance said. "We lost the best part of a day and have to catch up."

"So you can get him to the poor farm all that faster."

Geronimo, chewing a handful of dried meat, moved his eyes between them. But he didn't say anything. Sundance guessed the old man knew what a poor farm was. A place for half-dead old people.

"Just drink your coffee," Sundance warned her. "Drink it or leave it. We're moving out of here in five minutes."

Geronimo growled that he was all right. "You see I am alive. I am chewing meat and drinking coffee."

They moved out, Dora Baxter in sullen silence, and they headed north again. By nightfall they were thirty miles closer to the Oklahoma line. Sundance sat up all night to watch Geronimo who was regaining his strength fast. After Geronimo rolled up in his blankets Sundance wondered what would become of him. There was no reason he couldn't live a lot of fairly good years if he stayed on his farm and worked it. Even so, he felt a kind of pang as he looked at the huddled figure of the last of the great Apache warriors. This had been a man, as they said; he was a man still.

Dora Baxter had nothing to say and Sundance didn't offer any conversation. She went to sleep with her back turned to him.

By late afternoon the next day they met a line of freight wagons on the road and one of the teamsters said Fort Cobb was less than twenty miles ahead, just over the line. If they traveled late into the night they could be there in time to see the soldier boys putting on their pants.

Dawn was breaking when they saw the fort in the distance.

CHAPTER FIFTEEN

Fort Cobb was an old log fort standing on an elevation far out on the prairie. Cobb River made a half circle around the fort and flowed toward a distant lake. There were hills in the distance; between the fort and the hills were homesteads. It was a hazy morning, with the sky overcast. There would be rain soon. The homesteads looked small, Sundance thought, but prosperous enough for this part of the Territory.

Geronimo looked at the fort with ancient hatred. "I do not want to go in there," he said. "I lived with the soldiers for too long."

"We have to go in," Sundance told him. "How else are we going to find out where your land is? Anyway, the army has to be notified that you're here. Move on now. You're not going back to prison."

"This whole place is a prison," the old man said.

At the gate Sundance showed his safe conduct to the sentry, but he called the first sergeant anyway. The first sergeant was a veteran of at least fifty and he gaped at Geronimo.

"Is that really him?" the sergeant said. "If I didn't see it I wouldn't believe it, Mr. Sundance."

"That's Geronimo sure enough," Sundance said. "He's going to be farming in these parts."

"You sure? I never fought against him but a brother of mine did. Said it was the worst campaign he ever was through."

"Who's in command?"

"Major Flint. You'll be wanting to see him."

The sergeant led the way across the parade ground to the commandant's office in a two-story building with a wide veranda and a gallery on the second floor. Parade had just been dismissed and the men were going about their barracks chores.

Inside, another sergeant was writing at a desk. But he was a young man and Geronimo's face didn't mean anything to him. The floor was still damp from recent scrubbing and there was a smell of strong soap in the air.

The sergeant knocked and was told to come. "Geronimo is here," the sergeant told a tall man standing by the window.

"All right, Burns," the major said.

"You're Sundance, I'm Major Flint," the commandant said.

"This is Miss Dora Baxter, a newspaper reporter," Sundance said. "She's been with us all the way from Texas."

Major Flint bowed stiffly in military fashion. But he smiled. "Amazing!" he said. "It's just amazing. I won't ask you if you had a pleasant journey." The major smiled again. "From what I hear the first part of it was pretty bad. I won't ask you about those men you're supposed to have killed. The odd thing is, there are no charges against you."

"The Indian Ring doesn't like to get into the courts," Sundance said. "Too much might come

169

"That's Geronimo sure enough," Sundance said. "He's going to be farming in these parts."

"You sure? I never fought against him but a brother of mine did. Said it was the worst campaign he ever was through."

"Who's in command?"

"Major Flint. You'll be wanting to see him."

The sergeant led the way across the parade ground to the commandant's office in a two-story building with a wide veranda and a gallery on the second floor. Parade had just been dismissed and the men were going about their barracks chores.

Inside, another sergeant was writing at a desk. But he was a young man and Geronimo's face didn't mean anything to him. The floor was still damp from recent scrubbing and there was a smell of strong soap in the air.

The sergeant knocked and was told to come. "Geronimo is here," the sergeant told a tall man standing by the window.

"All right, Burns," the major said.

"You're Sundance, I'm Major Flint," the commandant said.

"This is Miss Dora Baxter, a newspaper reporter," Sundance said. "She's been with us all the way from Texas."

Major Flint bowed stiffly in military fashion. But he smiled. "Amazing!" he said. "It's just amazing. I won't ask you if you had a pleasant journey." The major smiled again. "From what I hear the first part of it was pretty bad. I won't ask you about those men you're supposed to have killed. The odd thing is, there are no charges against you."

"The Indian Ring doesn't like to get into the courts," Sundance said. "Too much might come

"Small but sturdy. The man who lived there was killed by a kick from a horse. The place is in good shape. There are apple trees. A creek runs through the place."

"Where's it located?"

"Not too close to any neighbors, if that's what you're thinking. We thought it would be best to put Geronimo off by himself. The farm is way over by the hills. Nobody will bother him there."

The major turned his attention to Geronimo, who still refused to look at him. "You must listen to me, Geronimo," Major Flint said slowly. "You are under my protection here, but it is my duty to watch you. You are no longer a prisoner of the military, but until you have proved yourself you must not leave your farm except to come here. If you run away, you will be brought back. I must say this. If you give too much trouble, you will be shipped back to Florida. If you are sent back, you will remain there for the rest of our life. That is the order of the War Department. This is not your country, but it is good country. You can live in peace here and no one will molest you. No matter what you think of the Territory, it's better than the Florida swamps. Do you understand what I'm telling you?"

Geronimo grunted.

"He understands," Sundance said.

"Very well then," Major Flint said, picking up a ruler from the desk. He tapped a large map of the military district he commanded. "This is the fort, the hills are over there, ten miles away. See the creek there. The X there is where Geronimo will have his farm. That's the only X—the only farm—in that part of the country. The rest hasn't been settled yet." Major Flint traced the line of the road going

171

out toward the hills. "Just follow on out till you get to the creek. Past the creek about a mile you'll find the house. It's built on a slope with fields running down to the creek. You better stop off at the supply building and stock up before you leave. Anything else I can do for you let me know."

Sundance told Dora Baxter to go to the supply building with Geronimo. "I'll be over in a minute."

Sundance closed the door when they went out.

"What is it, Mr. Sundance?" the major asked.

Sundance said, "I don't think the Indian Ring will try to kill him here, but it's possible. I'm going to stay with him for a week or so. What about your patrols. I'd like you to keep an eye on him."

"We'll watch him all right," the major said. "Until he settles down, at least. You think these men—these gunmen—would have the gall to trespass on land governed by the army?"

"They have enough gall for anything."

"I'll tell you this, Mr. Sundance. If they come here and try to harm the old man I'll hang them and take the consequences. Is that good enough for you?"

"It's fine," Sundance said. He found himself liking the tall, lean soldier. There was something about Major Flint that reminded him of Three Stars. He would do what had to be done, and no nonsense about it.

Major Flint gripped the ruler with both hands. "I must have your honest opinion, Mr. Sundance. Do you think he'll try to make a break for it?"

"I don't know, Major. I honestly don't know. When he sees his land—knows it's his—maybe he'll change. You warned him, I warned him what will happen if he runs. He'll have to weigh that against spending the rest of his life in the swamps."

"Then we'll have to wait and see," the major said.

Sundance went to the supply building and found Geronimo piling up blankets. There was a redheaded corporal behind the counter and Sundance gave him a list of supplies. The corporal skipped several blank pages in a big record book and wrote GERONIMO at the top of the page and added a number.

"Now all he is, is a number," Dora Baxter said.

"He's alive," Sundance said. "He's not rotting in the Everglades." He asked the supply corporal about the shotgun.

"You'll have to wait till the new shotguns come in," said the corporal. "We're all out right now."

Sundance thought that was just as well. Time enough for the old man to get a gun in his hands, even a small-gauge single-barrel.

When he got through, the corporal put the supplies in a canvas bag with *U.S.* stenciled on the side. "He has to make his mark or sign his name, if he can write." The corporal turned the book around on the counter.

"Write your name, I know you can write." Sundance said.

Scowling, Geronimo dipped the steel pen in the inkwell and slowly wrote his name in large copperplate letters. The colonel's lady again, Sundance thought, but didn't smile.

They headed out from the fort. On the way there was a sudden downpour that lasted only a few minutes, and when the sun came out in force the horses began to steam. The road ran through fields of late Indian corn and there were hayracks in places. Sundance knew Geronimo was interested, though he pretended not to be. So maybe there was hope yet. There were Indians working in the fields and Dora Baxter said, "They sure look tame enough. Or is the word 'beaten-down'?"

"Enough of talk like that. It's their land and they're working it. They don't look so bad to me."

"It depends how you think of it."

"I think you better change the subject."

It was an easy ride to the creek and they crossed it in a shallow place. The hills were closer now, brushy and brown in the sun. Beyond those hills, a day's ride away, was Texas. Sundance wondered what the old man was thinking about. You could only guess wth Geronimo. He could be thinking of escape. He could be thinking of his dinner.

They had to cross a series of long slopes before they could see the house. And it was no log cabin with rough, chinked walls but a real house of carpentered lumber. The man who built it had dug a flat place into the slope for the house. Fields, now untended, ran down to a creek with trees along its banks. There was a sturdy lean-to for cordwood built onto the side of the house. It was stacked high with seasoned wood and there was an unfinished wall with rose bushes climbing through it.

"You say this house is mine?" Geronimo said, pretending indifference.

"That's what I say. That's what the United States Army says. It belongs to you. It will in six months. No one can put you off this land, Geronimo. The Territory isn't like other parts of the country. White men who trespass in the Territory are driven out by the calvary."

Geronimo just grunted. Yet when they were in the

house he walked around looking at things. The house was one room, with a bunk against the wall, a cast-iron stove, a table and chairs. A kerosene lamp with a tin shade hung from the beam in the ceiling. Wood cut to stove size was in a box beside the stove. In the corner there was a cupboard for dishes and cooking utensils. The wide planked floor had clean sand on it.

"Home sweet home," Dora Baxter said.

Sundance wondered what the hell was getting into her. There was an edginess about her that he didn't understand. She had her goddamned newspaper story and it was a good one. What else did she want? More excitement, he guessed. Well, the excitement was over. He hoped it was. If this woman wanted more excitement she'd have to go back to Cuba, or somewhere. Find herself another war.

"Get the fire going," Sundance told Geronimo.

The old man muttered something.

"It's your house, it's your stove. Look, it isn't woman's work to make a fire in a stove. You better get used to it. You're going to be doing it for a long time. If you want to cook and stay warm on cold nights, you have to make a fire."

Sundance put his rifle away and opened the bag of supplies. Dora Baxter threw her cigarillo in the stove and said she'd do the cooking. She mixed flour and water and melted lard and put the first batch of flapjacks on to cook. In the other fry pan she laid strips of bacon. Then she went down to the creek to get fresh water for the coffee.

Instead of sitting with them at the table, Geronimo took his food and ate it in the sun.

Looking at the open door, Dora Baxter said, "I feel sorry for him."

"You keep coming back to that. Why? What's the good of it? Other Indians have learned to live here. Why can't he?"

"Because he's Geronimo."

"He's also an old man. What you don't understand is this is no reservation with some crooked agent gouging the Indians for every cent he can get. Major Flint looks all right to me."

"The local Great White Father."

"Flint is doing the best he can with what he has. I'll say it again. If Geronimo settles down here the Indian Ring will let him alone. If he doesn't he'll have more than the Indian Ring after him. I don't know. He doesn't seem to mind it too much. You saw the way he looked around. And he isn't eating outside because he hates our company. What he's doing is looking at the land."

"His twenty acres. That can't seem like much to a man who roamed at will."

"Not for the past fifteen years. You didn't see that prison camp. You don't know what it's like. The soldiers stationed there hate it as much as the handful of prisoners."

"I don't care what you say, Sundance. I hate to see Geronimo penned up like this."

Sundance finished his coffee and stood up. "You better be thinking of New York. You have your story. Why don't you get on your horse and head for the nearest railroad. Go to New York and be famous all over again."

"Where are you going?"

"To look for some rabbits for supper. I suppose you'll be wanting to come along?"

"No. Have to write in my book while my memory is fresh."

176

Outside Geronimo was sitting on his heels, looking down at the creek.

"Mind if I kill a few rabbits on your land?" Sundance asked him.

Geronimo said, "Do not talk like a fool. But I will go with you. You will give me a weapon? The throwing hatchet?"

"All right. The throwing hatchet. Think you can drop a rabbit on the run?"

"I can do it, halfbreed."

They went down toward the creek and crossed it to where there was trees and brush. Then, on the edge of a grassy clearing, still wet from the rain, they waited, standing perfectly still, hardly breathing. After a while a jackrabbit came out of a burrow and nibbled at the grass. Another rabbit came out, and then another. Sundance looked at Geronimo. "Ready?"

Geronimo nodded. He threw the hatchet as Sundance fired. The long-bladed hatched flashed from his hand and the rabbit screamed and jumped into the air and came down dead. Sundance killed a rabbit with the first shot, swung the rifle and killed another.

"It will be better than bacon or salt pork," Geronimo said.

Back at the house they skinned and cleaned the rabbits, making cuts above the paws and around the neck, then pulling the skin off like a coat. Geronimo turned the wet side of the skin to the sun and set it out to dry. Sundance washed the carcasses in an iron pot.

"You can raise your own goats here," Sundance said. "A whole herd of goats. I will give you the money for the goats. Then you can eat goat chops five times a day."

"That would be good."

"What do you think? Will you stay here?"

"I am thinking about it, halfbreed. Is it the woman who taught you how to talk so much and say nothing?"

"Think of the winters in the high peaks," Sundance said. "A time when the wind blows cold and the belly growls for food. You remember what it was like in the mountains?"

"I lived there for fifty years, halfbreed. I would be there still if not for you. There is no need to bribe me with talk of goats. I will decide if I want to remain here. And you will not stop me if I decide to go."

"It's up to you," Sundance said.

Later, with the lamp lit and the rabbits frying on the stove, Dora Baxter continued to write in her notebook. She frowned at what she was writing, as if it displeased her. The door was closed against wind and the good smell of frying rabbit filled the little house.

When the rabbit was cooked Sundance forked it onto plates and put them on the table. He set the coffee pot on to boil. Now and then Dora Baxter looked at him as her pencil raced across the paper. She seemed to be trying to make up her mind about something.

"Rabbit's going to get cold," Sundance said.

"In a minute." She stared at him again, then at Geronimo. Her eyes had a strange, excited look. "I'll just put my notebook away."

When her hand came out of the leather bag it was holding the cocked .45. Sundance heard the sound of the hammer going back. By then it was too late.

The Webley was pointing straight at his heart.
"Put your hands up," she said.

CHAPTER SIXTEEN

The untouched food steamed on the table and Geronimo's black eyes glittered in the lamplight as he took his eyes from the cocked revolver in Dora Baxter's hand to Sundance's face. A knot of wood exploded in the stove; that was the only sound for a moment.

Looking at the gun, Sundance repeated the question. "What the hell do you think you're doing?"

There was no need to ask it; he knew what she was doing. All the craziness in her had come to the surface in a single moment.

The five-shot Webley remained steady in her hand and her voice was calm. "I'm letting Geronimo go. I don't want to shoot you but I will if you try to stop me. Geronimo is going to be free."

Geronimo hadn't made a move yet.

"So you can write a better story?" Sundance said. The pistol was a .45, it was cocked, she was too far away to jump her. "All that's been done you're going to undo, is that it? You got what you came for, isn't that enough?"

"You wouldn't understand," Dora Baxter said. "It all came to an end so quietly. There ought to be more. I thought there would be more. But a better story isn't the only reason. I want Geronimo to get away. Take his weapons, Geronimo, and take my horse. Take his money and get back to your mountains."

There was nothing Sundance could do. The big bore of the .45 was centered on his belly. This woman knew how to use it. He guessed she would. And while she held the .45 on him Geronimo came around behind and plucked the long-barreled Colt from his holster. As soon as the Colt was in Geronimo's hand Sundance heard the hammer going back.

"Unbuckle that belt of yours," Dora Baxter ordered. "Don't go for the knife or the hatchet. Between two guns you don't have a chance."

"I'll make you sorry for this," Sundance said quietly. He didn't turn. "Old man, you are betraying a friend who saved you from the hangman, got you out of prison. You don't want to do this to a friend."

"Drop the belt," Dora Baxter said. "Then kick it away from you. You're wasting your breath. Geronimo is going back where he belongs."

"Three Stars is our friend," Sundance said to Geronimo.

Geronimo pulled the weapons belt away from Sundance and picked it up. "I have no friends," he said, buckling on the belt. "My only friends were my children. My children are dead, murdered by you and Three Stars. This woman is right. I am going back to my own country. I spit on your farm and your gutless tame Indians, your growers of corn. Tell your friend Three Stars that he will find me in the mountains. You will find me in the mountains, Sundance."

Sundance said, "I will find you, you pitiful old man without honor. They will spurn you when you get back to Arizona. You are past your time. But old man or not, I will find you—if you do this—and I will kill you."

"Brave words, halfbreed," the old Apache said. "You will have to find me first. There is still the Mexican gold I offered you and you would not take. You call me an old man, but an old man, however old, is still a man. I am without honor, you say. In time to come I will show you what honor means."

"Go on, Geronimo," Dora Baxter said. "There is too much talk. I'll hold him here until you get a long start. I will write your story and tell . . ."

Geronimo was at the door with Sundance's Winchester in his hands. "Do not talk so much, woman. Do not explain things so much." And then the door opened and he was gone to the horses.

The pistol in Dora Baxter's hand didn't move. "Stand easy," she said. "He's going to get away and there's nothing you can do about it. This place, this miserable homestead . . . I couldn't let you pen him up here."

She had him, Sundance knew. She had him cold. But there would come a time when she had to let him go. He guessed he'd kill her for what she'd done. Somebody ought to kill her before she caused any more harm. The guff she spouted about wanting Geronimo to be free was just that. Guff! All the danger on the long journey from Texas hadn't been enough for her, and maybe it wasn't even the newspaper story she wanted to write. Some of it was that, but not all of it. He doubted that she knew what she wanted.

Outside there was the movement of horses and he

heard Geronimo's voice, soft in the darkness. A bullet broke the window. Sundance grabbed at the gun in her hand and twisted it away. She cried out with pain as bullets from different positions began to rain on the house. One of them broke the lamp and the light flamed out but the lamp didn't explode and then, for a moment, the shooting moved from the house as Geronimo galloped away. Out in the darkness there was yelling and even with all the yelling and shooting Sundance heard Geronimo's wild, high-pitched Apache war howl, and he knew they hadn't hit him with all the bullets they were throwing.

"You got us in good, Miss Baxter," Sundance said. The yelling went on for a while and then they started shooting at the house. Shards of glass were torn from the windows and fell clinking on the floor. The pot of coffee on the stove flew against the wall, spattering scalding coffee on them. Dora Baxter screamed and clutched at Sundance. He pushed her away as more bullets ripped through the door and thudded into the wall above the stove.

"Stay down," Sundance asid. All he had was her five-shot revolver, a gun with real stopping power at short range but no good for distance. There were plenty of shooters out there. Four or five? It was hard to tell. Some had rifles. The firing went on.

He was close to the door now and bullets splintered the wood just above his head. He thought of the weapons that were going away with Geronimo. A bullet broke a dish on the table and it banged off the wall with a clatter. Lying beside the door, he reached up and opened it. A bullet nicked the back of his hand, but now it was open. The shooting started up heavier than before, as if some signal had

183

been given, and when it reached its peak he saw two men running at the house. The shooting kept on and he let them get close because there was no other way to use the short-barreled gun. They ran up close while the others gave them cover and then he shot the one out in front. Sundance fired at the runner behind him and missed and the man threw himself flat and when he did there was nothing more to shoot at. Sundance fired at him when he raised up for a shot and he missed because the Webley was no good at that distance.

Two bullets gone from five, Sundance thought. One dead. Over his head he asked Dora Baxter, "You got any reloads?"

"Only what you have," she said. "We're going to get killed, aren't we?"

A bullet showered more glass on them.

"Looks like it," Sundance said. "Just stay down."

The shooting stepped up again. Bullets tore into the house as if the shooters wanted to take it apart with lead. Sundance fired twice at a man who came running and dropped him with the second shot. He might be dead, or just wounded.

Four bullets gone. Two men down. One bullet left.

There was no chance of getting out of this, Sundance knew. No chance at all. Making a break for the horses wouldn't do any good. They'd be cut down before they got ten feet. The firing picked up again. At last they had him, he thought. After all the years they had him trapped. He knew they wanted him more than they wanted Geronimo. Once he was dead they would have a free hand, could do what they liked. There was no one else to stop them.

He knew they must be wondering why he wasn't shooting back. His weapons had killed so many of them in the past, so now they must be wondering. They had lost two men; they would be cautious for a while. Then they would realize that for some reason he didn't have his weapons. When they knew that they would all come at the same time. So far they hadn't been able to come close enough to fire the house. But that was only minutes away, and when the house began to burn they would have to die in it or run out and be shot.

There could be no surrender no matter what happened. His death would not be quick if they took him alive. These men were the worst in the world, the scum of the outlaw world, and they would have their sport with him before he died. He would have sent out the woman if he thought they'd let her live. But their rule was no witnesses. A newspaper reporter was just as dangerous to them as he was, in a different way.

Sundance guessed they would let the news of his death get out to the public, as a warning to other enemies of the Ring. As a warning to anyone who might become an enemy. If we can kill Sundance, we can kill anyone, would be their message. Get in our way and you're dead, too.

They were still holding back, firing an occasional shot at the house while they made up their minds. Dora Baxter hadn't moved since a bullet broke the lamp. But she wasn't dead. He could hear her breathing.

"You all right?" he said.

Behind him he heard the scrape of broken glass. "I'm all right. I'm sorry. You should have killed me back in Beaumont.''

"Too late for sorry," Sundance said. "And the killing is all here. You have to get ready for it. They'll burn the house soon and you don't want to die like that. When you go out run straight into their bullets. It won't be so bad if you run right at them. You don't want to let them take you. They'll kill you anyway.''

"I'm going to die after all," Dora Baxter said in wonder.

"No way to get out of it," Sundance said. "We can't get to the horses. They may be dead by now.'' Sundance thought of Eagle and hoped the big stallion was dead. If they captured his horse they would never break his spirit, but these men were capable of any outrage.

Bullets broke what was left of the glass in the windows. The firing slacked off.

"You don't hate me for what I did?" Dora Baxter said. More glass flew and she gave a sharp cry of pain.

"You hit?"

"No. The glass cut my face. It's nothing.''

"Get ready," Sundance said. They were moving in the darkness, but he couldn't see them. A match flared and firebrands began to burn. He saw shapes moving in the light, but didn't fire. Not yet. Too close.

Someone yelled a command and a hail of lead tore into the house. Now they were spread out and coming in fast, firing as they came. Sundance held his fire. Just one more, he thought. Then he heard the horse coming at a gallop, heard Geronimo's wild Apache howl. By the light of the firebrands he saw the old man coming full tilt. The attackers wheeled and opened fire on him but he came ahead, blasting with the long-barreled Colt. A man with a firebrand staggered and died and another went down under Geronimo's bullets. The horse screamed as a bullet hit it in the neck. It ran on a few more yards, carried forward by its own momentum. As it crashed down in death Geronimo went right over its head but came up on his feet, still holding the Winchester and Colt. A man raised a rifle to his shoulder and steadied. Sundance fired the last bullet in the Webley and brought him down. He kicked open the door and Geronimo tumbled in with bullets chasing him. Dora Baxter screamed as a bullet hit her.

Hunkered down on the other side of the door, Geronimo threw the Winchester to Sundance. Then he reached into his pocket and began to thumb fresh loads into the Colt. There was no time to see to Dora Baxter. She hadn't made a sound after the first scream.

"I couldn't let you die, Sundance," the old man said. "So many things came into my mind and I couldn't let you die. Is the woman dead?"

"She's hit. I don't know how bad."

Out in the darkness the leader of the attackers was trying to rally what was left of them. Sundance guessed there must be four or five.

"I think we must go out to face them," Geronimo said. "The two of us."

Sundance could see the glitter of the old Apache's eyes. "The two of us," he said. "You ready? They're coming back."

With a wild howl the old man sprang out the door. There were five men and they were coming in fast. Geronimo ran straight at them screaming like a

187

madman. Sundance ran too, firing, levering, firing again and again. Two men went down and the darkness was filled with orange flashes and the stink of gunsmoke. Geronimo fired pointblank into a man's face and blew his head to bits. The old man howled as a bullet hit him, but he kept firing. Sundance killed another man and the two others turned and tried to run. He killed another, then the pin fell on an empty chamber. The man was running and Geronimo fired his last bullet. There wasn't time to reload. The running man turned and fired and Sundance's leg buckled under him. Geronimo was screaming. "Throw me the hatchet! The hatchet!"

Sundance tossed the hatchet to the old man and he caught it and began to run. In a moment the darkness swallowed him up. Then he heard a wild scream and the sound of a falling body. Geronimo came back with the hatchet. There was blood on the blade.

There was blood on the old man's shirt. "A bullet burned my ribs," he said. "Is the bullet in your leg?"

"Went right through," Sundance said. "The bone isn't broken. Help me up."

The grass was burning where a firebrand had dropped. There was fierce satisfaction in Geronimo's face. "The great Sundance asking for help."

"And glad to get it," Sundance said.

Geronimo pulled him to his feet and he hobbled into the house, Then Geromino went out and got one of the firebrands and took it in and propped it against the stove. The flames licked up, throwing eerie shows in the room. Dora Baxter lay in a pool of blood, but she was still alive. Sundance raised

188

her head and she opened her eyes. She smiled up at him.

"I'll never get to write my story," she murmured, still smiling.

"Afraid not," Sundance said. "But you lived it. Maybe that's a consolation."

"Yes," she said, her voice growing very faint. "Some consolation. You don't hate me."

"No," Sundance said. "I don't hate you. Knowing you was an experience, Dora."

"Will you do something for me?" A wheezing sound came from the hole in her chest.

"Tell me what it is," Sundance said. "I'll get it done." He guessed she had less than a minute to live.

"Send my notebook to the *Sun*. Say I was sorry I couldn't get back there. . . ."

Dora Baxter died without saying anything else.

"That was much woman," Geronimo said simply. "A little crazy like all the women who make their mark on men. But she is dead now and you are bleeding."

Still looking at Dora Baxter, Sundance said it was just a flesh wound.

"Do not be stupid, halfbreed," Geronimo said, lighting the stub of a candle by touching it to the guttering firebrand. "I will see to your wound and you will see to mine. Sit in the chair and slit the leg of your pants. In my house I will give the orders."

They burned the bodies of the Indian Ring gunmen just before first light. They hauled dead wood and brush into the cornfield and piled it high. Then Geronimo splashed everything with coal oil and touched a match to it. Flames sprang up and a column of oily black smoke curled up into the sky.

"I will use what is left to fertilize my fields," Geronimo said.

Later they buried Dora Baxter under a tree by the creek. It was still early, with mist on the water. Even with his ribs bandaged, the old man dug the grave while Sundance stood by supporting himself with a stick.

"I will cut a marker for her," Geronimo said. "But there is no hurry. She will be here forever, and so will I."

"What made you change your mind? You don't have to explain if you don't want to."

"I will say it," Geronimo said. "Riding away from here suddenly there was a tiredness in me. I tell you this and you will not smile."

"I'm not smiling," Sundance said.

"I am an Apache," Geronimo went on. "And when I broke through I thought, I am alive and they are dead. I knew they could not catch me. And yet I knew I could not leave you to die. The woman did not matter. Then when I thought of what I had to face—the weeks, months, of getting back to the mountains, the great tiredness came. I knew then that I had been away too long. The faces of people long dead came before my eyes and I knew that all I loved was gone into memory. I knew I did not want to kill anymore. Those men who were killed will be the last to die by my hand. So I will stay here, in this place you say is mine, and I will farm the land. I am not so old that there are not some years left. I am in a strange country, and alone, but I will survive. And when my time comes I will be buried here. You will come and bury me, halfbreed?"

190

"That's a promise, Apache."

Moving slowly because of their wounds, they made their way back to the house.

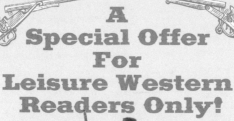

GET YOUR 4 FREE* BOOKS NOW— A VALUE BETWEEN $16 AND $20

Mail the Free* Book Certificate Today!

FREE* BOOKS CERTIFICATE!

YES! I want to subscribe to the Leisure Western Book Club. Please send me my 4 FREE* BOOKS. Then, each month, I'll receive the four newest Leisure Western Selections to preview FREE* for 10 days. If I decide to keep them, I will pay the Special Member's Only discounted price of just $3.36 each, a total of $13.44 ($14.50 US in Canada). This saves me between $3 and $6 off the bookstore price. There are no shipping, handling or other charges.* There is no minimum number of books I must buy and I may cancel the program at any time. In any case, the 4 FREE* BOOKS are mine to keep—at a value of between $17 and $20!

*In Canada, add $5.00 Canadian shipping and handling per order for first shipment. For all subsequent shipments to Canada the cost of membership in the Book Club is $14.50 US, which includes $7.50 shipping and handling per month. All payments must be made in US currency.

Name _____

Address _____

City_____ State_____ Country_____

Zip_____ Telephone_____

Tear here and mail your FREE* book card today!

Get Four Books Totally
F R E E* —
A Value between
$16 and $20

Tear here and mail your FREE* book card today!

PLEASE RUSH
MY FOUR FREE*
BOOKS TO ME
RIGHT AWAY!

LeisureWestern Book Club
P.O. Box 6613
Edison, NJ 08818-6613

AFFIX
STAMP
HERE

BUFFALO WAR

CHAPTER ONE

There were the pale moon and the cold night wind of the high plains country. Coyotes yipped and howled far away and the sound was carried on the wind. The wind rattled in the tall dry grass and even now, at night, there was dust in the air. Earlier there had been no moon at all because of the great banks of black clouds that shut out the light, and there had been heavy firing then, because no one—the attackers or the besieged—could be sure of where anyone was; but after the moon came out and flooded the country with cheerless light the shooting ebbed to a few sporadic shots, and in a little while it stopped altogether.

Sundance knew it would start again as the night dragged to an end. The shooting would pick up then, he knew, because the men under siege were better shots, and they would use the light to show how good they were. They knew it. So did he. So did his men.

He had told his men how it would be, and they had accepted it in the telling, but now here was the reality and they were angry and impatient, wanting to prove to him how wrong he was.

One of the men, angrier than the others, raised up against orders and fired at nothing. He fired again and then from the darkness in front of them came the boom of a heavy rifle and the man who had been firing was blown away from where he was by the big-caliber bullet. The bullet struck him squarely in the chest and killed him instantly and sent him rolling. He hadn't kicked his way to death, as he might if some other rifle bullet had struck him. The instant the big rifle boomed he was dead, swept away as if by a gust of wind.

The big rifle boomed again, but now there was nothing to shoot at. All the sombreroed heads were down, hugging what cover they could find.

"What will we do if you have figured wrong?" the man beside Sundance said. "If they come out too soon."

"Fight as best we can," Sundance said, hoping the other man was wrong. "I do not think they will come out in the darkness. If they do that, their big rifles will not mean so much. They are single-shots. They will lose their advantage if they leave their position."

"They have repeaters," the other man said.

The cold moon sailed across the sky.

"They have them," Sundance said. "But the big rifles are their strength. I think they will stay where they are for now."

"My men will kill you if you have guessed wrong," the Mexican-hatted man beside Sundance said in the same stiff, formal English. "My men are good men and they are not afraid of the big rifles you have brought them to face. But they don't want to die because you have guessed wrong. I cannot help you if my men turn against you, Sundance. I must take the side of my men."

The big rifle boomed again, but no one was hit.

"If it goes wrong you can shoot me," Sundance said. "Just tell them to keep their heads down and be ready for anything. Tell them no more shooting. We just lost a man for no reason. No more shooting. Tell them."

The Mexican-hatted man hissed the order and it

was relayed to the end of the line. The big rifle hadn't fired for several minutes.

"My men will do more than kill you if you are wrong," the man beside Sundance said. "They do not trust you. They have never trusted you. I have tried to explain to them what you are doing here. But that will not mean anything if this goes wrong. I will not be able to hold them."

A man moved and the big rifle blew the hat off his head. After that it was silent again.

"Enough of this warning and threatening," Sundance said. "I will take my chances with your men. I knew what I was getting into. Now I'm in it."

"Enough then," the other man said. "What next?"

Sundance said, "They will not come out and attack us until they have to. The water they took from the creek is all they have now. They can't go back to the creek."

"They have plenty of whiskey, Sundance."

"Then let them drink all the whiskey they want. I hope they're full of whiskey when they come out. You ever try to fire a rifle when you were full of whiskey?"

"Yes," the other man said. "I fired at a man and I hit the sky."

"Do your men understand how these men must be killed?" Sundance said. "If it isn't done right all this will be for nothing."

"They know," the other man said.

"They know but will they do it right?"

"I have told them. We must wait to see what happens, Sundance. The men in there know now that you are behind this. You know some of the men in there. How does it feel to kill men you know?"

"It has to be done," Sundance said, not wanting to think about Billy Dixon. The others didn't matter much, but Billy Dixon had saved his life. Now Dixon had to die with the others. They all had to die.

"I do not think I would like to be you," the man beside Sundance said. "But every man has his reasons." His name was Lone Wolf, and he was principal chief of the Kiowas.

Sundance didn't answer. In a few hours it would be dawn, and then the killing would start. . . .

CHAPTER TWO

"Moore's got Dutch Henry Brown with him," Sundance said. "And he's got Jimmy Doolin, Shad Dameron, Shotgun Collins and a lot of other hardcases. You may have heard of some of them."

From where he was sitting in front of General George Crook's desk, Sundance could see the mountain peaks, snow topped, high above Pueblo, Colorado.

"I know who Dutch Henry Brown is," Crook said sourly. "That man could steal a horse out from under Queen Victoria and she'd never know the difference. Doolin and Dameron are just as bad. That Doolin is one of a kind all right. Imagine a white man who steals horses from the Indians. Usually it's the other way around. If you could bottle nerve that Irishman would be a millionaire. I don't know the other names."

"Moore has some of the worst men in the Southwest working for him," Sundance said. "Some are worse than others, but they're all bad. The point is, Three Stars, they're all experienced buffalo hunters. That's their main business. All the horse-stealing and gun-running and whiskey-running is just a sideline. First and last, they're buffalo hunters, and now Josiah Moore has promised to make them rich."

"How is that? They just work for Moore, you say."

"Moore is going to put them on shares," Sundance said. "That will take some of the sting out of the danger they face, not that they'd give a damn anyway. Moore has picked his men well. Every man with him is a dead shot. To them death is just another side of life. When they left Dodge it was said they all carried .50-caliber shells filled with cyanide. They know what they can expect if the Kiowas or Comanches take them alive."

"My God," Crook said. "They're ready to take their own lives just for money."

Sundance smiled at his old friend George Crook, known to him and to the Indians as Three Stars, the number of stars he rated as a general in the United States Army. Soldiering meant everything to Crook; money meant nothing.

"They'd do anything for money," Sundance said. "And Moore is showing them the way to where the money is. They left Dodge City six weeks ago. Thirty wagons loaded with hundreds of pounds of powder and lead. Enough supplies to last them for months. Enough men and guns to stand off anything the Indians throw at them. This is no raid south of the Red River, Three Stars. No quick raid on the buffalo country of the South Plains. They mean to stay. They're so sure they're going to stay on Indian land that they even brought along a storekeeper, a blacksmith and a man who plans to start a saloon. Their names are Myers, O'Keefe and Hanrahan. They can't be considered fighting men, but they can shoot guns."

"You learned all this in Dodge?" Crook said.

Sundance said, "You sent me to get information about the Moore expedition. Dodge was the place to get it. The town's been talking about nothing else for months. Newspaper there was full of it. How Dog Kelley, the mayor, gave a big dinner for them the night before they left. A lot of speeches."

"That Kelley," Crook growled. "That tinhorn has more fleas than his hound dogs."

"They were guests of honor at the annual Dodge City shooting contest," Sundance said. "One of Moore's men, the youngest, Billy Dixon, took all the prizes. Beat out Old Dad Willgerly who was the favorite to win."

"Old Dad was the best," Crook said.

"I mention Dixon to show the kind of men Moore has with him. Dixon's only twenty-one, but he may be the best shot in Kansas. He's been a buffalo hunter since he was fifteen. The Kiowas and Comanches may not be afraid of much, but they're afraid of the buffalo hunters, especially hunters like these men. The South Plains Indians see these men as their doom, a sign that their way of life is finished. That's one reason. But they fear them for another and very sensible reason—they never miss."

Crook said, "I'd like to hang the lot of them."

Sundance went on. "Every man in the Moore party carries a .50-caliber Sharps. But some have .60 and even .70 calibers, and from what I hear they're all using overloaded shells. With 110 grains of power instead of the usual 90."

"Great Scott!" Crook was a man not given to profanity of any kind. "That makes a big rifle a small cannon."

"The Sharps has a heavy barrel and can take the overloaded shells," Sundance said. "The barrel of any other rifle would split like a bamboo shoot. Moore knows what he's doing all right. The Indians are afraid of the big calibers. They're even more afraid of the telescopes they're equipped with."

Crook got up and paced about, puffing furiously on his long-nine cigar. "The nerve of these men! In all my years on the frontier I never heard of

201

such impudence. According to the terms of the Red River Treaty no man—absolutely no white man—is supposed to hunt buffalo on Indian lands. To hell with calling it a treaty. It was a deal and I was a party to it. I signed the treaty on behalf of the United States government, and now they're going back on it. I thought that once—just once—Washington would keep its word. I must be getting old. I should have known better."

Crook kicked a spittoon, causing it to rock on its weighted base. Then he turned to Sundance with a rueful smile.

"Sorry, Jim. It's not my way to behead the bearer of bad tidings. It's worse than I thought, isn't it?"

"Very bad, Three Stars. You said yourself the buffalo herds on the South Plains are about the last herds left in the West. That's why the Moore brothers have organized this expedition. But the Indians won't hold still for it. There's nothing you can do to stop the Moores?"

Crook got another long-nine going. "Not a thing, Jim. Phil Sheridan commands the military division of the Missouri. That takes in all of Texas, as well as other districts. I'm stuck here in Colorado and officially what happens in Texas is none of my business. But—blast!—it is my business. I brought the South Plains tribes together and talked them into signing that treaty. I gave my word."

"You think Sheridan wants an Indian war?"

"If anyone else asked me that I'd have to deny it," Crook said. "The fact is, he does. Phil doesn't trust the Indians and never has. With good reason at times. You know that. There isn't a day goes by that he doesn't say the South Plains Indians are going to break out again. Hit the enemy first, has always been Phil's motto. Some of the Indians on the South Plains have been making trouble. No use denying that. Phil Sheridan wants to force a showdown. Phil's an honest man, but he's got a one-track mind. Smash the enemy is all he knows. Knock him down and keep kicking him after he's down."

"Kicking the Kiowas and Comanches won't be that easy."

"Sheridan knows he can do it with enough men," Crook said. "And that's what he'll get from Washington. That's what he'll ask for. Phil's a bit of a showboater, like all cavalry officers. He got so used to winning battles in the Civil War that he can't bear to lose a skirmish. It's no secret that Phil's got his eye on the Presidency. But the War's been over for ten years and maybe he'd like a big Indian war to put him back in the public eye. A lot of young voters were just kids when the War ended. I think Phil would like to remind them what a great hero he is. Confound it, Jim, I don't know that it's such a good idea having these soldier-Presidents. I mean professional soldiers. West Pointers. Hang it! This isn't Mexico or one of those Central American countries where they have admirals but no navy. Be that as it may, Phil Sheridan is always looking for a way to kill Indians."

"In Dodge Moore bragged that he had the army's blessing," Sundance said. "That makes sense. He'd never dare to cross the Red River without it."

"Of course he had it," Crook said impatiently. "That's what's so rotten about this whole thing. The army is supposed to patrol all along the Red to keep trespassers out. Moore should have been stopped, but he wasn't."

"You think Sheridan gave orders to let them through?"

Crook said no. "Foxy Phil's too smart to do that. When you're a general you don't have to give direct orders when you want certain things done. You let it be known that certain things would not be displeasing to you. Junior officers are quick to take the hint. They know they'll have to take the blame if trouble comes. That's how it works. However, if things work out well, then so do their careers. And don't give me that look, you heathen. I didn't invent the system."

"Sorry, Three Stars," Sundance said.

"No sorrier than I am," Crook said, slapping cigar ash from the front of his uniform. "In a way, Phil Sheridan's just taking advantage of the feeling back East—most of it from the Secretary of the Interior, that's Delano—that it would be for the Indians' own good if the last of the buffalo herds were wiped out. That way they would be forced to become farmers or stock raisers instead of no- mads. The missionaries, God . . . bless . . . them are of the same opinion. They'd like to have the Indians in one place, where they could thump their Bibles at them."

Sundance smiled. "You haven't said anything about the Indian Ring, Three Stars."

"Now don't you go tying Phil Sheridan in with that gang of thieves, Jim. The man may be a fool in some ways, but he's no crook."

"The Ring has to be tied in, Three Stars. I didn't say with Sheridan."

"And so they are." Crook sighed with exasper- ation. "The South Plains, one big pie and just so many slices for all these ravenous people. I feel so downhearted about the whole thing, I think may- be I should just resign and go back to Ohio."

"Wouldn't do a bit of good, Three Stars. Tell me the rest of it."

"It makes my head spin," Crook said. "But here it is. Sheridan and the Ring are on same side in this. For different reasons they want the herds wiped out so the Indians will be reduced to beggary. Sheridan would like to exterminate the Indians. The Ring would like them subdued but alive, because you can't steal from the dead, although they've done that, too. So there's a conflict there. Then you have the Texans, who hate the Indians just as much as Sheridan but hate the buffalo hunters more, because they may start a war that will spread to the settled areas. The last few years Texas hasn't had too much Indian trouble. Years back, as you know, the Texans tried to wipe out the Kiowas and Comanches, and failed. So they made peace with them. If you're going to get any help from whites, it will have to come from Texas people."

Crook paused. "How'd you like all the sour apples, Jim?"

"They're pretty sour," Sundance said, smiling at his old friend.

"There's more," Crook said, smiling too. "You said you wanted to know everything."

"Thanks, Three Stars," Sundance said.

"There's bad blood between Sheridan and the man under him," Crook said. "That's General Pope—John Pope—who commands north Texas. It seems Sheridan and Pope are from Massachusetts and it's rumored that Sheridan's father worked as a laborer for the Pope family at one time. The Popes are big landowners and have mills and factories and so forth. Old Yankees that employ a lot of Irish and treat them pretty bad, I guess."

"What about Pope?"

"A good man, a bit weak," Crook said. "No favorite of Sheridan's, that's for sure. Last year he caught hell when he refused to go to the aid of a party of buffalo hunters from Kansas. They raped and murdered an Indian child and the Indians trapped them, but they were well armed and the fight went on for days. One managed to get clear and ran into a column commanded by Pope. Pope could have saved them just by lifting his hand, but he didn't. They were slaughtered—executed, if you want to give it the rightful term. Officially Pope was in the right in refusing to risk his men's lives to save a gang of murderering trespassers. Sheridan read him out for it just the same. Old Phil's words: 'White lives and property must be protected wherever they are found. The character of these men is of no consequence. You should have come to their aid.' Pope was in the right, and you know how much that means to the military mind. Phil Sheridan never did concern himself with civilian law of any kind."

"Where is Pope now?" Sundance asked.

"He has his force camped near the Kiowa agency run by John Miles. That's by Sheridan's order. Pope's orders are to see that the Kiowas don't run off."

"What's Miles like?"

"A tough Quaker." Crook smiled. "That doesn't sound right, does it? But that's what he is. What they call a fighting Quaker. Led a company of fighting Quakers in the Civil War. That got him in dutch with the Quaker body in Philadelphia. I guess he's still in dutch with them. Six months ago he ran off a bunch of horse thieves from Kansas and killed two of them. I guess his bosses back East think he should greet these thieves with open arms and all kinds of brotherly love. So they are trying to get him removed, the blasted fools. As if they know anything about what's going on out here."

"Is Lone Wolf still the principal chief of the Kiowas?" Sundance asked.

Crook nodded. "You ever met the man?"

Sundance said no. "I know who he is."

"There's a lot more to know than that," Crook said. "Lone Wolf isn't just principal chief of the

Kiowas. The Comanches and the Southern Cheyennes listen to him, too. You might say he's principal chief of all the tribes on the South Plains. More than any man he's been responsible for keeping the peace south of the Red River. Time after time he stopped trouble before it got out of hand. So far he's even been able to control the Dog Soldier societies. You ought to know how hard that is."

As a young man Sundance had been a member of the Dog Soldier warrior society of the Cheyennes, the crack fighting force of all the tribes on the Northern and Southern Plains. Trained for nothing but war, they lived for war, and they longed for it as elite troops did in all the white armies of the world. In time of peace they perfected their fighting skills by constant effort. The young men were tested constantly by the older warriors, and it was nothing for a young Dog Soldier to be left without weapons, without water, in hostile country many days' travel from his tribe. If he survived he won no praise. If he died it just proved that he wasn't quite good enough.

"I know what they're like," Sundance said.

"The worst of it is," Crook said, "that the tribes on the South Plains—Kiowas, Comanches, Cheyennes—have formed a real alliance for the first time in their history. I'm partly responsible for that. God help me, I was the one who persuaded Lone Wolf to band the tribes together so he could speak for them as one voice. It wasn't easy for him to do that, but he managed because he's a clever and resourceful leader. Now—if he goes to war—he will have the most formidable Indian army ever seen on this continent."

"You're sure he'll fight, Three Stars?"

"Take my word for it, Jim. What else can he do? And mark you, old friend, this won't be just another isolated Indian uprising with the other tribes waiting for the outcome before they decide what to do. If it comes to war, Lone Wolf can put nearly two thousand men in the field, and there won't be any pitched battles where Sheridan can mow them down with Gatling guns and artillery. Lone Wolf will split his forces and strike hither and yon. Sheridan seems to forget that Lone Wolf and his Kiowas fought as Union auxiliaries in the Civil War. Not so much to help the Union but to get back at the Texans."

"No wonder the Texans hate him."

"With good reason," Crook said. "In the four years of war Lone Wolf learned to be a fine irregular commander. What he didn't know when the War started he learned from white officers attached to his forces. We taught him well, Jim, and now he's ready to use it against us. He may even carry the war into Kansas. That's how the irregular fights. Stab at the soft spots. We taught him to spread terror in the Texas settlements so that more and more Rebels would be tied up defending the West. Now it's our turn to experience the same thing in Kansas."

"Will the tribes go to war even if Lone Wolf holds back?"

"I was coming to that," Crook said. "You ever hear of a medicine man called Red Moon?"

Sundance said no.

"That figures," Crook said. "I never heard of him till recently. It's the old story. One messiah is killed or discredited and another one pops up. I got word of this Red Moon and didn't pay much heed at first. Now I'm worried. It would appear that Red Moon, a Kiowa, is a younger version of our old friend Wovoka on the North Platte. The same mad talk of being able to stop the bullets from leaving the rifles of our soldiers. . . ."

Crook was bringing back memories all right. Years before the wild-eyed Cheyenne medicine man Wovoka had talked the Northern Cheyenne into the bloodiest uprising up to that time. The Cheyennes could not be killed by the bullets of the white soldiers, he ranted. They could defy death as long as they wore the "ghost shirts" over which he had cast a spell. As proof of his words he had performed feats of magic, or what appeared to be magic—a clever medicine man was as skilled in conjuring tricks as any white tent-show performer. But Wovoka was different from the other power-mad fakers in that he believed his own lies; and before a trooper's bullet ended his life, he caused a bloody war that wiped out a third of the Northern Cheyenne. Sundance remembered the last day of the campaign when the Cheyenne warriors, still believing in the madman's magic, came at Crook's infantrymen in waves. They came over flat ground that offered no cover, yelling their defiance. It was a slaughter.

"You're thinking about that last day, aren't you?" Crook said.

Sundance said yes.

"I think of it too," Crook said. "I don't see it as my great hour of glory. Well now we have this Red Moon and he's as big a threat as Wovoka ever was. He's more of a threat because he wants to send the tribes against Phil Sheridan. Phil won't let them surrender the way I did. Right now it's kind of a stand-off between Lone Wolf and Red Moon, with Red Moon gaining a little every day. No, sir. No ghost shirts this time around. Red Moon isn't as modest as that. All he claims is to be able to raise the dead, and not just all the Kiowas that have died in the last fifty or a hundred years but all the Kiowa braves who have died for all time. How many Kiowas is that?"

"A lot, Three Stars."

Crook chewed on his long-nine. "And did you know Red Moon can vomit—that's the word:

209

vomit—up all the ammunition the Kiowas will ever need. Yes, and listen to this. Red Moon can make the sun stand still. Just like in the Bible. The hell of it is, he even has witnesses to some of his magic tricks."

"You have to have witnesses when you're getting started in the medicine business," Sundance said.

"You don't say? The word is that Red Moon got his start last year when some Texans caught him and two other Kiowas stealing horses and proceeded to hang them as a lesson to other thieves. The way I heard it, they were about to haul him up first, the two Kiowas waiting their turn, when he started cursing the lynchers and calling on God or whatever to destroy them. The Texans were jeering at him and his curses when suddenly a bolt of lightning struck the tree and split off the branch he was supposed to hang from. The Texans got killed by the branch, but Red Moon and the two Kiowas weren't even hurt. Of course it was just the start of a summer thunderstorm, but Red Moon seized on the incident as a sign of his divinity or some such nonsense. He had asked God to help him out of a tight spot and God obliged. After that the story spread far and wide, with Red Moon helping it along, naturally."

Sundance smiled. "They say P.T. Barnum is part Indian," he said.

"Is that so?" Crook growled. "I'm afraid I have no reliable information on how Red Moon had the sun stand still."

"After the first big miracle they stop asking for proof," Sundance said.

Crook looked tired. "I don't know that I can tell you much more about this. There's nothing I can do. I'm stuck here and can't move. If you think you can't do anything, just say so."

"Not yet, Three Stars. Josiah Moore told everybody in Dodge he was going up on the Staked Plains because that's where the last of the buffalo herds are. That's where I'll go, but I have to have an excuse for being there. Moore won't believe I just happened along, not in that wild country. I can't just drift into his settlement and say, 'Nice day.'"

"Then you mean to go in spite of all?"

"That's right, Three Stars."

"Because of me?"

"Sure. That's the best reason I can think of. You gave your word to the tribes, to Lone Wolf. I'm keeping it for you. No need to talk about that part, Three Stars. I still need an excuse."

"I have an idea," Crook said. "Early this year a band of renegade Kiowas attacked a small wagon train headed by a man named Amos Germaine. Murdered the whole party except for two sisters, Sophia and Catherine. Both grown girls. They still have them but where nobody knows. The newspapers have been drumbeating the Germaine incident for months, mainly because the two girls are said to be very good looking. They've been making a real cause out of the Germaine girls, although dozens of women are abducted every year. You could be searching for the girls, for the rewards."

"How much?"

"Close to a thousand apiece, last I heard," Crook said. "Two newspapers in Kansas pledged a thousand in all. The rest is by popular subscription. The combined bounty will be paid by the honorable and flea-bitten Thomas 'Dog' Kelley of Dodge City. So say the newspapers, here in Colorado."

"You know who leads the renegades?"

"Medicine Water," Crook said. "Now there's a man so bad he should have been killed the minute he was born. He was hanging material long before he murdered the Germaines. I'd like to be there when they catch him so I can help pull on the rope. What he did to the Germaine party is beyond description. He even tortured the older women, and no Indian's ever done that. Kill them, yes, torture them, no. The army's been hunting him for years. So has Lone Wolf and his Dog Soldiers of the Cheyenne. But it seems he's a hard man to catch. Those poor Germaine girls!"

In a sudden fit of rage Crook clenched his fists and stared at the brown spots of the back of them. Then he looked at Sundance. "It's awful to be getting old," he said. "If I were twenty years younger—even ten—I'd go after Medicine Water myself. But listen here, Jim. I've been talking and talking and you haven't said a word about what you're going to do. You have any idea?"

Sundance stood up. "It's better that you don't know, Three Stars," he said.

General George C. Crook grunted his annoyance.

Sundance smiled and went out.

CHAPTER THREE

There was a shower that lasted only a few minutes, and now the country steamed in the sun of early summer. Far away he could see the Red River, sluggish and brown, and beyond it the plains stretched away as far as the eye could see. Cottonwoods and alders grew along the banks of the river, and shooting stars, waving in the wind, made bright patches of color.

He was in the middle of the river when he saw them coming a long way off. A cavalry patrol coming full tilt. Out of the river, he waited for them to get close. They rode in hard and surrounded him, their holsters unflapped, staring at him with curious eyes. The man leading them was a major with the puffy face of the hard drinker. His eyes were streaked with red and he was sweating and looked angry about something.

The major had a loud, hoarse voice and an odd way of biting off his words. "What's your business here?" he asked.

"I just crossed the river, Major. I'm going south."

"That's no answer. I asked you what your business was. You look like a buffalo hunter to me."

"You see any wagons, Major? If it's any of your business I'm going south to look for two girls taken by renegade Kiowas. The names of the girls are Catherine and Sophia Germaine. There's a reward for their return and I'm going to try to collect it."

"So you say," the major snapped. "What's your name?"

Sundance told him, and when he did the major's eyes examined him again, taking in the beaded buckskins he wore, the weapons belt from which were slung a long-barreled Colt .44, a thick-bladed Bowie knife and a straight-handled throwing hatchet. But it was Sundance's face that interested him most: the copper skin, the pale blue eyes; the shoulder-length yellow hair that framed it.

"You still look like a buffalo hunter to me," the major said.

"I've hunted buffalo," Sundance said.

"Who did you work for?"

"General George C. Crook. A plague of grasshoppers destroyed the crops in south Kansas. General Crook fed the farmers. I shot the meat. I was General Crook's chief scout in three campaigns. I still have the papers if you want to see them."

Sundance wanted to tell the whiskey-faced major to go to hell, but there was nothing to be gained in trading hard words. It wasn't his way to get along by using Crook's name, but this was different—he was on Crook's business.

"Give them here," the major barked.

Sundance found the papers in his warbag and gave them to the major, who shook them out impatiently.

Finally he gave them back. "My name is Dodge," he said stiffly. "I guess you're who you say you are, but I'd like to remind you that what you did in the past doesn't count here, not if you've come to Texas to hunt buffalo."

"I'm looking for two girls, Major."

"Or you could be scouting ahead for some buffalo outfit. Listen to what I'm saying. If that's what you're doing you might as well ride back and tell them they'll be placed under military arrest if they cross the river. And if they do manage to cross without being seen, I'll find them before they've gone very far."

So that's it, Sundance thought. The major let the Moore expedition cross the river and now he's keeping out the competition.

"I'm still looking for the Germaine girls," Sundance said.

"I know about the Germaine girls," Major Dodge said. "What makes you think you'll be able to find them?"

"There's a reward of two thousand dollars, Major. That means I'll try very hard. Anything else you want to know?"

"I could turn you back if I wanted to."

"On what grounds, Major?"

"I don't need a reason," the major said. "I'll say it again. The fact that you worked for General Crook doesn't mean anything here. This is General Phil Sheridan's command and I take my orders from him. Crook has no say here. You'd do well to remember that. If you run afoul of the army in Texas, Crook can't help you. Is that clear?"

"I get you, Major," Sundance said, deciding the major was sorely in need of a drink. Well, the army was made up of all kinds of officers; by any standard this man was a blank cartridge, a genuine dud, the kind of pompous fool George Crook would have eaten for breakfast.

"Ride on," the whiskey-faced major said.

Sundance could feel them watching him as he touched Eagle's flanks and the big stallion broke into a canter and the river fell away behind them. He guessed the major knew who he was, although there hadn't even been a flicker of recognition.

On the face of it, there was no reason why the major shouldn't believe his story about the kidnaped girls, and yet he knew the major would start asking questions about him. He was too close to Crook to avoid that. So many officers of the political kind hated Crook. The newspapers called Crook "the conscience of the army," and that in itself was enough; for the army worked best without a conscience. And now, here in Texas, it looked like General Phil Sheridan and his cringing subordinates were carrying out a plan to start a war that would put Sheridan in the White House at the next election.

South of the river Sundance looked for signs of the Moore brothers' wagon train, but he found nothing until he rode west, parallel to the river, and then five miles from where he started he found the ruts made by heavily loaded wagons. He followed the wagon tracks south until he came to a place where they had camped for the night, a hollow with a bald hill on one side of it. Empty cans were strewn about and there were the cold embers of cook fires. Something shone dully in the grass. He picked it up. The brass casing of a .50-caliber shell. Beside one of the fires he found traces of lead spilled, he knew, from a bullet mold. There was no longer any doubt that he was trailing the Moore expedition and not some large party of emigrants. All he had to do now was follow along. The wagon tracks were as easy to follow as a road, and when the tracks stopped there he would find the men he had come to Texas to kill.

There was no use in hurrying: they had a two-month start on him, and when he found them he wasn't sure how he would kill them. But he knew they had to die; there was no getting around that. From what he'd learned in Dodge, there was a hard core of about twenty-five marksmen in the

Moore party. Dutch Henry, Doolin, Dameron, the new man Billy Dixon, and the others. The rest were skinners and wagon drivers, and the storekeeper, the blacksmith, and the saloonkeeper. Well armed and confident of the army's support, they would stand like a rock. But even the biggest rock could be moved, and there was no man who could not be killed. He had an idea of how he would kill them, but for now that's all it was—an idea. He hadn't told Crook about it because it wasn't clear in his mind. He wasn't even sure how he would go about it. So many things depended on so many other things. At the moment there was nothing to do but trail them to where the wagon marks stopped.

All through the day he moved on, checking his back trail now and then, to make sure he wasn't being followed by the major's cavalrymen. But even when he crawled up on a high hump of ground on the table-flat plains and glassed the country behind him, there was nothing to see.

That night he camped in a hollow out of the ever-present wind, and sometime in the night he woke up and knew his camp was being watched. The fire was dying and the wind was cold and he waited with the Colt in his hand. Eagle had whinnied and that was what woke him. They were out there in the dark and they weren't troopers, and he knew they could kill him if they wanted to, because they knew where he was, and he could only guess. There was nothing to be done about it, so he went back to sleep.

Nothing else happened during the night.

For a week he followed the wagon tracks south across the plains. At the end of the week the trail turned toward the west. Always at night there was the feeling of being watched, and in time the feeling was so constant that he almost got used to it. During the day it was there, too, but never so strong as it was once darkness closed in. Then the feeling of danger seemed to quiver in the dark night air. Eagle sensed it as much as he did; it made the stallion uneasy, not knowing what was out there.

Kiowas or Comanches, Sundance knew. But not renegades. If they were renegades and they meant to kill him they would not have waited this long. They knew he was following the tracks made by the Moore party.

Finally they showed themselves early one morning at the end of the second week. He had a fire going and was heaping coffee beans into the pot when they seemed to rise out of the ground, although there was little cover, and came walking in. Eagle whinnied his alarm and Sundance knew they were there.

"Easy boy," he said to Eagle. He dropped the last of the beans into the pot and set it on a bed of raked coals. There was nothing else to be done; they were coming in from four sides. He didn't look up until they were all around him. A Kiowa chief who seemed to be of no discernible age looked down at him.

Sundance stood up keeping his hands well away from his weapons belt. He spoke only to the chief, as if the fifteen or twenty Kiowa braves weren't there.

"Why have you been following me?" Sundance said. "For two weeks now you have been following me. Watching my camp at night, trailing me far back by day."

"You are Sundance?" the Kiowa said.

"I am Sundance."

"I am Lone Wolf of the Kiowa. Why do you follow the wagon tracks of the buffalo hunters? You have followed them and we have followed you. You knew you were being followed. I could feel it in the way you moved. Answer me,

218

Sundance."

The coffee pot was bubbling on the fire.

"I am looking for two girls taken by the renegade Medicine Water," Sundance said.

Lone Wolf's face remained expressionless. "You think you will find the two women with Josiah Moore's wagons? I think you lie, Sundance."

"Maybe I do," Sundance said. "You want coffee? What say we drink coffee and talk about this? What you think I'm doing and why you're following me."

"Coffee will not buy your life if I decide to take it."

"In two weeks you could have taken it at any time."

"Yes," Lone Wolf said. "And maybe the time to take it has come. But first we will drink your coffee and we will talk."

The morning wind blew cold and the bending grass of the prairie looked like yellow waves on the sea. In the clear morning light, with the sun full up without being warm, you could see for miles, and in the distance the plains rose up with an abruptness that was startling, and there, high above them, lay the Staked Plains, the great plateau that squatted in this waterless corner of West Texas: a vast region blasted by summer suns and swept by blizzards.

Lone Wolf, though not a young man, squatted easily on his heels and took the cup of coffee Sundance handed to him.

"Why do you come here, Sundance?"

"To keep Three Stars' word to you."

"I think it is too late for that."

"You think Three Stars' word is no good?"

"Good or bad, I think it is too late. It is too late for everything. The buffalo hunters have come to kill the last of our herds. Thirty wagons. An army.

And soon there will be more."

"No more," Sundance said. "The army will keep out the others. The men who bribed their way across the Red River want to get their money back. So there will be no more buffalo hunters. If the men who are here now can be killed, there will be no more hunters for a while."

"What is 'a while'?"

"A while is better than right now. It's next week or next year. Peace is better than war, Lone Wolf. Any kind of peace."

"Peace without honor?"

The Kiowas covering Sundance with their rifles understood nothing of what was being said. On the wind there was the smell of prairie flowers. The wind was warming in the sun.

"Any kind of peace," Sundance said. He nodded toward the great escarpment of the plateau. "The men up there can be destroyed and there will be no war."

"Four years ago Three Stars said there would be no war. We signed the treaty and there was to be no more war. There were no buffalo hunters on the South Plains at that time. Now they are here and you say they must be destroyed. You ask my help in destroying them. Then where is the Americans' army?"

It was hopeless to try to explain, Sundance knew.

"Will you trust Three Stars again?" he asked the Kiowa.

"I cannot," Lone Wolf said. "I think it has gone beyond his power to control. My soldiers would jeer at me if I offered them the word of Three Stars again. Three Stars does not command here. Sheridan does. That is the difference between life and death for the Indians of the South Plains. Sheridan hates us and wants to destroy us. That has always been his way. But I will tell you this, he

220

will not destroy us so easily."

It was hard to say it. "You will be destroyed when the buffalo herds are gone."

"Then we will live off the white man's cattle," Lone Wolf said. "We will live off his farms and settlements and even his towns. We will go to our graves, but many Americans and Texans will go with us. I know what the American armies can do. I was part of their armies once. My two brothers died fighting for the Americans. This is our reward."

Sundance pointed at the immense plateau that lay in front of them. "The war can still be stopped. The men who will cause it are up there. Help me to destroy them. It can be done, for all their guns and supplies."

"How?"

"A plan can be made. They are just men," Sundance said.

"I do not trust you, Sundance," Lone Wolf said. "I can trust no one now but my own people. I trusted Crook—Three Stars—and now war is as close as tomorrow's sunrise. Sheridan's soldiers are everywhere. More and more soldiers have come to the garrisons in Kansas. If Sheridan has spies, then so have I."

"You won't help me?"

"To help you would be to hasten this war. I do not know if that is what you are trying to do. You are of the Cheyenne and yet you are not. You move between two worlds without any true allegiance to either. It is true that you have not fought the Kiowas, but you have fought against the Apaches. And it is said that you even fought against your own people."

"I did that to keep all from being killed."

"So that they might lives as slaves?"

"The Cheyenne are not slaves," Sundance said. "If you do not help me to destroy the buffalo hunters I will find a way to do it by myself." He looked at the impassive faces of the Kiowas, at the rifles trained on him. "Or am I to die here because you think Three Stars has broken his word?"

There was sudden anger in Lone Wolf's eyes. "Why has not Three Stars come? When he came to talk of treaty he came with many officers and tents. Men ran to do his bidding. He brought the cannon and the Gatling guns to show what would happen if the treaty was not signed. Where is all that now? Why is he not here instead of Sheridan?"

"It's not his command now. Three Stars is in Colorado and cannot interfere. So he sent me."

"One man against Josiah Moore and all his guns?"

"I would not be one man if you would help me."

"I do not know what to make of you, Sundance. The words roll off your tongue and I do not know what to make of you. You are a madman or a liar. But I will tell you this. I will not help you to attack Josiah Moore. War is coming and I must prepare for it. I must have time. It will come too soon— before I am ready—if I help you to attack Josiah Moore."

Lone Wolf stood up. Sundance remained hunkered by the dying fire, with twenty rifles pointing at him. The long-barreled Colt was holstered on his hip. There would be no time to draw it and he wouldn't even try. Lone Wolf was right. The Kiowas and the Comanches had been betrayed. He knew he could kill a few before the hail of lead crashed into his body. But what was the use of that?

He waited and nothing happened. Then they moved away from him and suddenly he was alone. A yell brought the braves who had been guarding the horses below a dip in the prairie. They rode away and were lost in the heat waves that shimmered over the waving grass.

By noon he was climbing up to the high country, still following the wagon tracks. Here the grass was gone and the earth was bare and churned up by thousands of buffalo hooves. The buffalo trail was half a mile wide, and the tracks of the buffalo were older than the tracks left by the wagons. But they all went the same way, to the high plains, the plains the first Spanish explorers called *Llano Estacado.* The Staked Plains.

The setting sun was red when he found a place where they had made another camp. From high up he could see out across the plains. He moved on long after the sun was gone and it was well after midnight when he made camp, chewing on dried meat and sipping water before he rolled himself in his blankets. Up so high the wind was cold; on the high plains the wind never stopped.

Another day passed and then another, the daylight hours nothing but sun and hot wind; at night the wind was cold. He knew they were looking for water; there could be no settlement without water.

The next morning he saw smoke and when he got closer he saw that Josiah Moore had built what amounted to a small village. There were six main buildings, all of them "soddies," built by standing logs on end in trenches and filling in the chinks with sod. The roofs were wooden frames covered with sod, good insulation against the fierce summer heat yet to come in July and August. The windows had no glass, but he knew they could be covered by thick wooden shutters and barred from the inside. It was morning now and the shutters had been removed. He moved the binoculars down the line of buildings. Myers's store was at the north end of the line, and it even had a crudely lettered sign that said trading post and general store. Hanrahan's saloon was in the center of the line, O'Keefe's blacksmith shop at the far end. It looked like the talk in Dodge City hadn't been just wild frontier gossip: these men meant to stay. There was even a watch tower made of crisscrossed logs, and it stood high above the other buildings. The whole place had a substantial look. Sundance didn't know much about Josiah Moore except that he had grown rich in Kansas, in the buffalo trade. One thing was sure: he knew how to organize. Linked together, the houses made one long building.

Down from the settlement there was a creek and plenty of timber: willow, cottonwood, chinaberry, and hackberry. Another building was being constructed; so far only the logs had been set in place. He moved the glasses to the watchtower. There was a man in it, and only his head showed above the well protected sides.

Sundance put the glasses away and waited until the sun was full up. It was all right for a man to make an early start, but it would look suspicious if he walked in on them before breakfast time. Dutch Henry Brown was the one who would give him the most trouble. Some years before Dutch Henry and a bunch of hardcases had been stealing horses from the San Carlos Indian reservation run by John Clum. Clum's Indian Police hadn't been able to stop it. Sundance set a trap for them and the only one who wasn't killed was Dutch Henry. Since then they hadn't tangled, but from all reports the Dutchman, so called, hadn't changed. Sometimes he stole horses and sold them and then stole them back. In a long career of all-around villainy Dutch Henry hadn't spend a day behind bars; when things got too hot in one section of the country, he moved on to another. At times even the army dealt with him, because he knew where good horses were and how to get them. Now he was back where he started, in the buffalo trade.

The other men were little more than names; he knew Doolin and Dameron by sight, and that was all. They were a bad pair, but they didn't have the name of being rabid killers.

Sundance mounted up and started for the settlement. Before he had gone half a mile the rifle boomed in the watchtower.

CHAPTER FOUR

Sundance reined in and waited. The first shot was
just a signal; the bullet hadn't been fired at him.
Now he could feel the sights of the big Sharps
lined with with his chest. It was at least six
hundred yards to the watchtower, but the telescoped rifle could blow him out of the saddle
without the slightest trouble to the shooter.

There was yelling as the rest of the buffalo
hunters poured out of the log houses. Now they
were all in position, ready for anything. He saw
the flash of a telescope. They were sizing him up,
trying to figure out who he was, what he was
doing so far back in this wild country. They were
armed to the teeth, but they weren't taking any
chances. He could be scouting ahead for a war
party.

Then the man in the watchtower waved at him
to come ahead. The telescoped rifle moved with
him as he rode in. Now he was close enough to see
a bearded face behind the rifle. One by one, they
came out from cover and trained their rifles on
him. There must have been forty of them, not all
hunters but all had rifles. It was easy to tell the
hunters apart from the skinners and the wagon
drivers. The hunters were wilder looking than the
others and they handled their big rifles with easy
familiarity. Wagons piled high with hides stood a
distance from the settlement and they stank as

227

only buffalo hides could stink. The whole settlement stank of blood and death. Sundance saw Dutch Henry Brown and he was grinning like the mad dog he was.

A skinny man in a worn black suit smeared with dirt and blood held up his hand and told Sundance to stay where he was. Dutch Henry said something to the skinny man, but he didn't answer. Sundance guessed he was Josiah Moore, the Vermont money-grubber, leader of this rank-smelling expedition.

"My name is Moore," the skinny man said in a Yankee twang. He jerked a thumb toward Dutch Henry, who was still grinning. "Mr. Brown here says you go by the name of Jim Sundance. Would that be right now?"

"Mr. Brown is right," Sundance said.

"What you been doing, Mr. Sundance?" Dutch Henry said.

"This and that, Dutch. Been a long time since San Carlos."

"Not so long, Sundance. Not so long that I don't remember what happened there."

Josiah Moore waved Dutch Henry into silence. "What brings you up this way, Mr. Sundance? We don't get many vistors so far off the beaten track. You don't mind me asking? But we have to be careful, you see."

Sundance said he was searching for the Germaine girls.

"Yes, I heard about that," Moore said. "A terrible thing. A genuine tragedy, sir. But why are you searching for them on the Staked Plains, Mr. Sundance? No Indian movement in these parts, none that we've seen anyhow. It's seems to me you're searching in the wrong part of Texas."

Sundance realized that Moore wasn't being sarcastic. The Yankee businessman seemed to be devoid of humor, bitter or good natured; there seemed to be no shadings to this man's character. Old-fashioned Yankees were often like that: they said what was on their minds, they stated what they took to be facts.

"The Indians will come now that the herds have moved up here," Sundance said. "The Indians follow the herds. The renegade Kiowas who have the girls may turn up. The army has been making it hot for them on the lowlands, and the other Kiowas are just as eager to kill them as the army."

Josiah Moore's was the only clean-shaven face in all that shaggy bunch. He had a long bony chin and a rat trap of a mouth. His eyes weren't pitiless, just hard. His religion was dollars and cents, the cents being no less important than the dollars.

"I doubt that last part," he said. "About the Kiowas searching for the renegades. For my money, they're all renegades, sir. But you're right about the tribes coming up here after the herds. There's a reward for these poor girls?"

Sundance said two thousand dollars.

"A goodly sum of money," Moore said. He shouted up to the man in the watchtower. "You see anything, Jimmy?" The man in the tower said there was nothing to see.

"Why don't you dismount," Josiah said to Sundance. "Maybe you can tell us what's going on in the rest of the world. You can stop pointing those rifles, boys. When all's said and done, there's no harm Mr. Sundance can do. Come down and get your breakfast, Jimmy!" Moore yelled to the man in the tower.

They crowded into the big log house that Hanrahan called a saloon. There was a packed-dirt floor and the bar was a wide plank laid across two barrels. A shelf had been built against the wall and on it were whiskey bottles, a few bottles of tequila and mescal. There were four kegs of beer with spigots. Hanrahan looked like every other Irish saloonkeeper: burly and red-faced and mustached. He even had an oiled forelock and a watch chain across his broad belly. The man from the watchtower came in carrying his rifle. It was Jimmy Doolin hiding behind a three-month growth of whiskers.

Moore fanned himself with his hat. "There's no air in here, boys. Some of you clear out. You stay, Dutch Henry. You too, Jimmy. Where's Dameron?"

"Taking a piss, Mr. Moore," Doolin said.

Dameron came in and stared at Sundance. Hanrahan was frying steaks in a lean-to attached to the back of the soddy saloon. In a while there was the smell of coffee. Moore looked well pleased with himself and rubbed his bony hands together, making a dry, papery sound.

"You like buffalo steaks, Mr. Sundance?" the Yankee asked.

Sundance said he liked them fine.

"I'm sick of them," Moore said. "So are the boys. But they're what we have, so we eat them. They're better than salt pork. Anything's better than salty pork. Why don't you tell us what's been going on out there in the great world. By that I mean what's going on in the rest of Texas?"

Hanrahan brought in the coffee and platters heaped high with smoking buffalo meat.

"The Kiowas and Comanches haven't gone to war yet," Sundance started. "But all the signs say they will."

"Let them," Dutch Henry said, spearing a steak.

"Right you are, Dutch," Doolin said. "They better not start a war with us."

Dameron didn't say anything.

Moore said, "They may start a war but they can't win it. You think I'm wrong, Mr. Sundance?"

Sundance said no. "Sheridan's been moving troops all over. The Texans aren't happy about it, but there's nothing they can do. They'll have to bear the brunt of the war if it comes."

Moore's smile was bleak. "The Texans forget they're part of the United States now. I grant you they'll suffer a bit, but when Sheridan wins the war—and he will—there won't be any more Indian trouble."

"The Texans are putting a lot of blame on you," Sundance told Moore. "They say you're killing off the last of the herds. If not for that the tribes might remain peaceful."

"Is that what your friend Crook says?" Dutch Henry spoke with his mouth full of hot buffalo meat. Dutch Henry was more like an animal than a man. He had a wide face and small gray eyes and a body like a bear. His real name was Henry Born and there were traces of Pennsylvania German accent left in his growling voice. His wiry black beard grew high on his cheekbones. It looked like a mask.

Dutch Henry said to Moore, "Sundance fetches and carries for General Crook. Crook's an Injun-lover from way back. Why don't you ask Sundance the real reason he's up here?"

Moore looked at Sundance.

"I'm looking for the Germaine girls," Sundance said. "It's got nothing to do with Crook. I need the money."

"The best reason there is," Moore said. "How do you feel about this war, Mr. Sundance? You're right, though. We are killing off the last of the herds."

"Maybe it's a good thing," Sundance said. "When the herds are gone the tribes will have to settle down, learn to farm the land the government gives them. They've learned to do it in Oklahoma, they can learn to do it in Texas. If you know anything about me, Mr. Moore, then you know I've fought long and hard for the Indians."

231

"I know something about you," Moore said.

"He's lying," Dutch Henry growled and his hand dropped below the level of the table. "He's a stinking halfbreed liar."

Sundance didn't move. "You've got a big mouth, Dutch. A big dirty mouth when you have forty guns to back you up. You want the forty guns to back off? We can go outside and finish this. Just the two of us. You call me a liar again and I'll blow your dirty face off. You decide."

Sundance knew he could kill Dutch Henry and hoped there would be time to kill Moore before Doolin and Dameron killed him. Maybe he could kill three of them. Four was too many. And even if he did kill all four the men outside would blow him apart with their rifles. Dutch Henry leaned forward in his chair, but he didn't have the nerve to draw. He knew Sundance would kill him first.

For a businessman, Josiah Moore had plenty of nerve. He looked at Dutch Henry. "You heard what Mr. Sundance said. Is that what you want to do? Face him alone?"

"I'm no gun slick," Dutch Henry said.

"Then don't talk like one. Don't call a man a liar unless you're prepared to back it up. Don't try to drag my men into your quarrel with this man, whatever it is. What is the quarrel, Mr. Sundance?"

"A private matter," Sundance said.

"Then drop it," Moore said. "This is my settlement built with my money. That makes me the mayor. You think you'll find the Germaine girls, Mr. Sundance? How long have you been looking for them?"

Sundance said three months.

"That's one quarter of a year," Moore said. "If it takes you another three months, it will be hardly worth your while. For a man like you, I mean. I doubt very much that you'll find them at all. I think they're dead, sir. Raped to death, starved to death, stoned to death. Facts, Mr. Sundance. Life on the frontier. I think you're wasting your time."

"Maybe I am. Anyway, thanks for the breakfast. I better be moving on."

"What's the hurry, Mr. Sundance?" Josiah Moore asked. "I'm told you're an experienced buffalo hunter. You're here and I need all the men I can get. By your own word you've been searching for these girls for three months and haven't earned a dime. Why don't you come to work for me? Or with me, I should say. All my men are on shares, not just wages. Prices are going up as the buffalo get scarcer. We have the last of them, we can name our own price. I can, that is."

Sundance looked at Dutch Henry. "I don't know that it would work out, Mr. Moore."

"Fiddlesticks, Mr. Sundance," Moore said. "You're making too much out of your quarrel with Dutch Henry. There's money to be made here, and we're going to make it. Everything else comes second." Moore paused to give Dutch Henry a hard look. "In my settlement, it does. You spoke of forty guns, Mr. Sundance. Those forty guns work for me. Anyone who makes trouble will find those forty guns pointing at him. So there will be no more quarreling. What do you think?"

"I think I'd like to earn some money," Sundance said.

"Sure you do," Moore said in his nasal Yankee voice. "You can always look for the Germaine girls. They've lost their maidenheads by now, sir. They'll keep."

Sundance wanted to kill Josiah Moore, the bland Yankee businessman. Dutch Henry and the rest were heartless men; in a way, Josiah Moore was worse. The man seemed to have no feelings at all. The smug son of a bitch was the moving force behind all this. It would be good to

233

kill him when the time came.

"All right," Sundance said, thinking that he could trust Moore less than any of them.

"Capital, sir," Josiah Moore said, rubbing his hands. "These may be the last of the buffalo herds, but they're big ones. We don't have enough wagons to take out all the hides we've shot. The wagons that are loaded now will start back for Kansas. Others are already on their way."

"I was stopped by a cavalry patrol at the Red River," Sundance said. "A Major Dodge. Dodge said he was turning back any hunters that tried to cross into Texas."

"Major Dodge is a sensible man," Moore said complacently. "My wagons will get through."

Dutch Henry was watching Sundance while he stuffed his belly with buffalo meat. No matter what Moore said, Sundance knew the trouble was far from over. Behind the makeshift bar Hanrahan was picking his teeth with a sliver of wood. The wind blew dust in the door. At the far end of the settlement the blacksmith was pounding iron.

A big man, very young and yellow bearded, came in with a big Sharps under his arm. There was dust on his hat and all over him and he went to the plank bar and told the Irishman to draw him a mug of beer. Hanrahan looked at Moore and Moore nodded that it was all right. The young man gulped down the beer and turned around with the empty mug in his hand.

"The Kiowas are moving up here," he said. "Comanches too, Mr. Moore. Not as many Cheyenne, but some. They're all together now."

"Let them come," Doolin said.

"Why don't you shut your mouth, Doolin?" the blond man said. "I wasn't talking to you. I'd just as soon never talk to you."

"The hell with you, Dixon." Doolin glanced at

234

his sidekick, Dameron, to make sure he had support. "You think you're so great, but you're not. Am I right, Shad?"

Dameron grunted. "Right as rain, Jimmy."

"Shut up, Jimmy," Moore said to Doolin. "Let the man talk. Now this about the Indians moving up?"

"I'm hungry," Billy Dixon said, dragging a chair to the table. He gave Sundance a quick glance before he forked a buffalo steak onto a plate. "A big party of Kiowas and Comanches came up the day before yesterday. Yesterday more Kiowas and Cheyennes."

"How many?" Moore asked.

"The two days, about a hundred," Dixon said. "I think that's just the start of it. They're well armed, the whole lot of them. It gave me the shivers to see them all together."

"You got the shivers, did you, Billy?" Dutch Henry said.

"You'd get the shivers, too, if you weren't so dumb," Dixon said. "Kiowas, Comanches and Cheyennes, all on the same side."

"You think I'm dumb, do you, kid?" Dutch Henry said.

"Dumb enough," Dixon said. "Sometimes you talk dumb. That'll do for dumb."

"Peace, boys," Josiah Moore said. "I don't know I ever ate a breakfast with so much hard feeling in it. What about the army, Billy? You see any patrols?"

"Not a sign," Dixon said. There was dust in his eyebrows and in his ears. "They'll be along when they get up the nerve. When they outnumber the Indians five-to-one, that's when they'll be along."

"Billy has no respect for our boys in blue," Moore said to Sundance. "I'd like you to meet Jim Sundance, Billy."

Dixon nodded. "I know who he is."

Dixon had a strange innocence about him, Sundance thought.

"I think I'm a better shot that you are," Dixon said. "Maybe you don't know I won the last Dodge City shooting contest."

"Billy Dixon is not a modest man," Dutch Henry said to Sundance. "Tell him about the time we shot for the big money in Las Cruces. I had a whiskey head that morning. If not for that I would have whipped you."

"Maybe you would have," Sundance said.

"I was just a hair off," Dutch Henry said. "You know that. Tell this kid."

"You lost, that's all that matters," Dixon said. "In Dodge City I didn't lose."

"How are you when you aren't shooting at targets?" Sundance said. "Targets don't shoot back. There's a difference." Sundance liked Dixon.

Doolin laughed. "That's telling him, Sundance, me boy."

Josiah Moore stood up and wiped his mouth with the back of his hand. "Time is money, boys, and we've wasted too much of it. It's not like when I first came out here from Vermont. Back in '60, the buffalo covered the Great Plains like a carpet. No end to the critters. Money on the hoof. We used to shoot till our trigger fingers got sore. I knew a man once killed a hundred buffalo before breakfast. At three dollars a hide, that man made himself an easy three hundred before his coffee boiled."

Moore looked doleful. "That kind of money beats digging for gold any day of the week. I'll be sorry to see the last of the buffalo, boys."

"Meaning you'll have to go to work, Mr. Moore?" Doolin said. Doolin was the clown of the outfit.

"Making money is the hardest work there is,

Jimmy."

"Cheer up, Mr. Moore," Doolin said, winking at the others. "You'll always find a way to make money. If the money is there, you'll find it. They tell me there's a lot of money to be made slave trading in the South Seas."

"Slavery's agin my principles," Moore said. "All joking aside, boys, we have to work harder than ever before. Thus far we've had the Staked Plains pretty much to ourselves. Now Billy says the Kiowas and Comanches are heading up from the lowlands. So we have them to contend with. They'll try to scatter the herds to spite us. Drive them as far back in the Plains as they can. Other hunters will be along, you'll see. Our friends in the army won't be able to keep them all out. It may come to swapping bullets with other hunters before this is over. Now let's go out there and make money before the other feller takes it away from us."

The hunters went out, leaving Sundance with Moore. Billy Dixon stayed too.

"We'll be working in five parties," Moore said. "I take it you'd rather not work with Dutch Henry?"

"He can work with me," Dixon said.

"Suits me," Sundance said.

"All right," Moore said. "I'll fix you up with a Sharps and ammunition. The price will come out of your share. But you can trade it back when we're done here."

"He can use one of my rifles," Dixon said.

Moore frowned at the thought of losing the profit on the rifle. "That's mighty generous of you, Billy. Looks like you made yourself a friend, Sundance. Billy's awful tetchy about his guns. To work, boys. The day is wearing on."

Dixon had his own covered wagon and he bunked in it instead of in the soddies like the rest

237

of the men. The tailgate was down and the inside of the wagon was clean and the bedding had been rolled up and secured with a rope. Three .50-caliber Sharps rifles, a .50-caliber Remington rolling block, and two Winchesters were chained to a rack. One of the Winchesters had the longest barrel they made.

Dixon unlocked the chain and handed Sundance one of the Sharps. It was fitted with a telescope.

"That's the same as the Sharps I'll be using," Dixon said. "Bought both of them new the day I won the shooting contest in Dodge."

Sundance said thanks.

"Don't have to thank me," Dixon said. "I want us to be evenly matched, is all. That way we'll discover who's the best shot."

"You mind dropping that?" Sundance said, deciding that this strange man had as little humor as Josiah Moore. "You can be the best shot if you like. Doesn't bother me."

"That wouldn't be fair." Everything Dixon said was dead serious, an odd thing in a man so young. "I wouldn't want to take advantage of a man of your age."

Sundance smiled. He was thirty-eight. "I'll try not to fall over my feet, son."

Dixon locked the guns again. "I'd just as soon you didn't call me 'son.' I may be young, but some day I'm going to be as famous as you are. And probably a better shot."

If you live that long, Sundance thought.

"Call me Billy," Dixon said. "We're going to be together a long time. It's like Mr. Moore said. We're going to have to travel out far to find what we're going to shoot. We shot everything close to home. But now the herds are moving away. Maybe three or four days—longer—before we get enough hides to start back. Nothing Mr. Moore

238

hates more than to see wagons come back half empty."

They started out. Dixon, Sundance, two hunters named Ives and Hackett. There were three wagons and three skinners. One of the skinners was a one-eyed black man with bushy gray hair and a filthy beard. The two other skinners were twin brothers who never spoke. They wore canvas suits like miners and they stank. The hide wagons were crusted with inches of blood baked black by the sun, and now that the sun was hot, they buzzed with flies.

As they pulled away from the settlement, Dixon said with the same serious air, "I'm glad to make your acquaintance, Sundance." He didn't smile. He never smiled.

"Likewise," Sundance said.

Billy Dixon, for all his solemn manner, was an easy man to like. It wasn't going to be so easy to shoot him when the time came. But Sundance knew he would do it.

There was no other choice.

CHAPTER FIVE

All day they traveled south of the settlement without seeing any buffalo. But there were buffalo chips and the grass had been cropped down to the roots. Dixon hung down from his saddle and picked up a chip without dismounting. He snapped it between his fingers and it was dusty and dry.

"They're a good piece ahead of us," he said. "I doubt that we'll see anything before the day after tomorrow. They'll be looking for water along about then. You ever been through this country?"

"Not this part of the Plains," Sundance said. "More to the south. There's not much water anywhere. No real rivers, just creeks. A few ponds that start to dry up in July."

"Buffalo are dumb to come to this country," Dixon said. "But that's what they are—dumb. If God made a dumber animal than the buff, I don't know what it can be. They just don't never learn a thing. Other critters have learned to fear the hunter. Now you take the wolf . . ."

For a young man, Dixon had done an awful lot in a few short years. He told Sundance he had hunted wolves for bounty in North Dakota and other places.

"Traps were no good a-tall," he said. "The sly bastards learned to spring the traps and eat the bait. Poison worked for a while, but they learned to avoid that, too. In the end, we just had to do it the hard way—hunt them down and shoot them. Winter was the best time for that. Hard on them, hard on us."

"Hunting wolves is a hard dollar," Sundance agreed.

"That's why I came back to the buffalo trade," Dixon said. "Didn't want to do it, but that's where the money is."

"Not for long, Billy."

"Don't I know it. That's why I been following these shooting contests. Not enough of them though. You saw my wagon. I been traveling around in that. I'd do all right if they had more of these shooting contests, but they don't. And some of the ones they do have ain't exactly honest. Was in one in Hays City, Kansas, and I knew I won fair and square but the judges decided agin me."

The sun was hot and even though they were ahead of the hide wagons the smell reached them. Ives and Hackett rode in silence, chewing and spitting.

"What'll you do when Moore gets through here?" Sundance asked.

Billy Dixon considered the question in his solemn way. Finally he said, "Maybe sign on with the army as a scout. I hear the army is offering three-month contracts to likely men. Course the army pays beans, but it's better than nothing. Bill Cody got his start as as scout. Today that old boy is rolling in gold. Started with one Wild West show. Now they tell me he's got three."

Billy Dixon tugged at his blond beard. "People have told me that I look something like Buffalo Bill when he was young. You think maybe I do?"

"Somewhat," Sundance said. Every kid in the West wanted to be another Bill Cody, the old fraud. "You have to remember there's more to the circus business than being a good shot. Bill Cody never was that good a shot anyhow. Bill's a showman more than anything else.

"You sound like you know him."

"I worked under him when he was shooting meat for the army."

"By gosh!" Billy Dixon said. "I'm talking to a man that knew Buffalo Bill. What do you remember about him?"

"He drank a lot," Sundance said. Then seeing the hurt look in Billy Dixon's eyes he added, "Of course Bill could handle it. It didn't get in the way of his work."

"That sounds more like Bill," Dixon said.

Sundance said, "You ever think you should clear out of here, Billy? There's a lot of things you can do. Deputy sheriff. Not in some helltown. A decent town where the gunmen don't run wild. Maybe you know I'm a friend of George Crook, the general. Right now he's in Colorado in charge of a mapmaking expedition that's good for a year's work. If I give you a letter he'll take you on."

Dixon was solemn but he wasn't dumb. "What's all this about, Sundance? I'm working for Mr. Moore. By the time we're finished here I'll have a lot of money. Mr. Moore is kind of tight with a dollar, but he always pays up. You sound like you want me to duck out on Mr. Moore."

"No such thing," Sundance said. "Your business what you do. You were talking about jobs, is all."

Sundance knew he had gone too far and was trying to repair the damage as best he could.

Dixon's momentary suspicion seemed to go away. "I thank you for the consideration," he said. "But I signed on with Mr. Moore and I plan to stay to the end. This is the last big hunt ever will be, and years hence I'd like to be able to say I was in on it. It's like it's a part of history. I'd be honored

243

to work for General Crook after it's over."

"Sure," Sundance said, pretty sure that Billy
Dixon wouldn't be working for anyone by the end
of the summer. It was too bad a straightforward
boy like this had to get tangled up with a weasel
like Moore. But for good or ill he had made his
choice, and so he had to go down with the rest of
them. Billy Dixon had chosen the wrong side, and
there was no use thinking about it.

In the early afternoon they halted the wagons
and ate cold flapjacks and dried buffalo meat.
The Plains stretched out flat and featureless except for a ripple of hills in the distance. There were
mourning doves in the grass and they flew away.
Dust was carried on the wind; in another month,
in the high country, there would be dust all the
time.

They were just about done eating when a mule
deer darted from a thicket of gambel oak on the
far side of their camp. Sundance and Dixon fired
together and the deer was bowled over by the
bullets. Reloading their rifles, they walked toward
the dead animal. They stooped to look at it. The
wounds were about two inches apart.

Dixon looked disappointed. "This don't prove
a thing."

"Sure it does," Sundance said. "It proves we
don't have to eat buffalo meat tonight."

The next day they saw a small party of Indians
watching them from a hill, making no attempt at
concealment. By the time they got close the
Indians had gone.

Dixon handed the binoculars back to Sundance. "Some of them were Cheyenne," he said.
"We'd best be on our guard once it gets dark."

They made camp in a scatter of rocks that would
give some cover if an attack came in the night.
Ives and Hackett, the hunters, stood the first
watch. Sundance skinned the mule deer, and cut

it in sections. There wasn't enough water to wash
the carcass, but nobody cared. Dixon said he
didn't trust the skinners to stand guard. The one-
eyed Negro went out in the dark to take a piss,
stayed a long time, and came back drunk. He lay
down under his wagon, wrapped himself, even
his head, in a buffalo robe and went to sleep.

"He's half wild," Dixon said.

Nothing happened during the night except that
the Negro woke up sober and got drunk again. It
got cold in camp after the baked earth gave up the
heat of the day. They kept the fire going with dry
buffalo chips but slept well away from it; if an
attack came the light would make them targets.
The cold wind of the high plains had a lonesome
sound. Toward dawn there was a brief, heavy
shower that drenched them; when first light came
they were still wet. Huddled around the fire they
drank coffee and ate all the deer meat they could;
the rest was thrown away because it would grow
rancid once the sun came up strong. The two
skinners were in a bad mood and they began to
taunt the Negro for his all-night drinking. Ives
and Hackett took no part in it, but the two skinners kept it up. It got wearisome after a while
and Dixon told them to shut up or he'd flog them
out of camp.

"Let the man alone," Dixon warned. "Drunk or
sober, he does more work than you two put
together."

And once again Sundance knew he wasn't
looking forward to killing Billy Dixon.

Late that day they found a buffalo calf with a
broken leg. The herd had crossed a rocky place
and the calf had stepped in a hole. Dixon shot the
calf and the Negro skinned it and put the hide in
his wagon. Blood dripped from the body of the
wagon.

"We're catching up," Dixon said. "Herd can't

be far ahead or that baby buffalo would be dead long since. If we travel late and get up early, could be we'll have something to shoot."

Before it got dark, Dixon broke open some buffalo chips and they hadn't dried in the center.

"Looking better," he said.

Again they caught sight of Indians, a larger party this time. "Looks like the truce is still holding," Dixon said. "I guess they know Phil Sheridan's reputation, all right."

"That won't stop them from going to war," Sundance said. "When they're ready they'll fight. Sheridan may end the war. He won't prevent it from starting."

"Mr. Moore is counting on the army to keep the Indians busy while we take out the hides. We have enough men and guns to beat off even a big attack. You saw how the settlement is built. A clear field of fire on all sides of it."

Sundance had been thinking about that. He knew, too, that fire arrows wouldn't be any good. The sod-covered roofs wouldn't burn.

They stood watches in pairs during the night. Dixon went out before first light and came back in an hour. "There's a fair-sized herd in a hollow about three miles ahead. There's a pond down in the middle. I got the leader spotted already."

They rode out ahead of the wagons and even before they got close they could hear the movement of the herd. Then they tethered their horses to ground pegs. There was no need to tether Eagle. Sundance just told him to stay. They went ahead on foot and when they got closer they crawled. Down from where they were the pond had a dull shine in the early light. Some of the buffalo were standing in the muddy water, with the rest of the herd pushing from behind.

"They've just about drained off all the water," Dixon said, measuring the distance with his eye as he set up his forked rest stick. "I make it about three hundred yards."

Ives and Hackett had moved away along the rim of the hollow and were getting set up to shoot.

Dixon sighted along the barrel of his scoped rifle. "You see the leader?"

Sundance had the big bull in his sights. "I see him. Which of us takes him?"

"You do it," Dixon said, looking over to where Ives and Hackett were. They were ready.

Sundance fired and the leader went down in the mud. The others fired together. The boom of the heavy rifles echoed and rolled, but all the herd did was to move around uneasily. Without a leader to start a stampede, they would stand there while they were being killed. Round after round of .50-caliber shells crashed into the herd. They loaded and fired, loaded and fired, until the rim of the hollow was wreathed in powdersmoke and the ground was littered with empty shells. Sundance guessed they were killing about twenty buffalo a minute. Dixon loaded and fired faster than any man he had ever seen.

Soon the edge of the pond was strewn with thousands of tons of dead buffalo. The sun came up and they were still firing. They continued to fire as the herd finally moved away and then, as if by some signal, the herd started to stampede, heading for a gap in the hollow on the other side of the pond. Dixon yelled at Ives and Hackett to stop firing.

"Damn fools," he said. "We already shot more than we can fetch back."

They went down into the hollow and shot the buffalo that weren't dead yet. There weren't many. Their fire had been deadly. No wonder the Indians were afraid of these men, Sundance thought. A bullet that could drop a bull buffalo blew a man to bits. An overloaded shell could rip a man's leg

247

from his body. He'd seen it happen.

They were counting the carcasses when the rumble of the hide wagons sounded on the wind.

"I make it a hundred and seventy," Dixon said. The water in the pond was thick with blood. There was blood everywhere, their feet squelched in it. A lot of food going to waste, Sundance thought. Buffalo robes for the ladies back East, and while the ladies kept warm, the Indians starved.

The wagons came over the rim and down into the hollow. Ives and Hackett were collecting the empty cartridge casings.

"Damn! I thought we'd take two hundred," Dixon said. "It's pretty good though. Mr. Moore says the price of a hide has gone up to five dollars."

"Indians over yonder on that hill," Ives said, coming down to the pond. "They're gone now but I saw them. I feel like giving them a few rounds. I'm sick of them sneaking about watching us."

The skinners were putting the first hides in the wagons. "Don't be a fool, Ives," Dixon said. "They're just waiting for us to leave here so they can get at the meat. There sure is a lot of it."

The canvas clothes of the skinners were slick with blood. It got into their hair, into their beards, and when they wiped their faces with the backs of their hands, their faces got bloody too. It looked as if they were sweating blood. The one-eyed Negro was faster than the others. He used two skinning knives of different sizes, switching them back and forth without pause. He made long clean cuts, taking great care not to damage the hides. Then he peeled off the hides, scraped the wet side, and dragged them across the blood-wet grass to the wagons.

Sundance was the first to see the smoke clouding the sky several miles away. Dixon saw him looking that way and turned to stare. They both knew what it meant. The Indians had started a prairie fire to keep the buffalo running.

"Bastards!" Dixon said without much anger. "I was thinking we'd ease up on them again. Catch the buffalo the next place they settle down. The hide wagons could go back, then follow us again."

"We'll have to travel a ways if the Indians keep them moving with fire," Sundance said. "No telling where the herd will get to."

"That's for us to find out," Dixon said. He pointed at Ives and Hackett. "You boys stay here till the skinning's done, then go back with the wagons in case they're attacked. Then get back here fast as you can and follow our trail. Tell Mr. Moore what we're doing. Tell him he better post a stronger guard on the settlement."

"What about our shares?" Ives said. "You'll be shooting buffs and making money. We'll be guarding wagons."

"Anything we shoot you'll get your share of," Dixon said. "Now get on with it."

The wind changed and the smoke was blowing in their faces when they rode out of the little valley and headed south. It looked like all the country to the south was on fire.

"Damn those Indians," Dixon said. "If that fire catches up to the herd a lot of good hides are going to get spoiled."

"The grass isn't that dry yet," Sundance said. "The herd is well grazed and well watered. It can move fast enough to stay ahead of the fire. Anyway, if the wind doesn't shift again, the fire will burn itself out."

"We'd better try to ride around it," Dixon said, kicking his horse to a gallop. "It's starting to come our way."

Whipped by the wind, the fire was spreading out in a line more than a mile wide. They rode in front of the moving wall of flame until, three miles from where they started, they saw a long, shallow ravine with a stretch of shale on the far side of it. They skidded their horses down the sandy side of the ravine, picked their way through the scattered rocks at the bottom, then climbed up the other side. The fire roared up to the edge of the ravine, then jumped to the brush on the other side, and that was as far as it went.

Sundance and Dixon crossed the bare, rocky place the fire couldn't cross and followed the ravine south. The fire was beginning to burn itself out but the plain smoked for miles, and even with the wind the smoke blotted out the sun. They stopped to spill water in their hats for the horses. Their eyes showed white in their smoke-blackened faces. Dixon rinsed his mouth and swallowed.

"Bastards!" he said. "They think they're going to stop us, but they're not. All they can do is make it harder. No matter. They can run off the herd. They can't hide it."

"They can run them far enough," Sundance said. "We'll be a long way from the settlement if this war breaks out. We don't know that it hasn't."

"Then why didn't they attack? That last party we saw was big enough."

"Maybe they want to pick the right place. Besides, there were four of us with big rifles then. Now we're just two."

"You don't have to go, Sundance. You can catch up with Ives and Hackett and go back with the wagons."

Sundance knew Dixon would like him to turn back. "I need the money," he said.

They crossed the ravine again and rode in the direction the herd had gone. Smoke still drifted across the plain and patches of brush burned and sparked. Here and there were dead buffalo, killed by the fire or the stampede; their hides still smoldered, giving off a bitter smell. The smoke bothered the horses and they had to take it slow.

They were getting closer to the hills they had seen earlier in the day. The hills were hardly more than a ripple on the vast surface of the Plains, but Sundance had been south of the hills years before, and knew that they were facing rough country crisscrossed with brush-choked ravines. He knew the Indians would try to break up the herd and send it in different ways, figuring the hunters wouldn't know where to start first. It was a good enough plan, Sundance decided. Buffalo hunters liked to make their kills in open country, and with the herd all together. The hunters could go into the badlands; getting the wagons in to take out the hides would be hell even for the most experienced driver. Peace or no peace, the Indians were starting to fight back though no shots had been fired yet. That would come, he knew, unless he found a way to drive Josiah Moore off the Staked Plains. That was hardly possible because Moore was too greedy, too stubborn. He wondered how many men it would take to overrun Moore's settlement. A hundred men wouldn't be enough, and maybe two hundred wouldn't get it done, not when you considered the way the place was set up, not when you considered the men who would defend it. Every hunter there had at least two rifles; the skinners would act as loaders so there would be continuous fire. And these men were no farmboys and store clerks and drifters turned soldier for a bed and three meals a day. They wouldn't panic because they took pride in their brute courage; and they wouldn't surrender because they knew what they could expect.

Anyway, even if the Indians won the fight Sheridan would be glad to see it as an act of war. His armies would move, with their Gatling guns and their cannon.

There had to be some other way. But what?

Killing Moore wasn't the answer. That could be done and maybe he'd get away, but the death of Moore wouldn't change anything. In fact, it might make it worse. At the moment, Moore was able to maintain some control over the wild bunch he had put together. In his way the skinny, money-loving Yankee was a sensible man. It would be different when the hardcases like Dutch Henry and Doolin and Dameron took over.

"The bastards have split the herd," Dixon said when they crossed more than ten miles of burned-over grass. He pointed. "See there and there, where the tracks are different. "They drove into the herd like a wedge and split it in two."

"They'll split the two halves into quarters when they get to the hills. We haven't come to that yet, but we will."

"You sound pretty sure."

"I'm sure. They wouldn't go to all this trouble to keep the herd in one piece so we could just follow along and find it. They'd be doing us a favor if they got the whole herd penned up in some dead-end. Fish in a barrel, like they say. It won't be that easy."

Billy Dixon was indignant. "They got no more right to the buffalo than we do. Who made them the owners?"

"They sort of took it for granted, Billy. They've been on the Plains a long time."

"Like hell, Sundance. Mr. Moore said the Apaches were here long before the Comanches and the Kiowas. Mr. Moore says they drove the Apaches out and stole their country. Now Mr. Moore says the Apaches are starving down in the deserts. So what makes their cause so holy?"

"They're just hungry, Billy." Sundance caught himself again. His anger was causing him to say the wrong things. All that mattered was putting an end to Josiah Moore and his gang of thieves.

But maybe Three Stars was right: the situation here was next door to hopeless. Billy Dixon, in all his ignorance, was right, too. The Kiowas and Comanches had driven the Apaches from the land they had lived on and hunted over for hundreds of years. And who was there before the Apaches? The hell with history! This was the here and now and the Indians were being starved by a skinny Yankee whose only concern was to line his pockets.

"There's enough light left to start in," Sundance said. "But we'd best leave markers for the skinners. If the country in there gets too rough they may have to pack the hides out on mules."

Dixon considered the problems connected with packing out wet hides by muleback. "Damn things wet weigh a ton," he said. "Mules are stubborn and they're smart. They're clean critters for all the mean things they say about them. Clap wet hides a-drip with blood on their backs and they'll kick up holy hell. You wouldn't like to carry wet hides on your back, would you?"

"Wouldn't like it one bit," Sundance said.

"Neither would I, neither would a mule," Dixon said. "Well, we'd best start in and see what it's like."

When they got to the start of the badlands it was just like Sundance said it would be. The Indians had split the buffalo herd four ways, and they had done it well because no one section of the herd looked bigger than the other.

"How many do you figure in all?" Dixon said.

"We killed nearly two hundred at the pond," Sundance said. "Maybe about a thousand left."

"That's about my guess," Dixon said. "Wouldn't be so bad if they were all in a bunch. Now some are going to get lost, get killed in there. Which way you want to go?"

"One way's as good as another," Sundance

said. "Or as bad. There's not a whole lot we can do tonight. It'll be dark soon. Maybe we'll catch up to the buffalo come morning. What do you think?"

Looking at the badlands that lay in front of them in the gathering darkness, Billy Dixon said, "I'm thinking they ought to have more of these shooting contests."

CHAPTER SIX

They were about to move out the next morning when the shooting started far back in the hills. The firing was ragged, building to sustained volleys, then dying away to single shots. For a while there was no shooting at all. Then it started again.

"That's no hunting party," Dixon said, kicking dirt on the fire. "More like a gun battle. Let's go see. If the army's up here it could be an ambush."

The ragged firing continued as they rode into the hills, staying on the slopes because the ravines were too broken and the brush choked. They didn't have to cover that much ground, but it was all bad. In places they had to dismount and lead their horses. The firing was closer now, right over the next ridge. The left their horses on the safe side and crawled to the top. When they got there they were able to look down into a wide draw strewn with rocks the size of houses.

"I'll be damned," Dixon said, keeping his head down. "Injuns fighting Injuns. What in hell do you make of it?"

Sundance looked through the telescope fitted to his Sharps. "Kiowas," he said. "One bunch has the other trapped there in the middle."

The firing started again. Most of it was coming from the attackers, who were shooting from three sides. Sundance moved the telescope to where three dead Indians lay sprawled among the rocks.

"Two of them are Cheyenne," he said. "The other is a Kiowa."

The men who were besieged began to fire back as the attackers moved down from the rocks. Sundance moved the telescope again and got a quick look at Lone Wolf raising up to fire a rifle. Bullets splintered the rock beside his head. The fire from the attackers grew heavier.

"That must be Medicine Water," Sundance said. "Lone Wolf and his men have been hunting them all over. They found them in the wrong place. You want to mix into this, Billy?"

"Let them fight it out. Who the hell cares?"

"After Medicine Water and his band finish this, they'll still have the girls. Lone Wolf and his men don't stand a chance. Looks like they're outnumbered three-to-one. There's no way they can break out."

"All right. But I'm mixing in because of the girls. The hell with Lone Wolf."

The attackers were down from the high ground, getting ready to rush Lone Wolf's position. The others were moving in from two sides. Dixon sighted through the scoped rifle.

"No," Sundance said. "Wait till they make their rush. Here it comes."

Sundance and Dixon fired together and two renegades went down. The big rifles sounded like cannon. They fired again and killed two more men. The running Kiowas, caught in the open, began to howl their surprise. The men trapped in the rocks opened fire with everything they had as Sundance and Dixon rained heavy bullets into the attackers. With the scoped rifles there was no way they could miss. The renegades turned and began to run back toward the steep sides of the draw. Five of them died before they got there. One man ran up the side of the draw like a goat and he was close to the top when Sundance followed the man's run and killed him before he reached the rim. The attackers were still coming from the other side, but they wavered and ran for cover as the two buffalo rifles killed those out in front. They turned and ran like the others. Sundance and Dixon fired carefully but fast. By now Lone Wolf and what was left of his men were out from cover, blasting the retreating attackers with bullets. For an instant Lone Wolf looked up at where Sundance and Dixon were firing. Then he ran, thumbing bullets into a repeating rifle.

When the renegades got to the far side of the draw they rallied for a while, and they might have made a fight of it if it hadn't been for the two buffalo rifles. Dixon had a fierce look of satisfaction on his boyish face. A renegade raised up to fire and Dixon's bullet blew his head to bits.

"Damn!" Dixon said. "We're like the damn artillery."

Sundance saw Lone Wolf stagger and fall. He looked through the scope. Lone Wolf was still moving: a leg wound. Howling, two renegades sprang from cover and ran toward the fallen man. Sundance killed one, Dixon killed the other.

Then, suddenly, it was over. The renegades vanished into the rocks, leaving their dead and wounded behind. Sundance and Dixon loaded their rifles and came down the slope. Two of Lone Wolf's men had lifted him and he was lying on a flat rock gripping his thigh. Blood leaked through his fingers and his face had the stony look of a man who won't admit pain. Only six of his men were left; at least nine or ten had been killed. The survivors turned their rifles when Sundance and Dixon got close. Lone Wolf spoke to them and they lowered the rifles but remained sullen and suspicious even though Dixon and Sundance had saved their lives. Now they owed something and they hated it, Sundance knew. He could understand that, but Dixon didn't.

"Thank you too," he said to a glowering Kiowa.

"Give it up, Billy," Sundance said. "They don't know how to say thanks. How bad are you hit, Lone Wolf?"

"The bullet is still in there," the Kiowa said. "I have other bullets in me."

"This one can't stay or you won't walk again. You want me to take it out?"

"I would like to walk," Lone Wolf said.

Sundance nodded. "That was Medicine Water we shot at?" He took a handful of sulphurhead matches from his pocket and struck them against a rock. Then he took the long-bladed skinning knife from his belt and held the blade in the flame. He wiped the soot from the blade. It was thin, razor sharp, with an upturning point.

"The renegade, yes," the Kiowa said, holding the edge of the rock with both hands. He braced himself and didn't move again as Sundance began to probe in the wound. He stared at the sky while the point of the knife went in. His voice remained steady though sweat dripped from his face. "Medicine Water surprised us. He is like a starving wolf now, crazy but cunning."

Sundance felt the point of the knife scrape against the bullet. He dug into a little deeper, getting the curved end of the blade under the lead slug. Lone Wolf continued to stare at the sky. Sundance kept on talking. "I do not know what Medicine Water looks like. Did he die in the fight?"

Now the point of the knife was under the bullet and he began to take it out. It couldn't be done fast. A doctor would have done it with a forceps; a knife was all he had.

"Medicine Water got away," the Kiowa said.

Sundance turned the knife and brought the

bullet out on the flat of the point. He threw the bloody slug away. "It's out," he said. "But the bleeding won't stop if I don't burn powder in the wound."

Lone Wolf's voice had no strength in it. "Now we will have to hunt him again. I had been told that some of his band deserted him. I did not think he had so many men. And so he took us by surprise."

Sundance took a .50-caliber shell from his pocket and began to work the lead free of the brass casing. He pressed the lead against the rock and turned it. It took a while to extract the lead from the casing. Then he sprinkled the powder into the wound. Lone Wolf heard the sound of the match rubbing against rock, but he didn't move. Sundance touched the flame to the powder-clogged wound and there was a hissing, sputtering sound and the stink of burning flesh. The burnt flesh closed over the wound like the puckered eye socket of a blind man, and the bleeding stopped. There was no need of a bandage. The scab that would form in a day or two would be protection enough.

Sundance stood up and wiped off his knife. "You won't be hunting Medicine Water just now," he told the Kiowa. "Stay off that leg, give the torn muscles time to heal. I can't say you won't limp for the rest of your life."

Lone Wolf stared at the fire-blackened wound. "I will not limp on a horse, Sundance. There will be another time for Medicine Water."

"You ran off the buffalo, didn't you?" Sundance said.

"Moore will not find them so easily now," Lone Wolf said. "They are scattered in the hills. Enough to keep us alive."

"You know if Medicine Water still has the white girls?" Sundance asked.

"That was what drew us into the ambush." Lone Wolf's men watched in silence as he eased his wounded leg off the rock. "We had been hunting him for a week, thinking he did not have so many men as he had. His band is starving and they came to the high country to hunt buffalo. We followed him from the lowlands. We killed some of his men who lagged behind. I think he betrayed them, left them to die as part of his plan. Then he sent one of his men to say that they were starving, with little water left, and he was willing to give up the girls if we would call off the hunt."

"Where were you to meet? To get the girls?"

"Not in this place," Lone Wolf said. "South of here by a tall rock that looks like the face of a man."

"You trusted a man like Medicine Water?"

"No, Sundance. But I wanted to return the white captives to their people. The killing of their family, the taking of the girls has made much trouble for the Kiowas, for all the tribes. They are just two women but their capture has caused more trouble than anything else."

What Lone Wolf was saying was true. The newspapers in south Kansas were using the abduction of the Germaine girls to whip up war feeling against the Kiowas and all the tribes on the South Plains. Nothing like two pretty young girls to get the public interested. And yet no matter how bad the newspapers made it sound, it had to be true. If the Germaine girls were still alive, they had gone through hell, for by all accounts, Indian as well as white, the renegade Medicine Water was a demented killer. And when a compassionate man like Crook said he'd be glad to pull on the rope that hanged the renegade, there could be no doubt of how evil he was.

"Had you any proof the girls were alive?" Sundance asked. He guessed there must have been or an old campaigner like Lone Wolf would not have been trapped so easily.

"There was proof," Lone Wolf said, kneading the muscles above the wound. "The renegade who came with the offer of a trade had a letter from the girls. I have it."

Lone Wolf reached inside his shirt and gave Sundance a penciled note on a scrap of brown paper:

DEAR MR. CHIEF LONE WOLF,
    WE ARE ALIVE AND THEY HAV NOT HARMED US. MEDISIN WATER WILL LET US GO IF YOU LET HIM GO. PLEASE HELP US SIR.
    WE WANT TO GO HOME.

It was signed Sophia and Catherine Germaine. Sundance gave the note to Dixon. He read it and gave it back.

"You want to go after them?" Sundance said.

Dixon took in a deep breath and blew it out. He made a gesture of exasperation. "Yep, I guess I do. But we'll do it, the two of us." He waved his hand. "I don't want these Injuns along. They didn't do so good here. They'll only get in the way."

Only Lone Wolf knew what he was saying. The Kiowa's eyes, flicking to Dixon's face, held no expression, but Sundance could feel Lone Wolf's hatred for Dixon. Hatred mingled with shame, for Lone Wolf knew that he had led his men into a trap where more than half of them had been killed.

Lone Wolf looked at Sundance. "Your young friend has a hard mouth," he said.

"He's an honest man, Lone Wolf. He speaks the truth. We will rescue the girls in our own way. You cannot be there to command your men. They will not take orders from us. You must wait here until we free the girls."

"Medicine Water will kill them if there is no way out for him."

"We have to see that he doesn't. If we can take the girls alive, then you must take them back. It will be a gesture of good faith. The army can not disregard that."

"You think the army will believe a Kiowa? Any Kiowa? They will say we have had the girls all the time."

"The girls will tell the truth."

"No," Lone Wolf said. "If there is enough hate in them, they will not tell the truth. I do not mean to be hanged because two crazed women refuse to tell the truth."

"Then how did you intend to get them back."

"I would have left them near a settlement or an army post."

"That's no good, Lone Wolf. The army has to know that you rescued them."

"Then you must come with me," Lone Wolf said. "Your hard-mouth friend can come with you."

"Oh no, sir," Dixon said. "I'm in this as far as I want to go. I work for Mr. Moore."

"Two thousand dollars reward, Billy," Sundance said. "Half of it is yours. Leave me out of it. You can be the hero. I don't recall that Bill Cody ever rescued any white women captives. Do you?"

"Can't say that I do. You sure you want to give up the glory?"

Glory! To Sundance glory meant as much as a bucket of sheep dip. Looking for glory was what got you killed. The Sioux showed Custer the price of glory.

"I got enough glory," Sundance said.

"I could use some," Billy Dixon said with no trace of humor. "I'll go with you and then I'm going back to Mr. Moore. I gave my word to stick with him. You say I'll get a thousand?"

"That's right. You get a thousand I don't see you have to go back to Moore."

"Like hell I don't! I got a lot of money tied up with that man."

"Do what you like." Sundance knew there was no use talking to Billy Dixon. Smart in some ways, he was thickheaded in others.

They moved south, leaving Lone Wolf and his men in the draw. Thinking of the fame that was going to accrue from the rescue of the Germaine sisters, Billy Dixon was inclined to brag.

He said, "If that's the principal chief of the Kiowas back there I don't see that Phil Sheridan has much to worry about. Neither does Mr. Moore. I'd like to see Lone Wolf lead his ragtag Injuns against Mr. Moore's settlement. When I say ragtag Injun I'm of no mind to include you, Sundance. A ragtag Injun is what you're not."

"Thanks," Sundance said.

A mile south of the draw they found a dead Kiowa who had been badly wounded and had bled to death. He sat against a rock with a cocked rifle and the ground under him was soaked with blood. Sundance took his rifle, an old Henry repeater with a brass frame, and smashed it, breaking the stock and bending the barrel out of shape. Dixon watched him while he did it.

Dixon said, "How many men you figure the renegade has left?"

"Maybe eight or nine," Sundance said. "More than enough for another ambush. Medicine Water has horses and they're going to slow him down. We'd make better time if we leave our horses behind. Medicine Water will keep the girls alive just as long as he thinks they'll give him some bargaining power."

"I figured that already," Dixon said.

They gave the horses water and left them in a

ravine. After that they made better time. Dixon was big but he was sure-footed and he kept up with Sundance as they ran from ridge to ridge and fought their way their brushy draws. It was hot and still as they went deeper into the badlands; the renegades had a start on them but they were catching up. At least one of the fleeing Kiowas was wounded and there were drops of blood on the rocks.

They crossed another stony ridge and Sundance pulled Dixon down into cover when he saw the wounded Kiowa staggering about two hundred yards ahead. The wounded man dragged his rifle by the barrel. The back of his shirt was soaked with blood and he fell and got back on his feet and kept running.

Dixon eased his head up and started to push his rifle over the top of the ridge. "I can drop the bastard easy."

Sundance's hand closed over the breech of Dixon's rifle. "Let him go. He won't be any good to Medicine Water. If they know we're this close they may kill the girls as soon as they get to them."

"Then how in hell are we going to get them out?"

"They must have some kind of hiding place in there, maybe a cave or a deep ravine. That's where their suppy of water will be."

That's still not saying how we're going to rescue the girls."

"The quickest way to get the girls killed is to let Medicine Water know we're following him. Pretty soon he's going to leave a few men behind to cover his back trail."

"Won't be so easy to sneak up and kill them."

"We're not going to do that. That's what they'll expect and they'll be watching for it. What we have to do is get past them without being seen. If Medicine Water doesn't hear any shooting maybe he'll think his backtrail is covered."

"How the hell are we going to get past them? They'll be spread out wide and watching like hawks. Maybe we can do it, but if it takes too long the rest of the renegades could be clear out of the country, and the girls with them."

Sundance knew Dixon was right, but he couldn't think of any other way to do it. The girls were the prize in this game. If the girls died, there wouldn't be any profit in killing Medicine Water. Of course they might be dead by now, for it was entirely possible that Medicine Water had murdered them after they wrote the note. Still, he had to hope that they were still alive, no matter how battered and dirty and degraded they were.

Sundance took off his hat so its outline wouldn't show against the top of the ridge. The wounded renegade was making his way between two big rocks when suddenly he fell and didn't get up again. Two Kiowas ran from cover and dragged the dying man out of sight.

"That makes two we have to get around," Dixon said. "How many more you figure?"

"Two more. Four men and Medicine Water have gone on ahead. I'd say he left one or two men with the girls."

"That makes seven," Dixon said. "Six or seven. Maybe we can get past Medicine Water's rear guard, but that means we'll have four men behind us. Six or seven in front, four behind. I don't like that so good. You don't know that isn't part of a plan, to catch us in the middle. If we can get close enough to use the knife there wouldn't be any shooting. Use the knife on them and move on fast."

"No way to surprise four men by daylight, Billy."

"You don't know there's four down there."

"We have to figure on four. At least three. It

can't be done, not by daylight."

"Then we wait for night to do it."

"They'll be gone by night. Medicine Water doesn't want to make a fight of it. A fight he can't win. All he wants is enough time to get away."

Dixon eased his head up, but there was nothing to see. Dust blew and the brush creaked in the wind. Otherwise there wasn't a sound.

"I still don't like it."

"Neither do I," Sundance said.

"How far back do you want to join up again?"

Sundance pointed. "You see that tall split rock? All right. We'll join up again the far side of that. Go slow, Billy. Crawl a bit, then stay still even if there isn't any cover. But always head for something that offers some cover. Then wait and move on."

Sundance took one side of the slope and Dixon took the other. They went out wide and started down in opposite directions. The end of the ridge where Sundance was ended in a drop of about fifteen feet. There was nothing to hold onto, so he went down on his back, sliding at first and then falling. He landed on his feet, then lay back against the bottom of the ridge until the dust he raised stopped blowing, and then he crawled to where a shallow ravine began and ran south for about a hundred yards. Before he started down he lay behind a rock with the sun hot in his face.

The ravine was grown over with thorn bush that started close to the ground. His hat offered some protection against the black-bayonet brush but his back was torn and bleeding by the time he crawled and rested in the hot sand. When he started again a big kangaroo rat hopped away from him, then turned and looked at him, unafraid because he had never encountered a human being before, then hopped away without haste.

It took Sundance thirty minutes to get to the end

of the ravine. There the sides had collapsed and tons of rock and sand stood in his way. The top of the slide was bare and he had to crawl over it. He crawled up part of the way and waited, the Sharps cradled across his arms. He raised his head and could see the top of the split rock where he was to join up with Dixon. Dust blew hard and his eyes were gritty and hot. He noticed that the wind, blowing from the south, was increasing in force. A high plains duster, he thought. Maybe not.

The wind blew harder as he crawled across the top of the slide and down the other side where the ravine took up again. If there were sounds other than the wind, he didn't hear them. He had no way of knowing if the renegade rear guard was watching the ravine. He gritted his teeth as the black-bayonet thorns ripped his back and decided they weren't.

He came to a place where he couldn't get through. The thorn bush was too dense, too tightly packed. It would have been easier to crawl into coils of barbed wire. The only way out was to climb up the side of the ravine and take his chances on being spotted, but when he got to the top, after sliding back twice in the sand and shale, he knew he was behind them. Not far behind them—but behind them. Lying still, he wondered how Dixon was making out. No shots had sounded, but that didn't mean anything: a knife in the right place wouldn't cause any outcry. Dixon knew how to shoot as well as any man Sundance had come across, but he didn't know much about Indians. The way he tried to downgrade Lone Wolfe showed that. Holding the enemy in contempt could get you killed faster than anything else. If the enemy had a gun then you had to beware of him.

In the bottom of the ravine the wind hadn't been much. Now that he was out from cover the wind blew dust in his face with something approaching gale force. It was early in summer for a duster to be blowing, but there it was. Once the freeze of winter ended and the topsoil was loosened you had to expect a duster at any time.

There was some distance left in the ravine; he stayed out of it. The dust wasn't so bad yet that he couldn't see the split rock where they were to meet. He thought he heard a cry and then when the high howling sound remained constant, never changing in pitch, he knew it was just the wind whistling through a hollow place in the rocks.

The sun was shining, but the light was thick and gray because of the dust. He was well past them now and it had taken the best part of an hour. The approaching duster would give them cover. But he wasn't sure that the renegade rear guard wouldn't pull back before the wind worked itself up to a fury.

Another twenty minutes took him behind the split rock, and he waited with the Sharps cocked and ready. The wind was howling now and the wind was cold, the way it always was when a duster was blowing up hard. He heard the scrape of metal on rock and he brought the big rifle to his shoulder. Something was crawling toward him.

It could be Dixon. It could be anyone.

CHAPTER SEVEN

Sundance set down the hammer and Billy Dixon
said, "I passed so close to one of them I could
have wiped his nose for him. The dust was
making him sneeze. You think we're in for a real
blow?"

"Looks like it. No use looking for tracks while it
lasts."

"A hell of a thing," Dixon said. "It was bad
enough before."

They pulled their bandannas up over their
mouths and went ahead in the dust-laden wind.
The wind buffeted them as they leaned forward
and staggered into it, and sometimes it drove
them back until they recovered and dug into it
again. As the wind grew stronger everything lost
its shape and the sun was just a yellow blob in the
sky. The wind-driven dust stung their faces like
birdshot and it was hard to breathe.

They were resting behind a rock and Dixon
said, "We don't even know where we're going."
He was gasping. "Why don't we dig in and let this
blow away? They won't move out in a dust storm."

"That's the best time to move out," Sundance
said. He was gasping, too. "Any tracks they leave
will be covered. If they get deep enough into the
lands we may never find them."

They battered their way through the shrieking
wall of sand, turning their backs on it to breathe.

It could have been any time of day, any time of night. Sometimes they stumbled and fell over rocks in their path. Everything became a trap: a hole with jagged rocks at the bottom, a patch of thorn bush. After a mile they rested again and tried to keep their lungs from filling with sand. The hell of it was they could have bypassed Medicine Water's hiding place by now. It could be anywhere to the right or left; they would not have seen it in the storm. And then Sundance heard the frightened whinny of a horse. For an instant it was borne on the wind. He knew Dixon hadn't heard it and maybe he hadn't heard it either, yet the sound had a different pitch than the howling of the wind.

Sundance turned his head and waited to hear it again. But there was nothing but the remorseless banshee howl of the wind. Even behind the rock where they were the sand drifted up against them, soft and sinister as snow. They struggled on for another five hundred yards and when Dixon fell and seemed to want to lie there, Sundance dragged him back to his feet and shoved the fallen rifle into his hands. He could barely see Dixon's face. They were moving on, hardly able to put one foot ahead of the other, when he heard the horse again. This time he knew the storm wasn't playing tricks on him, and although the storm seemed to rage as before, he sensed a lessening of its fury. By sheer will power they had walked through the worst of the storm, and now the wind was dropping.

Sundance saw the rock wall ahead of them and he pulled at Dixon's arm and pointed. Not more than fifty yards head of them was the black mouth of a cave. It seemed to waver in the wind, as if it might not be there at all, but as the wind died by stages it took shape again, dark and threatening. The wind faded as softly as a kite drifting to earth, and although the sky was olive colored and dusty, the light grew stronger.

Dixon's eyes were red and staring above his bandanna. Sundance pulled him behind a rock and when he spoke what came out started as a shout. Sundance clapped his hand over Dixon's mouth and forced him to be still. The wind dropped to nothing. All around them it looked as if grey snow had fallen and there was that strange peace that comes always after a storm of any kind.

Dixon shook himself free and his eyes had lost their wild, staring look. His voice didn't seem to belong to him.

"You think they're in there?" he said.

"I think they're in there," Sundance said. "They have the horses in there, too. It looks big enough for all of them." He pointed again. "There's the tall rock that looks like the face of a man. They'll be coming out soon. You all right, Billy?"

"I could use a drink of water," Dixon said.

"After we kill them you'll get water. The one to get is Medicine Water. The girls are his ace and he'll be sticking close. He's the one to kill. The others will scatter."

"We don't know what he looks like."

"You'll know him when you see him. Makes no difference. We kill the men closest to the girls, then go after the others. They'll try to kill the girls the minute we open fire. You ready?"

Dixon nodded and took the plug out of the muzzle of his Sharps. The hammer made a grating sound as he moved it back and forth. Sundance felt in his pocket for shells. It would have to be done fast if the girls were to live. He took the long-barreled Colt from its holster and blew dust from the barrel. The cylinder turned when he thumbed back the hammer to half cock and worked it by hand. But it made a rasping sound he didn't like. He knew he could count on the Sharps, though. It

271

was a workhorse of a rifle and not even a dust storm could keep it from functioning. In a while he heard them coming out.

They brought the horses out first and they stood quivering in deep sand. There were five Kiowas and they stood waiting with the horses. Medicine Water—it had to be him—came out last with the girls. Somehow Sundance expected him to be a bigger man than he was. That was all the stories, he guessed. But the leader of the renegades was no taller than the others, and yet he was different. Across the fifty yards that separated them Sundance could see the madness in the renegade's face, in his eyes. There was great cruelty in this man, and there was a madness that had been with him from birth or had been earned through bitterness and betrayal. He pushed the girls ahead of him with the muzzle of a Winchester and in his belt were stuck not one but three pistols.

Billy Dixon began to raise up. Sundance pulled him back.

One of the men holding the horses spoke to Medicine Water and he let out a mad, shouting laugh. He pushed one of the girls and tripped her by hooking his moccasined foot around her ankle. But when she got up she was smiling. He dragged her to her feet by her hair and they laughed together. Then Medicine Water pointed at the other Germaine girl and they laughed again. Dixon turned to stare at Sundance, who made no response at first. Then he nodded for Dixon to get ready.

Medicine Water came forward, still laughing and talking, and one of the Kiowas handed him a buffalo bladder filled with water. He was holding it high above his face when Sundance shouldered the rifle and blew his head away. It shattered like a rotten melon and he remained standing, the water-filled bladder still in his hands, after his

272

head was gone. Dixon killed a Kiowa who sprang toward the girls with a knife. Medicine Water dropped and the girl who had been smiling threw herself on top of his headless body. She was screaming. The other girl remained standing, making no effort to hide or to run. A Kiowa whirled and pointed a rifle at her. He pulled the trigger and the dust-clogged rifle blew up in his face, taking out an eye and part of his skull. Dixon fired and killed another man. Sundance was pushing another cartridge into the Sharps when a bullet from behind clipped the top of his head, burning a path through his scalp. Dixon whirled and killed a Kiowa who was running at them from behind. He dropped and then another Kiowa came running behind the dead man. He fired a rifle and missed and then he sprang forward. Dixon smashed him in the kneecap with the Sharps, then grabbed the Kiowa by the throat and smashed his head against the rock. Out in front one of the renegades vaulted onto a horse and Sundance fired and killed him. The remaining Kiowas ran, leaving the horses. Blood ran into Sundance's eyes from the scalp wound and he sleeved it away. He stood up and they came out from behind the rock and before they got to the girls the one who had thrown herself on Medicine Water's body began to howl. The other girl hadn't moved.

Dixon looked from the howling girl to Sundance and his eyes didn't understand any of it.

"What in hell is going on here?" he said.

It would take too long to explain, so all Sundance said was, "He captured her four months ago. She's been with him a long time."

"Shit," Billy Dixon said.

The Germaine girls were as dirty as railroad tramps, their clothing in rags, and the one who hadn't moved was barefoot. Dirt had worked itself

273

deep into their hands and faces. They looked wilder than the wildest, half-savage ridgerunner of the Kentucky mountains.

Sundance guessed they had been driven crazy in different ways. All the renegades had used them many times over; the raping wouldn't be the worst part of it, for the Indians were no strangers to perversion. To degrade white women, to reduce them to howling, crawling animals, was the Indian's best idea of revenge.

Sundance went to where the first girl was standing as if paralyzed with shock. Her eyes moved to him with a sort of careless curiosity. Then she smiled like an idiot.

"Are you Catherine or Sophia?" Sundance asked her. The other girl tore at the dead renegade's blood-spattered shirt and continued to howl. Maybe they'd be better off dead, Sundance thought. He had seen too many white captives who had never recovered from what they'd been through. Shame was a big part of it; the sneers and whispers of the whites took care of the rest. One woman he'd heard about in Kansas developed a mania that no doctor could cure. Throughout her life, before she hanged herself, she scrubbed her body raw with hot water and lye soap. He knew cases where husbands had rescued their wives after years of searching, then refused to sleep in the same bed because they were "dirty."

"Tell me your name," Sundance said, taking hold of the girl's arm and shaking her.

"Why I'm Sophia," she said in a light pleasant voice that did more than hint at madness. She touched her matted blond hair with a dirty hand, yet it was a very feminine gesture. She held her dirty hands out in front of her and smiled at them. "Back home everybody said I had such nice hands. My mother used to scold me for being so vain. Putting corn husk oil on them before I went to bed. My mother used to say I'd better let my hands get tough if I planned to get married and raise a family. You must think I look terrible."

Dixon was trying to pull the other girl away from Medicine Water's corpse. He drew back in confusion when she hissed at him like a maddened cat. For all his traveling around there were things that Billy Dixon hadn't seen before.

"Let her be and come over here," Sundance told him.

Sophia Germaine touched her hair again and smiled at Dixon.

"Billy, I'd like you to meet Miss Sophia Germaine. She'll be going back with us, so you two should get acquainted. Take good care of her, you hear?"

Billy Dixon bent his big body in an awkward bow. "Miss Germaine, ma'am," he said gallantly.

"Mr. Dixon, sir," Sophia Germaine said, touching her hair again.

Sundance went over to the other girl. She was more afraid of him than she was of Dixon. He wondered if the frontier would ever stop tearing human lives apart.

"Get up and come away from there," he ordered her in a flat, hard voice. "I told you to come away from there. I'll drag you if I have to."

Catherine Germaine had pale blue eyes like her sister's. She glared at him, twisting her mouth in her anger. Blood from Medicine Water's shattered head was all over her.

"Did you kill him, you son of a bitch?"

"I killed him," Sundance said.

Suddenly she sprang at him with clawing fingers. He grabbed her wrist and backhanded her across the face. He slapped her again and again. She took the blows and screamed her defiance. Then with a furious movement she

275

broke his hold and turned to run. Sundance rabbit-punched her across the back of the neck and caught her before she fell.

"My sister is very excitable," Sophia Germaine said to Dixon. Smiling, she offered it as a casual comment.

Sundance picked up the unconscious woman and slung her over his shoulder. "Let's go," he said. "I want her to be away from here when she comes to." He jerked his head toward Medicine Water's body. "Take his moccasins and put them on Miss Germaine."

"That's very kind of you," Sophia Germaine said.

They hadn't gone more than a mile when Catherine Germaine began to kick and struggle. Sundance put her down and handed her a canteen. She stared at him while she drank. He had to grab the canteen away from her, or she would have emptied it.

"Don't start up again," Sundance warned her. "What happened to you is over. You can't go back to it. You're acting crazy but I don't think you are. Like it or not you're going back."

"Back to what?" She spat the words.

"Get moving," Sundance said.

By nightfall they were close to the draw where Medicine Water had staged the ambush. A big fire glowed in the gathering darkness. A buffalo rifle boomed and then Dutch Henry's growling voice came at them from behind a rock.

"You better be Dixon and Sundance," Dutch Henry shouted. "Answer up quick."

Sundance called back. So did Dixon.

"We got the Germaine girls," Dixon said.

"Come ahead then," Dutch Henry said. "Bring the ladies down by the fire where we can see them."

There were ten buffalo hunters around the fire

eating meat and drinking whiskey at the same time. Doolin grinned at the girls and dug his partner, Dameron, in the ribs. Josiah Moore wasn't there.

Doolin got up unsteadily and swept off his shapeless black hat. "'Tis an honor to have you in our company, ladies. Before you start supper would you be caring for a drink? To take the edge off your dreadful ordeal, is what I mean."

Dutch Henry was looking at Catherine Germaine in a way Sundance didn't like.

"Sure," Dutch Henry said. "Why don't they have a drink?"

Sophia smiled at Dutch Henry. "Gosh no. I tasted it once. It tasted terrible. But thank you for the kind offer."

"Give the bottle here," Catherine said in a rough voice. "I could use a goddamned drink."

Doolin winked at his partner. "That's the spirit, little lady. I always say there's nothing little a cup of cheer at the end of the day."

He started to hand the bottle to Catherine, but Sundance shoved it back at him. "The lady doesn't drink, Doolin. What the lady needs is food and coffee."

"I'm powerful hungry," Sophia said to Dixon. Dixon forked a buffalo steak onto a tin plate and gave it to her. She sat down and ate as if the others weren't there. Dixon sat beside her.

Dutch Henry took a swig of whiskey from Doolin's bottle. He looked at Sundance over the top of the bottle. "Since when did you join the Temperance League? What's it to you if the lady wants a drink? You know the trouble with you, Sundance? You're always butting into other people's business."

"I said no drink, Dutch. Whiskey isn't good for this lady."

Doolin sniggered. "I'll wager she's had worse

things in her mouth than whiskey. If I know my Injuns she's had a lot worse things to suck on these past months."

Billy Dixon stood up holding his rifle with the stock turned toward the runty, sniggering Irishman.

"Keep that up and I'll break your face," Dixon said. He pointed at Shad Dameron. "I know you, friend. You put words in this bogtrotter's mouth, then you hang back and laugh behind your hand. You want some too?"

Dixon raised the upended rifle.

"Who are you calling a bogtrotter?" Doolin said indignantly. "A man like you that can hardly read and write."

Dameron took the bottle from Doolin and drank from it.

"You'll go too far one of these days," Dameron said. "You and your goddamned shooting contests. Jimmy just offered the women a drink. What the hell's wrong with that?"

Dutch Henry was still grinning at Catherine Germaine. Sundance took her arm and pushed her toward Dixon. "See to this lady, Billy. She's hungry."

Catherine shook off Sundance's arm, but there didn't seem to be much strength left in her. What she needed was food and sleep. But she needed a bath more than anything. He guessed there were lice in her hair.

"The hell with you," she said in a dead voice. But she didn't offer any resistance when Dixon made her sit beside her sister.

"Hello, Catherine," Sophia said.

Dutch Henry took another drink. "The lady doesn't like you, Sundance. Smart lady. Who could like you? I know I don't like you." Dutch Henry waved the bottle. "You like him, boys?"

The only one who answered was a man Sundance recognized as Shotgun Collins, another Irishman who had ridden shotgun for Wells Fargo at one time. His leathery face was pitted with old smallpox scars and he had the quick darting eyes of a ferret. A shotgun lay beside his Sharps.

"I don't like him," he said to Dutch Henry. "I don't hate him, but I don't like him."

Dutch Henry laughed loud. "You'll hate him when you get to know him better. Everybody does. The rest of the boys don't like him either, but they're too bashful to say so. It must be hard on a man not to be popular. Me, I'm very popular, right, Jimmy?"

Doolin hiccuped. "I'd vote for you, Dutch. So would Shad."

Sundance, still standing, was glad to see that Catherine Germaine was eating. Dixon handed her a cup of coffee and she took it.

"You sure are talky tonight, Dutch," Sundance said, wondering if the trouble that was right under the bullshit would settle down.

Dutch Henry had plenty of whiskey in him. "That's because I like to talk when I'm among friends. That doesn't include you and it doesn't include the winner of the Dodge City shooting contest. You know why I'm popular? It's because I like to enjoy myself and let the other man do the same. Live and let live. Scratch my back and I'll scratch your back. The way I see it, if you don't like to pepper your meat, that's no reason to stop the other man from peppering his."

"You like pepper, do you, Dutch?" There were ten of them, Sundance thought. If it came to killing, the two Irishmen and Dameron would throw in with Dutch Henry. It all had to do with the women, and nothing else.

"Pepper's all right," Dutch Henry said. "But you have to know it's not my main interest in life.

"Good grub, good whiskey's more to my liking. And, lest we forget—a woman."

Dutch Henry looked at Catherine Germaine whose fierce angry eyes were hooded as she hacked and stabbed at the meat on her plate.

"I like a wild woman," Dutch Henry said. "The wilder the better."

"Plenty of wild women in Kansas," Sundance said. "When Moore pays you off, you can go wild yourself."

Dutch Henry grinned and looked again at Catherine Germaine. "Payday's a long way off and so is Kansas. I was thinking we might have a little party here and now. It's not like the ladies haven't been well broke in."

Sundance slapped Dutch Henry across the face. The slap sounded like the report of a small-caliber pistol. Dutch Henry started to reach for his beltgun and found himself staring into the muzzle of Sundance's Colt. The hammer was back.

Collins got up with his sawed-off shotgun. Doolin and his partner stood up, too. Doolin was too drunk to be afraid, but Dameron's eyes darted around, looking for support.

Dutch Henry had a trickle of blood at the corner of his mouth and his eyes glittered with hate. Yet, when he spoke, his voice retained the same deadly, bantering tone.

"Listen to me, boys. We have the whiskey and the women. That's all we need to have a party. There's eleven of us and two of them. What say we get to it?"

Two more hunters stood up, men Sundance didn't know. Another man stood up. That made seven, Sundance thought. But they all wanted the women and they'd join in when the shooting started. There was no chance of coming out of this alive if they decided to make a fight of it.

"Your choice," Dutch Henry said. "You backed

280

me down in front of Moore, but this is different. Us boys mean to have those women."

"Then you'll have them dead." Sundance pointed the cocked pistol at Catherine Germaine who stared at it with an utter absence of fear. "Billy will kill the other one. One way or another you'll be having your party with dead women."

"Jesus Christ, the man is crazy," Doolin said.

Collins had the shotgun ready, but his eyes said he wasn't so sure he wanted to use it.

"Dead women aren't so bad if they're still warm," Dutch Henry. "I've seen it done."

"And done by you," Sundance said. "Everything dirty's been done by you. The rest of these men may not be so sick in the head. I'll tell you again so there's no mistake. I'll kill these girls before I let you have them."

Sundance spoke to the others without turning his head. "How about you, Collins? You want to take your pleasure with dead women? There's no way the story can't get out. Then where will you be? No decent man will drink with you, even talk to you. When the whores hear about it, they won't want you either. Answer me, Collins. Dutch is counting on you to blast me with that scattergun. You like to stick it into dead women, do you, Collins?"

Collins lowered the sawed-off. "Who the hell said anything about that? You're crazy, all right." Collins's voice cracked with an abrupt rage. "What the hell do you think I am, talking to me that way? Dead women, for Christ's sake!"

"Ah well, we still have the whiskey," Doolin said, sitting down again. Dameron looked like he was glad to join his loudmouth partner. Doolin gave him the bottle and he drank from it.

"Why is everybody looking so mad?" Sophia Germaine said.

"Looks like you'll have to settle for whiskey,

Dutch," Sundance said.

Doolin hiccuped. "Poor old Dutch," he said.

"For now I will," Dutch Henry said, drinking more whiskey. When he got it down he began to sing *Jesus wants me for a sunbeam*. He stopped the hymn singing to look at Sundance. "We're going to have it out one of these days. I guess it'll keep."

"Where's Moore?"

"Not here, friend. Back at the settlement is where that old Yankee is. When Ives and Hackett came back and said the Injuns had drove off the buffalo with fire old man Moore got mad. Teach the red varmints a lesson, Moore said, and sent ten of us to do just that." Dutch Henry pointed out past the fire. "Mr. Sundance, sir, you mind telling me what all these red niggers are doing here? Red niggers killed by other red niggers, not much sense in that. The ones had the ladies, God bless 'em, ambushed the ones was looking for them. Am I right, sir?"

"That's what happened," Sundance. "We got here and drove the renegades off. Then we got the women."

"And fine women they are, Mr. Sundance." Dutch Henry looked at Catherine Germaine. "However dirty they may be. I had a pet pig once."

"What was the pet pig's name, Dutch?"

The question came from Doolin, who dug into Dameron's ribs but got no response because Dameron was asleep, felled by too much whiskey.

"It was an Irish pig, Jimmy," Dutch Henry said. "So I called the pig Doolin. It was a coward of an Irish pig. That's why I called her Doolin."

Doolin took the bottle from his partner's yielding hands and drank what was left in it. "You say the pig was a her," he said. "You took special note of that, am I right, Dutch? I take it then that you had carnal knowledge of this she pig, as square-head farmers have been known to do."

Dutch Henry was drunk enough to start shooting. "Are you asking me did I put the pork to this pig?"

"This Irish pig," Doolin said.

Sundance gave the runty Irishman a hard look. "Drop it or I'll drop you. I was talking to Dutch before you stuck your nose in."

Dutch Henry was drunk enough to like that. "Right you are, Sundance, my friend. Life's too short. Am I right or wrong?"

"You never said a truer word," Sundance said as Dutch Henry's eyes began to close. "You see any Indians when you came down in this draw?"

Dutch Henry said, slurring his words, "Indians here? Yes, sir, Mr. Sundance. But they run off when they heard us coming. Too bad about that, sir. I would have been honored to kill a few."

Dutch Henry's head bobbed on his chest and he began to snore.

Sundance saw Catherine Germaine staring at him.

CHAPTER EIGHT

"They may not be as drunk as they sound," Sundance said when Billy Dixon came over by the fire. "You notice the two on guard aren't drunk at all. They have a whole night to try something with the women."

Dixon gripped his rifle. "They better not try anything with Sophia."

Sundance said, "She's got a sister, remember. There are two sisters."

"Oh her," Dixon said. "You can look after her, the wild one. I like the other one better."

"Sure," Sundance said. "I'll take the first watch. Wake me in four hours."

"I didn't like you saying you would kill Sophia. I don't care about the other one."

"Why not, Billy? She's been through it, too. It takes women different ways."

"Like hell! I saw her wailing over that dead savage. She took the easy way out and then she got to like it."

"Don't be so pious," Sundance said. "A lot of things you don't know about women."

"What the hell do you know about them?"

"A few things. More than you do. Now go to sleep or let me go to sleep."

"What about taking the girls back to Dodge? Lone Wolf isn't here."

"It's better that he's not. The girls are in no

shape for a long journey. If we bring them back the way they are there will be a worse outcry against the Indians."

Dixon always said what was on his mind. "Sophia's a bit addled, I guess. Keeps talking about her mother as if she's still alive."

"That's shock," Sundance said. "I'm hoping time will take care of it. Food, clean clothes may help. Look after her, Billy. You're closer to her own age than anybody here. The girl has had a bad time. They both have."

"The other one survived pretty well. It's like she took a fancy to that killer."

"That's where you're wrong. She's just as much a victim as her sister."

Sundance sat by the fire with the Sharps across his knees. The Winchester, in its beaded scabbard, lay beside him. If they came at him in a rush, the Sharps wouldn't fire fast enough. He cleaned the Colt, getting the dust out of the moving parts. Then he oiled it and reloaded. He set the hammer at half cock and spun the cylinder. It turned quietly and smoothly.

The fire of buffalo chips gave off a not unpleasant smell and they burned hotter than wood. Sophia Germaine cried out in her sleep and threw off her blanket. Dixon got up and covered her again. After that it was quiet except for the snoring of the men.

Sundance looked up when Catherine Germaine came to the fire. After four months with the renegades she seemed to move with the stealth of an Indian. Her pale eyes looked strange against the oily dirt of her face. She was more subdued now, but he wasn't sure she would stay that way. He guessed he was going to have a lot of trouble with her.

"What do you want?" he asked, knowing that soft talk wouldn't work.

"I'm not going back to Kansas," she said, staring at him. "I'm not a slave and you can't make me go where I don't want."

"You can't stay on the Plains. These men are no better than the renegades. You saw what they were like tonight."

"I saw they all wanted to have a go at me."

"Both of you."

"What difference would that make?"

"It would make a difference to your sister."

Ignoring that, she said in a dead voice, "Yesterday I had something. Now I have nothing. You killed the only man I ever cared about."

"Medicine Water was a vicious animal. The army would have hung him where they found him. That man you cared about murdered your whole family. That was just one of the things he did."

Her pale eyes were indifferent in the firelight. She smelled of sweat and dried mud. "The hell with my family. My father was a psalm-singing brute. Not a day in my life I wasn't worked from dawn till dusk. The same with my sister. He whipped her too, but I got the worst of it because he knew I hated him. That son of a bitch prayed while he used his belt on me because I wasn't working hard enough to suit him. I watched him die and I'm glad he's dead."

"What about your mother?"

"I have no feelings about her. She prayed a lot. You never saw such a family for praying. There wasn't one thing that wasn't sinful. We couldn't even go to a dance like the rest of the girls in our county. One time a boy—just a boy—gave me a necklace he made out of Mexican coins. Just a little necklace this boy made on a cattle drive. My father took it away from me and tossed it in the stove. He said only fallen women wore such sinful trash. Then he came at me with his belt. I grabbed up a shotgun and said I'd blow his head if he hit me. I guess he knew I meant it because that was the end of the beatings. From then on he never spoke another word to me. If there was something he wanted done, he'd tell my mother and she'd tell me."

"They're dead," Sundance said. "What's the use of going on about it?"

"You can say that because you didn't go through it. The minute I saw them lying dead I knew I was free. All the preaching and hymn singing was over for good."

"You didn't have to stay there and be beaten. Why didn't you leave home and find work in a town? What was there to stop you?"

Her voice remained flat, her eyes without expression. "When you have a father like that it's hard to make a break. Medicine Water made the break for me. I don't care what you say about him—he was a man."

"He'd have sold you to the Comancheros when he captured some other white woman. You'd have been a hag in a year. Your teeth would fall out from the food. When the Comancheros got through with you they'd sell you south to a Mexican whorehouse. They wouldn't get much for you. They'd get something."

"I would have settled for a year," Catherine Germaine said. "I didn't think about time. I was dirty and hungry, but I didn't have to think. One day was the same as another. We kept on moving from one place to another."

"Why are you telling me all this?"

"Because I don't want to go back to Kansas. There's nothing to go back to."

"You must have some folks there."

"My uncle is just like my father. And for all his praying he was always looking at my legs."

"You're going back just the same," Sundance

said. "Do what you like when you get there. If you're thinking about money, there's a reward posted for your return. Two newspapers and some local people posted the reward. Two thousand dollars in all. You can have my share of the money."

Catherine Germaine gave a sneering laugh. "I never thought I was worth that much. What do I have to do to earn it? Tour with a carnival show and tell the farmers how many times I was raped?"

This woman didn't want to be helped, Sundance knew. He had no way of knowing what she'd been like before her capture by the renegades. But she couldn't have been so hard and twisted in her mind.

"You don't have to stay in Kansas," Sundance said. "I'll give you the money and you can go where nobody knows you. Why don't you stop whining and think of your sister?"

"My sister is a fool. Instead of fighting back the way I did, she let my father break her spirit."

"Your sister is a nice girl."

"Meaning I'm not. I don't care what you think. Take my sister back to Kansas if you like. I'm not going."

"What do you figure to do on the Staked Plains?"

Catherine Germaine looked around at the sleeping hunters. "This must be a big outfit if they can send out this many men. How many are there? You might as well tell me. I'm going to find out anyway."

Sundance said about forty men.

"Do they have any women in this settlement?"
Sundance said no.

The sneering laugh came again. "Then I'll be their woman. I could get rich servicing forty men."

"You don't care about the money," Sundance told her. "You just want to get back at your father. You may be grown, but you have the mind of a kid. Take the money I'm offering you and leave Kansas."

She gave him a curious look. "If you don't want the reward money, why are you doing this?"

"To help stop a war. That's why you and your sister have to go back. The whole frontier is worked up about you."

"Is it now? There's a catch to your plan you don't know about. That's me. I don't give a damn what's happening in Kansas or anywhere else. You'll have to settle for simple-minded Sophia. Back in Kansas she can simper and say pretty things. The sons of bitches will like that."

Sundance shook his head. "Can't be done like that. You have to go too."

"Like hell I do. I told you I wasn't a slave or a bond servant. You can't make me do anything."

"I can make you go back. Listen to me so there's no misunderstanding. What you want or don't want isn't important. People are going to die if you aren't returned. I'll rope you to a horse if that's what it takes."

Living with the savages had almost turned her into one. Four months hadn't been long enough to make the change. But she was well on her way. It showed in her eyes.

"You won't take me any place. I'll turn these men against you. Here and back at the settlement. You think you can stand up to forty men? Men that haven't had a woman in months?"

"I won't let you be a whore to spite your father. Not here anyway."

Her mouth was set in a stubborn line. "None of your business how many men I spread my legs for. I won't go back to Kansas to be gawked at."

"You must be deaf or stupid. I said I'd give you

290

money to get away from Kansas."

Her eyes narrowed with suspicion. "How do I know this reward of yours isn't a trick?"

"I don't have printed proof, if that's what you mean. You'll just have to take my word for it."

"No," Catherine Germaine said. "I don't have to take your word for anything. I don't, you know, and hope to see you dead for what you did. That's what will happen if you try to take me from forty woman-starved men. You'll get killed and so will your friend."

She was right about the forty men. It was something he had been turning over in his mind. When it came time to leave with the girls, there would be trouble.

"What happens to your sister if we get killed?" Sundance said. "If we're dead, what's to stop them from using her, too? Your sister never did anything to you. Why does she have to suffer because you want to be a whore?"

"Sophia will have to make her own way in the world. I guess she'll get used to it. What the hell does it matter what happens to us? You were ready to shoot us tonight. Would you have done it?"

Sundance said yes.

"For our own good?"

"That's right."

"You sound just like my father."

"It would be easy to get sick of you," Sundance said. "Right now there are dozens of women captives would be glad to have your chance."

"Oh quit your preaching," Catherine Germaine said. "I'm going back to sleep."

In the morning they started back for the settlement. Catherine Germaine avoided Sundance's eyes, but she smiled at Dutch Henry, knowing he

291

was the one who would lead the others in any final showdown. Doolin, red-eyed and whiskey sick, tried to make jokes. Only Dameron made an attempt to laugh.

At breakfast Sophia Germaine ate everything Billy Dixon heaped on her plate. Sundance could see that the shock hadn't worn off and maybe it never would.

Looking at her dirty hands and ragged dress, Sophia said, "My mother would have a fit if she could see me like this. I'm badly in need of a bath, Mr. Dixon."

"We all are," Dixon said. "You sure you had enough to eat?"

"Oh Lord yes. I'm stuffed. My mother always says breakfast is the most important meal of the day. Get a good breakfast in you and you can work the whole day through, my mother always says. My mother . . ."

Sundance noticed that she never mentioned her father. Religion was a hell of a thing when it ruined people's lives.

Josiah Moore, trailed by hunters, came out to greet them when they got back. The hunters eyed the girls and whispered back and forth. Sundance knew Moore had them under some kind of control because he was the means to money. But there might come a time when money was of less importance than rape. If Moore hadn't been so greedy he would never have allowed Hanrahan to set up a saloon. Moore's love of money could get him killed or crippled if he got in the way.

"My goodness, what have we here?" Moore said. "Would these be the Germaine ladies of which I've heard so much?"

"Sundance and Billy found them wandering in the wilderness," Doolin said.

"Sundance and Billy are genuine heroes," Dutch Henry said.

"But they don't want to share," Doolin went on with his joking. "That's not very democratic, Mr. Moore."

Moore waved Doolin to be quiet. "That's no way to talk in front of ladies. I'd like to hear what went on out there."

Sundance told him about the fire, the ambush in the draw, the killing of Medicine Water.

Moore frowned when Sundance told of saving Lone Wolf and his men from being massacred. "You've been busy," Moore said. "I don't know that it was so smart to save Lone Wolf. That Kiowa is a menace. It would have been better if you had le. them fight it out. You could still have trailed the renegades."

"Nobody but Lone Wolf can prevent a war," Sundance said. "Without him West Texas will go up in flames."

"That would be terrible," Moore said, not meaning a word he said. "Oh well. What's done is done. Make yourself to home, ladies. I know you'll want to freshen up."

Moore didn't mean it as a joke, but Doolin laughed. "That's a good one, Mr. Moore."

"Be quiet, Jimmy," Moore said mildly.

"You can use my personal tin bathtub, ladies," Moore went on. "Freighted all the way from Dodge City. I'm afraid we don't have any feminine attire on the premises, but Mr. Myers has a right good supply of men's wear. You'll pay for the clothes, Sundance. I don't want to seem inhospitable, but business is business, you understand. Of course you do."

Sundance said he'd pay for the clothes.

"Good man," Moore said vigorously, rubbing his papery hands.

Moore's tin tub was in a lean-to beside the sod house where he lived by himself. It was half filled with dust from the storm. Sundance emptied it

293

and asked Catherine Germaine if she wanted to go first.

"Yes, Catherine, why don't you bathe first," Sophia said. "Mr. Dixon is going to fix me something to eat."

The hunters had gone into the saloon to talk to Moore. It was plain that Moore wasn't happy about the saving of Lone Wolf's life. It was just as plain that Moore wanted a war as much as Sheridan and the Indian Ring.

There was a three-legged iron pot to heat water for the tub. Sundance carried buckets from the creek and filled it and lit a fire of charcoal under it. The mesquite charcoal burned hot and bright in minutes. Then he went to Myer's store and got boots, socks, pants and shirts for the girls. Along with the clothes he bought a bar of yellow soap, a can of coal oil and a finetooth comb.

"The coal oil is for the lice," he told Catherine Germaine who was waiting for the water to heat.

She flared up. "You bastard! I don't have lice."

"You have lice. The coal oil is to get rid of them. The soap isn't enough. Rub the coal oil in where they are and let it soak for a bit. Then use the soap and the fine comb. Of course you'll get the cooties back if you stay on with the hunters. And maybe you'll get worse than lice. Some of these men are rotted clear through."

"Get away from me. I'll brain you with a rock if you don't get away. I don't want to listen to any more of your filthy talk."

Catherine Germaine looked like another woman when she came out of the lean-to and saw Sundance sitting on a barrel. Her yellow hair was damp, but it was bright from the washing, and now that her face was clean, freckles showed across her nose and on her cheekbones. She was dressed in a dark blue flannel shirt and brass-studded Levis. The store boots made her two

294

inches taller, and that suited her, too.

The bath had improved her looks but not her humor. "Nobody asked you to stand guard over me."

"I invited myself. Some of the boys might decide to do a little peeping."

"Let them peep. What's there to see they haven't seen before?"

"I doubt if they've seen many like you."

"You can save your sweet talk, if that's what you think it is. If you want me to spread my legs you'll have to pay like the others."

"Now who's talking dirty? At least the rest of you is clean."

"Cleaner than you."

Sundance smiled. Women, all women, were funny. They had so little to fight with in a hard world, that they tried to turn everything to their advantage.

"You're positively shining," Sundance said. "You want something to eat?"

That didn't please her either. "You don't have to watch over me like a mother hen."

"That's the first time I've been called that. I guess you'll eat when you get hungry enough."

Billy Dixon stuck his head out of his wagon. "Is the other one through with the tub?"

"What does he mean 'the other one'? You tell that bastard I have a name."

Sundance called back to Dixon. "Miss Catherine Germaine of Kansas has just finishing bathing." He looked at the girl. "Is that formal enough for you?"

She told him to go to hell.

But she went with him when he went into Hanrahan's dirt-floored saloon. There was some sort of argument going on between Moore and Dutch Henry. They broke it off when Sundance and the girl came in.

"Why 'tis an angel come down to earth," Doolin said, pretending to shield his eyes with his dirty hand.

Dutch Henry passed his tongue over his thick lips, but didn't say anything. Some of the other hunters began to act bashful in the presence of the girl, but Sundance knew that wouldn't stop them from raping her if they got the chance. All it would take to get them started was whiskey. And there was plenty of that. Buffalo hunters, most of them, were the scum of the frontier. They gloried in their dirt and drunkenness and the fact that people hated them wherever they went. There might be a few men here with some decency left. Even so, they would band together when trouble came.

"Scat boys," Moore said. "Time is money and you're not making any sitting here."

Dutch Henry, Doolin and Dameron stayed on without being told. These men and Shotgun Collins, who wasn't there, seemed to be Moore's bodyguard. They would do his bidding as long as it didn't interfere with their own plans. For the moment they were ready to follow orders.

"Mr. Hanrahan has a nice stew cooking up," Moore said. "I'm sure the young lady would like some of that."

Catherine Germaine nodded.

"You have any plans for starting back?" Moore asked Sundance.

"Not for a while. The girls need a few days' rest. I'll let you know when we're ready to leave."

"I'd like for you to do that," Moore said. "It will be pleasant to have the ladies' company in this dreary place."

Doolin laughed. "Ah it's not so dreary, Mr. Moore. We have a fine saloon and plenty of grub, even if it is buff meat. You know what I think, Mr. Moore?"

"What, Jimmy?"

Doolin looked at Catherine Germaine instead of Moore. "I'm thinking the ladies will like it so much here they'll want to stay on. Bemis can play the concertina and Farquarson the fiddle. Cripes, Mr. Moore, we could have dances and all kind of fun, if you get my meaning. How do you feel about that, Dutch Henry."

Dutch Henry wiped his mouth with the back of his hand. "I'm always for a little fun, Jimmy."

"Am I right, Mr. Moore?" Doolin said.

"Anything is possible," Josiah Moore said.

And Sundance heard in the dry Yankee voice more of a threat than anything else the others had said.

CHAPTER NINE

Dutch Henry spoke directly to Catherine Germaine for the first time. "You think you might like the rough-and-ready life, Miss Germaine?"

Catherine glanced at Sundance before she answered. There was malice in her quick smile.

"Mr. Moore says anything is possible," she said.

"Indeed it is," Moore said heartily. "Try your luck, is what I say. You never know where it will lead you. Miss Germaine, you're welcome to stay here as long as you like."

Sundance knew that Moore, cunning old bastard that he was, had detected some of the wildness in Catherine Germaine. Moore played on people's feelings, joshed them along, threatened when nothing else worked. It showed in the way he indulged Doolin and his stupid jokes. The result was that Doolin was devoted to the Yankee moneygrubber. Sundance guessed that Doolin was Moore's spy among the other men.

"What day is it anyhow?" Doolin looked around, but none of the hunters seemed to know.

"I believe it's Saturday, Jimmy," Moore said.

"By God now, isn't that a bit of luck," Doolin said. "And there I was thinking it was the middle of the week. Some week."

Moore's voice was blander than usual. "Was there some special reason you wanted to know?"

"Well sure this is. If it's Saturday why don't we have a dance? Nothing like a Saturday night dance to break the monotony, don't you know. Breaking up the floor is the best entertainment there is. A good shindig is what I miss out here on a long hunt."

Dixon came in with Sophia Germaine, yellow-haired and all clean like her sister. She wore the same clothes as her sister, except that her flannel shirt was gray.

"The lovebirds," Doolin said. "When's the wedding going to happen, Billy?"

Moore made a palms-down motion to Doolin. "Jimmy was telling us how much he liked dancing," Moore said.

"When did they ever let him into a dancehall?" Dixon got a chair for Sophia Germaine.

"If you mean the stink of the hides, sonny boy, I've been known take a bath once in a while."

Dixon sat down. "The last time you had a bath the Red River ran black."

Sundance wished to hell Dixon would drop it. There was no point in forcing trouble before they were ready for it.

Doolin ignored the insult, though Sundance knew it would stick in his crabby little brain.

"I'm a holy terror when it comes to the polka," Doolin went on as if Dixon hadn't said a word. "Not to mention the waltz and the Virginia Reel."

"How about the Irish jig?" Dixon said.

"Ah well, Billy, you know as well as I do they don't do much jigging in this part of the world. I know you're trying to get my goat, Billy boy, but you're not going to get it. I'm too full of good cheer to rise to your bait."

"You're full of something all right," Dixon said.

Dutch Henry looked at Dixon. "What's the matter with you, kid? You used to be easy to get along with. Now you're turning into a sorehead.

300

What's the matter with you? Can't you take a joke?"

"I don't like jokes, Dutch. Jokes are as dumb as the people that make them."

"Will you listen to the man," Doolin said.

"No, you listen to me, Doolin." Dixon pointed his fingers so far across the table that it was almost in the Irishman's grinning face. "You make any more jokes about Miss Germaine and me and I'll shut your dirty Irish mouth for good."

"Is that a fact now?" But Doolin didn't look so sure of himself.

Dixon said, "There's one way you can find out. Do it and we'll see what happens."

Moore hadn't said anything for a while. Sundance knew the Yankee was letting it go on, because he wanted to see how Dixon would hold up.

Now, at last, he stuck his Yankee nose in. "Peace, boys," he said. "There's no call for all this back-chat. In my opinion it's this lonesome, windy country that does it. Frazzles the nerves and sets one man agin the other. Ladies, I hope you'll allow me to apologize on behalf of my friend Jimmy Doolin. He's a man of high spirits, and sometimes he gets carried away, you understand. But the lad's heart"—Doolin wasn't less than forty—"is in the right place. Jimmy would like to have a dance and it might be a tonic for the whole lot of us."

A dance might ease the tensions, Sundance thought. At least for a while.

"What do you think, Sundance?" Moore asked.

"Depends how tired the girls are."

Catherine Germaine, looking at Sundance, spoke quickly. "I'm not tired. Not a bit."

Moore smiled at Sophia. "How about you, young missy?"

"I adore to dance," Sophia said in her light

301

voice.

Moore rubbed his hands together, a sure sign that he was pleased. "Then it's settled and we'll have our dance." He sniffed at the air and made a face. "Seems to me you fellers could do with a dip in the creek. Let the lovely ladies be an example to you. I don't know the name of the feller that said it, but he's right: Cleanliness being next to godliness, and the rest. Get a move on, boys, and I don't want to hear any grumbling or complaining. No matter what you were brought up to believe, a plunge in the creek won't kill you. Only do it downstream from where we get our drinking water. Wash out your duds wile you're at it. Plenty of sun left till sundown."

Sundance and Dixon took the girls to the creek, far downstream from the others, and Catherine complained about it.

"You've got rape on the brain," she said.

"Catherine says terrible things," Sophia said. "But she doesn't mean them. She thinks she does but she doesn't."

"I don't even want to look at you," Catherine told Sundance.

"Then look the other way."

Sophia giggled.

On the way back to the settlement Sundance motioned Dixon to drop back behind the girls.

"I'm agin all this," Dixon said. "This dumb dance."

"I don't know there's much we can do about it. I think Moore put the idea in Doolin's head. Moore pulls the strings and Doolin moves and talks. You a drinking man?"

"I like a drink. Yes."

"Don't drink tonight. If they start up I don't want you fuzzy-headed. It's plain that Moore doesn't want the girls to go back to Kansas. The longer they're missing, the worse the war talk will get."

Billy Dixon could be thick. "Why would Mr. Moore want to do that?"

"Money. That's what he lives for."

"You think Mr. Moore is that mean?"

"Not mean because he likes to be mean. Not mean like Doolin or Dutch Henry. Moore is just money mean. Hardly makes a difference which mean it is. Mean will do."

"Mr. Moore's always been pretty decent to me."

"That's because you made him money. If Moore ever goes into politics he'll give turkeys to the poor. All the poor that can vote."

Catherine Germaine turned and called back. "What's all that talking back there?"

Sundance answered. "We were just planning the decorations for your dance."

Catherine called him a name that was hard to find anywhere except privys behind saloons.

"I think she likes you," Dixon said. "When I was in a shooting contest one time an old drunk that sold hot corn to the spectators, a man that had been educated back East, and was doing fine till John Barleycorn got a hold of him, told me women, some women, like to keep the men they like hopping 'cause they like them so much. Do you get my meaning?"

Sundance smiled at Dixon. "Not when you say it like that."

"I thinks she likes you," Billy Dixon said. "You like her?"

"Since you're being so goddamned nosy, I'll have to say yes."

"All that business with the renegade doesn't bother you?"

"You should be a preacher, Billy."

"Not enough money in it," Billy Dixon said.

The dance was to be held in Hanrahan's saloon. It had the best floor and it was bigger than the other buildings. Moore and Hanrahan were talking about the cost of the beer and whiskey. Hanrahan, a large florid man, kept nodding his head as Moore talked. Hanrahan had his name on the sign outside, but Moore was the real owner.

Moore looked at Sundance and Dixon. "I declare everybody's clean enough to hold a prayer meeting. Come in, ladies. Your presence is a good influence on this bathless community."

Hanrahan started to move the chairs and tables back against the wall, so the floor would be clear for dancing. Then he swept out the cigarette ends and scraps of food that littered the place.

"I wish we had some decorations," Sophia said, looking around at the drab walls.

"Mr. Myers has ribbons and such," Moore said. "Why don't you and Billy go on down there and see what he has?"

"I'd like a beer," Catherine said.

"To be sure, young lady," Moore said. "Mr. Hanrahan, will you do the honors?"

Hanrahan filled a glass mug and brought it to the table.

"Nothing for me," Sundance said.

Hanrahan went back to blowing dust from the mugs and glasses. He wet a rag and wiped off the bottles. There was a lot of dust left when he finished.

"How do you like our little village?" Moore asked Catherine. Hanrahan was listening.

Catherine glanced at Sundance. "I like it fine, Mr. Moore."

Moore was pleased. "There may be a real town here someday."

Like hell there will, Sundance thought.

In a while Dixon and Sophia came back with spools of different colored ribbon. Sophia had picked a big bunch of prairie flowers: yarrow, monkshood, fleabane and gentians. She was smiling and happy.

"Don't the flowers smell nice?" she said to Sundance, who felt a twist of pity. His pity was mixed with a deep hatred for Josiah Moore, the miserable son of a bitch.

"They're nice flowers," Sundance agreed.

Catherine Germaine drank beer and didn't help with the decorations. Dixon, looking like a tame bull buffalo, walked around behind Sophia while she tied the flowers with ribbon and stuck them here and there in the sweat-smelling saloon.

The sun was still hot, but it would be dark in a few hours. Every time there was a gust of wind dust blew in the door and with it came the stink of the hides. Hanrahan rolled in a barrel of beer and bunged in a spigot and ran off a mug for himself.

Sophia was tying the last bunch of flowers when the two musicians came in with their instruments. Bemis was the concertina player, Farquarson carried a fiddle and bow. Bearded and shaggy headed, they were the most unlikely pair of musicians Sundance had ever seen, and by their smell they hadn't joined the others in the creek. Both men were in their late thirties, and they were lanky and somewhat stooped, like so many hunters.

"You're a bit early, boys," Moore said.

"We know that," Farquarson said in a cranky Scotch accent. "What we come for is to find out who's going to pay us."

"Pay us," Bemis said like an echo.

Moore's eyebrows went up. "This is a dance for the whole settlement. Surely you don't want to be paid?"

"Damn right we do," Farquarson said firmly. "Playing for a dance is hard work. You're always saying business is business, Mr. Moore. So how about it?"

"I'll get the boys to pass the hat for you," Moore

said. "Say a dollar a man. That'd earn you about twenty dollars apiece. That good enough for you?"

The musicians nodded.

"We better practice a while," Bemis said, dragging a long mournful wheeze from the concertina. Farquarson put the fiddle against his chest, in the manner of country fiddlers, and sawed off a few notes.

"Not in here, boy," Moore said with a pained look. "Get so you can keep in step, then come back when it's time for the dance."

The two men went out and soon the plaintive music drifted across the vast silence of the plain. It sounded to Sundance as if they were trying out a waltz. But they played so badly, it was hard to tell.

"Just so they don't sing," Moore said, getting up and rubbing his chin. "And now I think I'll run a razor over this old face of mine. Until we meet again, ladies."

Sophia giggled. Catherine didn't do anything except get another beer from the Irishman.

There was nothing else for Dixon to do, so he came over to the table. "How do you think it's going to go?" he said.

"Hard to tell," Sundance said. "I don't think real trouble will come until we leave."

"Not with me," Catherine Germaine said.

Dixon frowned. "What's she talking about?"

"Nothing. We've been having a debate and it hasn't been settled yet."

"There will be a few fights," Dixon said. "If Mr. Moore doesn't make them check their weapons there could be cutting and shooting."

"Most likely he'll tell them to leave the weapons with the saloonkeeper. You got a short gun in that collection of yours?"

Hanrahan was rolling empty beer barrels out in

back.

"I got a Sheriff's Model Colt. What have you got?"

"A five-shot English Webley. Keep your coat on and hide the short gun. I don't mean to go unarmed, no matter what Moore says. You can bet some of them will have sneak guns. Knives, too."

"You think Mr. Moore carries a gun? I never seen him with nothing but a rifle."

"Hard to tell with that baggy suit. Moore's no kind of shooter. Just don't turn your back on him if there's trouble. You're just as dead, no matter who shoots you."

Catherine Germaine drained her beer mug. "You're the one that seems to be looking for trouble. We're having a dance and you're talking murder. You're so fond of killing you think everybody is the same. If you don't want to come to the dance, why don't you go off and murder somebody?"

"I'm not getting any of this," Dixon said, staring at Catherine Germaine.

"The lady's had three mugs of beer, that's all."

Catherine banged the empty mug on the table. "I'll have three more if I feel like it."

"What you should do is get some sleep."

Sophia, still smiling, came over and said, "I think that's a very good idea, Mr. Sundance. Mr. Dixon says we can sleep in his wagon. He's got it fixed up real nice, Catherine."

"I don't sleep so good." But even as she said it, Catherine's eyelids began to droop.

Sundance went to the barrel and drew her another mug of beer. "Drink up and get some sleep."

She must have been bone-tired in spite of all her fierce energy, and she nodded off before the beer was gone.

"Poor Catherine," Sophia said.

Sundance picked Catherine up and she mumbled, but didn't wake up. Some of the men were coming back from the creek and they stared when they saw Sundance carrying the girl to the wagon. Dixon had unrolled the bedding and the two girls climbed in. Sophia covered her sister with a blanket.

"I'll just sit around till they wake up," Dixon said, picking up his rifle.

"Don't leave that short gun behind," Sundance said.

"What're you going to do?"

"Look around."

It just couldn't be done if he didn't get help from Lone Wolf, Sundance decided. Yet it had to be done; time was being used up fast. But how? He walked down to the creek and looked at the deep pool they used for their water supply. The pool was clear and had a sandy bottom. Beyond the pool the creek ran shallow again. Damming the creek farther up might work as part of an overall plan. If he could use some of Lone Wolf's men to pin them down in the settlement—if they went long enough without water—there might be a chance to finish them. But he knew that a frontal assault on the settlement would be bound to fail, not unless he had every warrior at Lone Wolf's command. That just wasn't possible because the Kiowa chief would never move his entire force and leave his villages unprotected. And once Sheridan learned that a large force of Indians was on the move, he would strike. No, somehow it had to be done with a fairly small group of fighting men. They would have to be good men—the best—because they men they would have to face would fight like tigers. Between the hunters and the Indians was a savage hatred built up over twenty years. Moore's men had all the advantages.

They had enough dried meat and canned goods to hold out for weeks; enough guns and ammunition to equip a small army. In fact, they were a small army. And if they held out long enough, Sheridan's soldiers would come with artillery and Gatling guns.

Somehow water was the key to the destruction of the hunters. None of it was clear in his mind; he knew it couldn't be put off much longer. Billy Dixon was something else he had to think about. There had to be a way to get him to break with Moore, and yet he could hardly tell him that he was planning to kill forty white men. Dixon was frontier born and bred; he would never be a party to the massacre of forty men, not even of men like these. Whatever they were, he had hunted with them, eaten with them, shared whiskey with them. He was, after all, a part of the outfit. It was too bad that Billy Dixon's misplaced sense of honor would get him killed. But there it was: it had to be faced.

And he still felt bad about Billy Dixon.

It got dark and Sundance got the stubby, five-shot .45 from his warbag. The English revolver had belonged to a woman who was dead now. He checked the loads in the cylinder and put a handful of bullets in his pocket. The five-shot was short and heavy, with tremendous stopping power. It was no good for any kind of distance shooting; a man shot at close range with the Webley went down and stayed down.

When he got to the saloon, it was filling up with hunters and skinners. Except for a few diehards who avoided soap and water at all costs, they had tried to clean themselves up. A few had even dug out fairly clean shirts and pants. Behind the plank bar, Hanrahan was busy drawing beers and setting up bottles and glasses. The two musicians came in and were greeted with a cheer.

Doolin was standing at the bar with his partner.

After knocking back a drink, he winked at Dameron. "'Tis said them fellers' music can turn a man to stone. Ah, I was only joking, boys. What will you have to drink? Whiskey, is it? Well boys, that's a very wise choice, for 'tis said Hanrahan uses beer to wash his socks, then pours it back in the barrel."

Sundance saw Dutch Henry watching him from a table by the back wall. Shotgun Collins was with him, but he didn't have his scattergun. As other men came in, Hanrahan collected their weapons and put them in a trunk behind the bar. Hanrahan looked at Sundance and he held open his fringed buckskin jacket to show he wasn't carrying a gun or a knife. The five-shot was at the small of his back, held there by his belt.

There was plenty of loud talk, but nobody paid much attention to what was being said. With the exception of Hanrahan, who was too busy making money, all their eyes kept drifting toward the door. The women were in their minds, and everything else came second.

Ten men were standing guard—Moore believed in a heavy guard—and they would be relieved after two hours. In the saloon there was an air of expectation. It was always like that at a frontier shindig; there were never enough women.

Moore came in with his old black suit smelling strongly of benzine. Most of the mud and blood had been sponged away; that was all he could do for a suit that looked twenty years old. Moore had shaved his bony face and was wearing a stiff-fronted white shirt with a brass collar stud—no tie. He got a cheer, too. He got a bigger one when he announced that he would buy a round of drinks for the house.

"One round," Moore said. "After that it's every man for himself."

"You still drinking barley water, Mr. Moore?"

Moore didn't mind tomfoolery as long as it came from Doolin. "Indeed I am, Jimmy. It's good for the digestion and you don't wake up with a bad head. But you boys drink all you want. Mr. Hanrahan can use the money."

Hanrahan gave Moore his glass of barley water. "Here's to money," Moore said.

Moore drank a mouthful of barley water and held up his hand for silence. "I've got a few words to say, boys, and I hope you don't take them in the wrong spirit. You've all worked hard and don't think I don't appreciate it. Now the time has come to have a little fun, and I'd be downright obliged if you didn't wreck the place in the process of having it. There's only two ladies and an awful lot of you. Our two musicians—take a bow, boys— are going to keep the dances short so everybody'll get a whirl around the floor. I won't stand for any horseplay, least not with the ladies. When your dance is over, that's it. Fellers that have danced can dance with other fellers that have danced. It's a fine old custom places where the ladies are scarce. Fellers that want to be asked to dance can tie a bandanna around their arm. If a feller doesn't want to dance, then leave him be. Keep it pleasant as you can. Those are the rules and I hope you abide by them."

"Sure we will, Mr. Moore," Doolin said. "But where are the ladies?"

"Strike up the band," Moore ordered. "They'll be along when they hear the music."

Bemis and Farquarson launched into a waltz that might have been *My Darling Clementine*. They sawed and wheezed away, fiddle and concertina, trying to make their music heard above the babble of voices, the crash of beer mugs on the bar. No one paid any attention to the music; eyes still drifted toward the door.

The noise dropped to nothing when the two

sisters appeared in the doorway, with Billy Dixon behind them. For all their boots and rough clothing, they were two very pretty girls. The music faltered, then resumed.

Dutch Henry got to the girls before any of the others. His coarse black hair was plastered down with grease.

"May I have the pleasure of this dance?" he asked Catherine. He didn't even look at Sophia.

Catherine gave Sundance a tight smile before she answered. "I'd be delighted," she said.

CHAPTER TEN

Dutch Henry was a terrible dancer, but he didn't seem to know it. Or if he knew, he didn't care. He knew the steps, and that was all. In contrast, Catherine was light and graceful, even in heavy boots, and she did her best to match her movements to Dutch Henry's bear-like lumbering. And she was doing more than that, Sundance knew. She smiled into Dutch Henry's swarthy face, nodding and laughing at whatever he was saying. Now and then Dutch Henry looked over her shoulder at Sundance, claiming ownership if only for the length of the dance.

A young hunter with a wispy red beard asked Sophia to dance and Dixon had to let her go. But he watched her all the time she was dancing. The hunter tried to get Sophia to talk, but all she did was make nervous little faces and look at Billy Dixon.

The music stopped and Dutch Henry went back to his table after whispering something in Catherine's ear.

"Don't you dance?" Catherine said, smiling meanly, when she came back to where Sundance was. "Or is that too silly for a big serious man like you?"

"My! You are a good dancer," she said when they were out on the packed-dirt floor. The band was bulling its way through *Lorena*.

313

"You know this is the first dance I've been to in my life," Catherine said.

"Then how did you learn to dance?"

"From a book. One time in Abilene I bought a book that showed how to do all the steps. My father didn't know about it or he would have tried to take it from me. I taught Sophia how to dance, but she was always fearful my father would catch us. I hummed the music. We danced in the barn."

"I like you better when you talk about things like that. Why don't you give yourself a chance?"

Catherine grew rigid in his arms, all her grace suddenly gone. "I told you to quit your preaching, Sundance. It won't do any good. This is where I'm going to stay."

Sundance said, "So far you've just said that to me. Dutch Henry and your other gentlemen friends would be glad to hear it."

He knew he was taking a chance, pushing her like that, yet he had to know if she really meant what she said. Her hatred for her father, if that's what it was, seemed to have been switched to him—the man giving the orders. She was a grown woman in some ways; in others more like an angry, defiant kid.

"Don't force it," she said as the music ended. "I'll say what I want to say when I feel like it. Are you that eager to get shot?"

"You could get shot too, if trouble starts," Sundance reminded her.

"That would be a big loss, wouldn't it?" Catherine, hard-faced, pulled away from him, went to the bar and demanded whiskey. Hanrahan gave it to her and she drank it in two gulps. Still sitting with Shotgun Collins, Dutch grinned over at Sundance. Sophia Germaine was dancing with one of the hunters, a big man who just walked around to the music. After she had another drink Catherine began to dance by herself. Lurching to his feet, Dutch Henry pushed a man aside and grabbed hold of her. Dutch Henry was breaking the rule laid down by Moore, but none of the other men tried to stop him. Moore, fingering the lapels of his rusty suit, just smiled.

Dutch Henry had Catherine in a bear hug and was spinning her around, sometimes lifting her off her feet. Two men, full of whiskey, got up and danced together, kicking up their heels and yelling. Dutch Henry danced Catherine closer and closer to the table where Collins sat drinking. Then, holding Catherine with one hand, Dutch Henry reached for the bottle and drank from it, spilling whiskey all over himself and Catherine Germaine. Still holding her, he pulled her head back and stuck the bottle in her mouth. She cried out in pain and Sundance started forward. Sophia heard her sister's cry and broke away from her dancing partner and ran in front of Sundance.

"Let her go, Dutch!" Sundance yelled, reaching for his gun. Collins, crazed with whiskey, jumped up and grabbed Sophia, pulling a hidden gun at the same time. Dixon fired at Collins and Sophia screamed as the bullet struck her in the neck. Dixon fired again and got Collins in the face. Sundance had his gun out, but he held back from firing. Dutch Henry's hand reached for a sneak gun, but before he could bring it out Catherine grabbed his arm and sank her teeth into it. Dutch Henry tried to shake her off, but she hung on like a wildcat. Some of the hunters had whipped out knives and were starting toward Dixon.

"Mike! Mike!" Josiah Moore shouted. "Jimmy! Shad! Get in there and stop this!"

Hanrahan reached behind him and came up with a 10-gauge shotgun with sawed-off barrels. He fired one barrel into the ceiling, then turned the fearsome weapon on the hunters. Doolin and Dameron had their guns out.

Moore was yelling so hard that spit flew from his mouth. "You're not going to wreck my saloon, you drunk sons of bitches! Stop this, I'm telling you. Let that woman go, Dutch."

"What the hell do you think I'm trying to do?" Dutch finally managed to throw Catherine away from him. She fell to the dirty floor and crawled to where her sister lay dead. Collins, just as dead, sat against the wall with his eyes open. For a moment there was no sound but shifting feet and Catherine's muffled sobbing.

Dutch Henry's pistol hung down by his side. His eyes flicked to the cocked Colt steady in Sundance's hand, then to Hanrahan's sawed-off. He pointed his left hand at Billy Dixon. "He's the one started it, Mr. Moore. He's the one killed the girl."

"Put up the gun, Dutch," Moore ordered. "All you men put away your weapons. There's going to be no more killing in here. That goes for you too, Sundance. Look, Sundance, Mike can blast you any time he likes. So put up the gun."

Sundance put the five-shot Webley in his belt and looked at Moore. "What happens now? The girl is dead and Dutch Henry killed her. I don't care who pulled the trigger. You think you can explain that away? A woman has been killed."

"I didn't kill her," Moore said.

"Dixon killed her," Dutch Henry said. "I was just trying to give the other one a drink."

Billy Dixon walked in front of Hanrahan's shotgun and took a bottle off the bar and drank from it. Now and then he looked at Sophia Germaine's body, at her sister crouched beside it. Catherine stroked her sister's dead face, talking quietly as if the others weren't there.

"What's done is done," Moore said. "What do you want me to do, Sundance? Shoot somebody? Hang somebody?"

Sundance said, "I want you to call off your guns. I'll go outside with Dutch Henry and we'll have it out. Nobody else gets in the way. The trouble between us is the reason for this."

Moore glanced at Hanrahan's shotgun. "Can't do it," he said, shaking his head. "I said no more killing. What happened here was a terrible accident. Collins grabbed the girl and got killed for it. I guess if he hadn't grabbed her she wouldn't be dead. Billy shot her and I know he feels bad about it."

Still drinking hard, Billy Dixon had a numb, frozen look on his face. Whiskey dribbled into his beard. "I didn't mean . . ." His voice became a mumble.

"Nothing can be done about it," Moore said. "We're far from law and sheriffs, so that's my decision. In the morning we'll give the poor girl a nice funeral. O'Keefe will burn a fine headboard for her. Drink up, boys. The dance is over. What the blazes is that?"

"Wagons coming," Doolin said. "Funny time of night for the boys to be coming back from Dodge."

"Maybe not," Moore said. "Yarbro always pushes his men hard. I told him to get a move on. We got to send back another batch of hides. Go see if that's who it is."

Doolin came back with a thick-bodied man wearing a shovel hat and a stringy beard. Outside there was the rattle and creak of wagons. There was shouting as the empty wagons were unhitched.

"You made good time," Moore said to Yarbro. "You bring back the supplies?"

Yarbro nodded, looking at the dead woman on the floor. "What the hell's going on here, Mr. Moore?"

"Poor girl got shot, Bro," Moore said. "Boys got wild and shooting started. No need to go into all that now. How was the trip over and back?"

Yarbro got a mug of beer from Hanrahan. "No Injun trouble if that's what you mean. That don't mean we didn't see Injuns. Saw a bunch of them late yesterday. That's how come we pushed on by night."

"Nothing else?"

Yarbro glanced at Sundance. "Something we got to talk about, Mr. Moore. The new price of hides, is what I mean."

"Sure, Bro," Moore said. "Take your beer and let's go sit over yonder. The rest of you men drink up and clear out."

"Not me," Billy Dixon mumbled. "I'm going to stay and drink."

Doolin, Dameron and Dutch Henry stayed where they were.

"Do what you like," Moore said. "But no more wildness, you hear. Come on, Bro. Let's have that business talk."

Yarbro took his beer to the table and leaned forward to talk to Moore. After a while Moore called Hanrahan over to the table. Hanrahan went back behind the bar where the sawed-off still lay. Yarbro went on talking to Moore.

Sundance went to Catherine Germaine and tried to pull her away from her sister's body. Suddenly she rose up with Collins's pistol in her hand and tried to point it at Dixon. She was screaming and she smelled of whiskey. There was blood all over her shirt. Sundance grabbed the pistol and twisted it out of her hand and hit her on the point of the jaw. He caught her before she fell and put her in a chair.

"I'm going to get a blanket for the dead girl," he told Moore.

"Good idea," Moore said.

Sundance turned and found himself facing Hanrahan's shotgun. Dutch Henry and the others drew their guns at the same time. He turned back to Moore. Moore wasn't pointing a gun, but Yarbro was. Hanging onto the bar, Billy Dixon didn't seem to know what was going on.

"You're full of tricks, aren't you, Moore?" Sundance said.

"Not as much as you, my friend."

"What do you mean by that?"

"You were sent here by Crook to spy on us, that's what I mean. And don't give me any more of that poppycock about searching for the women. I ought to have known a man like you wouldn't go piddling around for two thousand dollars. Not for as long as you said. My good friend Bro has just been telling me a few things about you."

"Such as?"

"I'll let Bro tell it," Moore said. "Seeing as he got it straight from the horse's mouth. Speak your piece, Bro. Let this dirty spy hear what you told me."

For such a rough-looking man, Yarbo had a oddly shy manner. He cleared his throat several times. "Well, it's like I told you, Mr. Moore. Coming back from Kansas we ran into a column led by Major Dodge. Crossing the Red River, is where it was. The major said he had a message, real important, for you, Mr. Moore. Said he'd been checking back on this Sundance for weeks back and finally got some answers. The major said Sundance had been in Dodge asking questions about you, Mr. Moore. You and this whole hunting party. Too many questions, so it wasn't like he was just curious. Then after he got through with his questions he went all the way to Pueblo, Colorado, to report to General Crook. Major Dodge has a friend that's an officer in Pueblo, and he gave him the whole story. Looks like Sundance has been working for General Crook the whole time."

319

Moore raised his hand to stop the wagon master. "Well told, Bro," he said. "You did good bringing me that story. Wouldn't have missed it for the world. You can deny it all you want, my friend. It's true just the same. You came here with a lying story about two captive girls. Dutch Henry warned me not to trust you. He was right and I was wrong. Apologies all round, Dutch Henry."

"That's all right, Mr. Moore," Dutch Henry said, grinning at Sundance. "We all make mistakes."

"Not any more. I'm not a man that gets mad too often, but this sneaking spy makes me mad. For my money, there's nothing rottener than a spy. That's you, Sundance. You came up here and I gave you work, food to eat, a warm place to sleep. And all the time you were plotting our ruination. That young man drinking over there let you use his bought-and-paid-for rifle."

Moore raised his papery voice. "You hear what I'm saying, Billy Dixon? I'm talking to you, Billy."

Dixon wiped his mouth and stared at Moore. "What're you talking about?"

Dixon listened while Moore explained. "That's the long and short of it, Billy," Moore said. "General Crook is the real enemy here. Nothing we can do about him—not yet, anyhow—but we do have his spy. What galls me about Crook is he's the same color we are. But that's always been his way, taking sides against his own people. The hell with Crook! All I have to know is he sent his spy up here to destroy us. How he meant to do that I have no notion. Nobody's going to drive us out of here as long as there's buffalo to be killed. Am I right, boys?"

Doolin chimed in as usual. "Damn right, Mr. Moore. Attacking this place would be the same as committing suicide."

Billy Dixon's eyes were bleary and he scratched his head with the back of his hand. "The whole thing sounds crazy."

"Crazy or not, this halfbreed meant to kill you too. You think Bro would make up a yarn just for the hell of it."

Dixon's face twitched and he stepped up close and slapped Sundance across the face. Sundance didn't move and Dixon slapped him again.

"I saved your life, you son of a bitch," Dixon yelled, blowing whiskey fumes in Sundance's face. "I thought you were my friend. I think I'm going to kill you right now."

"Easy, boy," Moore said, pushing Dixon back with the tips of his fingers. "We'll take care of the spy in our own way. Now you go and fetch a blanket for the poor dead girl. I know you had a great liking for her."

Dixon swayed on his feet. "That's the truth, Mr. Moore. Sure I'll get a blanket for her . . . least I can do."

Moore pushed him again. "Then go do it."

Dixon went out to his wagon, taking the bottle with him.

"You broke that boy's heart, Sundance." Dutch Henry grinned and Doolin sniggered. "What do you want done with him, Mr. Moore?"

"I'm figuring that."

"What is there to figure?"

Moore rubbed his hands together, always a sign that he was pleased with his own thoughts. "I want him dead, but not in the settlement. My thought is for some of you boys to take him down to the lowlands and make it look like he was killed—scalped and mutilated—by Injuns. His Injun friends. Crook's Injun friends. How's that for an idea?"

"It's a corker, Mr. Moore," Doolin said. "If that ain't justice, I don't know what is. But what about the girl?"

"Her too," Moore said. "What's the matter,

Dutch Henry? You got something agin killing the girl? I see her as no better than a dirty squaw."

Dutch Henry looked at Catherine Germaine, who lay unconscious in the chair, and passed his tongue over his lips. "Squaw woman or not, she's all we got."

Sundance bunched his fists and Hanrahan raised the scattergun.

"Sorry to disappoint you, Dutch Henry," Moore said. "She goes with the halfbreed. When you take them down, make you leave them where the army will find them. I want the Injuns to get the credit for it."

Dutch Henry wasn't ready to agree. "We could kill her when we pull out of here and go back to Kansas. Hell! We can say we found her dead on the trail. Meanwhile, we can make use of her for the next two months."

Moore considered Dutch Henry's idea and decided against it. "Was she less crazy and wild I might go along with you, lad. There would be killing and more killing if she stayed her. I didn't know how wild she was till I saw her tonight. Don't argue about it. I say she goes with the halfbreed."

Doolin sniggered, a sound that Sundance had come to hate. "You don't mind they have fun with her on the way?"

"Just so they make it look good when the time comes," Moore said. "Anything else is a bonus."

Billy Dixon came in carrying a blanket, and they watched him while he wrapped Sophia Germaine's body in it. Blood dripped on the floor. He lifted the body without effort and started for the door.

"Hey, Billy," Doolin called out. "You forgot the other one. You want to tuck her in too?"

Billy Dixon spoke in a dead voice, with his back turned. "The hell with her. The hell with you, you

Irish bastard."

"You'll say that once too often, Billy boy."
Doolin had a cocked pistol in his hand, so he felt
safe enough.

Moore told Doolin to be quiet. "Go on, Billy. See
to the girl."

"The poor lad," Doolin sneered after Dixon
went out.

"Oh for Christ's sake, will you put a cork in it?"
Josiah Moore looked old and gray-faced. Murder
wasn't his usual line of business—just grubbing
for money. "No more of that talk, Jimmy. It's not
needed and not wanted, you understand. It's bad
enough we have to do this without joking about it.
All right, Jimmy me boy?"

"Sure thing, Mr. Moore," Doolin agreed.

"You may kill us but you'll get yours," Sundance said to Moore. It was a stupid thing to say,
but he said it. There was more hope than truth in
the statement.

Josiah Moore allowed himself a tired smile.
"You think I'm going to get mine? No such thing
is going to happen, and you know it. There's a
popular notion that men that do bad things come
to bad ends. Me, I plan to die in bed at the age of
ninety, surrounded by all my grandchildren. You
just can't take what's coming to you, Sundance. I
don't know why that is. You been asking for it a
long time."

"Longer than that," Dutch Henry said.

Josiah Moore rubbed his eyes and yawned.
"Lock them in the shack where Hanrahan stores
the beer. Tie them good, hands and feet. Guard
them till it gets light. You'll be in charge of this,
Dutch Henry. Take a couple of men and get an
early start. I'd like to get this over with. Then we
can get back to making money. That's what we
came for, boys, and nobody's going to stop us. But
listen to me. I'd like the halfbreed and the girl

gone by the time I get out of bed."

Dutch Henry jerked his thumb toward Catherine Germaine. "Pick her up and carry her," he ordered Sundance.

Outside, Dutch Henry dug his pistol into Sundance's back. "Why don't you drop the squaw woman and make a run for it? You're supposed to be so smart, why don't you do that? You'll be wishing you had once I get you out on the trail. My dear sweet Jesus! When that time comes you'll beg for a bullet in the brain. Moore says kill you first, then scalp you and cut off your balls. But who says you have to be dead when that's done?"

"Hey, Dutch," Doolin said. "All Moore said was kill him. That other talk . . . you don't have to talk like that. Moore said nothing about torture."

"What's it to you? You won't be there. You'll be right here spying for Moore and kissing his ass, like always." Dutch Henry pushed Sundance again. "You sure you don't want to make a run for it, red nigger? Make a break for it and I'll kill you quick for old times' sake. Case you don't recall the old times, I'll remind you. San Carlos is old times. You near to got me that time. Now I got you."

"Moore said to wait," Doolin said.

Dutch Henry spat. "Moore says. Moore says. Why not? I can wait. The halfbreed will have that much more time to think. So will I. I know a few tricks even the Injuns don't know. You got the goddamned key, Doolin?"

Hanrahan's storehouse was a windowless shack made of split logs. It had a log ceiling and that was topped by strips of sod like the rest of the buildings in the settlement. Doolin got the padlock loose from the hasp and went inside to put a match to a lantern hanging at the end of a chain. The storehouse stank of stale beer; empty beer barrels stood against the back wall. Otherwise, the shack was empty.

Dutch Henry held his gun on Sundance while Doolin roped his hands and feet. Catherine Germaine lay on her back on the dirt floor, damp from beer dregs. She muttered when Doolin finished roping Sundance and started on her. While he was roping her wrists together Dameron came in.

"What the hell do you want?" Dutch Henry said, looking at Catherine Germaine.

Dameron said, "Mr. Moore said I should stand the first watch. Mr. Moore says I'm soberer than you fellers."

Dutch Henry spat on the floor. "What's the real reason, Dameron?"

"He doesn't want you starting up with the girl. Just lock them up and guard them, Mr. Moore says. Do what you like on the trail, Mr. Moore says."

Dutch Henry spat again. "You're beginning to sound like Doolin. What if I decide to start up with the girl? I mean here, tonight."

"Mr. Moore wouldn't like that a lot," Dameron said. "The rest of the boys will want to make use of the girl, if you do. They're not asleep, Dutch. Nor likely to be. Mr. Moore says he don't want the girl killed by rape. That's what'll happen if all the men take turns with her. You'll have a lot of guns pointing at you, maybe killing you, if you go ahead with what you're thinking. In the settlement, is what Mr. Moore means to say."

"How about your gun, Dameron?"

"I work for Mr. Moore."

"Me too," Doolin said, standing up. "You'll have all the chances you want, Dutch. Out on the trail you can have this woman for breakfast, dinner and supper. Do what Mr. Moore says and get some sleep. That's what I'm going to do. Shad here will watch them good."

"That's the truth, Dutch," Dameron said.

Dutch Henry, still half drunk, winked at Dameron. "Well I know that's true, don't I, Shad. You never did care for women, is what I recollect about you. Why should you, me boy? You got all the woman you want in Doolin. Now will you be so good as to tell me, is that truth or falsehood?"

"You got a dirty mouth," Dameron said, angered beyond his fear of Dutch Henry. "However did you get such a dirty rotten mouth?"

Dutch Henry hiccuped. "It's a gift," he said.

The door of the shack banged shut, and after that there wasn't even a glimmer of light. Lying on the floor beside Catherine Germaine, Sundance didn't try to wake her. If she woke up up total darkness, she might start screaming. He heard Dameron moving outside. Even if he could work free of the ropes, Sundance knew there was no way out of this place. Not without help. He felt Catherine stirring beside him.

He rolled close to her until his mouth was next to her ear. "It's Sundance," he said. "Don't scream and don't cry out when you open your eyes. You can't move your arms or legs because you're tied. So am I. Do you know what I'm saying?"

He kept on saying it.

Even so, she struggled furiously when she found herself in darkness. But she didn't scream. She remained still for a while.

"Sophia's dead," she whispered at last. "It's clear now in my mind. Sophia's dead."

"She's dead. Keep your voice down. We're in a storehouse behind the saloon. You better know all of it."

Her voice didn't hold much interest. "Tell me anything you like. I don't care. Are they going to kill us?"

"They mean to. Moore's plan is to have men take us down to the lowlands. Kill us, blame it on the Indians."

At first he thought she was crying when her

326

body began to shake. Then he realized she was shaking with silent, hysterical laughter. He bumped her with his thigh and told her to shut up.

But she continued to shake. "What's the matter? You afraid to die?"

"Nobody wants to die."

"I don't care if I die. I don't care what happens to me. You want to know why?"

"Might as well."

Catherine Germaine began to cry and there was nothing to do but wait until she had cried herself out.

"Sophia wouldn't be dead if not for me," Catherine said. "A month back Medicine Water and his men killed some whiskey traders and stole their wagon. A whole wagonful of whiskey. They stayed drunk for a week, more than a week. Couldn't walk, couldn't ride. They drank and slept, drank and slept. We could have escaped at any time. Took ponies and escaped. At least I knew we could. Sophia didn't know that—my sister didn't know anything—but I did. I stayed because I wanted to stay. And now my sister is dead."

"So she is."

"I know what you think of me."

Sundance said, "All I know is we're in here waiting for morning."

"You hit me, knocked me out," Catherine said. "That was a rotten thing to do."

"You were trying to kill Billy Dixon. Listen to me. You have to listen to me. Dixon's bullet may have killed your sister, but Dutch Henry made it happen. Or Moore, or Sheridan and his connivers—or maybe you."

"You think we're going to die?"

"There's a fair chance of that."

The wind had been rattling the padlocked door, but now there was another sound. Something falling. Maybe a body. Sundance knew it could be Dutch Henry come back to pay a visit, with his pants unbottoned, a pistol in his hand.

"I'm afraid, Sundance," Catherine whispered. "Please don't let them kill me. I thought I didn't care if I died and now—"

He bumped her with his thigh and she stopped talking. A key grated in the lock and the man who opened the door held it so that it wouldn't bang. Now there was some light and Sundance knew it was Dixon. It was Dixon and none too steady on his feet, and when he came in, leaving the door open, dull light shone on the knife in his hand.

"I hit Dameron on the head," Dixon said, kneeling beside them. "You have to get out of here. This is the last chance you'll get."

Sundance held up his hands and Dixon cut the ropes that bound them together. Then he gave the knife to Sundance and let him cut the ropes around his ankles.

"Make it quick," Dixon said. "Dutch Henry is still up and around, still drinking."

Sundance cut the ropes that bound Catherine Germaine. She sat up rubbing her wrists, but remained silent. Sundance helped her to her feet.

"What about the rest of the men?" Sundance asked, rubbing his own wrists.

"Some asleep, not the whole lot. They know what Dutch Henry has in mind. They'll follow his lead. You have to get away from here. Take Dameron's beltgun and rifle and get away from here. You don't have much time. I didn't dare touch your stallion. He'll come if you call?"

"He'll come," Sundance said. "You coming too?"

Dixon's breath was foul with stale whiskey. "Too late for that. I killed your sister, Miss Germaine. I liked her more than you know, but she's dead because of me. I'd do anything to bring her back. When you get back to Kansas, tell the truth of it."

"Don't be a fool, Billy," Sundance said. "Nobody can fault you for what happened here."

"I'd fault myself."

"That's what I'll do all my worthless life," Catherine Germaine said. "But I'm going anyway. If he doesn't want to go, let him alone."

"Too much talk," Dixon said. "Take Dameron's pistol and rifle and go."

Sundance stooped to pick up Dameron's rifle. "Dameron's dead," he said to Dixon. He stuck the dead man's pistol in his belt.

"You killed him, that makes a cover for me," Dixon said. "Get out of here, Sundance. I'm telling you for the last time. I don't know what to think about you. Everything Moore says isn't a lie. You were just as ready to kill me as the rest of them. I'm warning you—don't come back here, or I'll kill you myself."

Now Billy Dixon was gone and they were close to the corral. In all the houses there were lights. A bottle shattered against a wall and there was loud laughter.

Sundance told Catherine to stay where she was while he opened the corral gate. He called to Eagle and the rest of the horses moved uneasily. Eagle came forward at a walk. There was no time to find the saddle. Sundance was putting Catherine up when the rifleman fired from the watchtower and killed her. She was still falling when Sundance vaulted onto Eagle's back and he was nearly clear of the settlement when the rifle in the tower boomed again. The bullet burned a crease on the stallion's rump, but he kept running. Behind him Sundance heard men running from the houses. Bullets sang around him as he rode into the darkness.

Once he was clear of the settlement, he knew

there was no way they could overtake him. So for now he was safe, but there was no consolation in the thought. The two girls were dead and Moore was stronger than ever. Now he was alone on the Staked Plains, without water, without food, carrying borrowed guns that he hadn't tried yet.

But no matter what happened, he vowed he'd come back.

CHAPTER ELEVEN

There wouldn't be any more buffalo hunting for a while. Moore would send out all the men he could spare to look for him, and he wished the Winchester he had taken from Dameron was a buffalo gun with a scope. With the scoped rifles, they could reach out and kill him at incredible distances. He had done the same sort of shooting himself. But the big rifles weren't the only advantage they had—they had water.

A man could go for weeks without food, but not many days without water. All the old tales about men sucking pebbles and coins were true enough in their way. But after a day or two of that, a man was finished.

Darkness still covered the Plains; it would be morning in another hour. With enough water he could outdistance them at any time. Eagle could run like the wind—if he had water.

So he took it fairly slow as a means of conserving the stallion's enormous strength. For now he stayed on the trail that went down to the lowlands and from there back to the Red River and Kansas. He knew there was no water anywhere along the wagon trail. This wasn't true desert country, but a man could go many days and many miles without finding enough water to wet his lips. In winter there might have been snow; now, in early July, the Staked Plains were swept by hot winds by day, cold winds by night. And there was no water.

What he had to do was find a way back to the creek without being killed. By now there would be men strung out along the creek; their orders would be simple: kill him on sight.

There was no way to know how long they would hunt for him. Maybe not more than a day or two. Josiah Moore didn't see him as that much of a threat, not by himself. Moore was sure that nothing could drive him from the settlement. But he knew he was just guessing; there was no telling what Moore would do.

Resting Eagle along the trail, he listened for sounds of pursuit. There were none. That didn't mean they weren't just a few miles back. Dutch Henry knew how to handle horses so they'd make the least noise. Doolin was just as good.

The need for water wouldn't make itself felt until the sun burned hot in the sky. There was dust on the wind—always dust on the Plains in summer—and it gritted between his teeth. There was hardly any shade on the Plains; in the few patches of broken country there were a few caves and rock overhangs.

He left the trail about ten miles from the settlement and rode south across flat country. That would take him back to the creek at some point.

He wasn't glad to see the sun come up; it would be a long day before it set again. During the long hours of daylight he would never know when some scoped rifle had him in its sights. Five hundred yards was nothing to a big Sharps with a scope. It could reach out so far that he would never know the man who killed him.

But what would he do even if he found water? All he could do was drink as much as he could, let Eagle do the same. Without a canteen the thirst would come back before many hours.

After three hours he knew he was close to the

creek, where it made its meandering way down to flat country. Here, closer to the edge of the immense plateau, there were small canyons walled by cliffs. A day or so past there the drop to the lowlands would begin.

He rode through a waterless canyon, but after it curved south for a mile, it came to a dead end, and he had to backtrack. He crossed a wide expanse of shale that sloped down to the canyon wall. When he finally came to the creek it ran deep through the rocks, and it took him a while to find a way down. He knew they could be waiting anywhere along the creek.

So far south of the settlement, the creek was more like a small river. He led Eagle down to a sandy place that made a small beach below the rocks. He watched while Eagle drank, then he lay on his belly and drank himself. The water ran over jagged rocks, and that was the only sound. Out of the wind it was hot by the creek; he drank until he couldn't drink any more.

If it had been possible, he would have stayed in the creekbed. Instead, he had to lead Eagle back up into the wind. After that he followed the creek as best he could, staying as close as he could; but there were times when he had to ride out far to find a way across great fissures in the rock that went down to the water. Right now his only plan was to stay alive, to find a place where he could hole up for a few days, maybe longer. He could trap small game or kill it silently with the throwing hatchet. Above all, he had to make Moore think that he was gone from the Plains.

During the day he checked his backtrail, scanning the country behind him with binoculars. But there was nothing to see. Toward afternoon the country ran on a downslope and after he picked his way through more than a mile of rocks he saw a narrow canyon, well grassed and dark even in

333

the sun. There were cliffs on one side of it, a broken slope on the other. The creek ran through it and out through a V-shaped opening at the far end.

From the place he entered the canyon, it took him more than half an hour to get to the bottom. It wasn't until he got down on the flat that he saw it would have been easy to come around the side of the broken slope from the south. He let Eagle drink and moved on into the shade of the cliffs. From the creek there were stepped-back slopes that went up to the base of the cliffs. He was starting up, looking for a cave, when a rock rolled down in front of him. He was reaching for his beltgun when he saw the rifles pointing at him. He took his hand away from the gun and put his hands up.

Lone Wolf came out from behind a rock with a rifle in his hands. He was limping badly from the thigh wound he had suffered in the ambush in the badlands.

"Why have you come here, Sundance?" he said.

"I am trying to stay alive," Sundance said.

The Indians with Lone Wolf were mostly Dog Soldiers of the Southern Cheyenne, fierce, muscular men with suspicious eyes. The few Kiowas there were the men who had survived the ambush. Sundance recognized all of them. They stared at him with flat eyes, but it was the Dog Soldiers who showed the most hostility. They didn't know who he was, not yet, but they knew he was dressed like a Cheyenne, and it puzzled them. There were at least twenty-five of them.

Lone Eagle gave Sundance a leather bag of dried buffalo meat, and he ate while the Dog Soldiers watched him over the barrels of their rifles.

"They think you have led the buffalo hunters to

this place," Lone Eagle said.

"If they're close behind they mean to kill me," Sundance said. He told the Kiowa what had happened at the settlement, the dance, the killing of the girls. He told him about the wagonmaster named Yarbro.

"Moore will blame the killing of the girls on your people," Sundance said. "He will send the lies back to Kansas. The men he sends will swear to the lies. Then there will be war."

"It had to come," Lone Wolf said. "I brought the Dog Soldiers to the Plains to continue to search for the women. A small force, but these men are the best fighting men on the South Plains. Now we will attack the settlement and Moore will have his war."

"You couldn't take the settlement with three times as many men. More than that. It's too well defended. I'm telling you the war can be prevented."

"But you say Moore will send men back to Kansas with lies."

"Yarbro and his wagons will lay over for a few days," Sundance said. "The hides they send back have to be checked for rot. Rotten hides don't bring any money. Then after the hides are checked, they have to be loaded."

"You say a few days?"

"All right. Maybe two days at most."

"We can ambush the wagons after they leave. There cannot be so many men with the wagons," Lone Wolf said.

"The settlement is more important. If we move now the settlement and the wagons can be wiped out. Even with the rifles your men have, it can be done."

Sundance looked at the rifles pointing at him. Some had repeaters, some of them new. The others were armed with old Henry repeaters, a favorite of the Indians because of its bright brass frame. The Henry was a handsome weapon, but not too reliable when it got old. A few Dog Soldiers carried Spencer carbines. Two Dog Soldiers were armed with revolvers. All in all, this was not a formidable array of weapons when compared to the big rifles of the hunters.

"We will have better weapons tomorrow," Lone Wolf said. "Comancheros are coming from the south with guns for my people. A rider came to say they are on their way. Early tomorrow."

"Comancheros this far north?"

"I sent word to them. They will be well paid. We hate the Comancheros, but we deal with them."

Sundance knew all the Indians on the Southern Plains hated the dreaded Comancheros, all the scattered bands of renegades—Mexican, half-breed, white—who traded and plundered throughout West Texas. They traded in women, horses, guns, whiskey—anything to make a dirty dollar. But they had their uses. They supplied guns to the Indians, white slaves to the Mexican whorehouses; their strongolds at the far southern tip of the Staked Plains were a haven for killers and outlaws from both sides of the border.

An idea formed quickly in Sundance's mind.

"Why pay them at all?" he said. "Why not take the rifles and kill them?"

"Why do you say this? You know that is not how trading is done. Say what is in your mind."

Sundance said, "If the Moore settlement is wiped out somebody has to be blamed for it. The Comancheros are capable of such an attack. To get the buffalo guns would be reason enough. There are many other guns there, but the buffalo guns with the telescopes would fetch the highest price. You know how much rifles like that would fetch in Mexico?"

"And in Texas," Lone Wolf said. "You are

speaking of great treachery, Sundance. The Comancheros have kept their word in their own way."

"They keep their word as long as it suits them. They would turn on you like lobos if there was enough money in it. Think of this. How many times have they traded guns that were no good, traded whiskey that drove your people blind. Far south and west of here they have made slaves of Hopis and Pimas and sold them to the haciendas in Sonora. Kill these men who are coming and take the guns. You think the guns will be any good?"

Lone Wolf nodded. "Yes. They know I am not some drunken sub-chief. They have promised good guns. You say blame the attack on the Comancheros. How would the Comancheros get close enough to do that? The big rifles would kill them as surely as any other men."

Sundance said, "They'd get close enough because they're traders. They could say they had young Indian women to sell. They could have horses. Any reason is good enough. It's well known that Moore will deal with anyone."

Lone Wolf thought for a while. "This attack, how can it be made? If there is a long siege we will be in more danger than they are. If they counter-attack—I have a force of twenty-six men—what will happen them?"

"It can't be a real siege," Sundance. "It will have to be done fast, or not at all. First, we will cut off their water supply. It comes from this creek, far up on this creek. They get their water from a deep pool down the slope from the settlement. If the creek runs dry only the water in the pool will remain."

"Dam the creek?"

"If it can be done."

"But the water will remain in the pool."

337

"Until the sun dries out the pool."

"But it will remain for a while. It will remain for many days even with the sun."

One of the Dog Soldiers yelled and ran down to the creek where a pony was grazing in a patch of locoweed. The pony whinnied crazily as the Dog Soldier whipped it away from the poisonous weeds.

That was it, Sundance thought. That was how they would do it.

"We will poison the water in the pool," he said. "We will drive the hunters crazy with locoweed. You know it drives horses crazy. There are horses that like the craziness so much that they hunt for the weed. Some can be cured of the craving. Others crave it so much they have to be shot."

Lone Wolf looked at the pony now inching back toward the patch of weeds. The Dog Soldiers drove it away with rocks.

"It sounds like madness," Lone Wolf said. "I do not think it can be done. You have done this, or heard of it being done?"

Sundance shook his head. "I will have to think about it. What about the Comancheros?"

"You must think about the weed. I must think about the Comancheros. You are welcome in my camp, but the Dog Soldiers will not look on you with kind eyes when they learn who you are. My Kiowas know, and they will tell them. You must be ready for whatever happens. Are you ready?"

"Ready enough," Sundance said.

Still watched by the Dog Soldiers, Sundance went down to the patch of locoweed by the creek. He picked one of the purple flowers and crushed it between his fingers. The crushed flower had a sharp alkaline smell and its juice left a purple stain on his fingers.

The Dog Soldiers were camped in a huge cave under the hang of the cliff. It was getting dark and

Lone Wolf was sitting by a fire in the middle of the cave. The smoke went up through a fissure that went to the top of the cliff. Tied-together blankets covered the narrow entrance to the cave and prevented the firelight from being seen. The Dog Soldiers sat in silence, watching every move Sundance made.

"Do any of them speak English?" Sundance asked.

"None," Lone Wolf answered.

"Then we can talk. You asked how the pool can be poisoned. It can be done if we find enough locoweed and take the juice from it. The poison will have to be strong, the pool is deep."

"I say it is madness," Lone Wolf said. "I think you are a madman to say it."

"War is madness," Sundance said. "You will not take a chance to stop this coming war? Think what it will be like. You can't retreat to the south, because there you will have to face the Apaches. If you get as far as the border, there will be the Mexicans and more Apaches. There will be the Texas Rangers, the Texas militia."

"Yes, I fear the militia more than the others," Lone Wolf said. "The volunteer soldiers are the worst. They are farmers and ranchers who want to take our lands."

"Take the chance, Lone Wolf. There is nothing to be lost by following my plan. There is no way I can do it alone. Moore's settlement isn't just a lot of sod houses. It's a sign that men like Moore can do what they like. The law hasn't stopped him, and the army hasn't stopped him. There is only you and me and your twenty-six men."

"And they don't even trust you, Sundance."

"They trust you, Lone Wolf."

"My Kiowas trust me because they know me. The Dog Soldiers of the Cheyenne are my allies. That is not the same thing. If they did not need the

Kiowas, they would not be our allies. They have not forgotten the wars we fought before the white men came to this country."

"But they obey you."

Lone Wolf smiled bitterly. "They obey me, but they watch me. Some of them would like me to make a mistake. It is the same as in the white man's armies. Often the man who commands is more hated than the enemy. If I follow your plan, and it fails, the alliance between the Cheyenne and the Kiowa may come to and end. If there is a war, a broken alliance would be bad for everyone."

"Then don't let it happen," Sundance said.

"All right, I will follow your plan. Even if it takes me to my death. We will commit this act of treachery toward the Comancheros. We will ambush them when they come. All will die."

"I'd like to keep a few alive," Sundance said.

"They will be killed when we attack the settlement. Their bodies will be left for the soldiers to find."

Lone Wolf stared into the fire. "The buzzards will feast on the bodies before the soldiers come."

"The buzzards won't eat their clothes. There will be no dead Kiowas, no dead Dog Soldiers to say how the hunters were killed. You will take the bodies far away."

"It is a strange way to fight," Lone Wolf said.

"We have to fight any way we can. The only way to win is to win."

Lone Wolf stared at Sundance, at his copper skin and light blue eyes. "If the attack fails and there is a war, will you fight against us, if you survive? That is just a question. You will not survive if the attack fails. The Dog Soldiers will be too many for you."

Sundance had asked himself the same question a number of times. In the past he had scouted for

340

the army during several bloody Indian campaigns. In Sonora. In the Arizona desert. On the North Platte. But in all those campaigns he had served under Crook, a soldier who waged war only to end war. But Crook had no part in this. Sheridan outranked Crook and would make sure he stayed with the mapmaking expedition in the Colorado mountains. Everything had changed, he thought.

Sundance said, "If there is a war I hope to live long enough to fight in it. But this time I will fight for the Indians, if that is possible. What I learned from the army I will use against it. I will show your men how to fight in the white soldier's way."

"This will bring great sadness to your friend Three Stars," Lone Wolf said.

"I don't think so. Three Stars will understand my reasons. Maybe it would have been better if I had fought the army all these years."

"You will never see Three Stars again if you live to fight with us. You will be a hunted man for as long as you live. There will be no amnesty, no reservation for you. The army will hang you."

"It hasn't happened yet," Sundance said. "Neither has the war. Will you tell the men about the ambush tonight?"

"In the morning," Lone Wolf said. "If I tell them now, they will have the whole night to think. Some will find arguments to oppose the killing of the Comancheros. Some of our people—renegades or not—are with the gun-runners and whiskey traders. The Dog Soldiers hate the Comancheros, but they like the whiskey they bring."

"We can't let them get at the whiskey. I know what you're thinking. It has to be done just the same."

Lone Eagle smiled. "We may have our own war before we leave this canyon. I will sleep now. I hope you will be alive in the morning. If the Dog

341

Soldiers decide to kill you, there is nothing you can do but die."

Sundance rolled himself in his blankets and was asleep in minutes. There was no use being on his guard, so he slept well. He woke up once during the night, but the cave was quiet except for the sounds of sleeping men. The cave smelled of sweat and the grease the Dog Soldiers smeared on their bodies to make it hard for an enemy to get a hold during a hand-to-hand fight. He went back to sleep.

The sun was coming up when he went outside; it was good to get the smell of the cave out of his lungs. The Dog Soldiers standing guard looked at him without expression, but they knew who he was by now. Watched by the guards, he went down to the creek and drank from it. Then he scrubbed his body with clean river sand. The Dog Soldiers stared at the many scars on his body. He knew the scars that interested them most were the scars put there by his initiation into Cheyenne manhood. They knew the scars, and what they meant, for they bore them, too.

There was no sun at the bottom of the cliff where Lone Wolf had called the men together to tell them about killing the Comancheros. Listening, Sundance decided that the Kiowa was a pretty good leader. Before he got to the part about the killing, he reminded the Dog Soldiers of the many crimes the Comancheros had committed against all the tribes on the Plains. He said they feasted on war, thrived on misery.

"Now they are far from their own country, and we will kill them," Lone Wolf said.

A Dog Soldier, taller than the others, stepped forward to challenge Lone Wolf's decision. All the Dog Soldiers were dangerous men; to Sundance, this one looked more savage than the others. His face was intelligent but set in a permanent scowl.

"Speak, Long Rifle," Lone Wolf said.

"If we kill these men the others will not trade with us." Long Rifle clenched his fist and raised it in the air, a gesture of defiance and anger. "We have need of many more rifles. Where will we get them if not from the Comancheros? What we take from dead soldiers and the ranches will not be enough. You are saying we must kill the only men who can keep us supplied."

Lone Wolf pointed to the walls of the canyon. "They will die here and word of their deaths will never leave here. This place is far from their country. Other Comancheros will never come here. No one will ever come here. Not even the buzzards will find them. Before we leave here the bodies of the Comancheros will be deep in the cave."

"There is no honor in this," Long Rifle shouted.

"Honor means nothing to the Comancheros. Would you pay for guns when there is no need?" Lone Wolf spat his contempt for the other man's foolishness. "We will keep the money—the gold—and use it to buy more rifles. If there is a war we will need all we can get."

"Are you saying there will not be a war?" This time it was Long Rifle's turn to spit.

"War or no war, we will need rifles. The more rifles we have, the stronger we are. Now and always. I say we will kill the Comancheros and take the rifles. And not just the rifles but their horses, gunbelts, everything they have. The Comancheros wear gunbelts stitched with silver and gold. There will be money in their pockets, gold coins hidden in their boots. Would you pay for all this, Long Rifle?"

"We will do what you say," Long Rifle said, narrowing his eyes. "But the Cheyenne is not deceived by the clever tongue of the Kiowa. I think there are other meanings behind your words. We will make you sorry if there are too many meanings."

Lone Wolf shouted in sudden anger, "You will not threaten me. I am principal chief of all the Kiowas and Comanches."

Long Rifle spat again. "There are no Comanches here and only a few Kiowas. Here you are chief if we say you are chief."

"Then what do you say, Long Rifle?"

"For now you are chief and we will do what you say. What is the plan you have made?"

"There is no plan," Lone Wolf answered. "Some men will show themselves so the Comancheros will feel no suspicion. The rest will hide in the rocks and kill them. I want three Comancheros kept alive. That will be explained to you after the others are dead. They will be coming soon and we must be prepared."

Lone Wolf sent one of the Kiowas to the end of the canyon to signal the arrival of the Comancheros.

"Around the side of the far slope is the only way they can come in," Lone Wolf said. "One of my men is with them and will show them the way."

"How many men and wagons?" Sundance asked.

"Some wagons," Lone Wolf said. "But always the Comancheros travel together in large bands. That is their protection. All will be heavily armed. They will fight well if we give them a chance. If they get into cover, it will take many hours and cost many lives before they are killed."

"Then we have to get them in the first few minutes. When will you tell the Dog Soldiers about the rest of the plan? The locoweed?"

"When they have the possessions, the horses, the guns of the Comancheros. When they have food and tobacco, that is the time I will tell them. If they do not obey me then there can be no plan."

One of the Dog Soldiers shouted and Sundance saw the lookout at the end of the canyon waving a white cloth tied to the end of his rifle barrel. Lone Wolf raised his rifle above his head and signaled back. The lookout climbed down from the rocks and started back along the creek.

Lone Wolf limped up the slope to a position where he could be seen. Three of the Kiowas stayed with him. Sundance ran up into the rocks where the Dog Soldiers were already in position.

Nothing stirred for a long time, then there was the rumble of wagons as they came around the side of the slope. A good part of the slope was flat, but there were places where the ground was broken, and the wagons could move only a few yards at a time. Mexican-hatted men rode behind the three wagons, holding them in place with ropes wound around their saddlehorns. Sundance counted fifteen men, not sure whether there were others concealed under the canvas tops of the wagons. He saw the Kiowa who had guided them in.

A Comanchero on a spirited white horse rode out in front of the wagons and came down the slope at a reckless pace. At the bottom he waved to Lone Wolf and waited for the wagons to get down. With the brakes on and the guy ropes holding them in place, it took another five minutes to get the wagons to safe ground.

Sundance could see the leader's face as he got closer. It was a brutal face, swarthy and jowled. A thick mustache divided it like a bar. The leader's silver stitched sombrero glittered in the sunlight. He wore an embroidered vest and matching pistols with ivory handles. The wagons were coming along the side of the creek. Another few minutes.

Lone Wolf, limping badly, started down the slope. Sundance wanted to call him back. Then he

345

knew that Lone Wolf was doing what had to be done. If he hung back too close to the rocks, the Comanchero leader might get suspicious. These men lived their reckless lives in the shadow of the hangman's rope; for them suspicion was as natural as breathing.

The leader waved the wagons to a halt and rode forward to greet Lone Wolf. Sundance raised his rifle and knocked the leader out of the saddle. The Dog Soldiers opened fire at the same time, killing men right and left. Lone Wolf had thrown himself flat and was crawling for cover. The Comanchero closest to him opened fire with two pistols, but before he got off three shots, Sundance shot him in the head. The leader's horse had run into the creek and broken its legs. It lay there screaming. The men who were driving the wagons had jumped back inside and were giving return fire. Six or seven men had died in the first volley from the rocks. The firing that came right after it killed another five. The others, except for those in the wagons, were making for the creek. Out from cover, the Dog Soldiers followed them, running fast. The Comancheros, knowing they weren't going to make it to the slope, wheeled their horses and came galloping back, firing as they came. Two Dog Soldiers dropped but the others, trained well for war, dropped to their knees and brought down the last of the Comancheros on the far side of the creek. The three wagon drivers were still shooting back and Sundance yelled at them, in Spanish, to throw out their guns.

"You don't have a chance," Sundance yelled. "Throw out the guns and we'll let you live."

A Mexican voice called back. "We have your word of honor?"

"My word of honor," Sundance shouted. "Come out now or we'll kill you."

A moment passed and then the first driver

threw his rifle out. Then he showed himself, expecting to be shot, and looking surprised when he wasn't. He called to the other two men and they came out. Sundance told them to jump down and keep their hands up.

"A big mistake happen here," one of the Mexicans said. "We are your friends."

Lone Wolf told his Kiowas to put the prisoners in the cave. "Tie them, guard them well," he said.

Sundance went to look for the wagon where the whiskey was. It was the last wagon and the bottles were packed in straw. There was straw on the floor of the wagon to soften the rough jolting of the trail. Without turning, he struck a match and tossed it in and the wagon went up in a sheet of flame. In seconds the bottles exploded and the rotgut sent liquid flame spurting in all directions. The Dog Soldiers yelled in rage when they smelled the burning liquor. Some of them raised their rifles, ready to kill. Sundance didn't move.

Lone Wolf limped forward until he was between Sundance and the angry Dog Soldiers. Raising his clenched fist, he threw his rifle on the ground and thumped himself on the chest.

"If you kill him, you kill me," he shouted. "You have the guns, the horses, everything. Take them. They are yours. Are we to be killed or not?"

Muttering angrily, the Dog Soldiers turned away, more eager to loot than to kill. The last bottle of whiskey exploded and the burning wagon began to sag to one side. It fell over with a crash. It smoked for a long time after the fire died out.

The Dog Soldiers had broken open the crates of rifles in the lead wagon. Two crates were filled with Winchester repeaters, all old '63 models that had seen hard use. The third crate contained old Army Springfields.

"We better test these guns," Sundance said.

"They're old, but they don't look too bad. Better check the ammunition too."

There was plenty of food in the second wagon: salt pork and bacon, canned fruit, dried beef, sacks of coffee beans, coarse brown sugar. But the Dog Soldiers craved tobacco more than anything else, and they whooped when they found it.

Lone Wolf looked at Sundance. "I think now is the time to tell them the rest of your madman's plan."

CHAPTER TWELVE

The faces of the Dog Soldiers were stony as they began to collect the locoweed. This was something they had never done before, and they didn't understand it. And what they didn't understand they didn't like to do. Sundance's plan, even when it was explained to them by Lone Wolf, seemed as loco as the weeds they were sent out to gather. They knew its effect on cattle, but since men did not eat locoweed, they had no way of knowing what the result would be. Sundance wasn't so sure himself, but he did know that in the fur-trading days there were mountain men who chewed on the weed as a way to forget their loneliness. It drove them slightly crazy, not in the same way as alcohol, but they were known to run naked in the snow, to jump off high places thinking they could fly.

Sundance had to give his orders through Lone Wolf, for the Dog Soldiers knew who he was, and did not trust him. He had fought against the Northern Cheyenne, under Crook, and in their eyes he was a renegade. Worse than that, he was a halfbreed with divided loyalties. He knew they disdained all this planning and scheming. If they had their way, he knew, they would make a direct attack on the settlement, and they would be wiped out. But that was the way of Dog Soldiers; trained for battle they were ever eager to prove their courage, and all lesser men were held in contempt. They might not be so easy to control once the siege began; only Lone Wolf could keep them in check, if they were prepared to listen to him.

All milkvetch was called locoweed, but it wasn't all poisonous. Sundance showed Lone Wolf the varieties that were not; the kind he wanted had purple flowers. Lone Wolf relayed the order to his men and their faces grew stonier. They had to range out far to get enough of the right weed; an hour later Sundance said there was enough. The mixture had to be strong.

"The Dog Soldiers do not think this is a manly way to fight," Lone Wolf said. "They no not want to kill men who are crazy, not even the buffalo hunters."

"They won't stay crazy for long," Sundance said. "One way or another, they'll fight like crazy men. They won't run around barking like dogs. Now tell the men to beat the weeds into a pulp and put the pulp in the buckets and pour in water. Not too much water."

"Then what, Sundance?"

"Let the pulp steep for a while. Then they are to squeeze out the pulp and throw it away. I will do the rest. Tell them they'll have plenty of killing to do before we get rid of Moore and the hunters. That ought to cheer them up."

Watched by Lone Wolf, the Dog Soldiers pounded the locoweed on flat rocks. Their hands turned purple as the pod-like flowers were crushed with the rest of the weed. They began to fill the buckets with the pulp and to cover it with water.

"Now wait," Lone Wolf told them. "Smoke the tobacco of the Comancheros and wait."

Squatting on their heels in sullen silence, the Dog Soldiers smoked the foul-smelling trade tobacco known as "nigger hair." All Indians craved tobacco, the stronger the better; the destruction of the Comancheros' whiskey had left them in an angry mood; Sundance hoped the head-splitting tobacco would do something to make up for it. But there was no way they could be kept under control if they had whiskey in them, especially the rotgut traded by the Comancheros, which wasn't whiskey at all but raw alcohol colored with tobacco juice or molasses.

The three Comancheros who had been allowed to live sat against a rock with their hands tied behind them. They had no idea why they were there, or what was going to happen to them. Sundance felt absolutely no pity for the three men who were about to die within the next few hours. Two of them were Mexicans, the other was an American, but all wore the gaudy Mexican clothes, the silver-stitched sombreros, the bright-colored scarves of the Comancheros. As they watched they whispered in Spanish. The American, young and lanky, was more afraid than the others. It showed in his eyes, in the way he strained at the ropes that bound him. The others sat with the dead-eyed fatalism of most Mexicans. One of them had diamonds plugging up the holes in his rotting teeth.

"Hey, hombre," he called out to the Sundance in Spanish. "You would give us a cigarette? A small thing, a cigarette."

He spat out curses when Sundance didn't answer, and yet he continued to smile his diamond-studded smile. The American looked around wild-eyed and afraid.

"There must be no mutilation of the dead," Sundance said to Lone Wolf. "No castration, no scalping, nothing that will show that the killing was done by Indians. Those of your men who are killed must be taken away when it is over. We will burn the houses before we leave. The Coman-

351

cheros would do that. But I want the army to find nothing but the bodies of the hunters and the three Comancheros. If it is done right, the army will blame the Comancheros."

Lone Wolf nodded gravely. "Are the Comancheros to be killed before the attack?"

Sundance said no. "We will drive them out in front of us, let them make a run for the settlement. The hunters will do the rest. Before we leave we will take their boots and hats, anything of value they have in their pockets. The Comancheros would do that, too."

"It is a clever plan," Lone Wolf said. "But sometimes the simple plan is better."

"There can't be any simple plan. This is no farmhouse we'll be attacking. If you can think of a better plan, then tell me what it is."

Lone Wolf remained silent, but Sundance could see that he had doubts about the plan. During the Civil War Lone Wolf had been something like a colonel of irregulars. He could read and write and knew something of military tactics, yet he was unwilling to believe that the settlement could be destroyed with anything but orthodox warfare.

"The creek has to be dammed or its course changed by night," Sundance said. "There's no use poisoning the pool if the flow of the creek isn't stopped. The creek will run dry, but the water in the pool will remain. That will be their only supply of water."

Lone Wolf said, "Even at night the guards will know the flow of water has stopped. Even if they are close to the creek they will know some sound they know is missing. A man knows sounds without thinking about them. If they all turn out to see what is wrong, how then will you poison the pool?"

"It has to be done the moment the water stops coming. I will do the poisoning. Your men will open fire when it is done. Not all your men. No more than ten. That will be enough to pin them down for a while. But they must not think they are being attacked by a large force."

Lone Wolf thought for a minute or two. "If they are pinned down, how will they get water from the pool?"

"We'll let them get it. They have some water in the settlement, not enough if they think they're in for a siege. They have plenty of food, but food isn't as important as water."

"Then why have they not stored up water?"

"Because they're too confident. Any one of those hunters is a match for three soldiers, maybe more. They know how Indians fight so they think they're nothing they can't beat off. Too much confidence is their weak spot, Moore's weak spot, and we're going to use it."

Once again, Lone Wolf remained silent.

Sundance went on. "If the creek can't be dammed right, we'll have to change its course. Run the water off to a hollow place if we can find it. That means your men are in for a lot of rock moving and digging."

Lone Wolf looked at the sullen Dog Soldiers as they rolled one foul-smelling brown paper cigarette after another.

"You are asking a lot, Sundance. These men are warriors. What you speak of is for women."

"We don't have any women. Tell the brave warriors they'll have to get blisters just this once."

"I will tell them, but I will not say it like that. No matter how I say it, I cannot be sure they will obey me."

"They'll die if they don't."

"Death with honor is all that matters to them."

The whole thing might still fall apart, Sundance knew. The Dog Soldiers were in an angry, rebellious mood, and if they decided to follow their own course of action, nothing could be done to change their minds. Threats wouldn't do any good; persuasion wouldn't work either.

"Then let them die with honor," Sundance said. "If they rebel against your authority, then I am finished here. If they want a war that will wipe out their people, General Sheridan will be glad to give it to them. Courage won't be much good against rapid-fire guns. You were in the war, you saw what Gatlings can do."

Lone Wolf kneaded the muscles in his damaged leg. Sundance knew it was causing him a lot of pain, though he never spoke of it.

"You are talking to me when you say that. Is that not true, Sundance?"

"It's true. I can't talk to them, so I must talk to you. You must make them follow the plan. If one part of it goes wrong, the whole thing will collapse. There won't be time to get another chance at Moore."

"I will do what I can," Lone Wolf said.

When the locoweed pulp was squeezed out and thrown away, the water that remained in the buckets was thick and purple colored. It had an alkaline taste, but Sundance guessed that would not be noticed once it was mixed with the water in the pool. The creek itself was faintly alkaline.

The Comancheros and the Dog Soldiers watched him as he emptied the poison into one bucket; there was enough to fill two canteens. It was getting dark and nothing could be done until he scouted the creek upstream from the settlement. The best time to do that was when the hunters had finished the day's work. If he went there at first light, he might run into a party of them starting out for the kill.

"If it looks all right we'll do it tomorrow night," Sundance said. "While I'm gone, keep the Dog Soldiers out of sight. I don't care who comes along, they are not to open fire. Even if it looks like they can kill a large party of hunters, they are to hold their fire."

"I am listening," Lone Wolf said.

The next day, Sundance started out in the early afternoon. The settlement was a good ten miles away but, thinking of the watch tower, he stayed well clear of it. For the rest of the day he waited in a deep ravine until the sun started to slide down the sky. They'd be coming back from the hunt within an hour or two. He gave it another thirty minutes, moving out when the light was starting to get thick and red. Even a man with a telescope would have trouble spotting him now.

A mile past the settlement, he made his way to the creek looking for a place where it could be dammed. The flow of water could be stopped anywhere; if not done in the right place it would overflow the dam and the work would be wasted.

He rode upstream but no place he saw looked promising. What he was looking for was a place where the creek widened out. He crossed the creek and rode down from it and found a long ravine that twisted away for miles. This would have to be it, he decided. The only sure way to stop the flow of water was to change the course of the creek so it spilled into the ravine.

The ravine was at least two hundred yards from the creek, but they wouldn't have to dig a channel all that way. But the creek would have to be dammed after its banks were breached. A hill ran down to the ravine; once the water began to flow, it would start to cut its own channel.

It was well into the evening when he got back to the caves where the Dog Soldiers were. If anything, they looked more sullen than before. They ate their jerked buffalo meat in silence while he talked to Lone Wolf. The cave smelled musty as if the bones of some long-dead animal were moldering in the darkness. The three prisoners sat against the wall of the cave.

"Hey, amigo," the one with the diamond teeth called out when he saw Sundance. "A little food and water, *por favor.* Your friends have not fed us."

Sundance told Lone Wolf to get one of his men to stick food in their mouths. "Then let them drink, but don't untie them. They may try something and your men will kill them."

"You have found a place?"

"I have found a place. The course of the creek can be changed so it will spill into a ravine. But the men will have to work. Do all the things they won't want to do."

It was dark now and the only light in the huge cave came from the fire.

Lone Wolf got up using the barrel of his rifle as a crutch. The Dog Soldiers and the Comancheros watched him. All remained silent as he began to speak in the lingua franca of the Plains, a short, guttural language that was a mixture of the Indian languages, with an occasional word in Spanish or English. He said that Josiah Moore's settlement had to be destroyed, the men there killed, and the only way to do that was to follow the plan Sundance had made. He praised the Dog Soldiers for their courage, but argued that courage itself was not enough.

There was muttering, most of it angry, and Lone Wolf had to raise his voice to be heard. Soon he was shouting and so was a tall, muscular Cheyenne with glittering eyes and a furious manner. Like the other Dog Soldiers, like Sundance himself, this brave bore the terrible scars of the initiation rites that only the bravest came through without screaming in pain. Most of the opposition to the plan was centered around this man, whose name was Long Rifle. He was in his late twenties and had the arrogant strut of a man who considered himself better than anyone. He carried a Bowie knife with a thick blade at least three inches longer than the one slung from Sundance's belt. He looked like he knew how to use it.

Shouting angrily, he stalked back and forth in front of the fire, showing off for the others. It was clear that he resented Lone Wolf's leadership; a Kiowa giving orders to a Cheyenne was not to his liking. But, for now, he said nothing about that; for now they were allies. The plan, he said, was fit for nothing but cowards and old women.

"Are you calling me a coward?" Lone Wolf shouted.

"If you act like a coward, then you are a coward," Long Rifle shouted back, placing his hand on the handle of his knife. "You do not command any longer. Go and dig with your dirty halfbreed. We will not follow."

There it was, Sundance thought. Long Rifle's challenge to Lone Wolf was plain and unmistakable. If Lone Wolf didn't fight for his leadership, he would lose it. Sundance didn't know how old Lone Wolf was, but he couldn't have been much less than fifty, and though the wound in his leg was healing, he was in no condition to fight. Even without the injured leg, he would have been no match for a man twenty years younger and in top physical condition.

Sundance stood up and moved beside Lone Wolf, who had drawn his knife. The fire threw their shadows on the wall of the cave. The two Mexicans were grinning; beside them the American had his mouth open, not knowing what was going on, or why.

"Stay out of this, Sundance," Lone Wolf said in English. "The challenge was to me. The insult was thrown at me."

"And at me," Sundance said. "You know you can't win a fight with this man. If you were not wounded, he would not dare challenge you." Sundance knew this wasn't true, but he had to find a way to make the older man back off without losing face.

"What are you saying?" Long Rifle shouted in the language of the Plains.

"I am saying that you are the coward here," Sundance said. "It is easy to challenge a wounded man. If not for the wound, Lone Wolf would cut you to pieces. But you see I am not wounded. You called me a dirty halfbreed. Now I call you a sneaking carrion eater and a defiler of young boys. The buzzard smells better, the coyote is braver."

With a wild yell Long Rifle drew his knife and started to come around the fire.

"Move back," Sundance told Lone Wolf. "If he kills me, then you can have him."

After a moment's hesitation Lone Wolf moved back, but he levered a shell into the chamber of his rifle, a warning to the other Dog Soldiers not to interfere. Sundance knew they still might come at him in a bunch. According to the rules of their warrior society they were expected to stand back, no matter what happened to their comrade. But rules were fragile and men spurred by hate were likely to do anything.

After the first wild yell Long Rifle came on cautiously enough. They circled and the firelight glittered on the blades of their big knives. After they had circled twice, Sundance knew that Long Rifle had been in many other knife fights before this one. He moved in the *en garde* position of the swordsman, feet well apart, the right foot slightly advanced, body and head held well back, the knife pointing out and upward, the thumb

358

against the guard on the side of the blade.

Long Rifle sprang forward and Sundance blocked his thrust and turned it aside. The clang of the long, heavy blades was loud in the silence of the cave. Long Rifle thrust again, then jumped back, trying to draw Sundance in after him. Sundance moved in but not in a wild rush. Long Rifle attacked again and drew blood from Sundance's forearm with the three inches of razor-edged steel on the back of the knife. There was no pain from the thin wound, but he could feel the trickle of blood. Some of the blood was soaked up by his shirt; the haft of his knife had not yet become sticky. If the haft became too blood-slimed he would have to switch the knife to his left hand, and though he could fight lefthanded if he had to, his left was never as good as his right. Sundance chopped at Long Rifle's thumb, but he jumped aside and tried to open Sundance under-arm from elbow to wrist with an upward slash of his knife. The three inches of razor steel were what made the Bowie such a deadly knife. The three inches curved up to a point that could be used for ripping and a man could lose his intestines in a single tearing thrust. Brought up hard under the armpit, the tip of the heavy blade would just about sever a man's arm from the shoulder.

Long Rifle attacked again, seething with anger because he hadn't been able to penetrate Sundance's defense. He had started the fight with a fair amount of caution. Now his anger was getting the better of him. He lunged for Sundance's belly and as quickly as the thrust was turned he thrust again. He lunged too hard, let himself be carried too far forward. Sundance knocked the blade up and ripped the back of Long Rifle's hand. It opened the hand from small finger to wrist, but it wasn't enough to make the other man drop the knife. Sundance chopped at Long Rifle's wrist.

Instead of cutting flesh his blade sank into the soft steel just in front of the haft. He forced Long Rifle's blade downward, steel locked in steel, while Long Rifle tried to pull free. The knives were still locked, and their faces were close together, dripping sweat, when Sundance kicked Long Rifle in the knee and brought him down. Long Rifle fell and his head rolled in the fire and he yelled when his greased hair began to burn. He jerked himself back on one knee and blocked Sundance's chop at his skull. He thrust as Sundance's neck, at the jugular, and though he missed, the thrust and Sundance's response to it gave him time to get back on his feet. Long Rifle's face was contorted with the pain from his burning hair. Aware that he was losing the fight he attacked in a fierce flurry of blows. The two blades clanged like sabers as the two men fenced like duelists, advancing and retreating, circling all the time. Long Rifle's next attack was so fierce that he forced Sundance back to the wall of the cave. Brought up short by the rock, Sundance saw Long Rifle's blade coming in a sideways slash that would have split his face. He jerked his head to one side and the blade clanged against the rock. Sundance chopped at Long Rifle's head and cut off his right ear. Blood spattered Long Rifle's body as he jumped back, and for an instant he stood without moving, while the blood dripped from the side of his head. There was bewilderment in his face, and the beginning of fear. Gone was all the cockiness and the boasting. He seemed to know he was going to die. Staring, he retreated a few steps, holding the point of his blade out from his body.

Sundance hesitated but only for the blink of an eye. If he could have spared Long Rifle's life, while preserving his own, he would have done so. But to give Long Rifle back his life would have been worse than an insult. To the Dog Soldiers, mercy meant weakness. To give Long Rifle back his life would guarantee a bullet or a knife in the back. And it would come, as sure as sunrise.

Long Rifle tried for one last attack. Sundance beat it back without much effort. Then he went in for the kill, driving the other man back with relentless force. Long Rifle took a deep cut on his left arm and the Dog Soldiers began to edge forward. Lone Wolf pointed the rifle and yelled. Long Rifle made one last thrust that may have been an effort to meet a quick death. Sundance knocked his thrust aside and drove his blade upward under Long Rifle's ribcage. The upward stab was so powerful and penetrated so far, that he found it difficult to withdraw the knife. He jerked it free, with blood dripping from the blade, and Long Rifle, already dead, crashed to the ground and lay still.

Lone Wolf came forward into the firelight. "Who else questions my authority?" he shouted.

None of the Dog Soldiers spoke.

"We better get on with it," Sundance said, looking after the knife cut in his arm.

He wondered how long the Dog Soldiers would stay in line.

CHAPTER THIRTEEN

Three hours after they started they passed within a mile of the settlement and followed the creek to the place where the work was to begin. Even with the binoculars Sundance could see lights; it was too dark to make out anything else. The three Comancheros were roped and gagged to prevent any outcry. Now that darkness shrouded the Plains, the wind was cold, blowing dust in their faces even at night.

They rode in single file, with Sundance and Lone Wolf out in front. The death of Long Rifle had left the Dog Soldiers in a sullen mood, and at no time was Sundance sure that he wouldn't get a bullet in the back. Only Lone Wolf's presence was keeping him alive, he knew; if anything happened to the chief of the Kiowas, he was as good as dead. At times there was a moon, cold and bright until rolling black clouds drifted across its face.

"This is where we'll do it," Sundance said, pointing. "The ravine is down there. Here is what the men have to do."

As before, Sundance gave no direct orders to the Dog Soldiers; everything had to be passed on by Lone Wolf. Even so, the Dog Soldiers knew that Sundance was giving the orders, and they hated him for it.

"The bank of the creek must be breached before

it's dammed," Sundance said. "But first they must dig uphill until they are within a few feet of the creek. If they dig out from the creek itself they'll be working in water all the time. Half of them are to carry rocks up from the ravine to give the dam a foundation. Tell them to work fast. The night is wearing on."

Lone Wolf grunted. "Do not press too hard, Sundance. They are in an angry mood."

"Do what you can," Sundance said.

Unused to work of any kind, the Dog Soldiers were clumsy workmen, inept even at the simple task of digging, yet after an hour the channel that was to run off the creek was beginning to take shape, and the foundation of the dam was two feet high. The water ran over the rocks, but when the fill from the channel was dumped behind them, it would start to back up. Sundance looked up at the great banks of clouds that shut out the moon. The wind blew colder and he hoped it wouldn't rain. If it rained the dam and the channel would not be enough to stop the rush of water.

Another hour passed and the stones in the creek were higher and the channel, dug from below, was getting close to the bank. Sundance guessed it was past midnight, but he knew Lone Wolf was right about trying to rush the men. In time to come they would brag about the great trick they had played on the hunters; right now their backs hurt and their hands had blisters.

Sundance walked along the channel with Lone Wolf limping behind him. The channel was five feet wide and four feet deep behind the bank of the creek. It got shallower as it went downhill. There was no need, and no time, to dig all the way to the drop into the ravine. The soil was sandy as it got close to the ravine; the water would cut its own channel once the flow increased.

"Time's getting short," Sundance told Lone

Wolf, not liking the look of the sky. There was hardly any light left. He knew he was betting his life against the chance of rain. If it rained hard enough the plan would fail; the Dog Soldiers would kill him. Even Lone Wolf's stern authority would not be enough to hold them. There was even a chance that they would kill him too.

"Tell them to start filling in the dam," Sundance said. "As soon as the water runs off we will ride. Ride fast."

Lone Wolf looked at the sky. "How fast will not matter if it rains."

"Start them breaking loose the bank," Sundance said. "Tell them the only work from now on is killing."

The men standing in the channel were knocked over by the sudden rush of water from the creek. Floundering in the water, they yelled their surprise that, so far, the hated halfbreed's plan had worked. Already the water was tearing at the sides of the hole they had dug in the bank of the creek. There was a flood of water and sand and dirt and small rocks, but Sundance didn't move until, minutes later, he heard the first splash of water as it fell to the bottom of the ravine.

Then he said, "Let's ride."

Leading the others, Sundance could hear the drop of the water in the creek. Rocks were beginning to appear in the creekbed and pools were forming where there had been a smooth flowing surface. When they got close to the settlement, Sundance told Lone Wolf to take ten men in closer and wait until they heard a shot. That would be the signal that he had dumped the locoweed juice in the pool.

"Only ten men. Don't move in the others until we're ready. And tell them not to fire too fast. I'd like the hunters to think this is a small party and not too well armed. You're to be met with heavy

365

fire, so find the best cover you can."

"But what if they come out with their big rifles?" Lone Wolf asked.

"They won't come out in darkness. The settlement is their fortress. They'll stay in there. A few of them will make a run for the creek. The others will cover. The Dog Soldiers are not to kill the ones who run to the creek. Let them get the water, let them get back with it. Then we wait."

Lone Wolf said, "It is a plan with many pieces in it. Maybe it is a child's house of sticks that will fall when one stick is dislodged."

"Maybe it is," Sundance said, sliding to the ground with the canteens in his hands. He gave a command to Eagle and the big stallion obeyed instantly. He would wait in the darkness until a whistle brought him back. Lone Wolf spoke in whispers to the men and they all dismounted. So far, so good, Sundance thought. No matter how much the Dog Soldiers hated him, they were following orders. But the real test would come when the shooting started. Trained to kill, they would be impatient to finish it.

"You have to kill the man in the watchtower," Sundance said. "If it can't be done with bullets, we'll have to burn out with fire arrows. Try it first with bullets. The burning tower will give them too much light."

Lone Wolf and his men vanished into the darkness, and Sundance, holding the two canteens, ran toward the creek, then got down on his belly when the moon broke through the clouds. He lay still, waiting for darkness to close in again. There were no lights in any of the buildings. While he waited a match flared for an instant in the tower. A man lighting a cigarette. Getting at the man up there wouldn't be easy. The lookout post was a sturdy box atop crisscrossed logs bolted to-~ether. The sides of the box were made of planking many inches thick. Not even the biggest-caliber rifle was capable of penetrating the box and killing the man inside.

When it got dark again he crawled toward the pool. There would be other guards watching from inside the shuttered windows. But he saw nothing and heard nothing. He got to the bank of the creek and unstoppered the first canteen. Below him the pool was dark and deep, the night wind sending ripples across its surface. Holding the canteen close to the water, he emptied it, then swirled the water with the canteen itself. He emptied the second canteen, thinking again of the rain that might come at any moment.

Carrying the empty canteens, he went back toward the place where Eagle was waiting. He left the canteens in the grass and whistled for his horse. An almost inaudible sound that might have been made by some night bird. He led Eagle down the dry creekbed to where the rest of the Dog Soldiers were waiting with the horses. The Indian ponies whinnied at the menacing presence of the great fighting stallion.

"Stay here, boy," Sundance said.

He moved away from the cover of the trees before he fired the first shot. The crash of the exploding bullet had barely died away when the big rifle boomed in the watchtower. At the same time Lone Wolf and the ten Dog Soldiers opened fire, sending bullets into the tower and the line of darkened buildings.

"Attack! Attack!" the guard in the tower was yelling. The hunters turned out faster than trained soldiers, but there was no wild firing, just an occasional shot. Sundance crawled forward to where Lone Wolf and the ten men were deployed along a low ridge covered with grass and small rocks. A bullet from the tower tore into the ground ‹ few inches from his face. He lay flat, then moved on again.

"The rifle in the tower is more dangerous than the others," Lone Wolf said. "None of our bullets have been able to kill him. One of my men is dead, another is dying."

"The only way to kill the man up there, we have to fire at the same time." That might not work either, Sundance knew, but short of burning the tower, it was the only chance to get rid of the sniper. "Tell the men to hold their fire until he shoots again."

Lone Wolf passed the command down the line of men. The firing stopped and the rifle in the tower was silent. It remained silent until Sundance raised up to fire two quick shots from the Winchester. The rifle in the tower fired on the second shot and the Winchester was torn from Sundance's hands by the force of the bullet. The Dog Soldiers all fired at the same time. All along the ridge there were orange flashes and bullets ripped into the tower. There was a scream and after that there was no more shooting from the tower.

"Tell the men to stay down," Sundance said. "It may be a trick." Someone in the settlement was yelling at the man in the tower, but there was no answer.

"Tell the men to continue firing," Sundance said. "Tell them to go easy on the ammunition."

As soon as he spoke a rifle opened fire from one of the buildings in the center. To Sundance it sounded like a .60- or .70-caliber, the biggest rifle made. The huge bullet shattered the head of a Dog Soldier and sent the bloody corpse rolling in the grass. When the buffalo gun boomed again Sundance decided it was a .70-caliber, by the sound, and he guessed that Dutch Henry was at the other end of the barrel. Some of the other hunters owned .60-calibers; Dutch Henry was the only man there with a .70.

No more shooting came from the tower, so it was a good bet that the man there was dead. Sundance wondered if the man in the tower had been Billy Dixon. There was one chance in twenty-five that the dead man was Dixon; the only men exempted from night guard in the tower were the skinners and Josiah Moore. And Sundance remembered that Dixon had saved his life not once but twice. Somehow it wasn't so easy to convince himself that Billy Dixon had to die with all the others.

Sporadic firing dragged on for an hour, but no more of the Dog Soldiers were hit.

"They have not tried to get to the creek," Lone Wolf said. "This could be where your child's house of sticks comes apart."

"They'll try for the water after they talk it over," Sundance said. "They know we aren't a large force, but more men could be coming to join us. If that happened they'd know it would mean a long siege. They drank up all the beer at the dance. What's left is whiskey and a small store of water."

"You are gambling, Sundance."

"Yes, I am gambling."

The big rifle boomed again and suddenly the line of log houses erupted in a volley of gunfire. The sound of the big rifles, all firing together, was like rolling thunder. Sundance and the other hugged the ground. A Dog Soldier who dared to fire back was ripped apart by bullets. A second volley came right after the first. It stopped abruptly and a door banged open and shut. Sundance raised up and saw three men running with clusters of canteens hanging from their shoulders. Against orders, some of the Dog Soldiers opened fire on the running men. None was hit and then they were running down the slope into the cover of the trees. The fire from the buildings started again.

It grew heavier, a sign that the men with the water were coming back. There was so much noise that Sundance had to shout at Lone Wolf, who was only a few feet away.

"No more firing, let them get through," he shouted.

Some of the Dog Soldiers fired anyway, but by then the moon was dark. The door of the center house banged shut, and the firing stopped.

"Send a man to fetch the others," Sundance told Lone Wolf. "It's not long until first light. If our luck holds out it will be timed just right." Then he realized that no Indian believed in luck of any kind. In their entire history of dealing with the whites the Indians had never been lucky.

While they waited for the other Dog Soldiers to come up, Lone Wolf said, nodding his head toward the settlement, "The young white man who was with you when you found the women. You think he is in there?"

"He's in there."

"You were friends that day. You fought well together."

"Dixon's a good man, the best, but he's on the wrong side. I do not want to kill him, but nothing else can be done."

"Do you hate all the men in there?" Again, Lone Wolf nodded toward the row of darkened houses. No shots had been fired for a few minutes.

"No, not all of them. If I could drive some of them out, I would do so. But that's not possible."

"It must be strange to kill men you do not hate. I do not think I would like to be you, Sundance. I say that without insult of any kind. But your ways are strange to me. In my lifetime I have killed no men but those I hated."

Sundance looked up at the sky. This talk of life and death and a man's reasons had no meaning

370

here.

"Looks like it's not going to rain, after all," he said.

"The men are coming," Lone Wolf said. "Have you decided what you want to do with the yellow-bearded man. The man you call Dixon. It may be possible to spare his life, if that is what you want to do."

"I don't know what I want to do. This whole thing has been set up so the killing of the hunters will be blamed on the Comancheros. If Dixon lives and tells about what happened here, the soldiers will move against you. Sheridan wants a war. This will be his excuse."

"You are arguing with yourself," Lone Wolf said. "One side of you against the other. This man called Dixon. Would he keep his word not to talk? In exchange for his life?"

"He'd keep it if he gave it," Sundance said. "That's the kind of man he is. All this may be nothing but talk. It's likely he'll be killed in the first few minutes. Why would you be willing to take the word of a man you don't know?"

"Because you say his word is good."

"We'll have to see what happens."

By now all the Dog Soldiers were deployed along the ridge, belly-down in the waving grass. It was dark and cold, with the wind blowing hard. One way or another, it would be over in a few hours. If Moore's men didn't come out by dawn, continuing the siege would worse than a waste of time. All they could do was pull out. Soon after that the army would move against the Indians. A fast rider, dispatched by Moore, would see to that.

The wind rose and blew away the clouds that shrouded the face of the moon. Washed in pale, cold light, the Plains were like the unreal country of a nightmare. Sundance crawled along the safe side of the ridge to look at the rifles that lay near the Dog Soldiers who had been killed. One of the rifles was an old Spencer carbine with a cracked stock held together with copper wire. Beside the next dead man he found a .44-40 Winchester that looked all right.

Back beside Lone Wolf, he jacked the remaining cartridges and reloaded. Then he kicked out the spent shells from the long-barreled Colt and reloaded that, too. In the sky there were long red streaks; the moonlight was paler than before. Lying there, waiting for first light, he sensed the uneasiness of the Dog Soldiers despite their silence. Maybe Lone Wolf was right. Maybe he had made a plan with too many pieces. In trying to stop the war, could be he just hurried it along. Yet when he thought about it, he couldn't see that there was anything else he could have done. If they could kill the hunters and get away with it, then other trespassers, even the wildest, would think twice before they crossed the Red River, for if the Moore expedition—the biggest and best-armed ever mounted on the Plains—failed what chance would a lesser party have. Sure, Sundance thought with some bitterness, except that it was nearly dawn and nothing was happening. Except for an occasional shot, to remind them of what a buffalo rifle could do, the settlement remained silent.

Sundance looked at the sky. "We'll give it another thirty minutes, then pull out. Maybe I was wrong about the water supply. Looks like they haven't started on the water they took from the pool."

Lone Wolf said calmly, "We have come a long way and we have worked hard. We will wait. I will wait with the Dog Soldiers, but maybe it is better if you leave now. You will be gone before their anger becomes too fierce."

Sundance, still looking at the sky, said he

couldn't do that. "I brought you here, persuaded you to follow this plan. I can't leave you now."

"Even if it means your death?"

"We all have to die, Lone Wolf. This place is as good as any. I won't run out just to save my life."

Lone Wolf nodded. "I would do the same."

Just then a howl that sounded like that of a wolf came from the settlement. It rose up into the quiet morning air and before it reached its highest pitch, it was answered by another howl and then another. The sound was so strange, so night-marish, that Sundance felt the hairs bristle on the back of his neck. He had seen horses and cattle driven crazy by locoweed, but for all the stories he had heard, this was the first time he had experienced its effect on men. A murmur of astonishment ran down the line of Dog Soldiers. The door of the center house banged open and stayed open and a man ran out howling. He ran out and fell and picked up his rifle and, still howling, he fired at the first rays of the sun. Sundance shouldered the Winchester and dropped him with the first shot.

Other men followed the first crazed hunter, until the bare ground in front of the settlement was filled with armed men running in every direction. Some were howling, some were laughing, some were dancing. One man threw away his rifle and flapped his arms. Faced by such madness, the Dog Soldiers hadn't opened fire. Lone Wolf shot a dancing man. The Dog Soldiers began to kill.

It was time for the three Comancheros to die. Holding the Colt in their faces, Sundance cut the ropes that bound their wrists and ankles. One of the Mexicans spat at him. The other grinned. The young American fell down and lay whimpering in the grass. Sundance dragged him to his feet and pushed him over the top of the ridge. He staggered with the two Mexicans behind him. Bullets cut them down before they had gone more than ten yards.

Only minutes had passed, yet the settlement yard was littered with bodies. Firing fast, reloading fast, the Dog Soldiers let loose their bullets and their hate on the crazed buffalo hunters. Sundance saw Josiah Moore's face at the door of a house. The Yankee trader was waving his arms in hopeless desperation, yelling at the men to get back inside. Sundance fired at Moore just as the door banged shut.

Some steady fire came from the houses and Sundance knew that all the men there hadn't drunk the poisoned water. But most of them had, because the ground was covered with the bodies of the dead and dying. And they were still dropping under the relentless fire of the Dog Soldiers. A wounded man got up bleeding from a chest wound and shaking his head with the furious bewilderment of a bull in a bullring getting ready to make his last charge. It was Dutch Henry. It was time for Dutch Henry to die. Sundance aimed the Winchester and killed him. There was no sign of Billy Dixon.

Lone Wolf shouted at the Dog Soldiers when they jumped up from their positions and began to charge the settlement. They ran firing and screaming, and though the return fire was steady it wasn't enough to stop them. Four or five dropped as they ran, but then the others battered down the doors with anything they could find. After that the killing went on inside. Thinking of Dixon, Sundance ran fast, not yet knowing what he wanted to do. Then he saw Billy Dixon clubbing a Dog Soldier in the door of the saloon. The Dog Soldier went down with a shattered head and Dixon, wild-eyed, turned the empty rifle at Sundance. Sundance saw that he was wounded and barely able to swing the heavy rifle. As the rifle went up the last of Dixon's strength gave out and he began to fall. Sundance caught him before he hit the ground and shielded him with his body. Lone Wolf came limping behind.

A few last shots sounded and then it was over. Still crazed with killing, the Dog Soldiers who survived the attack pointed their rifles at Dixon, who sat against a stack of lumber with blood leaking from his shoulder. Sundance didn't know if bones had been broken, but the bullet had missed the lungs.

For a moment there was no sound but the wind. Dixon stared at Sundance. "You planned all this?"

Sundance said yes. "It had to be done, Billy. I urged you to get away from here."

One of the Dog Soldiers spoke to Lone Wolf.

"They're all dead but this man, your friend," Lone Wolf said.

Billy Dixon's eyes were full of wonder. "All dead," he said.

"You don't have to die," Sundance said. "Give me your word that you won't tell how Moore's men came to die. You give it, I'll take it. You're not shot too bad. I'll patch you up and you can go back to Kansas. Go anywhere you like. But I have to have your word I won't give Sheridan a chance to start his war, not even for you. Make up your mind, Billy. There isn't much time."

Billy Dixon looked at the faces of the Dog Soldiers, at the rifles aimed at him.

"Can't do it," he said at last. "Can't change sides at the last minute. I'm a white man and I have to stick by my people. Even these dead people. If I gave my word I'd have to honor it. Then where would I be for the rest of my life? Every time I heard of some white family being murdered by Injuns, well then my word would stick in my craw."

"All this fighting won't last forever. Everything comes to an end. Don't be a fool, don't die for nothing."

Billy Dixon smiled at Sundance. "You're the fool. You're fighting a lost cause, and I think you know it. There's no way you can win. You can delay what's going to happen, but you can't stop it. Sorry it had to come to this, Jim."

Billy Dixon closed his eyes and Sundance shot him in the head.

Sundance took no part in what came next. Lone Wolf told the Dog Soldiers what to do, and they did it. They dragged away the bodies of the other Dog Soldiers who had died. The bodies of the hunters were stripped of their boots, gunbelts, and all other valuables. By now the sun was up hot; buzzards wheeled in the sky. The three Comancheros were left where they had died. Feeling very tired, Sundance looked at what was left of Billy Dixon. The top of his head was gone. He had done that. In the years to come he would think about the killing of Billy Dixon, and it wasn't going to be easy to live with what he had done. But there was no going back on it. Not now.

The last thing the Dog Soldiers did was to splash coal oil and set fire to the buildings. Oily smoke boiled up into the sky. Limping, Lone Wolf came over to where Sundance was.

"Everything has been done. Everything you planned and ordered," the Kiowa said. "What is in your mind, Sundance? What will you do now?"

"I'm tired and would like to go away from here. So much has happened and I am tired."

"If war still comes, it will not come from me," Lone Wolf said. "That is my promise to you. We are going now. Goodbye, Sundance."

Sundance nodded. "Goodbye, Lone Wolf. I'll be on my way in a little while."

SUNDANCE

HANGMAN'S KNOT/APACHE WAR

PETER McCURTIN

Hangman's Knot. Sundance doesn't think twice about shooting the drunken coward in a saloon brawl. But Judge Isaac Parker, the infamous Hanging Judge, thinks differently. Sundance receives an instant death sentence, but if he captures the feared half-breed outlaw Joe Buck, he will be freed. There is only one problem: Buck is Sundance's old trail partner.

And in the same action-packed volume . . .

Apache War. Sundance is dispatched on a mission to Fort McHenry, Arizona, where an arrogant young Army major is itching for war. The major's "enemy," the Apache people, had been living in peace for years, but by the time Sundance arrives, the killing has begun again. The soldiers are out for blood, and only Sundance can prevent an all-out war in the desert.

___4561-3 $5.50 US/$6.50 CAN

Dorchester Publishing Co., Inc.
P.O. Box 6640
Wayne, PA 19087-8640

Please add $1.75 for shipping and handling for the first book and $.50 for each book thereafter. NY, NYC, and PA residents, please add appropriate sales tax. No cash, stamps, or C.O.D.s. All orders shipped within 6 weeks via postal service book rate. Canadian orders require $2.00 extra postage and must be paid in U.S. dollars through a U.S. banking facility.

Name_____
Address_____
City_____State_____Zip_____
I have enclosed $_____ in payment for the checked book(s).
Payment <u>must</u> accompany all orders. ☐ Please send a free catalog.
CHECK OUT OUR WEBSITE! www.dorchesterpub.com

WILDERNESS

BLOOD FEUD

David Thompson

The brutal wilderness of the Rocky Mountains can be deadly to those unaccustomed to its dangers. So when a clan of travelers from the hill country back East arrive at Nate King's part of the mountain, Nate is more than willing to lend a hand and show them some hospitality. He has no way of knowing that this clan is used to fighting—and killing—for what they want. And they want Nate's land for their own!

___4477-3 $3.99 US/$4.99 CAN

WILD BILL

DEAD MAN'S HAND

JUDD COLE

Marshal, gunfighter, stage driver, and scout, Wild Bill Hickok has a legend as big and untamed as the West itself. No man is as good with a gun as Wild Bill, and few men use one as often. From Abilene to Deadwood, his name is known by all—and feared by many. That's why he is hired by Allan Pinkerton's new detective agency to protect an eccentric inventor on a train ride through the worst badlands of the West. With hired thugs out to kill him and angry Sioux out for his scalp, Bill knows he has his work cut out for him. But even if he survives that, he has a still worse danger to face— a jealous Calamity Jane.

___4487-0 $3.99 US/$4.99 CAN

WILD BILL

JUDD COLE

THE KINKAID COUNTY WAR

Wild Bill Hickok is a legend in his own lifetime. Wherever he goes his reputation with a gun precedes him—along with an open bounty of $10,000 for his arrest. But Wild Bill is working for the law when he goes to Kinkaid County, Wyoming. Hundreds of prime longhorn cattle have been poisoned, and Bill is sent by the Pinkerton Agency to get to the bottom of it. He doesn't expect to land smack dab in the middle of an all-out range war, but that's exactly what happens. With the powerful Cattleman's Association on one side and land-grant settlers on the other, Wild Bill knows that before this is over he'll be testing his gun skills to the limit if he hopes to get out alive.

___4529-X $3.99 US/$4.99 CAN

Dorchester Publishing Co., Inc.
P.O. Box 6640
Wayne, PA 19087-8640

Please add $1.75 for shipping and handling for the first book and $.50 for each book thereafter. NY, NYC, and PA residents, please add appropriate sales tax. No cash, stamps, or C.O.D.s. All orders shipped within 6 weeks via postal service book rate. Canadian orders require $2.00 extra postage and must be paid in U.S. dollars through a U.S. banking facility.

Name_____

Address_____

City_____State_____Zip_____

I have enclosed $_____ in payment for the checked book(s).

Payment <u>must</u> accompany all orders. ☐ Please send a free catalog.

CHECK OUT OUR WEBSITE! www.dorchesterpub.com

WILD BILL

YUMA BUSTOUT

JUDD COLE

When the Danford Gang terrorized Arizona, no one—not the U.S. Marshals or the Army—could bring them in. It took Wild Bill Hickok to do that. Only Wild Bill was able to put them in the Yuma Territorial Prison, where they belonged. But the prison can't hold them. The venomous gang escapes and takes the Governor's wife and her sister as hostages. So it is up to Wild Bill to track them down and do the impossible—capture the Danford Gang a second time. Only this time, the gang's ruthless leader, Fargo Danford, has a burning need for revenge against the one man who put him and the gang in prison in the first place, a need as deadly as the desert trap he has set for Bill.

___4674-1 $3.99 US/$4.99 CAN

ATTENTION WESTERN CUSTOMERS!

SPECIAL TOLL-FREE NUMBER
1-800-481-9191

*Call Monday through Friday
10 a.m. to 9 p.m.
Eastern Time
Get a free catalogue,
join the Western Book Club,
and order books using your
Visa, MasterCard,
or Discover®*

Leisure
Books

GO ONLINE WITH US AT DORCHESTERPUB.COM